CW00449830

THE PROPHECY AND THE TEMPLAR SCROLL

Copyright © 2019 by Lina Ellina

All rights reserved. Published by Armida Publications Ltd.

No part of this publication may be reproduced, stored in a retrieval system,
or transmitted in any form or by any means, electronic, mechanical,
photocopying, recording, or otherwise, without permission of the publisher.
For information regarding permission, write to
Armida Publications Ltd, P.O.Box 27717, 2432 Engomi, Nicosia, Cyprus
or email: info@armidapublications.com

Armida Publications is a member of the Independent Publishers Guild (UK),
and a member of the Independent Book Publishers Association (USA)

www.armidabooks.com | Great Literature. One Book At A Time.

Summary:
On the eve of a new crusade, Cyprus, the last Christian stronghold in the Levant,
is torn apart when the Templars connive against King Henry in favor of his brother Amaury.

The enigmatic Lois, with the assistance of the Seneschal's scribe, Nicholas,
undertakes to spy on Amaury while a serfs' rebellion is underway.

The arrest of the Templars in Europe changes the status quo,
and the Templars on the island bury some of their possessions, drawing maps with their exact location.

Seven hundred years later, one such map resurfaces in Covent Garden and a treasure hunt begins.

Cyprus 2013. The banks raid their clients' deposits in the 'bail-in'. Michael Costa goes to bed a
millionaire and wakes up struggling to make ends meet. Unexpected help comes when
Lucy Hernandez buys his house. Unbeknownst to them, the location of the house is the
X-location on the Templar map.

[1. Mystery & Detective - Historical 2. Historical - Fiction / Medieval
3. Romance - Contemporary 4. Romance - Historical
5. Romance - Time Travel 6. Travel - Literary 7. Action & Adventure]

Cover images:
"The Arn Limited Edition Official Movie Sword" by Søren Niedziella.
This file is licensed under the Creative Commons Attribution 2.0 Generic license
and was only partially modified to fit the purposes of the cover design.

"Leiden, Universiteitsbibliotheek, BPL 25 (9th century)" – Photo by Erik Kwakkel - medievalbooks.nl
This file is licensed under the Creative Commons Attribution 4.0 International (CC BY 4.0)
and was only partially modified to fit the purposes of the cover design.

Photo by Timothy Dykes on Unsplash

*This novel is a work of fiction.
Any resemblance to real people, living or dead, is entirely coincidental.*

1st edition: March 2019

ISBN-13 (paperback): 978-9963-255-87-0

THE PROPHECY AND THE TEMPLAR SCROLL

A NOVEL BY

LINA ELLINA

ARMIDA

—◆—

To Andreas, the love of my life, and
our four wonderful children

In loving memory of my father, Nicholas

—◆—

I would like to thank
my historical editor, Dr. Nicholas Koureas,
my publisher, Armida Publications,
and all my friends who read
the manuscript for their invaluable feedback

THE PROPHECY AND THE TEMPLAR SCROLL

Introduction

This book consists of two parallel stories, set in the same place but in different centuries. Nevertheless, once one gets into the book one soon realises that despite the differences in time as well as in the characters figuring in each story, it is the similarities rather than the differences that spring to mind.

Anyone familiar with the medieval and modern history of Cyprus, even in a general fashion, cannot be but struck by the historical parallels between both periods. In the early fourteenth century Cyprus, a western kingdom ruled by a Frankish royal dynasty originating from Poitou in France and with a largely Greek population, was developing rapidly in economic terms, having become a major trading entrepôt after the loss of the Holy Land to the Saracens, was nonetheless bedevilled by war overseas and unrest at home. Expeditions from Cyprus attempted, albeit without success, to recover parts of the lost territory, with the failure to do so creating internal unrest and providing opportunities for the enemies of its ruler, King Henry II. The most ambitious and unscrupulous of them was none other than his own brother Amaury, who eventually usurped the throne in 1306 with the support of a section of the Frankish nobility and of the Templars, who themselves were to suffer arrest throughout Europe just one year later, in 1307 on the orders of King Philip IV of France and Pope Clement V, who had the Templar Order abolished in 1312. As for the usurper Amaury, he was murdered in 1310, with his brother restored as king shortly afterwards.

Likewise, Cyprus in the 1960s and early 1970s was also enjoy-

ing rapid economic development, largely through tourism, but
this took place against a backdrop of internal unrest. Many Greek
Cypriots desired *enosis* or union with Greece, despite British and
Turkish opposition, and blamed Archbishop Makarios, the island's
president, for the failure to achieve this aim. Like King Henry II in
1306, Makarios was overthrown by a Greek-inspired coup in July
1974. This coup, followed by a Turkish invasion of the island and
the occupation of over one third of its territory, led to his restora-
tion by the end of 1974, just as King Henry II had been restored.
Furthermore, both before and after 1974 Cyprus was regarded as
and indeed used as a springboard for Western intervention in the
Middle East. It was seen for decades as a strategic asset within the
context of the Cold War between the Soviet Union and the Eastern Bloc countries and the United States and its allies.

In this respect the parallels with the wider political context of
the medieval Lusignan kingdom of Cyprus are remarkable. The
kingdom of Cyprus was itself a product of the Third Crusade that
set out from Western Europe to reconquer Jerusalem, that had
fallen to the Saracens under the leadership of Saladin. One of
its leaders, King Richard I of England, conquered Cyprus in the
summer of 1191 on his way to the Holy Land from Isaac Kom-
nenos, a Byzantine rebel who in 1184 had proclaimed himself
emperor, and then sold it, firstly to the Templars and then when
they returned it to King Guy de Lusignan, the dispossessed king
of Jerusalem. Guy founded a dynasty that would rule Cyprus for
over three hundred years. During this period, as well as during
the one hundred years of Venetian dominion that followed it, Cyprus was likewise a strategic asset in the long drawn out conflict between Western Christendom and Islam. Pope John XXII
(1316-1334) described it as being located 'on the confines of the
Hagarene nation', while one century later the Cypriot chronicler
Leontios Makhairas depicted it, with a touch of melancholy, as 'an
orphaned realm' placed between Turks and Saracens. In the early
fourteenth century as in the late twentieth Cyprus was a border-

land but also a meeting place, not simply between rival political blocs but also between different cultures.

This is brought out very skilfully in the book. The romance blossoming in the early fourteenth century is between the Frank Nicholas and the Greek Lois. In a similar vein, the romance maturing in post-1974 Cyprus is between the Greek Michael Costa and the Englishwoman Lucy Hernandez. Political upheavals and personal tragedies impact on the lives of ordinary people, and the heroes and heroines of this story are no exception. Nicholas is the adoptive son of the fief-holder Ramon of Provence, for his own father, a bosom friend of Ramon, was killed in warfare. Lois, who loves him loses both her parents to the bloody flux and so is raised by her maternal grandfather George Contostephanos. Michael Costa likewise becomes an orphan, raised by his own grandfather after his parents are killed during the Turkish invasion. The tragedies scarring their lives reflect the greater tragedies and upheavals scarring Cyprus. Yet they find love and emotional fulfilment in the end, and so the book ends on a note not of depression, but of optimism, underpinned by a conviction that even the most fearsome odds can be overcome. On a final note I cannot refrain from remarking that Lina Ellina, besides producing a gripping and suspense filled story, has placed it in its wider historical context(s) in a truly masterly fashion, in the details as well as in general. Having recently written a paper on the production and export of soap in medieval Cyprus I was touched to see that Nicholas and Lois at the end of the story engage themselves in exactly the same enterprise to make a living. Readers of this book will find that the melding of romance and history herein is a very felicitous one.

Dr Nicholas Coureas, *a Senior Researcher at the Cyprus Research Centre, works on the history of Lusignan Cyprus and has published various books and articles on the subject.*

I

1280

An eight-year old boy tethered his mount to the trunk of a sturdy pine tree and ascended the steep cliff cautiously, oblivious to the drizzle and the cold. The muddy path curved and sloped upward abruptly, and he was mindful of each step he took on the slippery stones.

He came to a secluded cave and stared at it with trepidation. Its entrance was partly covered by the falling water of the cascade and partly by the large branches of an old willow. With reluctant steps, he reached the cave opening and took a moment for his eyes to adjust to the dim light.

"Come in, king's son," a rough female voice startled him.

He shivered, as if cold steel had brushed the back of his neck. How did she know who he was? For a moment, he was tempted to turn around and run away, but his desire to find out the answer to the question that niggled at him like a sore tooth was too strong to ignore.

He pressed a piece of silver in the woman's hand. "Tell me what you see," he said, assuming the air of authority kings are meant to have.

The woman looked him up and down, put the silver aside, and took his hand in hers. The boy felt the calloused hand studying his palm and the nails tracing his palm lines but told himself he had nothing to fear. The sheath with his knife was secured safely in his boot.

His father would probably punish him if he ever found out that he had sought counsel outside the palace and the Church. He forbade the old ways, but when young Amaury heard the servants in the kitchen talk about the seer in the wilderness, he could not help wondering what his future held. And God must have approved, for his father had decided to take him hunting with him in the vicinity of where the soothsayer dwelled the very next morning.

The woman with the ageless face fixed him with her gaze but remained taciturn.

"Well?" the boy asked eagerly. "Will I be king?"

It was unlikely. He was the fourth of King Hugh's sons. The four boys, John, Bohemond, Henry, and Amaury had been born within a difference of thirteen summers. But disasters happen, he thought. Warriors perish on battlefields. Even accidents and diseases occur.

The woman quivered and not entirely from the cold. The sun had vanished from the sky when the boy entered the cave. It was a sign of wroth gods. His hand foretold abhorrent deeds. She shut her eyes and chanted an incantation. Amaury stared at the unearthly creature in awe.

When the woman spoke at length, she chose her words carefully. "You will rule over the people of this island, but there will be blood on your hands. Ask me no more. Now, leave!"

The boy looked at her stunned. She seemed exhausted. He wanted to ask what she meant about the blood on his hands but did not dare. Not because she forbade him, but because he was afraid to find out. He was too stricken to attempt to ask, though he would wonder many a time in the years to come why she did not say the actual words: that he would be king.

Still dazed by the revelation, he scrambled to his feet. His heart beating like rumbling, distant thunder, Amaury sprinted back to his mount, balancing safety and speed, shielding his face with his arms from the branches. With trembling fingers he untethered his horse, jumped into the saddle, and dug his spurs into his flanks. He galloped back to the hunting party lest he be missed.

2

2013

The early morning sunlight peeped through the drawn blackout curtains on a March Friday, waking Michael Costa up. A lazy smile flickered across his face. He was in the best of moods. He caressed the smooth skin of the ravishing model lying by his side, his fiancée. She swayed her hips invitingly, and he indulged willingly.

"Promise you'll wake me up like this every morning for the rest of our lives," she said in a pussycat voice.

"If you're a good girl." He gave her a quick kiss on the lips and swung his feet out of bed.

Michael shaved and put on a navy blue suit. He struggled between a light blue and a yellow tie but decided he did not need one. He glanced at his thickset figure in the mirror, arranging his collar and went down the stairs sprightly where Lola, a stray brown and white beagle that followed him home one day, was waiting for him to show her affection.

Michael had only coffee for breakfast that morning. He checked on his grandfather in the small house adjacent to the back garden, got into his brand new silver convertible, and drove off, a smug smile on his lips.

Half an hour later, he was entering the main branch of the Cyprus Popular Bank on the commercially busy Archbishop Makarios Avenue in Limassol. An hour later, the sale of his gourmet restaurant chain, *Chez Michel*, was sealed and two million euros were transferred into his savings account. He had already made plans to start a gourmet catering business. Though he would worry about that after his honeymoon, he took out a loan of half a million euros to set up the new business, using part of the two million as collateral.

He was getting married next Saturday and he no longer wanted to work nights. Night life had a way of burning one out, and he had had enough of that. Instead, he meant to become a family man, have two children, preferably a boy and a girl, ideally in that order. At the moment, he was looking forward to surprising Adriana with a romantic fortnight away in Bora Bora.

Michael bounced out of the bank, sliding his dark shades on. He got into his convertible, lowered the roof, and turned the music on. He tapped his fingers on the steering wheel to the rhythm, cruising down the avenue toward the beach and the Four Seasons Hotel to discuss the last details for the wedding reception with the food and beverage manager.

Michael was pleased with himself, thinking he had all the answers. Little did he know that come midnight, through no fault of his own, he would have nothing left in his bank account, and he would still need to repay the loan of half a million, even though he would never touch the money.

*

In her Kensington apartment, Lucy Hernandez tucked a lock of her honey blonde hair behind one ear and emptied her coffee mug. Her brain cells still craving caffeine, she poured herself a second mug, turned on the TV, and put on her make-up. The news was on the bail-out in Cyprus which turned out to be a bail-in.

Only the previous evening she had heard how Troika was threatening to cut off the emergency liquidity assistance to the country unless their parliament voted for a levy on all bank deposits, including those of up to one hundred thousand euros. It was a package measure unheard of, its legality questionable, and the way it came into being rather unorthodox. Lucy had no idea if Cypriots had brought this misery upon themselves, though she suspected politics had something to do with it. The impossible ultimatum this small country had been presented with, she thought, was immoral. She pursed her lips. During shootings of the last episode of

'Med Cuisine', she had taken a liking to that sun-drenched place and its hospitable people.

The moment she turned off the TV, the problems of an island thousands of miles away were forgotten. Lucy slipped into a white silk blouse and peach pencil skirt that accentuated her petite figure, checked herself in the mirror, and smiled with satisfaction. The bright colors she had chosen lit up her face and made her look younger. It was William's birthday, and she had taken the day off to find him a present and meet him for lunch before his evening class.

William Sinclair was in his mid-forties, a dashing professor at UCL, teaching Medieval History. His academic résumé attested his numerous publications on the Order of the Knights of the Temple. Born to wealth and position, he exuded confidence and authority. Sinclair was also a man of sophisticated taste, and Lucy had dwelled for days on what to get him for his birthday. This would be the first birthday present she would be giving him, and she wanted it to be special. The mere thought was daunting, as if she was taking an exam, but she was determined to find a gift that would stand out.

In search of inspiration, she set off for Covent Garden's Jubilee Hall Market. Lucy always enjoyed a stroll there, a quaint place full of history, where she could find anything from antiques to food. After two hours of searching fruitlessly, she began to feel a twinge of disappointment. All she had come across were souvenirs, and she could only imagine William's distaste at them. About to switch to plan B, a bottle of *Château Margaux,* a medieval map caught her eye. She stepped closer and studied it carefully.

It was a map of the wider Grand Commandery feudal estate in Western Limassol, home to the oldest named wine in the world, *commandaria*. She only recognized it because of the 'Med Cuisine' shoot. Whenever she had visited a place for a film shoot, she had made sure to carry out thorough research and to use little bits and pieces of interesting information when demonstrating local products and recipes.

She turned the map around in her hands. It was a parchment with a broken wax seal that depicted two knights on a horse. The Templar seal; if she recalled William's description correctly. Like many historians, William was often caught in the manic grip of enlightening the laymen around him about all sorts of details that had no place in today's world, and Lucy sometimes had to make an effort to show excitement. It had been easy at first; everything was new to her. But then she sensed rather than saw his disenchantment when she could not retain all the knowledge he impressed upon her. In fairness, she probably got equally carried away when she talked about flavors and recipes, she thought.

What mattered was that the map would be the ideal present for him. Filled with a surge of exhilaration, she walked to the checkout counter and waited patiently in line, looking dreamily around and imagining his expression when he saw the seal.

With her valuable possession secured in a fine scarlet leather cylinder, she glanced at her Frédérique Constant wristwatch, his birthday gift to her last month. It was almost lunch time. She leisurely strolled to the Floral by Lima Restaurant where she was to meet him, unable to wipe the grin off her face. She had found the perfect gift for him!

3

1291

Sequestered by a dense cypress fence, the modest *casale* of Ramon of Provence was not more than a speck on the map, squeezed between the huge estates of the Grand Commandery of the Knights Hospitallers in Kolossi and the *casale* of the Count of Jaffa in Episkopia. At its narrowest point, where the Kouris River bordered the Provence *casale*, you could throw a javelin from one end of the estate to the other. The fief had been the king's reward for shielding him from a lunatic assailant during a hunting expedition, losing an eye in the process, and for a life of loyal service.

Still youthful at the age of fifty-one, Provence rode *Mistral*, his black stallion, across the fields, his long silver hair blowing in the wind. He kept a light hand on the reins, letting his mount set its own pace. Recently back from the defeat of the Christian army at Acre, Provence longed for the placid life on his estates. Eloise, his wife, had made him promise that this had been his last battle, a promise he made only too eagerly and one he had no intention to gainsay in the future. His serfs, sowing artichokes and peas, recognized his stalwart figure from afar. He slowed down and passed by them unhurriedly, raising a hand in greeting as they bowed their heads.

Provence reined his mount to a halt and readjusted his black eye patch when he reached Nicholas, his eleven-year-old squire, who was practicing with the pell. Provence had taken him as a page at the age of six; a little earlier than usual, as a favor to his dying friend and comrade in arms. The mother had died at birth. True to his word, Provence had treated the boy like his own son and even given him his name. And so, young Nicholas took up the study of courtesies and the craft of knighthood.

Eloise had borne Provence two daughters. The first was stillborn and the second died in her sleep when she was a baby. Then the Lord blessed them with four healthy sons, and for one moment in life, Provence was happy.

But within the last two years, he had lost the first two; his first-born, Bernard, at the siege of Tripoli, and Olivier, his second son, in a hunting accident. Their thread of life cut prematurely short was a nightmare without end. Provence was still praying for strength and waiting for time to pass until the pain and the sorrow became bearable. But he knew this day would never come. It was unnatural for a father to bury his sons.

The only distraction from grief had been Nicholas' training and a game of chess in the evenings with Kontostephanos, his Cypriot bailiff. The boy had brought life into the house and his training a sense of purpose. Peyre, his third son, spent almost his entire time in church, studying the Scriptures, and his youngest, Albert, was simply not suited for the military life. To Provence's concealed disappointment, the boy was more interested in clothes and spices than in weapons. But he was a good boy, handsome as well, and Provence loved him all the same. He was his son.

Provence cast an approving eye upon the young lad with the wavy black hair and the clear green eyes, as he got ready to strike his heavy wooden sword against the tree trunk of a century-old nettle tree for the hundredth time. A few paces farther away, four-year-old Lois watched his moves attentively. The little girl had been following Nicholas, the only other child in the manor, everywhere since she could put one foot in front of the other. She lifted the stick in her hand, and mimicking Nicholas, she charged at a nearby myrtle tree trunk but missed and fell over.

Nicholas laughed heartily, walked up to her, and offered her his outstretched arm. "*Vine aquí, pichòt!*" Come here, kid!

She accepted his arm gracefully, pushing the mop of thick dark curls from her face. "*Mercés,*" she thanked him in *lenga d'òc.*

Provence was not utterly surprised to hear Nicholas and Lois exchange a few more sentences in Greek. He had already noticed the boy's greatest potential, his linguistic aptitude, in his Latin lessons. "Interesting," he murmured, rubbing his chin, as a plan began to take shape in his mind.

*

George Kontostephanos was no ordinary man. He had a quick, inquiring mind and uncommon resolve. He was hard-working, forthright and governed in conduct by kind benevolence. Kontostephanos descended from an old Byzantine family of *archontes,* the landowning aristocracy. Their land taken away from them, the *archontes* had no place in the new kingdom of Cyprus under the Lusignans. Those who had not left for Byzantium had been degraded to serfs.

Kontostephanos' father had stayed but had been prudent enough to bestow on his son the knowledge of High Greek and Latin which had served him in diverse ways. Above all, Kontostephanos had been raised to a *lefteros,* a free citizen, a privilege granted to very few islanders. It also allowed him to stay on in what used to be his family estates as bailiff. His aristocratic lineage granted him deference among the Cypriots who looked up to him for guidance.

But Konstostefanos' life had changed in the last three years. Both his daughter and her husband had died of the bloody flux, leaving Lois, their baby girl, behind. Kontostephanos' sister, a nun who lived in the barren land south of the Salt Lake, helping in the construction of the nunnery at Cape Gata, had volunteered to take Lois into her care, but Konstostefanos believed that life in a convent was a choice Lois had to make for herself when she was older.

"You have asked to see me, my lord?" Kontostephanos' creased face appeared at the door opening of the great hall.

"Yes, come in, Kontostephanos. Pour us some wine while I prepare the chess board," Provence said.

Provence was a man of simple tastes and few pretensions. He led a quiet life, liked plain food, but had a weakness for wine. Kontostephanos offered him a chalice and took a seat across from him, as he was setting the last pawns on the chess board.

Provence raised his chalice. "*A la vòstra.*"

"*Eis ygeian,*" Kontostephanos matched the toast in Greek.

Provence moved the pawn in front of his queen and said, "I would like you to teach Nicholas Greek for an hour after practice every day."

Kontostephanos raised his eyes to him for a moment and inclined his head. "It would be an honor, my lord." He moved a pawn, saying, "Might Lois also attend?"

A man who always thought ahead, Kontostephanos had meant to teach his granddaughter how to read and count. She was perhaps a bit too young to start, but he could help her before their evening prayers. Knowledge had been his only means to ameliorate his own life. He hoped it would do the same for his little Lois.

Provence advanced his left knight, contemplating that women were not supposed to learn to read so as not to receive love letters from unwelcome suitors. Worse still, literate women were frequently perceived as the devil's handiwork. He decided not to take issue with Kontostephanos' request. Apparently, their views on the subject matter differed. He glanced up at his bailiff's thinning white hair.

"I see no harm in that. He could practice Greek with her."

"In that case, might Lois sit with the young master in his other classes as well?"

Kontostephanos was pressing, but he knew Provence was fond of him and his little girl. It would be an unparalleled opportunity for Lois. Who was to tell how she could use this knowledge? If she were married to a serf, not at all, Kontostephanos reflected; yet life was full of twists and turns.

Provence opened his mouth to deny Kontostephanos' request flatly but changed his mind. He had observed how Nicholas did his best when he knew someone was watching. "All right then. If Nicholas does well, she can stay. If he gets distracted or delayed, she will have to stop."

"Of course, my lord. You are very kind! Thank you."

"Your move," Provence said impatiently, eager to play chess.

*

Long after Kontostefanos bid him goodnight, Provence remained seated in the great hall, pressing the tips of his fingers together in a little steeple. The reflection upon the aftermath of the recent fall of Acre caused him many uneasy hours. The Christian army had been vanquished, and support from the West had dwindled as rulers seemed more preoccupied with fighting each other. It was pure luck that the Sultan of Egypt, who had sworn to destroy Cyprus after the siege of the port of Alexandria, had been murdered. To prevent one another from ascending to power, a lot more emirs took up killing their peers.

Provence sensed that Cyprus' near future lay not on battlefields but in diplomacy. The language used in the Levant, the Eastern Mediterranean, was Greek. There would be ample time to prepare Nicholas for a position in the palace while continuing his knighthood training. A combination of both skills would set him apart. The young lad seemed up to it.

*

In his manor in Strovolos, Amaury lay still in bed, his nightshirt soaked with sweat. With eyes wide open, he stared into the darkness and waited for John's ghost to leave him in peace. It had been six years now that his eldest brother's ghost haunted him, tearing his sleep asunder.

Amaury's despair was all the greater, for his was a burden he must bear alone; a secret he must take to his grave. He oftentimes wondered if John plagued Henry's repose as well. He assumed he did but had never found the nerve to ask. Some things were best left unsaid. Eleven years after the prophecy, he understood the part about blood on his hands only too well. He still had to figure out the part about ruling his people.

Despite his youth, he was only two months shy of his nineteenth birthday, Amaury was a seasoned battle commander. His reputation for bravery preceded him. What no one knew, however, was that his bravery, bordering on recklessness, was partly rooted in provoking the Grim Reaper to take him and put an end to his haunted nights.

His thoughts turned to the discussion he'd had with Henry earlier that day. In the fight against the Saracens, Henry needed to forge a stronger alliance with Armenia. He wanted Amaury to marry Zabel, one of the Armenian king's sisters. Amaury had heard of her legendary beauty and should have been pleased with Henry's choice, but he demurred. He shifted in bed, his mouth twitching. What would she think of his nightmares?

4

2013

Hunched over a steaming mug of coffee, Michael watched the financial analysts on TV. He pecked on his laptop, browsing from site to site for breaking news. The minister of finance had just returned empty-handed from a crusade to secure a loan. The country's immediate future seemed bleak. Rebuilding the shattered economy would take years, if not decades.

In the meantime, the little experiment carried out on Cyprus had been met with skepticism, and a new directive that guaranteed deposits of up to one hundred thousand euros was now underway. That was not much, but it was better than nothing. Michael had always adapted well to change and found himself ruminating on how to use best whatever money he would be left with when the banks opened again; he had a flair for business.

The breaking news at the bottom of the screen caught his eye: 'Cyprus Popular Bank Closing?' He gasped and held his breath. That was his bank! How was it possible that the second-largest bank could fail? How could anyone have the right to steal the money he had worked a lifetime to earn? Michael was furious with whoever was responsible for this mess, Cypriot or foreigner. If only he had not trusted his cousin, a branch manager at the bank. He had reassured him that the high interest rates on deposits were a means to attract more capital for the bank's overseas investments.

Michael passed a hand over his shaved head. Life as he had known it would no longer be the same. The realization bored down on him with a devastating impact.

He turned the TV down and picked up his ringing cell phone. It was Adriana. He took a deep breath to calm himself and did his best to smile when he spoke to her. "Good morning, sweetheart."

"Good morning, Michael." Her voice, though guarded, came as a pleasant break from all this distressing news.

"How was the fashion show in Paphos yesterday?" Normally, he would have gone with her, but she had insisted that he should best stay home and think of a way out of this mess. Michael was not sure that there was much he could do at the moment but did as she had said.

"Michael, there's something I have to tell you."

He took a sip of his coffee and put his mug down on the table. "I'm listening."

"I can't do this."

He did not like the sound of that. "You can't do *what* exactly?"

"I can't marry you."

"What?"

"You deserve someone better than me." She had picked up the line from a movie.

A pause.

"Oh, hilarious! You had me going there for a moment. Is this a joke? It's not April Fool's Day yet, is it?"

"I'm serious, Michael. I'm leaving. I have this new contract from a modeling agency in the Emirates. I'm sitting on the plane as we speak. It wouldn't have worked between us. I'm sorry."

"On the plane? Now? Really?" He breathed in slowly. Now he knew why she had not wanted him with her in Paphos. "How long have you been planning this? When were you going to tell me?" Michael snapped, his patience wearing thin.

"I'm telling you now."

"Over the phone! You couldn't even tell me in person?" His brows bumped together in a scowl.

"You'd make me change my mind. I know it's hard to believe right now, but I love you, Michael, with all my heart."

"You have a funny way of showing it!" he said, narrowing his lips.

"I'm sorry!" Her voice broke.

Michael tried hard to understand. Why was she doing this? Had he done or said something? He racked his brain but nothing came. Everything had been fine until a few days ago. And then it dawned on him. "If you ever loved me, answer just one question for me truthfully!"

"Michael, we're taking off. I must go."

"Just one question. I deserve that much."

"All right," she said reluctantly.

"Are you leaving because I'm broke?" There was a pregnant pause, and Michael became conscious of holding his breath.

"I can't be poor again. I'm sorry, Michael. I must go now. Good-bye." She ended the call and turned off her cell phone.

Michael tried to call her back, but his call went straight to voice mail. He tossed his cell onto the table, his nostrils flaring. He darted to his feet, thoroughly blindsided, almost too angry to think. He paced up and down, shaking his head in disbelief then threw himself down on the chair again, unable to shake the feeling of being dragged deeper and deeper into a Kafkaesque nightmare.

He wiped his face in a downward motion, looked up, and cast a perfunctory glance at the pendulum. *Pappou*, his grandfather, would be home soon from his morning swim, and Michael did not want him to see him like this. A cold shower would help, he thought, and rose to his feet.

*

"Oh, and don't forget the deadline for your assignment on the

Third Crusade next week," Professor Sinclair said, finishing his lecture on Richard the Lionheart.

The students drifted out of the auditorium, and Sinclair gathered his things when two female students approached him. "Professor Sinclair, we were wondering if you might have a moment to explain the importance of capturing Cyprus for the Third Crusade. I mean —" one of the girls began to say.

Sinclair flashed a smile at them that made them sigh inwardly. "I'm sorry, ladies. I'm afraid I'll have to disappoint you today. I have an appointment, and I can't be late. Why don't you come and see me during office hours?"

"Of course," the girls said and walked away, head down.

Sinclair had a gift for enchanting students, female ones in particular. Someone would always want to talk to him for a few minutes, but today he did not have the time for that. He left the auditorium in long, brisk strides and went past the main library and the Bloomsbury Theatre. He crossed Gordon Street and entered Christopher Ingold, the building that houses the Department of Chemistry. He took the elevator to the second floor and knocked on Professor Keller's door. Charlie Keller was the head of the department, a colleague and friend, but most of all, a fellow member of the Order.

"Hello, William," Keller greeted him with a smile. "What brings you here?"

"This," Sinclair said, handing over the cylinder containing the parchment with the Templar seal. "You might want to wear gloves," he pointed out meaningfully.

Intrigued, Keller grabbed a pair of gloves from a glove container and removed the parchment from the cylinder. His brows furrowed at the sight of the seal. He raised his eyes and looked at Sinclair. "Where did you get this?"

"Lucy found it in one of the stalls in Covent Garden."

"Ah! Lucy! Such a nice girl," Keller said. "And smart," he added, pointing at the parchment. He chuckled. Keller had been surprised at first that Lucy had outlasted the female competition on campus that long. But maybe she was a good match for Sinclair after all.

"Yes, that's Lucy," Sinclair nodded in agreement. "It's probably just another counterfeit, but could you run a check anyway?"

"I'd love to! I'll get back to you as soon as I have the results."

"Thank you, Charlie. I owe you one," Sinclair said and walked to the door.

*

The house was as still as a cemetery when Michael carried the empty boxes to the bedroom upstairs. In a way, it suited his mood. It was like the funeral for a relationship based on deception. He had been betrayed. Now, it felt like he was digging a grave without a tombstone, wishing for the grass to grow over it and cover it quickly so that it would be out of sight and out of mind forever.

Overcome with emotion, he let the boxes fall on the wood flooring. Everything in that room reminded him of her. He snorted bitterly. She never thought much of wearing clothes and would move around the room in the nude, swaying those lean hips teasingly in front of him, and he would always indulge in that pleasure. They had great sex together; he missed that already. And they enjoyed going out for the evening. Adriana turned heads wherever they went, and Michael could see men's lustful gazes but never felt jealous. He had always believed that beauty is to be admired.

He stared at the boxes with a sense of finality. She was not coming back. Did he want her back? In retrospect, Michael was not sure he had ever really loved her. He knew what love was. He had found true love once – many years ago.

He closed his eyes and sighed. He needed closure, yet gathering

Adriana's personal belongings for charity filled him with anger
and bitterness. The world around him was falling apart with lightning speed, but Michael was certain of one thing: he had done
nothing to deserve this; any of this.

5

1291

After the destruction of Salamis, the ancient name for Famagusta, Nicosia became the capital city of Cyprus in 965. With its modest palace and its beautiful Gothic Santa Sophia Cathedral, it struggled but failed to resemble, even remotely, other large Christian capitals with their impressive palaces and castles. Even Famagusta, the island's major port, was larger and richer.

In the Lusignan palace, Henry would often sit and marvel at the paintings of Cimabue and Cavallini adorning the walls in the solar. With a good eye for art, Henry had begun early to assemble his own collection. But today he was too distraught to admire the paintings.

A man of a small stature and delicate frame, Henry had been fifteen when he succeeded his brother John to the throne six years earlier; his second eldest brother, Bohemond, had died four years before that. Henry was handsome and determined to be a good king, but he was lately susceptible to poor health and sensitive to criticism.

He peered at the map on the table in front of him, his brows knitted in a frown. His reign so far had been ill-fated. After his success at capturing Acre from the Angevins only a month after his coronation, the Saracens had conquered one Christian stronghold after another: Tyre, Beirut, Tripoli, and now Acre. No one could have saved these places, but Henry sat on the throne, and the responsibility fell on his shoulders.

"My lord," the Seneschal, interrupted his thoughts, and Henry met his eye. "The lords are all here."

Henry nodded, draped a deep blue mantle, lined with gold silk, over his shoulders, and went down the stairs. He took a moment to arrange his face into a mask of royal serenity and strutted into the great hall where the members of the High Court had assembled. Whispers faded away as he assumed his place on the throne on the high stepped dais, embellished with an Armenian carpet.

"My lords, before we start discussing the matters of the day, let me remind you that as of today, we will be keeping written records of the High Court sessions for better future reference."

This was one of the novelties Henry had introduced, for which he felt very proud. Since most of his nobles had limited knowledge of Latin, he had decreed that the records be kept in Italian or French; another modernity. In his effort to make his administration more efficient, he had even extended the court's role from an advisory body to a true court, responsible for trying and punishing criminals.

Henry cleared his throat and went on, "The Holy Land has fallen. The entire Christian world is watching, holding its breath. Will Cyprus be next? Or will our tiny realm rise to the challenge of the times exemplarily and become the stepping stone for a new expedition? I would like to hear your views." His voice carried well, the tone factual and grave in equal measure.

In the sensitive equilibrium of uneasy coalitions, Henry knew only too well that his court expected him to act as first among equals. Although he had been nurtured on the ideal of the recovery of the Holy Land, the young king was not a man blindly enamored with war. His anxiety to prevent spilling the blood of his subjects for a city he could not hold made him look less wholehearted. His dilatoriness bordered on cowardice, his critics said, to his aggrievement. Henry was also well aware of what the Orders wanted: war.

"I would also like to hear your views on how to best deal with the influx of Christians, arriving daily to our shores from the Holy Land." The consequences brought about by the sudden increase of the population of the island were alarming.

"The Seneschal will have flour sent to the bakers in Famagusta to bake bread to be given out at the port. And the castellan will ensure that the loaves are apportioned to the right people. The queen and I shall distribute alms here in the capital," he went on.

There were some anxious whispers, but no one spoke for a while.

"My liege," Provence said, "perhaps we could enlist some of the poor knights and sergeants."

"Indeed, we should; as many as possible… Houses that stand empty can be used to shelter those who do not have a home to go back to," Henry added as an afterthought.

Provence wondered if the nobles who had houses standing empty would like that.

"It seems unfair that we should lift such a heavy burden alone," Amaury pointed out, and the nobles nodded in silent agreement.

"You are right. We shall write to the Pope, requesting support from other rulers and the Holy Sea," Henry said. The court members seemed pleased.

"My liege, there's another urgent issue," Amaury said. "You should claim to be the Titular King of Jerusalem or the title will be lost forever."

Henry smiled approbation at his younger brother's political foresight. Amaury was learning fast, and Henry was counting on him to have his back. A man who took chances where other men spurned, Amaury was also a man to be relied on to keep his head in the heat of battle. If only he could learn to master his temper like he mastered his sword!

"And so, indeed, I shall," Henry assented. The idea was first mooted once he was safe onboard on his way back to Cyprus after the great catastrophe at Acre.

"It is my belief that we need to start preparing for a new expedition," Amaury added with conviction, and the hall was filled with whispers. The magnitude of the moment was lost on no one.

Henry's impassive face did not give away his irritation. He had been expecting that argument from the Templars or perhaps the Hospitallers; not from Amaury, though he knew what a warlord his brother was. He had seen Amaury fight, unburdened by the fear of death that plagued most men.

With a difference of only two years between them, Henry and Amaury had been inseparable, like light and shadow. They had practiced their Latin and at the quintain together. Unlike Henry, Amaury was sturdy and had matched him, risk for risk, throughout their boyhood. They challenged each other to the most outrageous dares in horse racing, swimming, rock climbing, even in brothels.

But since the fall of Tripoli, Amaury's first battle command, his mood had become more and more mercurial. Henry had sent him in charge of a company of knights and four galleys. They had been heavily outnumbered. Defeat was inexorable. Henry suspected that Amaury faulted himself for the loss of the men under his command; perhaps even that he had failed him. No one could have fought more bravely. Henry knew that.

That same year, he made Amaury Titular Constable of Jerusalem and the year after that Titular Lord of Tyre. Yet Henry sensed a gap between them, one he was finding hard to bridge. He wished his uncle, Philip of Ibelin, were there. He could always rely on his counsel. But from his letters, it seemed that it would be several weeks before he returned to the island.

Provence saw the indecision in Henry's eyes and the quiet expectancy on the nobles' faces. There had been rumors that he had been too slow to go to war against the Saracens, but Henry, who had just come back from the calamity at Acre, dismissed these rumors as invective accusations of a cabal of malcontent, ill-willed nobles.

Provence cursed under his breath. Whatever his other faults, Amaury was not a fool. Why then would he bring the subject up now?

"Perhaps we should not rush, my lord," Provence said, adroitly steering the attention to him; his voice rising up above the whispers. He had an uncanny sense of alliances shifting.

"Why wait?" Amaury ranted, tilting his head back. "It might take months to gather an army again anyway." A man with little patience with people who contradicted him, Amaury spoke with emotion. The tension in the great hall was palpable.

Provence looked him straight in the eye with the serenity of a man who had long since made his peace with his Maker. "This is true, of course, my lord," he said. He had lost one eye, he reminded his listeners, but his good eye did not deceive him. "We cannot go to war with empty coffers, and at the moment they are severely depleted. We should use whatever money is available, levy a tax if need be, to improve our roads and bridges and make trade easier. Trade will fill our coffers. Then we will be ready for war."

Provence's gaze swept around the room; he could smell new enemies coming out of the woods. A pack of wolves was waiting to pounce.

"Such talk is a disgrace to Christianity, a blasphemy! God wills to protect His Son's birthplace against the Infidel," the Count of Jaffa carped at full throttle. Provence felt disgust when people spoke as if they knew God's will. "Then Jesus entered the temple and drove out all who were selling and buying in the temple," the count went on, quoting Matthew, as if delivering a sermon.

The count was ardently supported, the passion of opposing opinion evident. The Templar and the Hospitaller Grand Masters were quietly assessing the evolving situation. Discussion rose and ebbed till the king raised a palm and ceased it.

"I thank you for your views. You will all agree that we need to set the taking-in of fleeing Christians as our priority. There will be plenty of opportunity to discuss further action in the near future," Henry said, trying to maintain the equilibrium, trusting in Providence. War had been staved off for now.

*

The birds' chirping filled the air as Provence traversed the burgeoning greenery in the palace gardens, heading for the stables after the court session.

"Provence!" an abrasive voice called out his name. He stopped and looked over his shoulder as Enric of Roussillon caught up with him.

"Roussillon," he acknowledged him warily.

Enric of Roussillon was a bilious man. The smallpox he had suffered at the age of seven had left him badly scarred. People blinked and strove not to turn their eyes away at the sight of his repulsive face. Even his own wife demanded that all shutters were closed and all candles blown out before he touched her.

Roussillon had never come to terms with the king's change of heart about the *casale* at Kouris River. Right before the hunting expedition, in which Provence had saved the king's life, Henry had promised him that estate. In the end, he had given Roussillon another much larger, albeit arid, piece of land.

Roussillon, who reveled in dirty tricks and ambushes, tried to coerce Provence into exchanging their fiefs. Provence, a man who chose his battles wisely, knew he was no match for Roussillon's rich family if it came to a confrontation. So, he suggested a marriage between Bernard, his eldest son, who would inherit the estate, and Aceline, Roussillon's eldest daughter. What had seemed an ideal settlement at first, however, turned sour with Bernard's death. Provence then mentioned the possibility of another betrothal between Olivier, his second son, and Aceline. Everyone was satisfied for a while until Olivier's tragic hunting accident.

"It has been a while. Let us walk together," Roussillon said, and Provence feared he knew what he wanted to talk about. "It has been nigh on six months since Olivier's death." It had been only four, but Provence thought it wiser not to correct him. "I think you will agree that this was a respectful time for mourning. My Aceline is not getting any younger, and I have three more daughters to see settled down. So, why not have Peyre marry Aceline in Olivier's place?"

Subtlety in manners was an art Roussillon had yet to master, Provence thought. "This would be a wonderful arrangement if only Peyre had not entered the clergy."

He hadn't – not yet anyway. But he wanted to. A marriage would make him miserable. Provence would have to send him away as soon as he got back home.

Roussillon uttered an oath. "All right. You have another son, do you not?" He exerted himself to curb his temper.

"Indeed, but Albert is still a beardless boy, much younger than your fair Aceline," Provence pointed out calmly.

"Are you trying to insult me?" Roussillon's scoff of disbelief left little room for maneuvering.

Provence looked away uncomfortably then back at him. "No, of course not. I will speak to him."

6

2013

Michael stood by the large French windows in his living room and looked out into the distance. He was in a foul mood. The thought that Adriana had been with him only for his money stung; so did notifying everyone that the wedding was off. He texted a laconic message: runaway bride – wedding's off, hoping it would stop people from calling to find out what had happened. He did not want to talk about it. Next, he canceled the wedding reception and the honeymoon.

He shook his head, puzzled. Just a few days ago, he was a wealthy, happy man with a great future ahead. How did he get from there to here?

"You're a lucky man, Michael," *pappou* said, folding his newspaper, placing it on the couch next to him.

"You think?" Michael said, raising an eyebrow. He shrugged. "I guess it could have been worse. She could have let me wait for her at the front of the church," he said self-mockingly.

"You're better off without a woman who loves you for your money; she will walk out on you the moment she comes across a thicker wallet. Better now, before you have any kids," *pappou* concluded with the gelid detachment of a man who had seen it all before.

Michael bit back an irate retort. "Gee, thanks!"

Pappou looked at him kindly. His forbearance under provocation never failed him. "You're miserable because you're focusing on what you cannot have. Happiness is being grateful about what you *do* have: health, youth, a wonderful house, a gift for cooking. Happiness is a choice. Self-pity won't get you anywhere!"

"What? Has it occurred to you that I've lost everything in one night? Not to mention that I have no idea how to go about starting a new business without cash and with the banks closed! This is ridiculous!"

"You were, of course, too young to remember, but when we escaped from the Turks in '74, we only had the clothes we were wearing. We had literally nothing but one another, and that was plenty! We did it then, we'll do it again! It's a different kind of war. They didn't take our lives and land this time, but our money. Have faith! Have patience! Money comes and goes. They can take away our money, but they can't take away our smile! Now, I could use some help with the gladioli." *Pappou's* voice was authoritative and unwavering.

Michael looked at the old man with a sense of pride and admiration for his buoyant spirit. It was he who should be giving *pappou* courage, not the other way around. Experiencing a twinge of shame, he came abruptly to his feet and walked to the door.

"Well, come on! What are you waiting for? Let's plant the gladioli!" he said, giving *pappou* the most optimistic smile he could muster up.

*

William Sinclair walked the short distance to the heavy flying buttresses of Chartres Cathedral and looked for the small iron side door. It was unlatched, as they had said it would be. He winced when the gate jarred open against the stone floor, cast a cursory glance around, and stepped inside unnoticed as the bells chimed at midnight.

Though there was no time to marvel at the stained glass windows, he was awed by the mystic atmosphere surrounding him as he descended the narrow spiral staircase, careful not to bump his head on the low ceiling. This was the first time he had been invited to one of the Order's clandestine meetings. When he had first heard of them, he thought they were no more than a legend. Yet here he was!

If one looked closely, one could detect the remains of engraved hexagons and triangles on the stone wall. He moved toward the circle of the candlelit labyrinth. On the far side of the room, there were four heavy oak seats, covered with vermillion velvet. An eight-pointed cross *pattée* was carved in the center of the horizontal wooden surface at the top of each seat.

Sinclair proceeded to the inner circle, at the center of the labyrinth, as he had been instructed. Moments later, four dark suits marched in and took a seat, their faces concealed in the shadows.

"Professor Sinclair, you believe you're in possession of a Templar parchment," the Grand Master said, his voice resonating in the empty cathedral.

This had been the first time the Grand Master had addressed him, and Sinclair felt a thrill of excitement. "This! It's a map with the seal of the Order," he said, holding Lucy's birthday gift up, struggling to keep the triumph from his voice.

"And you're certain that this is not one of those imitations readily available in stores?"

"I had it authenticated by one of our own, Professor Keller at UCL." Sinclair was not discouraged. He had expected them to be suspicious.

"What does it depict in your opinion?"

"Professor Keller believes that the parchment dates back to the early fourteenth century. It's a map of the Grand Commandery, the area around Kolossi Castle that came into the knights' possession in 1306, shortly before the trials. An educated guess would be that 'X' marks the location where the knights hid a treasure, or maybe documents, before abandoning the island or being thrown into the dungeons. What's perhaps even more intriguing is the riddle in invisible ink." He deliberately did not give more away to trigger their curiosity, and it worked.

"A riddle?"

"Yes, it goes like this:

> 'You shall find your faith
> In Lorraine,
> On the tree whose seeds
> Weigh gold,
> Facing Ursa,
> Taking as many strides
> As Judas' pieces of silver.'"

"And have you solved the riddle?"

"I have a working theory about the symbolism, but it would be safer to visit the place first," Sinclair said circumspectly. "I, therefore, request permission to investigate this further on site."

"Very well, professor! Leave the map on the seat next to you. We will revert soonest," the Grand Master said.

The four men rose to their feet and walked in procession, retracing their steps. Sinclair left the map on a nearby seat and walked out of the cathedral, drunk on the illusion that he was now a part of the core of the Order.

*

In her Kensington apartment, Lucy stared at the laptop screen, experiencing a pang of guilt. A part of her was relieved that William had this conference in France. She had to finalize her proposal to UKTV for the next season, and she needed to concentrate.

Lucy did not know if the recent drop in the ratings was related to her effort to be available for William whenever he had time for her amidst his research, classes, meetings, and conferences abroad, but she had come up with a new angle, and she was confident that the board would go along with her suggestions.

She poured herself a glass of *Chablis* and returned to her proposal for the meeting on Monday.

7

1299

The journey from the Provence *casale* to Nicosia was long and arduous. Initially, the road ran along the coast until it turned a left-angled bend. Henceforth it meandered up and down the hills and into the plain.

Provence's breath turned to mist in the frigid air, but he rode oblivious to the cold and the snow, giving his mount its head to find its way through the mire. He contemplated the eight long years he had been deprived of his son Albert. The boy took off after Provence had tried to impose the marriage to Roussillon's daughter on him. Maybe it was better this way, for Albert at least, for Provence would have to guard his back for the rest of his life.

Roussillon had not taken the news of Albert's disappearance well. He had leaned forward belligerently, his mouth twisting in a line of resentment and hatred flashing from his eyes. "I hope you had a good night's sleep last night, Provence, for I shall make sure that it will be your last," he had said, spitting out the words, his eyes glittering with impotent fury.

When Albert sent word with Peyre several months later to let his father know that he was well and that he was making a small fortune for himself trading in Famagusta, Provence had urged him not to come home, at least until Roussillon found another husband for his eldest daughter. Let some time pass, he had said. Let the rage die down, and Albert did just that.

Eight years later, Roussillon was still looking for husbands for his daughters. Aceline had earned herself the unfortunate sobriquet 'the black betrothed', and as the years passed, it was impossible for Roussillon to find a suitable match for her, despite the large marriage portion he was offering. As the custom wanted the first daughter to marry first, he was reluctant to have his younger daughters marry before Aceline.

Roussillon loathed Provence. He made no secret of it. He blamed him for taking away the land that was rightfully his, or so he believed, and for the misfortune that had befallen his daughters.

But for Provence all that mattered was that Albert was finally coming home. He had said so in his letter; he was coming home with Peyre and Guilhelm Gascoigne, his partner in trade. Provence was counting the days, envisioning the entire family sitting around the table in the great hall, regaling each other with tales of lost years.

*

Smoke curled up from the chimneys of the capital. As Provence reached the square, the palace came into a full view. Riding through the gateway, he came upon Roussillonand acknowledged him with a nod.

Roussillon shot him the customary baleful glance. "Provence, any news of your boy Albert yet?" The tone was condescending, insulting. The menace lingered after all these years like an acrid smell.

"Not yet, Roussillon. I hope you and your family are all well," Provence said patiently, not rising to the provocation.

"I hope he gets what he deserves," Roussillon said, raking him with freezing contempt. Without waiting for a response, he spurred his steed and rode on.

Provence breathed in and out and took his time reaching the stables. He swung from the saddle, handed the reins to the groom, and left his horse in his care.

He walked to the palace and glanced up at the frieze, depicting the Lusignan coat of arms, a silver lion, armed, and crowned with gold, adorning the triangular cornice that was supported on four Corinthian pillars. He stepped inside, brushing the snow off his long silver hair. His heavy ash green cloak swished as he lurched to the stairs, wondering what the urgency was to summon the court on such short notice.

The nobles and knights drifted in, and the antechamber buzzed with the low rumble of anxious greetings and gossip. They seemed to be just as confounded by the assembly as he was. The floor shook as the last participant, Philip of Ibelin, waddled into the antechamber.

The king's uncle was a big man with a receding hairline, thick lensed spectacles sitting on his nose, and a protruding midsection. His mere bulky presence demanded respect even from his adversaries, and everyone turned around to greet him. Philip shook hands with some of the court members before noticing Provence. "Ramon!" he cried out.

"Philip, it is good to see you again," Provence said, and they patted each other's back.

They went back many years with many chapters in their history. The first time they had met was at the coronation of King Hugh III in December 1267 in Nicosia. Two years later, they attended Hugh's coronation as King of Jerusalem at Tyre and accompanied him back to Cyprus in 1276 as members of his council.

A servant opened the doors to the great hall, and the nobles' whispers faded away as they entered. Moments later, Henry walked in through the inner door and sat on the heavy carved oak throne.

Provence watched his face closely. He seemed well today. Stories that Henry was dying were unfounded, but he was more and more frequently ill, to the displeasure of his court. He neglected his duties, some complained. Others were disgusted when he foamed at the mouth. But the pink color of his cheeks attested to his good health today.

"My lords, thank you all for coming on such short notice." He paused briefly for good measure. "We are faced this present day with a turning point in history. Damascus has surrendered to Il-khan Ghazan, the Mongol of Persia, yet now he has retired to his homeland. This leaves the city vulnerable to new Saracen attacks, so I urge you to consider how easily it can be lost again. If we take no action, posterity will remember us as cowards. Worse, still, God will never forgive us!" He spoke with fervor, instigating them to war.

Henry saw Amaury's surprise. He had never been one to shield his thoughts effectively. His face was transparent, to Henry at least, who knew every nuance of his brother's expression. He only wished he liked what he read more, for lately displeasure and disrespect showed more frequently than he cared to admit. It stung. And it worried him. Despite his overtures, Amaury was distant, evasive, and slippery as an eel.

"We can send fifteen mounted men and twenty footmen forthwith; more in a few weeks' time," Molay, the Templar Grand Master, proclaimed. No consideration could bring him to swerve from the path of fighting to free Jerusalem. Eager to start a new expedition, Molay did everything in his power to push things in that direction, from writing to the Pope to pressuring the king and the nobles on the island.

Provence understood Molay's motives. The holy cause attracted men to enter their ranks and offer the mighty Order their properties as all Templars were required to take an oath of poverty. The king's banning the acquisition of new estates without his permission was a desperate move to prevent the Orders from becoming too powerful, as they had been in the Holy Land, but it also caused friction.

Provence had an uneasy suspicion that the Templars, along with some dour nobles, including Roussillon, denigrated the king. They had started spreading the rumor that Henry was a trimmer. He could have helped Ghazan take Damascus rather than wait to have it offered on a silver platter, they said.

"We can match that," said the Hospitaller Grand Master, affecting a solemn countenance.

"I wish I could fight one last battle, but I fear I'm too old for that. If my son, Nicholas, were here he would offer to go," Provence stepped forward. Nicholas would be dubbed knight in a few days. That would be an opportunity to offer his sword to his king. It would also enable Provence to find a way to secure him a place at the palace – should he make it back. Not wanting to be found lacking in courage, more knights came forward.

"I thank you, my lords," Henry said. "Here's what we shall do. We shall send two galleys and two *taridae* at once under the command of Captain la Naento." He met his brother's gaze, and saw his jaw tightening. "They shall rebuild the fortress in Nephin first to establish a basis," he went on. "Then I will come with a greater force to attack Botron until Ghazan returns to join us. This will show the Infidels that we are in earnest!" His voice was ebullient, inciting them to action.

Henry did not have much of a choice, Provence thought. The voices in favor of war had become too strong to ignore. Amaury's voice had turned out to be the strongest. This declaration of war was a way for Henry to save face, a way out of their checkmate.

*

"I would have a word with you, brother," Henry said to Amaury, as the nobles walked out of the great hall.

Amaury approached the dais, and Henry motioned him to sit next to him. He snapped his fingers for wine. The cupbearer filled two chalices to the brim, and Henry asked him to leave the flagon.

"How is your lovely wife Zabel?" Henry ventured to probe what he saw to be a sensitive subject.

"She is in Cilicia, in Armenia, in her brother Hayton's court. She is hoping to intercede on behalf of her brothers Sempad and Constantine. As you know, Hayton has locked them up for life. Her letters for clemency have come to naught, so she has taken it upon herself to plead for them in person."

Henry knew where Zabel was and why. What he did not know was whether Amaury had expected him to intervene. Could that be the reason of his rancor? "Have you ever heard of a king pardoning the usurpers of his throne?"

"No, but you cannot fault her for trying. For Constantine, the double traitor, she cares little, but she had been very close to Sempad, her twin brother. She would never forgive herself if she did not make the effort at least."

Henry had little compassion for Zabel's brothers, especially Constantine, a shifty lot, always with one eye to the prevailing winds. "That is understandable."

He perused Amaury's face. It was obvious that he was sympathetic toward his wife's plight, but he did not seem dismayed. He poured them some wine and tried another topic. "You know why I gave La Naento the command?" Did Amaury think he did not trust him after the fall of Tripoli and Acre?

"I think I do. He is a more seasoned battle commander. Look, I will not lie to you, Henry. I would have liked to have the command myself, but I cannot fault you for choosing him over me. If I were you, I would have probably done the same. But I do not have to like it."

"No, you do not." He paused, wondering what his grievance then was. "Remember how we had each other's help back then to escape our Lord Father's wrath whenever we got into mischief? Like the time when we put sleeping draughts into the guards' ale and sneaked out to go trout fishing? They thought we had been abducted under their noses. Father had every guard comb the area."

A smile hovered on Amaury's lips. He remembered well. Their father had strictly forbidden them to go out at night, but Henry was not inclined to give up on any pleasure in life. He had the gift of appearing most deferential, especially to their father, but going nonchalantly through life, doing whatever pleased him in the end, whereas Amaury had more often than not got into trouble when he argued his case with him, even though eventually he would do their father's bidding.

"I had never seen father seething like that. I was sure he would have us whipped," Amaury said.

"Luckily, we got away with fasting and prayer."

"It was fortunate that it was almost Lent time." Amaury chuckled and paused. Then, "Remember the day you put the nursemaid's hem on fire?"

Henry jerked his head back, laughing. Amaury joined in his laughter, a moment of ease between them. They gulped down their wine.

"I had forgotten about that," Henry said. "Well, she shouldn't have told on us. Our Lady Mother was so furious she had us confined for days!" For Henry that had been the worst of punishments.

"For an afternoon rather," Amaury corrected him.

"Mother never liked it when we teased John. But it was not to be helped. He always took himself so seriously. He could always be counted on to fly into a fury."

That was the first time they had talked about John after all these years. Henry watched Amaury's fingers twitch of their own volition and wine sloshing over the edge of his cup. He had long suspected that Amaury found it hard to come to terms with what they had done, but he hoped time would heal old wounds. He realized now that time only made numb.

He tested the waters again. "He had one of his fits of rage for sure, but I do not remember why."

"We called him a changeling," Amaury reminded him, no longer amused.

"Whatever gave us that idea?" Henry feigned having no recollection.

Amaury shrugged, summoning up a thin, mirthless smile. He loved Henry. He did not like being at odds with him, by God's Grace he did not, although nothing on God's earth could have induced him to admit that he was.

"He was different in so many ways: his coloring, his temper. But mostly, he was a weakling. He scared easily; afraid of his own shadow, John was." Remembering was painful and dispiriting, and it showed on his face.

John was a bit slow, too, Henry thought but there was no need to bring it up. "Aye, not quite fit for a king," he said softly.

Amaury shook his head almost imperceptibly. He drained his cup and filled it again. He could sometimes find merciful oblivion in wine, but not now. Keeping his eyes glued to his cup, he asked in a voice barely audible, "Does he ever come to you?"

"Who does?"

Amaury emptied his cup and wiped his mouth with his sleeve. He wished now he had not asked. He forced himself to answer. "John."

Henry observed Amaury's face with renewed interest. Was that it? What had tormented him and put distance between them?

"Does he come to you?" he asked gently.

Amaury shrugged, embarrassed. His tacit admission came as a surprise to Henry but not as a shock. He'd had his share of guilt, but in the end common sense always prevailed. Or so he chose to think to soothe his conscience. Henry wondered if there were any words to lessen his brother's misery. He found none. Did Amaury regret it? Obviously. Did Henry want him to spell it out? No. Some things were best left unsaid.

8

2013

Lucy finished her presentation for the new season of 'Med Cuisine' and looked around the table at the blank faces of the board members of UKTV. She secured a lock of her hair behind one ear, smiling hopefully at them. Some of them returned the smile politely.

"Well, thank you for your interesting ideas Ms. Hernandez. We agree that the show needs a bit of a lift, a new title; a new concept. We may take some of your ideas on board, but what we mostly need is a fresh face," the director said, and Lucy's energy levels went into free fall.

She heard them thank her for her time and cooperation; perhaps their paths would cross again in the future. She wanted to protest, but the appropriate argument eluded her. As in a dream, she managed a polite reply, rose to her feet, and staggered out of the room. A sense of dread hit her in the gut, and she reminded herself to breathe.

Lucy had not expected that her contract would not be renewed. It was true, the ratings had been falling, but she had worked hard and was certain her ideas would turn the numbers around. It did not matter. What they needed was a fresh face, she thought, suddenly feeling twenty years older.

She left the building and got onto the busy Hammersmith Road. A walk always helped her clear her mind. She had no idea how long she had been wandering around, trying to accept what had just happened and chewing over her future. This was a situation she was not prepared for. She had to rethink her life, rearrange her priorities; assess the possibilities. And what would she tell William?

When reality sank in, she was convinced that this was a sign. Lucy had always been open to signs and went where life took her. An

optimist by nature, she reminded herself that prospects were endless. If it had not been for William, she might even have considered
a fresh start away from London, but she wanted to give this new
chapter in her life room to unfold.

Her steps brought her to *La Petite Bretagne* on Beadon Road. In
need of comfort food, she went in and ordered a sweet crepe. Her
gaze glided around at the country style ambience, finally settling
on a table at the far end of the room. Was that William? She looked
more closely. He was not alone.

A smiling, young waitress came and served the crepe while the
woman at William's table got up. Lucy watched him do the same.
They exchanged kisses and the attractive blonde, dressed in a white
and pink Jackie O dress, passed by Lucy, leaving an unmistakable
trace of Chanel 5 as she ambled out of the café.

Lucy turned her attention back to William who was signaling for
the check. Had he not said he would be out of town until tomorrow? Having lost all interest in her crepe, she left some money
next to her plate, and walked over to his table.

"Hello, William!"

He looked up. "Lucy!" He flashed a debonair smile at her. "Will
you join me?" He gestured for her to sit down.

Lucy slid into the seat opposite him, and he gave her a quick kiss
on the lips. "You're in town!" she said.

"Yes, I was able to get away from the conference in France earlier
than expected." Sinclair had long ago come to realize that the easi-
est way to obfuscate the truth was to 'bend' it as little as possible.
"Tea?"

He was about to signal for the waiter, but Lucy stopped him. "Uh,
no, thank you. Already had some… while you were talking with
that woman."

"Julie," he said, casting his gaze on the empty cup on the table for a moment. "I've been meaning to tell you, but there never seemed to be a good time for this."

"I have time," Lucy said guardedly.

"Lucy, please hear me out before you jump to conclusions. All right?"

She nodded her head yes.

"Julie's my wife, but we're getting a divorce."

"You're married!" Lucy exclaimed loud enough for the couple sitting at the next table to peer over their shoulders with acute interest. She looked at William's hands. He was wearing a wedding ring!

"Technically; we're separated," William said in a low voice, as if encouraging her to be similarly reserved.

"And you wear your wedding ring when you're with your wife and take it off when you're not because...?"

"I just don't want to upset her. We're so close to reaching an agreement. I don't want to sound calculating, but I happen to be a wealthy man, and I wouldn't want her to become unnecessarily competitive. Surely, you understand that," he said with a confident smile.

Lucy nodded slowly. It was a plausible enough explanation, yet she had become painfully aware of how little she knew him. "You never said anything."

"I was already in the process of getting a divorce when I met you. The truth is that I hadn't expected it to take so long, but we couldn't see eye to eye as to who gets what at first and —"

"Do you have children?" Lucy cut him short. She could hardly breathe. She did not care about his financial settlement. He had lied to her! He had not trusted her. What's a relationship worth without trust?

"What? No, no children. One of the reasons we're getting a divorce. Julie's career always came first. She's happy not to have any, but I'd like to have a family." He thought that Lucy would want to have children one day.

Lucy glanced at her watch. "Look at the time! I have to get back to work."

Sinclair sensed her urge to flee and cupped her hand gently. "Lucy, I've never lied to you. It *is* true. We *are* getting a divorce. Trust me! You can talk to my lawyer if you like."

Seriously? "I really have to go now," she insisted, grabbing her bag and rising to her feet.

Sinclair cast a cursory glance around. He found scenes in public distasteful. "Dinner tonight?" he asked, flashing an alluring smile at her.

"Um, I have to work late. I need to present my ideas for the new show to the board, so I'm a bit busy these days." She clammed up. She was lying, something she was terrible at, and she was certain he could see that.

"Lucy, are you running away from me?" he asked quietly.

She sighed. "Yes and no. I have a lot on my plate right now and the fact that you're married, still, complicates things. I need some time, William. I'll call you. Goodbye now," she said and walked away.

*

Michael leaned back on the couch in his living room. He clasped his hands behind his head, elbows pointing forward, lost somewhere deep in his own world. He stared at the ceiling for the longest time and then out of the window at the blackness of the garden. After several amendments to his original business plan, he still needed cash every way he looked at it; here and now. The banks were still closed and the limit of one hundred euros on daily withdrawals from the automated teller machines was not helping. Neither were the long lines of frustrated people. Worse still, no one accepted checks. How was he ever supposed to bootstrap a business like this? The economy was suffocating; he too along with it.

He feared the inevitability of dominoes falling. As the crisis continued, an alarmingly increasing number of companies, big and small, had begun to let people go. Many small businesses had either closed down or were in the process. The Orthodox Church and the municipalities had set up programs to feed people. Entire families relied on them to meet their basic needs. From one of the wealthiest countries in the world just a few years back, Cyprus had become a nation close to penury.

Michael banished these fatalistic thoughts. There was not much he could do about the country, but perhaps he could save himself. He just had to figure out how. He rose to his feet and poured himself a glass of a local blend of oak-aged cabernet and *maratheftiko*, an indigenous red wine variety. He had another glass and felt his taut muscles relax.

Pappou looked over the newspaper in his hands and peered at him with a worried frown. "Michael," his gentle voice interrupted the young man's thoughts. He waited until he met his eye and then went on, "If things are so bad, why don't you sell the house and come and live with me in the small house?"

When Michael had bought the land, in the plans, he included a small house adjacent to the back garden for *pappou* to keep an eye on him in his old age. It was *pappou* who had brought him up, all by himself, and had been by his side rain, hail, or shine. He owed him. But most of all, he loved the old man that much.

"*Pappou*, this house is meant for you," he said reluctantly, though it made sense. *Pappou's* house was big enough for both of them, for the time being at least.

"Michael, we've always been a team you and I," *pappou* said. "I've given my life to you. Do you really think I'd mind sharing the house with you? Your gift by the way," he remarked.

Michael nodded assent and offered him an evanescent smile. "This might not be such a bad idea. The way things are now, I bet no one's buying anything here, but perhaps I can put it up for sale on line. Thank you, *pappou!*"

"One more thing, I have some money put aside. It's not much, but I don't need it. Take it. I saved it for a rainy day. You've always paid all my bills, so I never really got to spend my pension. It's yours. See if it helps you start your new business."

Michael felt a tenderness for *pappou* welling up inside of him. He had never been a particularly religious man, but if there were guardian angels, *pappou* was his definitely. "Let's see if I can manage without it. It's good to know that it's there. The banks are still closed, who knows for how long, so you have no access to it anyway. But thanks – again! I'll have a word with some friends; see if they're interested in becoming silent partners."

Michael did not really want to sell the house. It was his dream house. He had taken his time to find just the right location, with a view of the sea and only a short drive into town, and to have it built to satisfy his taste and lifestyle.

He closed his eyes for an instant before opening them again, breathing in and out. It would take a while, but he would have another house built one day, he promised himself. Now, however, he had to think about how to speed up the sale. He would need a Town-Planning-Housing permit to get a separate deed for *pappou's* house. He would set about it right away. But he could still list it on various sites to save time.

9

1299

Provence stood in front of the open window in the great hall, excited and aflutter in equal measure. He could hardly wait for Albert to ride through the gate after all these years and hold him in his arms again. He had already given orders to kill the fatted calf and bring out the best wine. Yet clouds of worry cast a shadow over him. He could only hope that Roussillon would not find out about Albert's return.

Inevitably, his thoughts drifted to the new expedition. It would be Nicholas' first battle, an opportunity to prove his loyalty to the king. He was well prepared; Provence had seen to that. But in a battle, a man's life is in God's hands. Eloise's illness had been one more worry on his list lately. He said a silent prayer and thanked the Lord for bringing his boy back and begged Him to spare his other son's life and cure his wife.

Provence was also concerned about the outcome of this new campaign that signified the end of the unsettling quiet that followed the fall of Acre. The long drought that had emptied the grain warehouses on the island did nothing to allay his misgivings. The grain that was imported from Crete and Apulia hardly sufficed to feed everyone. With the new expedition in motion, famine would blight the lives of the serfs, and that would affect his estates in ways he did not want to begin considering.

The noise of running footsteps outside distracted him. He peered through the window and saw Lois sticking her tongue out at Nicholas and laughing. The young man ran after her, reached her in two long-legged strides, lifted her up easily in his robust arms, and whirled her around. Then he let her down and tickled her.

Her laughter lilted through the orchard. A flicker of discomfort snaked across Provence's face. He would have to have a word with Nicholas.

*

The sun was sinking when Nicholas had finished his chores and come into the house for supper.

"Nicholas!" Provence called out.

"Yes, Father?" Nicholas came into the great hall.

"Have a seat, son." Provence waved him to a seat, and the strapping young man sat across from him. "It's time you stopped playing with Lois like that," Provence got straight to the point.

"Like what?" Nicholas asked, jerking his head back.

Provence's mouth twisted slightly as if he was having a hard time finding the right words. "You know, tickling her, touching her."

"What? It's just a game."

"I know. Still, she is twelve; almost a woman now."

"Indeed? Uh, Father, she's just a *pichòt,* a bairn," Nicholas said, allowing himself a wry smile.

Provence looked at his poised face. Nicholas would normally try to abide by Provence's wishes. But he was in the habit of listening respectfully, with unfailing politeness, and then proceeding to do what he determined to be right in the rare occasions they were not of the same mind. And as far as Lois was concerned, he had a scant regard for propriety.

"Anyhow, you are a man, a knight soon. You should be spending your time preparing for your first battle," Provence said impatiently, realizing belatedly that his words might strike a sensitive nerve, but Nicholas was not thrown off balance so easily.

"Do not fret about me, Father. I had the most adept tutor, the best mentor there is." The corners of his lips went up in a mischievous grin.

Nicholas had a way with words, and Provence could not always tell if he was serious or not, but now he was preoccupied with other matters. He glanced out the window. "Their galley must have moored at Episkopia by now. They should be home soon," he said, finding it hard to contain his restiveness.

"They are here!" he cried out, agog, moments later and walked vigorously out the door. His heart beat so fast, he thought it would burst in his chest.

The three riders left their horses with the groom and brushed the worst of the dust from their clothes. Albert took a good look around, taking it all in, drowning in memories. It had been so long; too long!

Provence and Nicholas appeared in the doorway.

"Albert!" Provence's voice broke. Words failed him, but the tight embrace he gave his son said it all.

"Father!" Albert fought back unmanly tears.

Provence held onto his son, wishing he could recover those eight lost years. Then he embraced Peyre while Albert turned to Nicholas.

"The return of the prodigal son!" Nicholas said teasingly, and Albert rubbed his knuckles on his younger brother's head playfully.

As Provence let go of Peyre, he glanced at the man accompanying Albert. He had waited patiently for the family moment to be over.

"Father, Nicholas, this is my dear friend and partner in trade Guilhelm Gascoigne. Guilhelm, meet my father, Ramon of Provence, and Nicholas, my little brother," Albert said.

"Welcome, Guilhelm. *Mon ostal es ton ostal,*" Provence said, intercepting the tenderness in the gaze Albert and Guilhelm exchanged.

Guilhelm thanked Provence, and Albert inquired after his mother. He was surprised she was not there to welcome him back home.

"She's not well, Albert," Provence said. "She is resting upstairs, anxiously waiting for you."

Albert nodded and rushed up the stairs.

*

The unpretentious great hall in the Provence manor was not more than a rectangular room with a large stone fireplace and a chimney in one corner and three large oak trestle tables with a bench on each side at the center of the room. The only ornaments on the whitewashed wall were the stuffed heads of a *moufflon*, the Cyprus mountain sheep, and a boar, left and right of a tapestry, depicting a deer hunt.

Provence stabbed a pigeon on the thick bread trencher with his knife, twisted its leg with his fingers, and chewed. He used the sleeve at his wrist to wipe his mouth and downed his wine. "So, Albert, what have you been doing these eight years?" Peyre had kept him informed, but he wanted to hear Albert's own account.

"Well, Father, Guilhelm and I buy and sell whatever people need or desire. We buy cowhides from al-Sham and sell them to Marseille and Montpellier along with wine and olive oil soap from Cyprus. On its way back, the galley may be loaded with saffron or French cloth. In fact, trade has been so good that we are considering borrowing money to buy one more galley."

Provence was thoughtful. He had never been fond of borrowing. The deplorable prospect of not paying his debts back in time scared him more than any battle he had fought, but he kept this to himself. Albert seemed to have done well without his counsel. "And you, Guilhelm, how long have you been in Cyprus?"

"All my life; I was born in Famagusta."

"Tell me about your family," Provence asked.

"My family is originally from Gascogne. My father and brothers are boat builders. They say the pines from Troodos make the best masts, but I would know nothing about that. Trade is my world. Nicosia may be the capital of Cyprus, but Famagusta is the capital of trade and the capital of my heart, the most vibrant place to be," he said lightly.

"Famagusta sounds like an exciting place," Nicholas said, his curiosity piqued. He had seen almost every other corner of the island while accompanying his father, but not Famagusta. Provence had meticulously avoided arousing any suspicion in Roussillon's mind about Albert's whereabouts.

"Indeed! Believe you me, we have seen a bit of the world, and I tell you, Famagusta is a merchant's heaven on earth. There is no other place I would rather live in," Guilhelm said, a complacent smile sprouting on his lips.

With the nascent desire for travel, Nicholas became aware that, unlike Albert and Guilhelm, he had never been beyond the shores of the island.

"The bishop is thinking of having a cathedral built in Famagusta. He has commissioned the famous architect Jean Landois to draw the design," Peyre put in, as Lois came in with a fresh flagon of their best wine and replenished the chalices.

"That is perhaps the only thing we do not have yet," Albert said. "It is true, Father. I have never seen so rich a place as Famagusta. Merchants' daughters have more jewelry than royalty! This is why I would like to make Nicholas here a proposal." He looked at him. "You should come with us to Famagusta and learn how to trade. We need someone we can trust, and I promise you it is good living."

"He will be dubbed a knight in a few days," Provence remarked quietly.

"He can be a knight *and* a merchant. Nothing wrong with being a rich knight, is there? What say you, Nicholas?" Albert said under the benign influence of wine.

Lois gasped and held her breath. The notion that Nicholas would go away one day had never crossed her mind. The sudden prospect of life without him on the estate seemed gray and dull.

Nicholas met Provence's eye. They both knew that he had completed his knighthood training out of respect and love for his father and that he was destined for a different kind of life, but they had not talked about this in so many words. Trade was perhaps not so bad, Provence mused. It had worked with Albert, yet he could hardly picture Nicholas as a merchant.

"I would not mind trying," Nicholas said at length, welcoming the possibility of broadening his horizons. "But I'm afraid that it has to wait until my return. We are sailing for Tortosa soon."

A chill of fear passed over Lois like a shadow. She shrank back in alarm. She searched for his eyes, but he was too engaged in the conversation to pay heed to little Lois. Nicholas' leaving for Famagusta was bad enough; the prospect of going off to war, from which he might never return, was unbearable! She felt her throat constrict at the very thought.

Guilhelm drained his goblet and said, "Fighting is for the bloodthirsty. Trading is for the gold thirsty. I, for one, prefer gold to blood. What is this nonsense about sending all these robust, young men to be slaughtered for Jerusalem? Does no one see how unattainable this goal is? Worse still, does no one think of the retribution of the Saracens? Just because they have been stupid enough not to go to war at sea, there is no guarantee that their stupidity is perpetual.

"These *oltramontani,* these foreigners, are fine ones to talk. Their countries are huge and beyond the reach of the Unbeliever; their families safe. Our realm is just a rock in the midst of the sea, surrounded by the Saracens. Who will come to our rescue, I ask you? The Christians have lost their footing in the Holy Land. How many more places must be sacrificed ere they wake up to reality? The recovery of Jerusalem is simply beyond reach," he belabored the issue.

Provence clearly disapproved of the effeminate, glib manner of his expression, yet he could hardly disagree with the argument.

*

Back in the kitchen, Lois managed to place the flagon on the table without breaking it and remembered to breathe again; her brain too busy sorting the jumble in her mind.

10

2013

"So you see, Brian, I've been dating a married man," Lucy said.

Comfortably seated on the pearl leather sofa in his Chelsea apartment, Brian, a friend and former colleague, listened to her account about Sinclair, nodding along, unable to add anything thoughtful or helpful. He shook his head disapprovingly. "My, oh, my! That bastard!" he said at last. He, too, had broken up with his partner recently, and it still hurt – so much that he had even begun looking for another job. "This calls for a drink."

He stood up, filled two glasses with *Sancerre*, and offered her one. "If I were straight, I'd marry you and have half a dozen kids with you to make sure you wouldn't leave me." His endeavor at a joke failed miserably; it did not register with her.

"Why didn't he ever say anything?" She shook her head.

"Maybe he wanted to surprise you with his divorce?" Brian shrugged.

"Oh, he surprised me all right," Lucy said, wrinkling her nose. "And all this time I thought I'd found Mr. Perfect. How could I have been so blind? I never saw this coming." She did not know if she was angrier with William or herself.

"I know it hurts now, but it won't hurt forever," Brian tried to sound optimistic. "Mr. Perfect's out there somewhere, but don't go looking for him just yet."

Lucy grimaced and sighed. "As if the whole William-thing isn't bad enough, I need to look for another job, too!"

"Well, here's to new beginnings," Brian said. He raised his glass, and she reluctantly picked up hers.

*

Lucy was calmer when she left Brian's apartment; he always had a soothing effect on her. By the time she got back home, she was convinced she'd had two signs in one day telling her to move on — or away.

She stood by the window and looked up at the clouds gathering in the gray sky that matched her mood. She began to visualize images of a nice place by the beach on some Mediterranean island, the sun shining brightly in a clear blue sky. Her last film shoot on Cyprus sprang to mind. Out of curiosity, she searched for properties on the island. She had time to kill.

Despite the financial crisis, real estate prices were still high. It seemed that people had not been forced to sell yet. Not that she wanted to take advantage of people in need, but finding a bargain wouldn't hurt. She might be helping someone in a hurry to sell, she persuaded herself.

It was already dark outside when a sudden pop up for a new listing drew her attention. She read it carefully. The price seemed reasonable for what she could see in the photos. Built on the edge of a cliff, the villa offered romantic Mediterranean vistas; floor-to-ceiling windows allowed unobstructed views. Lucy fell in love instantly with the lovely balconies, the low-pitched tile roof, and the arch motifs. Rooms opened onto a swimming pool and a garden. Inside the house, elegant, modern furniture was combined with minimalist décor. It was close to what Lucy considered perfection.

She stared at the pictures for a long time, seeing herself living there. She would have a word with her lawyer first thing in the morning, she decided.

Her cell phone buzzed next to her. It was William — again. She was itching to talk to him, yet she declined the call. Was there anything more to say? She turned her attention to the photos on the screen.

Temptation stronger than common sense, she grabbed her cell and texted him a brief message: Call me when you're divorced.

*

Sinclair looked like thunder when Lucy would not take his call. He had not expected her cold shoulder to sting that much. Was it because she had made him chase after her for so long, or had she grown on him while he wasn't paying attention, he wondered, shaking his head.

He heard the familiar jingle sound and read her message. There was a brief incredulous moment before he tossed his cell on the desk, cursing under his breath.

II

1299

After supper, Albert showed Guilhelm around the estate while Provence remained seated in the great hall with Peyre and Nicholas.

"Peyre, how long has this been going on?" Provence asked in a low voice.

"What has?"

"You know what!" He pointed with his head at the direction Albert and Guilhelm had left the room.

"Oh, that!" Peyre said, loosening his cassock with his index finger. Nicholas shifted his gaze between their faces, stunned that Peyre grasped what Father was alluding to, for Nicholas did not. "Eight years or so," Peyre said matter-of-factly, watching his father's eyes widen.

Was it his fault, Provence wondered? Had he been such a bad father, or was it the devil's work? "What do you think of ... this?" Sodomite was the word that came to mind, but he could not bring himself to say it out loud – not when he talked about Albert.

Peyre shrugged. "You know the official stand of the Church. Luxuria is *peccatum contra naturum*, a deadly sin."

"I'm asking my son," Provence pressed.

"Well, they seem happy together; happier than many people I know. They just need to go on hiding from the rest of the world, or it's the pyre for them." Nicholas began to comprehend.

"Hmm" was Provence's only reply. Nicholas was not surprised that Provence had not spoken ill of Albert. He was his son, and he loved him. Nothing had changed Nicholas' brotherly feelings for him either.

"Mother is not well," Provence changed the subject. "The physician's leeching therapy has not made her any stronger. On the contrary, I fear she is fading away." He paused briefly and then he went on, "Widow Emilia said this morning that she can treat her with her herbs. Kontostephanos says it's a good idea. What do you think? Should I place your mother's health in the hands of a serf?"

Peyre pondered briefly and then said, "Maybe you should. The herbs will do what they can. The rest we must leave to God."

"Let's hope God does not mind Emilia's old ways," Nicholas said, his eyes crinkling with humor. Peyre cast him a glance that mingled disapproval and forbearance.

Provence nodded. "You are right. We have nothing to lose. I will have a word with Emilia in the morning." New ways, old ways meant little to him if it meant saving Eloise, but he thought it wiser not to start such a conversation with Peyre.

"Father, Peyre, I think I will wish you good night now," Nicholas said, rising to his feet. He had the urge to pray. The pains of so many years would be rewarded soon, and he was grateful.

They watched him go in silence. As soon as he was out of earshot, Peyre said, "You are worried, Father?"

Provence took a sup of wine and met his gaze. "I would be lying if I said I'm not. Only a fool would not be worried to see his son off to war." He had already lost a son on the battlefield of Tripoli. "But I have taught him everything I know. He has been most diligent. And he is sharp-witted." He spoke in a matter-of-fact tone.

"I daresay, he does not rattle easily and has an easy assurance withal. Well, Father, we can only pray for him. I will be saying an additional prayer for him after vespers. We all should."

Provence admired, envied even, the serenity and comfort Peyre found in prayer, for he did not.

*

Nicholas entered the chapel, dipped his fingers into the holy water, and blessed himself. He genuflected, crossing himself, clearing his mind for God. He felt proud and excited and wanted to humble himself. He was proud, for he had completed his knighthood training, and excited about the new life that awaited him either as a knight or as a wealthy merchant in Famagusta. And the choice was his to make. He prayed for guidance, but mostly for the opportunity to justify his father's faith in him.

He was still wrapped up in his thoughts when he walked out of the chapel.

"So, you are leaving."

Lois' voice startled him. He looked up and flashed a warm smile at her. "Yes, this is something I have to do."

"Mm," Lois nodded, unable to bear the thought of losing her best friend. But she could not tell him that. She had no right to burden him with her fears and anxieties. She smiled bravely.

Attuned to subtle mood indicators, Nicholas sensed her unease. "I will miss you, too, *pichòt*," he said gently, pressing his forehead against hers briefly.

"Just come back in one piece," she said; her voice thick with emotion.

"This is my intention!" Shoving back at the black mood descending, he gave her an infectious grin and added lightly, "You had better be a good girl in my absence. Or else I might have to punish you upon my return."

"And what will my punishment be, my lord?" Lois played along.

"Oh, I'm sure I will think of something," he said, entwining his fingers in her hair, pulling gently.

Without warning, he snatched her and whirled her around. Just as quickly, he let her down again and tickled her until she cried out, "I surrender!"

"That's better!" he said and let go of her. "Let us get back now, lest everyone start looking for us!"

*

Lois was unable to fall asleep that night. She experienced a feeling of dread in her stomach at the thought of Nicholas embarking for war, and she lifted her gaze to the dark ceiling.

"God, if You are listening, there is something I must ask of You; not for myself. You know I have never asked anything for myself. I beg of You to bring Nicholas back alive. I promise I will never forget my prayers again if You do, and I will do my best to care for his sick mother. But if You don't, I will never pray again!"

12

2013

Lucy slid open the glass door and stepped onto the balcony, taking in the last vestiges of twilight seeping below the horizon in the brisk early spring breeze. Soon she would be enjoying the Mediterranean every day. She made herself comfortable on an armchair, marveling at the view. Her mind slowly emptying, she felt so tranquil that she almost fell asleep to the gentle splashing sounds of the waves rolling on the beach.

The sky had turned dark blue velvet when she got back in, rubbing her arms. She began unpacking, counting the hours until the appointment for the house the next day.

Lucy had always welcomed change into her life. She attributed this mainly to her childhood background. Back in the day, they never stayed in a place longer than a few years at a time. But, more than that, Lucy always felt an urge to take on new challenges, visit new places and meet new faces. She was close to forty, a good time to slow down; settle down. Just a couple of weeks ago, she had been almost certain she would – with William. But then she had had a brutal awakening.

No more William, she rebuked herself and wondered if the house was as elegant and cozy as in the pictures she had seen. She hoped it was; photos can be deceiving sometimes. Her heart was set on it.

It would be dinner time soon, and Lucy settled on her favorite floral summer dress for the evening. She meant to enjoy herself tonight. It felt as though she was filling the first page of an exciting new chapter in her life.

*

Through the large French windows in the living room, Michael watched the beauty of the red-gold sky. The flaming brilliance of the dying sun dazzled him, and for a moment, all worries were erased from his mind.

He nibbled on a dried fig and poured himself a blend of a local shiraz and *lefkada,* a red grape variety brought to the island by the Byzantines, and took a sip.

He slid into a seat and picked up a little note from the coffee table. He had crossed out the first three of the four names of potential silent partners. He would be meeting later that evening with Dino, the fourth name on the list. He glanced out the window again. The purple sky was turning dark blue velvet.

If Dino said 'no', selling the house would be the only way out of this financial impasse. What if the interested buyer got cold feet? A sigh escaped his lips. *Patience,* he reminded himself. He would find out soon enough.

He glanced at his watch. There was still time before the meeting. He picked up his cell phone and stared at it for a while before he began deleting all the photos of her. There! She was out of his life, though a part of him still felt numb inside.

*

The taxi pulled to a halt outside the *Cuba Libre,* the Latin bar the concierge had recommended to Lucy earlier. She paid the driver and got out of the car to the sound of *Mi Tierra.*

She walked in, glad she could still hear herself think, and sat on a stool at the bar. The bartender greeted her with a nod and a smile from the far side of the bar. Business was slow, but that did not surprise her. The clients were mainly foreigners. It seemed as though Cypriots were being careful with their money.

She glanced around, studying the dimly-lit ambience. The décor was elegant and the vibe relaxed, though the bar turned clubby after midnight, the concierge had said. True to its name, it was a vintage luxury of mid-century design intermixed with vibrant Cuban colors and sleek furniture.

Lucy studied the drinks list, tapping her foot to the beat. *Giannoudi,* a local red variety that had recently found its way back to wineries, caught her eye. Always in search of new flavors, she settled for that. The bartender placed a glass in front of her, and she tested the deep, rich color. She gave it a gentle swirl, and took in its bouquet; delicate notes of vanilla and berries. She took a sip, relishing its silky light tannins, balance, and aftertaste. Cypriot wines had improved immensely in the last few years, she thought, and made a mental note to take some bottles back as gifts.

*

Michael leaned back on the sofa at *Cuba Libre* and took a sip of his beer. He placed the glass slowly on the coffee table and tried to read Dino's face. "Well? What do you think?"

Dino took his own sweet time, draining his pint of golden lager, while eyeing the blonde with the cute little floral summer dress who had just walked in all by herself and settled on a stool at the bar. She caught him checking her out and looked up and away, turning her attention to the drinks list.

Michael leaned back on the sofa, exercising patience. Dino smoothed his thinning dyed hair that gave away his desperate clinging on to his faded youth. Eventually, he met Michael's eyes.

"As promising as gourmet catering may sound, quite honestly, I don't have that kind of cash right now, Michael. When we spoke on the phone, I thought we would be talking about less – a lot less. My money's all tied up. I'm sorry," Dino said, rejecting yet another call. "I'm sure you'll find someone else," he added, though they both knew it would not happen any time soon.

"Sure. I understand." Michael nodded impassively.

Dino checked the time. "I'm sorry, but I gotta run now. Babe's waiting." He winked and stood up. "Oh, and good luck!"

"Sure. Thanks. I'll see you around," Michael said, rising to his feet. He shook hands with him and sat back down, watching Dino's beefy figure move away. There was something about working nights that made infidelity commonplace Michael thought, twisting his lips in disgusted irritation. He finished his beer, grabbed his car key, and got up.

*

Lucy took a sip of her *giannoudi,* watching the bartender's confident flair moves, when a tipsy client bumped against a waitress. In her effort to balance the heavy tray in her hand, the waitress stumbled and almost knocked down Michael as he was leaving. He did his best not to fall on the blonde at the bar, but he startled her all the same, and she spilled half her wine on his black slacks.

"I'm sorry!" they said in one breath. He had an easy smile, she noticed. "It's all right," they said in unison, and he looked at her with covert amusement.

The waitress apologized, and the bartender offered them a round of drinks on the house and gave Michael a bar towel.

"I'll have whatever the lady's having," Michael said. The bartender filled two glasses and placed them in front of them.

Michael dried his slacks, casting a fleeting, stealthy glance at her décolletage. He took a seat on the stool next to her, studying her discreetly. Although he could not place where or when, he had the impression they had met before. He realized she was uncomfortable: he was staring at her.

"I'm sorry. Listen, this is not a line, but I could swear you look like a girl I used to know," he explained. "Only she had long brown hair." He recalled in a flash of memory the curls cascading down her back. "That was," he paused for a second or two, lifting his gaze to the ceiling. "Almost twenty years ago. Lucy was her name."

Lucy's lips parted as she took a closer look at him, wondering how he had guessed her name. His features looked distantly familiar, and the sound of his smooth voice evoked a glimpse of a far-off memory. "My name's Lucy," she said, cautious and enthralled at the same time. "And you are…?"

He grinned as if to say, 'so, you don't remember me.' "Michael," he said with becoming modesty and a dazzling smile.

In that instant she knew. A warm smile blossomed across her face. She rotated her stool toward him, and their knees touched slightly. "Michael! Michael Costa from college! My God that was a lifetime ago! I'm sorry I didn't recognize you at once. What happened to that bushy hair of yours?" *That I used to love.*

He passed a hand over his shaved head. "Not much left I'm afraid," he said with a coy smile, remembering how straightforward she had always been.

"I think I like your new look. It gives you a touch of…" She paused, half closing her eyes, searching for the right word. "Mystery," she concluded.

"Thanks, I guess. Well, here's to unexpected reunions." He raised his glass.

"I'll drink to that!" They clinked glasses.

Lucy finished her wine, and Michael ordered two more, then grinned and shook his head. He looked down as if enjoying a private joke.

"What?"

He raised his eyes and looked up at her. "Oh, Lucy!" He breathed a sigh, shaking his head again in incredulity.

"What?" She sounded intrigued this time.

"I was so in love with you back then. It took me a very, *very* long time to get over you."

She smiled at the memory. "Well, I recall being head over heels for you." A pause. "What happened to us?"

Michael hesitated, shrugged. "Life happened. I asked you to marry me and come to Cyprus with me, but you had other plans. A career in Paris. I couldn't blame you. I'd have done the same." *Or not.*

"Yes." A reflective pause. "If my memory serves me right, I did ask you to come with me. Remind me! Why couldn't you?"

"Because of *pappou,*" he said, reminiscing and reaching for his glass. *Pappou* had been in chemotherapy at the time, and Michael wanted to be there for him. He was all *pappou* had.

Lucy nodded. "How's *pappou?*"

"Getting older, but he's all right. Better than expected for his age. He's a tough nut."

"To *pappou,*" Lucy said, raising her glass.

13

1299

Lois and Kontostephanos wished Widow Emilia, the cook in Provence's manor, good morning, as she greeted them with a censer with burning blessed olive tree leaves. Emilia had been a beautiful woman once, but the deep lines on her prematurely wrinkled, weather-beaten face attested to the hardships of a life full of back-breaking work and sorrow.

They said a silent prayer, swinging their open hand over the censer three times, and made the sign of the cross dutifully. Every morning and every evening, Lois kept her promise to God and never once failed to say her prayers, serene in the conviction that the Lord would hold to their understanding, and Nicholas would return home safely.

They took the ration of bread, cheese, raisins, and walnuts that Emilia had prepared for them and a goatskin bag filled with fresh water and headed for the vineyards.

"Have I ever told you the story about these six terebinth trees?" Kontostephanos asked, pointing at a perfect row of trees, three on each side of the manor entrance.

"No," Lois said, eager to hear another one of his stories.

"My great-grandfather planted them; one for each of his children on the day of their birth. That was before the Lusignans bought Cyprus from the English and made us serfs."

Lois nodded slowly absorbed in contemplative consideration of the noble's life she would have been living if all these Franks had never come to Cyprus.

"Why did we allow them to make us serfs in our own land?"

"We are just a handful of people, no match for their strength and wealth. But we should be vigilant, for the day will come when they are weak, and that will be our opportunity to strike."

Lois frowned. "What do you mean?"

"All these Franks, they come from so many different places. One day, they will turn against each other. Divided, they are not so strong." He paused briefly. "Do you think we are more like the oak or the reed?"

"The reed?" she said, shrugging.

Kontostephanos' lips broke into a complacent smile. "Yes, Lois, Cypriots are like the reed. A life of toil and hardship has made us modest enough to bend over in tempests and stand up straight again when it is all over. We will still be here when our conquerors leave, worshiping the Lord in our Orthodox way, speaking our own language. Cyprus has been Greek for thousands of years. For-eigners come, conquer, plunder, and leave; but we remain. It is the fate of the small and the weak. You can embrace it or vanish from the face of the earth! And we, who were once *archontes*, have a duty to our people to lead by example."

"But the Provences are kind to us. They have freed us, made us *lefteroi*," she said.

"Indeed, they are noble and kind. But we are the only *lefteroi* in the *casale*; everyone else is just a serf. In a way, they need us. We are the only ones on their estates who speak their tongue, the former owners of this very land. This appeases the locals when we collect taxes for the Provences."

They reached the vineyard and began to walk along the rows of vine. The ploughing already done, the serfs were busy pruning. Soon they would cultivate, cut off the shoots, and layer the run-ners. Lois could hardly wait for summer to come. Trampling the grapes was her favorite thing to do in the vineyard; it signified the safe bringing in of the crops, and it was a good excuse for a feast.

Despite the stultifying dullness since Nicholas had left, Lois tried to focus on her daily chores and *pappou's* teaching, a distraction from worrying constantly. Now she could smell and taste the difference in the wines from various crops, as Kontostephanos had taught her. She had earned the moniker 'the nose' because she could judge one vintage from another, and perhaps because her nose was a bit large in proportion to the rest of her face.

14

2013

A sliver of light filtered through the edge of the blackout curtain. Lucy made an effort to open her eyes and get her bearings, not an easy task with her head throbbing as though she was wearing a hat three sizes too small for her. She struggled to focus as she looked around at the unfamiliar setting until her gaze stopped at the arm resting on her hips. For an infinitesimal moment she plunged into panic. And then she remembered.

She checked the time and cursed silently. She pushed his arm gently away and got out of bed slowly, fighting back a nail-in-the-temple feeling. She slipped back into her dress, grabbed her jacket, and cast one last glance at him. After all these years, he still had that quiet charm and affable manner. There had been a sweet sadness in his eyes that drew her to him, a sadness that had not been there before.

Enough, she told herself! She picked up her high heels, closed the door gently, and walked barefoot into the living room. It was ablaze with light. Through the floor-to-ceiling windows, she marveled at the view of the Mediterranean giving way to verdant fields, studded with wildflowers.

"Ruff!"

The stuttered bark made Lucy freeze, but when she looked down at the brown and white beagle with its front legs flat on the ground and its rear held high, she grasped that the bark was an invitation to play. She let the dog sniff her hand, and it wagged its tail.

A voice speaking in Greek startled her, and Lucy looked up to face a rather short, elderly man with thinning white hair and a gentle face with rosy cheeks. She guessed that he was Michael's grandfather.

"Good morning," she said, feeling busted.

"Good afternoon, rather," the old man snickered sympathetically, pushing his round spectacles on the bridge of his broad, flat nose. "I see you've already made Lola's acquaintance. I'm making coffee. Would you like some?"

Lucy looked into his eyes and saw neither judgment nor mockery. Those were kind eyes, and his smile was gentle and reassuring. "Um, no thank you, but I could use a taxi." Lola stood on her hind legs and placed her front paws on Lucy, wagging her tail, and Lucy patted her on the head.

"Nonsense! Michael will drive you. I'll send Lola to wake him up."

"No, no," Lucy said, shaking her head. She winced as her headache returned. "It's all right; really. We should let him sleep," she added quickly before the old man could make a move. She was not sure that the romance of the night before would survive the daylight scrutiny, not after all these years and all that wine. "A taxi would be just fine."

He inclined his head with an understanding smile. "In that case, I'd better call a taxi then." He picked up the receiver, dialed a number, and said a few words in Greek. Then he turned to face her. "It'll be here in about fifteen minutes. How about that coffee?" His tone was encouraging. He intercepted her anxious glance at the closed bedroom door but made no comment. "Sugar?" he asked, already halfway into the kitchen.

"No, thank you." Reluctantly, she followed him into a bright room with large windows that looked onto a beautiful rose garden.

He placed a bottle of water, a glass, and some aspirin on the table. "Drink lots of water. It's the best remedy." He winked. Lucy poured herself a glass and took the aspirin.

The scent of coffee filled the air as he brought two small cups to the table and took a seat across from her. "*Geia mas*," he said, raising his cup as in a toast, the Cypriot way, and slurped his coffee. "I'm

Michael, by the way, Michael's grandfather. He's my namesake. You can call me *pappou* to avoid confusion. That's grandpa in Greek."

"I'm Lucy. Nice to meet you, *pappou*." She extended an arm.

Pappou shook her hand. "The pleasure's all mine."

"I see Lola's used to total strangers," Lucy blurted out more dryly than she had intended. The dog was accustomed to women walking out of Michael's bedroom, she thought for no apparent reason.

Pappou studied her face and finished his coffee. "She's friendly, but Michael's not in the habit of surprising us with strangers. It took him almost a year before he brought his fiancée home."

Lucy almost choked on her coffee. "He's engaged?"

"Was."

Lucy felt sick. What had she been thinking? She did not know the first thing about Michael after all these years! She finished her coffee and tried to stay calm and manage the pain in her head.

Relieved to hear the sound of a horn, she got to her feet. "That's my ride, I guess. Thank you for the coffee. You're very kind, *pappou*."

"So are you," he returned the compliment and walked her to the door.

Lucy got into the taxi and gave the driver the name of the hotel, stealing one last glance at the old man standing on the porch and waving at her. She waved back.

*

Michael was wakened by the taxi horn. He rolled onto his side with a pillow over his ears. A vaguely familiar perfume hit his nostrils. He opened one eye. Was that a bra? He had a sudden recollection to the night before and smirked. His eyes scanned the room for Lucy, but she was not there. He had a quick shower, slipped into a pair of jeans and a shirt, rolled the sleeves up, and went to the kitchen to look for her.

"*Kalimera, pappou,*" he said.

Lola barked, demanding his attention, and Michael got down on one knee. "Hey, sweetie. No, no licking." He pushed her muzzle gently away, wondering if Lucy had left without saying goodbye.

"Good afternoon, rather," *pappou* said, folding his newspaper. He got up to make him coffee. "You've just missed Lucy."

"I see you two met," Michael said, smothering a smile. "Where is she?"

"She took a taxi. She didn't want to wake you. If I'd known you had company, I wouldn't have used the house key so freely," he said apologetically.

Michael realized just then that he had no way of getting in touch with her. She had walked back into his life, wakened long lost emotions, and walked out again.

"It's all right. You couldn't have known," he said, wondering whether she might be at the *Cuba Libre* again in the evening.

"She's a nice girl," *pappou* said approvingly, placing the coffee on the table in front of Michael. He had never quite liked the model's cold eyes, though of course he never shared this with Michael.

"And you can tell how exactly?" he asked teasingly.

"When you reach the age of eighty-six, you'll be able to tell, too. She's sweet and tender-hearted." He knew that Michael had become cynical, that his faith in women had been shaken.

"So, I chose well. Good to know," Michael said, sipping his coffee. So long as he could find her again!

15

1299

Waiting for the next batch of heavy stones to be loaded for the rebuilding of the crenellations, Nicholas leaned over the parapet, looking around him at the fortress of Nephin. A great moat had been cut, all the way across the peninsula, for more than a hundred yards, through the living rock, leaving only a small spur in the center to support the drawbridge. The thick walls and the sea-swept battlements of the citadel offered additional protection against attack. The fortress was quasi-impregnable.

When the stones were loaded onto the pallet, the footman inside the treadwheel began to walk laboriously. As he did, the rope attached to a pulley turned on a spindle, hoisting the pallet. Nicholas and Poitou, his slightly-built new friend, shivered but willed the chilly breeze and the drizzle out of their minds and began unloading the heavy stones next to the Armenian masons.

Poitou staggered, but Nicholas was fast enough to give a helping hand. "One more," he said encouragingly. Poitou looked wan and exhausted. Nicholas would have done the work by himself if he could, but the stones were too big and too heavy. Poitou nodded, taking a moment to catch his breath.

"Watch out!" the footman in the treadwheel shouted as the rope snapped. The pallet crashed to the ground, men jumping out of its way just in time.

"It seems like we have a few minutes to rest after all," Nicholas said, catching his breath, and Poitou threw himself on a crenel with a rush of relief.

A sudden clamor erupted in the inner bailey, and Nicholas glanced down at the men assembling and a knight directing them to draw near. "Come on! We have to go, too!" he said, and they hurried down.

Captain La Naento appeared at the keep entrance. "Men, stop what you are doing and get some rest. When the sun goes down, we shall march to the fort of Mont Pèlerin. Local Christian peasants have told us that it has been abandoned since it was set ablaze by the Saracens, so it will be easy to seize. We can wait there for the main forces to arrive from Cyprus. God willing, it will be ours in the morning."

La Naento disappeared into the keep, and the men followed his advice to rest only too eagerly. Nicholas joined them with a sense of unease, wondering if the local peasants could be trusted. To him, swapping the safety of the fortress in Nephin for the unknown fort of Mont Pèlerin made little sense, but he held his tongue. He had neither the rank, nor the age or the experience to voice his thoughts.

*

A rooster squawked as forty mounted knights and turcopoles and sixty arbalesters and archers reached the bottom of Mont Pèlerin with the deeply rooted conviction that God was on their side. They did not see the hundreds of Saracens lying in wait behind thick bushes, left and right of the steep, narrow path that led to the fort. They, too, believed that Allah was on their side, and if they were to die, bright-faced angels would descend from heaven for them.

Suddenly, deafening and daunting war cries sounded, "Allahu Akbar!" The ferocious Saracen battle cry made the blood freeze in the veins of the soldiers of Christ. A storm of arrows whistled at them like a menacing cloud. They lifted their shields in confusion. The earth shook under the pounding hooves of the Saracen cavalry, four hundred men charging down the hill. Thick clouds of dust kicked up in their wake, as they mushroomed all around the Christians with the arrogance of numerical supremacy, the advantage of terrain, and the element of surprise on their side.

Amidst fiercely clashing swords, Nicholas' pulse spiked; his stomach heaved, but he stood his ground. Out of nowhere, an enemy sword came dangerously close to cutting off his head. At the very last instant, Nicholas warded off the thrust, raising his sword while leaning so far to his left that it seemed ineluctable that he would be unhorsed.

Swiftly, Nicholas sat in the saddle again, an impressive harmony between horse and master, and turned his mount around, parrying another blow. He'd had no time to think. Those were moves Provence had made him practice over and over again till his hands bled and he was saddle sore. Nicholas thrust his sword into his foe's chest.

From the corner of his eye, he registered a soldier running, axe raised high. With a lightning-fast reflex, Nicholas cut off the Saracen's arm, as he was about to lunge at unsuspecting Poitou from behind. Shocked, Poitou turned around and inclined his head in acknowledgement.

Nicholas looked around him at the panicked, loose, and riderless horses careening hither and yon. The battlefield was strewn with bodies, blood spurting from their wounds. He was astounded to find himself unharmed. It was as if God had raised a hand and deflected the enemy arrows. Roland, his white stallion, was less lucky. An arrow had wedged in his gambeson. The poor creature neighed in protest but obeyed his master's firm hand.

A few paces farther away, Amaury noticed the peasants in flight. They scattered, some into the mountains and some toward the coast. Even the peasants could see they were losing the battle, Amaury thought. For the love of God, what was La Naento doing?

"Retreat!" Amaury shouted. "Retreat!"

The Christians ran in disarray. The Saracens laughed; a sound carried in the wind that would haunt them long afterward. Only La Naento and his companion, Bertram Fassan, stood their ground, defending themselves till the bitter end, providing their comrades with a chance to get away.

*

The survivors reached Nephin with heads held low. Their situation was now precarious. Ghazan was not coming to their aid, and it was impossible to stay where they were. There was little choice but to sail for home.

Amaury leaned on the railing of the galley. He looked at the dark horizon, almost as bleak as his thoughts. He had always been one to act upon impulse and instinct. Instinct stronger than reason had told him to advise La Naento against endeavoring to take Mont Pèlerin. Why then had he kept his mouth shut? Was it because he wanted to prove Henry wrong for not giving him the command? Had he allowed his overweening pride to blind him?

Amaury jerked his head with a start. "Damn your catlike tread, Simon," he said as his friend materialized out of the shadows.

Simon of Montolif chuckled. "Cannot sleep?"

"We lost so many men today," Amaury said grimly, staring at the horizon.

"We would have lost a lot more if you hadn't given the command for retreat. The men know it. You kept your head, Amaury. You took command when chaos prevailed." Amaury was taciturn. "You look awful by the way," Simon said lightly, patting him on the back. "Try to get some sleep now or you will give Zabel a fright when she sees you."

"Heaven forbid," Amaury said with a half-smile, and Simon followed his own advice.

Amaury was not the only one passing a wakeful night. Nicholas was by Roland's side, treating his wound lovingly. There had been a special bond between them since the day Nicholas helped deliver him. He had looked after him when everyone thought the foal would not make it. But Roland fought to live, and Nicholas named him after Charlemagne's heroic nephew. He stroked his mane, whispering encouraging words, and the stallion whinnied in response.

Nicholas grieved for the fallen Christians and wondered what the point of going to war was without a stratagem. Perhaps Guilhelm was right; a life of peace and trade had more meaning.

16
2013

Lucy looked around her stupefied, as the taxi came to a halt right outside Michael's house. "This is it?"

"This is it," the driver confirmed.

She paid the man and walked up the short flight of steps to the porch, wondering what kind of a sign this was. She took a moment to collect herself before ringing the bell.

It was *pappou* who answered the door. "You're back! Come on in." Lucy gave him a small smile. "Michael, look who's here!" *pappou* cried out, and Michael appeared in the hallway.

"Lucy!" Michael was grinning from ear to ear.

"Were you expecting someone else?" she asked, tilting her head to the side.

"Uh, as a matter of fact, I was. I have an appointment, but please, stay. Coffee?"

"I'm on it. No sugar; I remember," *pappou* said, already heading for the hallway.

"Thank you!" Lucy cried out behind him.

"My pleasure," he shouted from the kitchen.

"So, you have an appointment. About the house?"

"Yes, how...? Wait! You? You're the buyer?"

"Potential buyer," she corrected him. "I need to see the place first."

"Wow!" Michael passed a hand over his shaved head. "Look at you! After all these years, you're thinking about moving to Cyprus!"

She shrugged. "Life's full of surprises! Will you show me the house?"

"Sure. That's what you're here for." He stretched out an arm.

"Have your coffee first," *pappou* said from the hallway. "It'll get cold. The house can wait. It won't go anywhere."

*

"And this is the master bedroom," Michael said, throwing the door open. He had left his room for last deliberately and was astonished to see her tucking a strand of hair behind one ear, lowering her gaze, blushing like a schoolgirl.

"About last night," Lucy said, clearing her throat.

"Something happened last night? Other than being loaded?" Michael offered helpfully. He decided not to mention the bra she had forgotten in his bed.

She locked eyes with him. "No, of course, not," she said, relieved he could read between the lines.

He was a little stung by the rejection, but he reminded himself that she was there for the house, not for him. He smiled. "Is it okay if I tell *pappou* you are *the* Lucy I once wanted to marry?"

Lucy thought for a moment. "No harm in that," she said, shrugging her shoulders.

Pappou put his head around the door. "Lucy, you're staying for dinner."

"Well, this is very kind, but –"

"No buts. You're staying. I'll make my specialty for you, sea bass – my way. Michael, show Lucy the gardens and the swimming pool until I prepare everything, will you?"

"You can't argue with *pappou;* you'll be insulting his hospitality," Michael said. "Besides, he makes the perfect sea bass. He used to have his own fish tavern, you know. He'd catch the fish himself and then serve it."

"In that case, *pappou*, thank you for the invitation, but I'll help you prepare. You might not know this about me, but that's what I do for a living."

"Actually, *pappou*, do you remember when I was in love with a girl during my studies in London?" Michael said, and Lucy wondered if *pappou* could see her blush.

Pappou tilted his head almost imperceptibly toward Lucy, his gaze inquisitive, and Michael nodded, giving him a crooked half-smile.

"It's twice a pleasure to have you home for dinner then," *pappou* said. "How about we make a contest out of it? Each of us will prepare sea bass in a different way. Deal?"

Michael and Lucy exchanged a glance. "Deal!"

"If this is a contest, we need a prize," Michael remarked.

"How about a kiss on the cheek?" *pappou* suggested.

"I'm in." Lucy said.

"Me too," Michael agreed.

*

To the sounds of the three tenors, Michael's kitchen had been turned into a battlefield, wafting a medley of ambrosial and balmy aromas, as the trio raced against the clock. In their rush, they kept bumping into one another, and it was hard to keep their dishes secret.

Pappou made sure their glasses were never empty, although Lucy noticed that he drank in moderation. "Good wine is a source of inspiration," *pappou* said, topping up their glasses.

Dinner turned out to be a delight, and the pairing with *promara,* a local white variety, successful. The pendulum chimed nine times in the living room when *pappou* said, "It's time to vote for the best dish of the evening. It goes without saying that we can't vote for our own. As I'm the eldest, I'll cast the first vote. Let me start by saying that this is not an easy decision," he said formally. "I can't begin to describe how pleased my taste buds are this evening."

He turned to Lucy and added, "Not half as pleased as we are with your company, sweet girl." She rewarded him with a smile. Then turning to his grandson, he added, "I'm sorry, Michael, but I'll have to vote for Lucy's grilled sea bass."

"Oh, this sounds like a fix to me!" Michael said, leaning back in his chair and shaking his head in mock protest.

"You'll have your chance to cast your vote after Lucy. Ladies first," *pappou* said.

"Mm, it's hard to tell if I liked Michael's sea bass in *kataifi,* shredded pastry, with the creamy lime dressing more or *pappou's* sea bass in vine leaf." She paused dramatically. "I think I'll go for *pappou's* dish. It's somehow brought out more…" She paused, fumbling for the right word, "… authentic flavor. I'm sorry, Michael," she said, turning to him and making an apologetic grimace.

"I accept defeat," Michael said, making a theatrical gesture.

"Your turn now," *pappou* prompted.

"Before I cast my vote, the decisive vote," Michael said, raising his eyebrows playfully, "I'm asking for a rematch."

"Granted," *pappou* agreed.

"Uh, not sure when. I'm leaving the day after tomorrow."

"Tomorrow then," *pappou* said, seeing no problem there. "We'll have a lamb competition!"

"Do you have better plans?" Michael asked.

"No, not that I can think of."

"Or I could take you out for dinner," he said, seizing the chance to be alone with her again.

"Um, actually, the lamb competition sounds quite challenging," Lucy said and lowered her gaze for a moment. Michael gave her an unexpectedly warm and understanding smile, for which she felt thankful.

"Great! My vote then. Lucy," he said solemnly, "I did like your grilled sea bass. It was cooked to perfection," he spoke slowly, as if preparing her for disappointment. "But I must confess that *pappou's* sea bass," he paused for a moment or two, "doesn't stand a chance."

The two men looked at each other and laughed heartily. "My sentiment exactly," *pappou* said. Turning to Lucy, he added, "And now your prize." He leaned closer and gave her a quick peck on the cheek.

"Congratulations," Michael said, staring into her eyes a second longer, before planting a kiss on her cheek.

"What are you doing tomorrow, Lucy?" *pappou* asked.

"I thought of going sightseeing."

"Michael could be your guide," *pappou* suggested casually.

"I don't mean to impose," Lucy said.

"I'm not doing anything tomorrow," Michael lied. "I'd love to show you around."

"All right, then. Thank you!"

"Lucy, please excuse me," *pappou* said a few minutes later, stifling a yawn. "I need to get my beauty sleep."

"What? No dessert? Don't you want to try my lemon sorbet?" Lucy asked.

"*Pappou* never eats sugar," Michael explained.

"Never?"

"I usually like cheese or fruits, but not tonight."

"*Pappou* lives a very healthy life. He's a cold water swimmer!" Michael put in.

"Wow! Hale and hearty; hats off to you!"

"Thank you, Lucy," *pappou* said, standing up.

"It's late. I should be going, too," Lucy said.

"It's late for an old man like me who'll get up very early in the morning, but not late for you two," *pappou* said and wished them good night.

*

When the door closed behind him, Michael asked Lucy if she wanted dessert.

"No, I'm full, but I'll help with the dishes. Then I'll call a taxi."

"Let's have a coffee, and I'll drive you back."

She nodded and they took to clearing the plates away. Michael could see she was tense. He recalled how mortified she had been earlier at the mere thought of their love making. She could be married for all he knew, though there was no wedding ring on her finger.

They poured themselves some coffee and sipped it slowly. Michael did not want her to leave. He wanted to ask so many questions. In the end, the question he asked was a practical one. "What do you think of the house?"

"It's a dream house, spacious, bright, great view of the sea! The garden will be beautiful when the trees grow. I'll have my own swimming pool. It's just perfect," she said, her eyes glistening.

"So, is this a deal?" he asked lightly, wishing her to say 'yes', not just for the money, but because he would have her near, a prospect that thrilled him.

"It's a deal. I'll take care of the formalities when I go back. I've already put my own apartment up for sale."

"You're sure about this? That you want to live here? What about your career in London?"

"Um, the truth is that I'm between jobs right now." And boyfriends, she thought. "This will give me a fresh perspective of what I want to do next. I'm already working on some ideas." She cast a glance at her watch. "Shall we?"

"Sure," Michael said and grabbed his keys from the coffee table.

17

1299

Lois came back from the orchard, carrying a basket of apples on her head. She placed it on the kitchen table and took to peeling and slicing the apples. Tedium had closed in from all directions since Nicholas' departure. The worry about him kept her company in the interstices of the day's chores and all through the night.

Her long strolls and solitary evenings at their secret place by Kouris River were her only comfort. She loved the timeless peace of the grassy swards, sheltered by giant reeds, elms, and plane trees. But it was still the afternoon, and she had to be patient. In the evening, she would play the flute.

When she was little and had no chores, Lois enjoyed lying by the river, listening to the soft breeze sigh through the reeds. That music spoke to her, and she had asked Emilia's brother, the musician, to teach her how to play the flute. On warm summer evenings, Nicholas would lie on the grass by the river with his hands locked behind his head and listen to her play.

The chapel bell chimed, bringing Lois out of her reverie. She resumed the slicing of apples when Emilia burst into the kitchen. "The young master is back!" she announced excitedly.

Lois' heart skipped a beat, and she almost cut herself. Putting the knife down, she thanked the Lord Almighty. She dried her hands on the square of cloth tied at her waist and scurried out of the kitchen.

He was not in the great hall, and Lois lifted the skirt of her dress and dashed upstairs, two steps at a time. It did not take long before she heard his familiar, firm voice in his parents' chamber. She pressed her ear against the door and heard him give them a brief account of the expedition. In her mind's eye, Lois could see him in the heat of battle.

"Father," Nicholas paused to give his words more impact, "Surely, you will agree that I have been tested on the battlefield." Provence nodded. He could foresee where he was going. "With your blessing, I would like to take Albert upon his offer to teach me about trade in Famagusta."

Lois covered her mouth with her hand, her legs buckling under her. He had just come back, and he was intent upon leaving again! He was a master, of course, free to come and go as he pleased, free to pursue whatever goal he set in life. And she? The fates had decreed that she was no more than a *lefteri,* a freed serf. But what sort of freedom was it when she had nothing in her own name and could go nowhere without a husband! She could do nothing on her own, she thought dejectedly.

Lois heard Emilia calling her and knew she had to help prepare a festive supper to celebrate Nicholas' return. She forced herself back to the kitchen.

*

As soon as supper had been served, Lois disappeared into the bed-chamber she shared with her grandfather. At least, she had the room to herself. Kontostefanos was still in the great hall. She said her evening prayers half-heartedly and got into bed but found it impossible to unwind. Her mind was too busy. She punched the pillow, tossed and turned several times before she bolted out of bed, got dressed, and sneaked out. Voices and laughter from the great hall spilled over the creaking sound of the heavy oak door as she pushed it open.

She headed for the river, cutting through the vineyards. The sound of the gently flowing water had a calming effect on her, and she sat down on the grass by the tall reeds, marveling at the sky that was artfully embroidered with stars.

*

Nicholas listened to the heated discussion in the great hall with a faraway look in his eyes. He found it hard to block red-stained battle images from his mind and felt the need to be by himself.

Just at the moment that he thought it proper, he wished everyone good night and strolled down to the river, the most serene place on earth. It felt good to be home. He knew each stone; each casuarina was rooted deep in memory. It was comforting to know he would be carrying these images wherever he went.

He noticed Lois sitting by the river. A half-smile crossed his lips as he sneaked up behind her.

"So, this is where you've been hiding," he cried out suddenly, making her jump.

Her cheeks blushed crimson, and she gasped for breath. "I'm not hiding!"

"Right, *pichòt,* you've only been avoiding me since I got back," he said, settling himself next to her on the ground and giving her shoulder a playful shove.

She met his eye, and in a moment of horror, she thought that he could see right through her. Did he ever miss anything? "I'm sad," she said at length, lowering her eyes and hugging her knees.

"Why?" Nicholas lifted her chin with one finger.

She looked at him and wondered how it was possible that he knew her so well, yet so little! "You are leaving again!" she said guilelessly.

Nicholas felt a surge of affection and smiled kindly at her. "That is true. What would you like me to bring you when I come back? A length of cloth? Or maybe a wooden side comb?" He reached out and brushed a strand of hair away from her face.

She tipped her head to the side, contemplating; looking into his green eyes that made her think of spring. "A book of spells!" she said at last.

Nicholas noticed the gleam of devilry in her eyes and the suggestion of a smile on her lips. He gave her a look of amused bafflement.

"Heaven forbid! You want to be a witch now? They burn witches you know," he scolded her gently, eyes alight with laughter.

What a Catholic thing to say, Lois was about to blurt out but managed to bridle her tongue. This was not the time for another discussion on what divided the two Christian faiths. "Only if they get caught," she said playfully.

"People would call you a blasphemer," he said lightly.

"But not you?"

"No, not me," he said and flashed a smile at her. "Whom do you want to cast your spell on anyway?" His expression showed faint curiosity.

You, of course!

"Oh, you never know when a spell might come in handy."

"I pity your foes," he joshed. His smile was both indulgent and affectionate.

Lois suddenly began to chant an incomprehensible incantation, and Nicholas looked at her mystified. She raised her fingers to her temples, closing her eyes and, in an imitation of an unearthly voice, she predicted, "You will make a fortune as a merchant in Famagusta."

Nicholas burst out laughing. "Have you turned soothsayer now?" She was smart and pert; funny and sweet. And she often surprised him with her crazy ideas.

"Yes, the Almighty has given me second sight," she quipped and went on chanting, "I see you returning to this very same *casale* one day."

His face became more serious. "I will miss you, too, *pichòt!*"

He casually placed an arm around her shoulders and kissed her forehead. She snuggled in his arms, enjoying the warmth of his skin in the chill evening. Life was not fair, she thought, and wished she could change that.

18
2013

The sun was peeking out of a blue sky when Michael kissed Lucy good morning; a peck on the cheek. He held the car door open for her, and she thanked him with a bright smile.

"Is there anywhere in particular you'd like to go?" He started the engine and pulled away smoothly.

"Um, not really. I thought you might recommend a place."

"All right; let's visit Akamas."

"Something special about it?"

"Oh, yes," he assured her but refused to elaborate further, merely saying that she would see for herself. He inserted the CD with nostalgic French songs he had prepared the night before, heard her humming, and was glad she still liked them.

"I didn't know that Limassol has a coastline of twenty kilometers… If I'd known the island's so beautiful, I'd probably have come with you then," she said lightly. Then, "If I remember correctly, I did ask you once to take me with you, and you said 'no!'"

"That's not exactly what happened. I told you that if you came with me, I'd have to marry you first, and you chickened out."

"It sounded a bit like a threat when you think of it," she teased him.

"Maybe," he said affably.

"Michael, we were so young! I just wasn't ready for commitment. There were a million things I wanted to do before settling down." She had explained all that twenty years ago. Why was she doing it again?

"I know, and I'd love to hear about them." He turned and smiled fondly at her. "So, how was Paris?"

"Oh, absolutely fascinating, but exhausting! Working as sous-chef for Alain Passard was the best university. The man's a genius, Michael, and he's got the utmost respect for Mother Nature. It was an amazing experience, but one that tests your self-discipline to the limit." She stopped abruptly, a sadness rolling over her face.

"What?" Michael asked softly.

"I got married in Paris," she said quietly.

Michael could not help wondering if she did the million things she had been planning before settling down. Why did it matter? That was all in the past now, he reminded himself.

"To Jean-Baptiste," Lucy went on. "He was also a sous-chef. He'd always have a drink and take his bike for a spin after work to unwind. One evening, he had a drink too many... Anyway, it was a happy marriage as long as it lasted. Eight whole months. And then I left Paris for good."

"I'm sorry," Michael said.

"It's all right. You couldn't have known. How about you?"

"I came back to Cyprus and opened up a fine dining restaurant. Business was good most of the time, so it grew into a chain which I sold just in time to lose everything in the bail-in. I'm trying to get back on my feet again. I have this plan for a gourmet catering business. That is if you buy the house and I have the cash to do it." He met her gaze for a second and focused on the road again.

"Hmm. Gourmet catering," she said, contemplating the potential of such an enterprise.

He glanced at her. "That interest you?"

A long silence.

"You're looking for a partner?" Lucy asked.

A smile dangled on the corner of his lips. "A business partner."

Her eyes lit up. "I gathered that."

"Yes, I'm looking for a partner."

"Hmm... I could do that. Let me settle things in the UK first. I'd need to sell my apartment. That might take a while." She paused. "Ever been married?"

Michael took the A6 to Paphos and a moment before he replied. "No. Some long relationships, but I never felt ready to take it to the next level. Until recently. For all the wrong reasons. She wanted it. And though *pappou* never said it, he'd love to see me finally settle down. All my friends are married with kids. Or divorced, come to think of it. Anyway, that's not going to happen now. A week before the wedding, she calls me from the plane to let me know she's leaving me." He snorted.

"And it still hurts."

"Well, my male pride got bruised. That's for sure. I could have done without telling my friends that the wedding's off 'cause the bride ran away. That was the second of the two women I proposed to who dumped me by the way," a touch of sarcasm, but light-hearted. "There's something wrong with women, I guess."

"That must be it!" Lucy grinned.

"Look to your left!" Michael said after a while. "This is where Aphrodite emerged from the foam of the sea, right there by that big rock," he added, pointing at a formation of huge rocks along the azure coastline.

"Amazing!" Lucy said, looking at the reflections of the sun on the gentle waves, licking the rock. She got the cell phone out of her bag to take a picture.

"On the way back, we can take the coast road. There are several spots where we can stop to take pictures if you like. Here you can see one of the most beautiful sunsets on the island."

"I'd love that."

They drove in companionable silence for a while before Lucy found the nerve to speak about William. "Now, this is going to sound weird, but bear with me."

"Okay," Michael agreed.

"Say you were in the process of getting a divorce. Would you be wearing your wedding ring when you met your wife to discuss the financial arrangements?"

"I've never been in this position, but I don't think I would. What would be the point?"

"Exactly!"

He locked eyes with her. "Care to elaborate?"

A sigh escaped her lips. "Well, I found out recently that the man I was dating for six months is married."

"Ouch!"

"Yeah, well. When I confronted him about it, he said that he hadn't expected the divorce process to last that long."

"I see." He gave her a glance that said, 'and you believed that?'

"Well, I know how it sounds. It's just that when he's close to perfect in so many ways, you don't quite expect that. And it hurts."

"I bet it does," Michael said gently, resenting the close to perfection part.

19

1300

At sunrise that mid-summer Monday morning, Nicholas reached the docks of the bustling harbor of Famagusta with a jaunty step. A flock of seagulls in flight dove for fish inches away from him. He breathed in the humid air of the coast and looked about at a galley being delicately nosed into mooring and ships being repaired. A swarm of serfs marched by, carrying sacks of carobs, grain, and pulses from the commune warehouses to the quay. Goods were headed for the Aegean and the Black Sea, or Venice and Ancona; some even farther away than that.

The oarsmen of the newly arrived galley disembarked noisily in search of the nearest tavern. A burly Genoese merchant lumbered by, shouting last-minute instructions to his galley captain. The vessel was loaded with butts of wine from Pelendri and Kilani to be sent to Rhodes. Nicholas had got used to hearing a cornucopia of tongues he did not understand. Daily, pilgrims and merchants from all the corners of the world stopped here on their way to or from the Holy Land, bringing goods and news with them.

Nicholas reached *La Sirène* and scrutinized its loading with cendal and samite to be sent to Marseilles. The Templars had rented her. She would sail to Limassol first; henceforth, she would travel alongside the Templar ship *Falconus* which carried powdered sugar, cotton, red dye, and camlet.

Nicholas had every reason to feel proud that Monday morning. This had been the first time Albert and Guilhelm had entrusted him with handling an item of business all alone. It was Nicholas who had found out that the Templars were interested in renting a galley and struck the deal with Pierre of Montpellier, a Templar knight, as well as with the cendal and samite weavers and embroiderers.

If all went well, they would make a small fortune. That would allow them to place the order for a second galley. Nicholas was confident that this time he had done everything right, from recording the transport of goods at the castellan's office to calculating the rate of tax. When he had first started, he'd had a hard time remembering the different taxes imposed on various goods.

Albert and Guilhelm did not teach Nicholas only how to trade. In this opulent city, the young man became more aware of his manner of dress. Following their counsel, he began to sport patterned chaperons and buttoned kirtles that he acquired from Paul of Nimes, the most famous cloth merchant on the island.

The three young men received regular invitations from the wealthy merchants with daughters of marriageable age, an opportunity for Nicholas to show off his new clothes at dances and feasts held in lavish houses. There was dancing, and there were secret places where young people could steal away. Albert and Guilhelm often teased him that his flair for coaxing women into his bed would get him into trouble one day, but Nicholas was a man of remarkable discretion. The city was vibrant, despite the threat of a Saracen assault or a pirate attack. Good things as well as bad things were possible!

Trading had opened Nicholas' eyes to the world. He had traveled. He had glimpsed the endless possibilities to enrich people's lives with products from distant places. And he had begun to amass a small fortune. Mont Pèlerin seemed remote and pointless. In Nicholas' new world, there was ample space for Christians and Saracens trading in peace. Trade served the king without bloodshed. The taxes merchants paid filled the royal coffers. But could wealth avert war?

*

The rapidly approaching hoofbeats awoke everyone with a start. Clad in a nightshirt, Nicholas reached for his sword hilt while Albert and Guilhelm sprang out of bed and peeped out of the window, as the castellan's men jumped down from their horses and banged on the door.

"In the name of the law, open up!" the hard-faced troop leader bellowed.

There was a moment of petrified immobility. Albert and Guilhelm exchanged worried frowns. They put on their robes, and Guilhelm opened the door with a shaky hand.

"Albert of Provence, Guilhelm Gascoigne, I have orders for your arrest. You are coming with us!"

"What?" Their jaws dropped; the color drained from their faces.

"On what charge?" Nicholas asked.

"Trading with the Saracens."

"That is preposterous! Says who? Who is our accuser?" Guilhelm asked, regaining his natural boldness.

"Not my place to say. You have been denounced. If you are innocent, you can explain that before the castellan, but now you are coming with us. Move!"

"When is the trial?" Nicholas asked.

"When the castellan returns from Nicosia."

Nicholas had no idea when that would be, and he suspected that the troop leader would not tell him, but he would find out soon enough.

He had warned Albert and Guilhelm about being in a dark gray area between the law and reason, but Guilhelm had failed to see what the Pope had to do with their little trade, miles and miles away from the Holy See. They could sell their pine in Alexandria for three times as much as in Rhodes or in any other Christian harbor. His Holiness did not need to know, Guilhelm had said.

Albert and Guilhelm would need all the help they could get, and Nicholas settled on starting with Guilhelm's family. They lived in town. He dressed quickly and sprinted to Roland.

*

Peyre left the archbishopric in Nicosia with Martis, Guilhelm's youngest brother. He would hardly catch any sleep again tonight, but he had got used to that lately. The archbishop was growing too old to attend to his duties, and Peyre carried his burden modestly, placidly learning to accept the fact that the job was never done by the end of the day.

All the way through the broad, sweeping plain of Mesaoria, Peyre prayed for strength and wisdom, as unanswered questions crammed his mind. They made slow but steady progress, riding warily with short intervals for their horses to rest and managed to arrive in Famagusta early in the afternoon the next day.

Gautier Gascoigne, Guilhelm's father, a round-faced hefty man with a fruity voice, joined them for supper and took a seat at the table. Gaston, Guilhelm's eldest brother, was sent to fetch Provence, but they were not expected until the next day.

"So, brief me on what you have done so far," Peyre said, rubbing the bridge of his nose and his tired eyes.

Gautier spoke first. "I have met with the consuls of Marseilles, Montpellier, and Narbonne as Nicholas suggested, but they say if there is evidence they traded with the infidels, their hands are tied."

He had not spoken to his son since he caught him kissing Albert, and now he felt torn inside. One part of him believed that this was condign punishment for his son's sin. Another part just wanted to save his boy. His fair wife's constant weeping, begging him to find forgiveness in his heart, might have softened him; or perhaps the fact that she had stopped sharing his bed until he did.

"I see," Peyre said, nodding. "And what about you, Nicholas?"

"I knocked on all the Provençal and Catalan doors, but nothing."
He shrugged. "I think they prefer to stay out of this for fear of being suspected of trading with the Saracens themselves." Since the
Provençals had helped the Catalans conquer Majorca, merchants
from the two communities had worked closely together.

"The charge of trading with the Saracens might be as severe as excommunication," Peyre confirmed their worst fears.

Nicholas knew that not being allowed to partake in the sacra-
ments was the least of Albert and Guilhelm's worries. They would
never marry nor have children to baptize. Guilhelm had always
said lightly, once they died, what difference would it make if they
were properly buried or not. But being treated as lepers, cut off
from society was simply bad for their families and bad for business.
Concealing their love was hard enough, and now this!

"Why them? Everyone trades with the Saracens!" Martis wondered
out loud, shifting his coltish frame on the bench.

"Not everyone, but most," Nicholas corrected him.

"If they start arresting merchants on this charge, there will be no
one left to trade!" Martis remonstrated.

"It seems we are allowed everything. We're just not allowed to get
caught." Nicholas' lips quirked up in a bitter smile.

"Is there anyone who would benefit from their punishment? Or
someone who feels wronged perhaps?" Peyre asked.

"I asked myself the same question," Nicholas said, "but I cannot
think of anyone."

The gloom around the table deepened. The food on the platter was
barely touched.

"If they appear penitent before the marine court, it would be in
their favor," Peyre said.

"I think this will not be a problem with Albert. I'm not sure about Guilhelm," Nicholas said, turning to Gautier. Guilhelm was known to bend and break any law that did not make sense to him.

"Leave Guilhelm to me," his father said gravely.

"Peyre, do you think that the Bishop of Famagusta could intervene for a milder sentence?" Nicholas asked.

"Perhaps we should pay Isol, the vicar of Syria and Palestine, a visit first. I hear he is close to the castellan. He could act as middleman," Peyre said, rubbing his chin. "If this does not bear any fruit, we can always turn to the bishop for help."

"Isol would help in exchange for what?" Gautier asked pointedly.

"He's a spendthrift, and he gambles with passion. He loses more often than he wins and owes money to several people," Nicholas said.

"From what I hear, he now has a new mistress, and he buys her dresses and jewels all the time," Martis said, snickering.

"So, we have something that he needs." Gautier saw the first glimmer of hope.

Gautier's family was far wealthier than his, Peyre thought, but that was of secondary importance at the moment.

*

Gaston galloped through the gateway of Provence's estate, dust rising up around him. His coarser neighed as he pulled the reins. In a flash, he leaped off his horse and sprinted up the three steps. He banged on the door with the urgency of life and death and asked to be taken to Provence at once. Moments later, Provence was giving instructions for fresh mounts and provisions, taking two steps at a time to the quarters he shared with Eloise.

He threw the door open with enough force to startle Emilia and

Lois, who were tending to their mistress, and reached the bed in two strides. "Eloise, I need to leave at once; urgent matters."

"Will you be long, my lord?" Her voice was still weak, but she no longer looked deathly pale.

"I hope not, my lady." He caressed her hair, and she managed to summon up a feeble smile. He kissed her on the forehead. "You get better in the meantime."

"God willing."

At the threshold, Provence beckoned Lois over. "Find your grandfather! I shall send for money. Tell him to collect all unpaid dues at once. And take care of your mistress while I'm gone."

"Yes, my lord. I hope everything is all right." She knew better than to ask a direct question, but Provence was not carried away by the obliqueness of her approach.

"Just do as I ask," he said and scurried down the stairs.

Lois closed the door behind him, praying silently for Nicholas' safety.

20

2013

The sun was high when Michael and Lucy reached the Aphrodite nature trail in the Akamas peninsula. They got out of the car and stretched their legs. It was a glorious day, clear and warm.

"Ready for hiking?" Michael asked.

"Sure! It's beautiful up here." Lucy marveled at the stunning view of the Bay of Polis from the top of the cliff.

After a five-minute walk, they came to the Baths of Aphrodite, a grotto with a big fig tree by the entrance. "So, Aphrodite bathed in this pond," Lucy said, her gaze gliding around the romantic cave with the waterfall.

"Not alone. Legend has it that this is where she first met Adonis. He was hunting in the forest and stopped here to quench his thirst. It was love at first sight." Michael gave her a comical smile.

"She wasn't called goddess of love for nothing," Lois remarked.

He put his hand in the water and sprinkled her legs with it. "They say the water of this pond is highly aphrodisiac."

"I bet it is," she said with an infectious smile.

They continued on the trail, alongside the curved coast line with amazing rock formations and strangely shaped boulders by the cliffs. The crystal blue waters were so clear, they could see all the way to the sea bed. The trail led through gorges and valleys.

Wandering in the viridescent fields of Akamas, abloom with redolent, rare wildflowers, Lucy took dozens of photos, careful not to step on the red poppies and the tulips that came in all shades of white, pink, and purple.

She lifted her chin up a notch in the early spring sunshine and spread her arms out like wings. A kaleidoscope of blue butterflies flew all around her, performing a little courtship dance. One of them sat on her hand for a moment or two before it flew away again.

"Oh, Michael, look at these butterflies!" she cried out excitedly. "I've never seen such vivid blue before."

"They're the emblem of Akamas," he explained. "I guess spring's the best time of the year to come here."

He had forgotten how magnificent this less visited part of the island was. Adriana had never been fond of walks in nature; she was a creature of the night.

"It's so beautiful and wild. Almost deserted, just amazing! Thank you for bringing me here." She smiled in a way that he remembered.

"The pleasure's all mine." He smiled back with unfamiliar ease.

He became aware that he was staring at her and cast his gaze on the tips of his shoes, shoving his hands into the pockets of his khaki chinos, before meeting her eyes again.

"Right! What do you want to do next? Get a 4x4 and go to Lara Beach and see the endangered turtles or go on a glass bottom boat trip? The blue lagoon's quite spectacular, pristine waters and all. Or we could go to Avakas gorge or have a bite to eat at the Anassa Hotel; great panorama of the bay from the terrace!"

"It all sounds great, but we can't do it all in one day. I'd love to come back again and do all those things, but right now I could actually eat something."

"Let's go then," he said, taking her hand in his, strolling back to the car.

A pair of blackcaps flew over their heads, the male chasing the female and singing its mating song. "All the things the poor male has to do just to get some attention," Michael said and grimaced theatrically.

Lucy's cheeks dimpled and the corners of her eyes wrinkled. He squeezed her hand gently and would have kissed her if she had only held his gaze.

An hour later, they were admiring the paradisiac panorama on the terrace of the luxury Anassa Hotel to the sound of a grand piano while savoring fresh grouper and sipping an oak-aged single vineyard *xynisteri*, a local white variety that Michael had chosen.

Looking at the view with Lucy by his side, Michael felt as though all worries had been lifted from his shoulders. Lucy seemed to be lost in the moment as well, he noticed; she would not take her calls.

*

Lola warned *pappou* of the approaching car, and he peered out of the window as Michael killed the engine in the driveway. *Pappou* opened the door, and Lola ran to them.

"Hello, *pappou*." Lucy flashed a smile at him, cuddling Lola's head.

"Did you have a good time?"

"Fantastic! Ready for one more contest?" she asked, as Lola turned her attention to Michael.

"Why don't you freshen up first, and I'll come round in about an hour?" *pappou* said discreetly. "Come on, Lola," he said, and the beagle followed him obediently, wagging her tail.

Michael opened the house door and let Lucy in. "Would you like to have a bath? It's been a long day. I could get you a fresh polo shirt if you like."

Lucy looked uncomfortable at first but then said, "Sure, that'd be nice. Thanks."

Michael took some towels out of a bathroom cupboard for her. "Take your time," he said, filling the bathtub with hot water, adding an aromatic blend of bath salts, the way she used to like it.

She caught a whiff of his after shave as he brushed up against her while reaching for the door. Their eyes caught, held until Michael broke the spell.

"I'll bring you a polo shirt." he said and left her standing there, filled with memories.

*

The tasting menu at the Ledbury in Notting Hill finished with brown sugar tart and stem ginger ice cream, accompanied by a 2006 rivesaltes ambré, Domaine des Chênes. This was Cynthia Ferguson's first time in a Michelin-starred restaurant, and she was bewitched by the cosmopolitan atmosphere.

When they had entered the restaurant, Sinclair noticed how all eyes were drawn to his sensual young companion, resplendent in an elegant emerald evening gown that matched her green eyes. He was unfazed. Her youth and beauty made the chase all the more challenging. Cynthia was a nice distraction from thinking about Lucy. He was irate she had not returned a single call. But that was history now.

Cynthia observed Sinclair thank the waitress for the cognac, wondering how she had got to be so lucky. An eligible bachelor, her debonair escort was every woman's dream. She did not care that he was old enough to be her father. Most young men could not afford to offer her a taste of the stars.

"Here's to Maria," he said, raising his glass.

"Maria?" she asked, frowning.

He looked at her with the confidence of a man who knew what he wanted and how to get it. "Maria Feodorovna, Dowager Empress of Russia. If it hadn't been for her special order to Hennessy to create an imperial cognac, Hennessy *paradis impèrial*, for her son's birthday, Tsar Alexander I, the world would be a poorer place."

"To Maria," Cynthia said, relieved, raising her glass.

Sinclair enjoyed a sip of his cognac and checked the caller on the screen of his buzzing cell. "I'm afraid I have to take this. Please, excuse me." He stood up.

"Of course," Cynthia said and watched him walk away from the table, wondering what could be more important than her.

"About the map," the voice on the other end of the line said, "it seems to be authentic, as you said. We want you to do some more research. Find out who the owner of the land around the *"X"* mark is. See if the place is for sale and report back to us."

"I'll get on it right away," Sinclair said, and the line went dead.

He would need to figure out the exact coordinates. That could be tricky, though Templar maps were noted for their accuracy. Then he would need to contact his lawyer and ask him to assign a local real estate agent to identify the property owner. He would need to remain anonymous, of course. One could never be careful enough.

He smoothed his thick blonde hair and returned to the restaurant, excited at the glittering prospect of taking Cynthia to bed.

*

Brian walked into the Ledbury a little earlier than his appointment with the chef. He wanted to get the vibe of the place. A stuffed deer startled him, staring at him from the wall, and Brian cast a glance around at the minimalist décor.

Hello, there, he thought to himself, when he noticed Sinclair leaning into the raving beauty by his side, caressing her knee under the tablecloth.

21

1300

"The vicar of Syria and Palestine will see you now," Isol's herald announced, and Peyre and Nicholas were shown into his office.

"I suppose you are here on account of your brother." Isol did not waste time on courtesies. He had just come back from delivering Gazan's renewed invitation to Henry to join forces in recapturing the Holy Land and had a lot to do and little time. He beckoned them to be seated.

"Indeed, we are, my lord," Peyre said.

"They are guilty of trading with the Saracens. There is substantial evidence from what I hear. They will be found enemies of the Church that you so humbly serve," he said, fixing his gaze upon Peyre.

There was a trace of sarcasm in his voice and a glint of cruelty in his eyes that made Nicholas nervous. How could the vicar be so certain of the outcome when the accused had not yet had a chance to defend themselves in court? Did he know something that they did not?

"So it would seem," Peyre said quietly. "I was wondering if the Church will benefit from their excommunication or if there is perhaps a way they could demonstrate their penitence." His unruffled countenance betrayed none of his feelings or thoughts.

"How?" Isol's eyes narrowed to crinkle slits.

"A pilgrimage perhaps?" Peyre suggested.

Isol's eyes were aglitter with excitement and avarice. The bribe he had received to unleash the castellan's men on young Provence and Gascoigne had come at a very propitious moment. Not only did he have to repay his mounting gambling debts, but his new mistress could not get enough gifts. The money was for having the two men arrested, not sentenced. There was no doubt in his mind that he had kept his end of that bargain. There was nothing to stop him from striking a new deal now.

"Out of respect for the archbishop and your father who has dedicated his life to the holy cause, I could perhaps be persuaded to suggest to my dear friend Brie, the castellan, not to take the case to court. After all, to err is human, and I would not like to cast the first stone," he added for good measure.

"What do you suggest?" Peyre asked.

"Take part in the next expedition," Isol said with a chilling effect.

"My lord," Peyre protested. "Albert and Guilhelm are not trained for war. They are merchants, not soldiers. They could not lift a sword if their life depended on it."

"Neither are all the peasants who fight for our Lord." There was a cool, ironic tinge to the tone of his voice.

"But they are not peasants," Peyre remarked calmly.

Isol remained silent for a moment, appearing thoughtful. "Perhaps they could make a contribution to the realm. I might be able to arrange for an audience upon the castellan's return from Nicosia. He is a very busy man," he said meaningfully.

"I shall make sure the archbishop hears of your ingenious plan to turn misguided Christians into supporters of the holy cause. We thank you for your time, my lord," Peyre said, rising to his feet, confident that his father would be able to see the castellan without having to pay Isol off.

*

"I cannot stop wondering who denounced them," Nicholas said as soon as they were on horseback and out of earshot. He could smell foul play and was incandescent with rage. The world of trade suddenly seemed less enchanting, filled with enemies, masked as friends. At least on the battlefield, he knew who the enemy was.

They reached the court and checked their mounts to the trunk of a sycamore fig tree. Neither of them had been inside the dungeons before, and they were ill prepared for the pungent stench of urine wafting from the stone walls. The darkness would have been complete but for a shaft of dim light, filtering through a crevice just below the ceiling and a torch burning in the corridor.

A warder unlocked the heavy iron door, and the four men embraced, emotions running high.

"For the love of God, you must get us out of here! I would rather die than spend another day in this hell on earth, I swear." Albert failed miserably to control the shaking in his voice.

Nicholas peered around and could see why. It was damp, cold, and filthy. At least, they were alone; he had feared they might have been thrown together with criminals.

"We will, brother. We are pulling strings, but you have to be patient. I will tell you all about it, but eat first. We have brought you some food and wine," Peyre said, handing him a satchel. Albert broke a piece of bread and passed it on to Guilhelm.

"Father is on his way here. We are expecting him before nightfall," Nicholas said.

Albert stopped chewing for a moment and swallowed, nodding. He broke a piece of cheese with his filthy fingers, and shoveled it into his mouth. Nicholas looked at the once respected merchants who had traveled freely and lived a wealthy life, and he felt outraged by the hypocrisy of the world.

*

In the castellan's office, Provence and his two sons waited with bated breath for the pronouncement on the penalty. Provence was weary. He had been in the saddle all day long these past two days and had hardly got any sleep, but he had insisted on going straight to Brie. His son should not spend a night longer in the dungeons if he could help it.

"Fifty bezants each," Brie said at last with an air of undisputable authority.

Provence's dark eye narrowed and the wrinkles in his forehead grew tighter. He was rarely flustered, but he could show a flash of anger that frightened everyone within twenty yards.

"Fifty bezants! This is preposterous! You can buy a slave for thirty."

"It is either that, or they can fight for their king. He is planning a new expedition soon as you know," Brie said, his aplomb deserting him.

"I wonder what the king would say about this extortion," Provence said. Peyre listened quietly, resolved to go straight to the Bishop of Famagusta when the meeting was over.

Brie shrank back and dried his sweaty palms on his lap. He cleared his throat. "Do you have another suggestion; a suitable punishment for going against the Church and the Pope?"

Provence had none. Even if Kontostephanos managed to collect all the taxes due and with the money he had set aside, he could hardly come up with thirty, let alone fifty bezants!

"I will take the punishment in their place," Nicholas seized the moment with confidence.

Provence stared at Nicholas, as if he could read his mind and soul. Should he have one son excommunicated or risk losing the other on a battlefield? That was a choice no father should have to make.

"I thought you were done fighting." His voice was hoarse. Fatigue finally caught up with him. He could feel it in every muscle and every sinew of his body. He was suddenly enfeebled by the burden of sixty winters and the multitude of brutal battles.

"If this means saving Albert and Guilhelm and serving the king and the holy cause at the same time, so be it." Nicholas' voice was firm.

"You can take only your brother's place. Gascoigne will still need to pay the fine. And they will have to sign a statement, declaring that they will never again trade with the Saracens. I will have them released when this is taken care of," Brie said.

*

That same evening, Roussillon stayed up, in the company of his best wine in the great hall of his manor. He savored the taste of long-awaited vengeance, like ripe red grapes melting in the mouth, an explosion of sweetness. Revenge was his favorite flavor he decided and chortled. He drew a great breath of triumph and joy. There was justice in this world after all!

22

2013

Michael's braised lamb shanks was the winning dish of the evening, and *pappou* and Lucy rewarded him with a simultaneous kiss on the cheek.

"To my worthy adversaries," Michael said, raising his glass.

"Mm, this wine's really good," Lucy remarked.

"*Pappou* has his own theory about wine, isn't that right, *pappou?*" Michael prodded, but *pappou* merely smiled.

"What's that?" Lucy asked.

Pappou shrugged and said, "White wine is like infatuation; red wine is passion, true love."

"There might be some truth there," Lucy said, smiling.

"In that case, I'll get us some more passion." Michael stood up and fetched another bottle from the wine cooler.

"Tell us about your family, Lucy? Where are you from?" *pappou* asked.

Lucy dried her lips on the napkin. "That's a long story." Her origins were far-flung by most people's standards.

"I love stories," *pappou* urged her on while Michael opened the new bottle and topped up their glasses.

"Well, it's complicated," Lucy said. "I have dual nationality: Spanish and Italian."

"So that's where your parents are from?"

"Not exactly. My grandmother on my father's side was Portuguese and my grandfather Spanish. They emigrated to France, chasing the dream of a better life, and that's where my father was born. Now, my maternal grandmother was Greek and my grandfather

Italian. They emigrated to Germany for the same reason, and that's where my mother was born."

Michael studied her face furtively. He recalled listening to the story before, one evening as she was nestled in his arms after making love.

"You speak all these languages?" *pappou* asked.

"I wish! Just some German and French."

"And how did your dad meet your mom?"

"While he was doing his military service, he was stationed in Germany, and that's where I was born, too; in Trier. It's a small city on the border of Luxemburg, the oldest city in Germany. It was a French military training area at the time. They were both very young. My mom used to be a ballerina, so we moved a lot whenever her contract was over. We were in the Netherlands when my dad told my mom to choose between him and her career. She wasn't ready to give up dancing then."

She shrugged and went on, "I haven't seen him since; a couple of birthday cards and then nothing. I was sent to my aunt in New York for several years till Mom finally married a Hungarian musician in Dublin. He was kind enough, but didn't try to play the role of a father. I'm afraid I didn't make them proud. I have no talent in dancing or music."

Lucy saw no reason to explain that she had loved dancing as a little girl, but her enthusiasm faded away soon. She could never have matched her mother's expectations. "I think they were relieved when I left for college," she added as an afterthought. She noticed that *pappou* was struggling to follow and patted his hand. "I told you it was complicated."

"Quite!" He nodded slowly.

"So, that makes you officially the personification of the European Union," Michael said teasingly.

"Never thought of it that way! Maybe." She was glad he had eased the tension. She glanced at her watch. "It's been a wonderful day and a lovely evening. Thank you for your hospitality, but I should go now. I need to pack, and I have an early flight to catch."

Both men rose to their feet, and Lucy hugged *pappou* goodbye. "I'll be back soon."

"Take care," the old man said, patting her on the back.

*

The humidity had dropped, and the sky had begun to clear when Lucy and Michael reached the hotel. He turned off the engine in the parking lot and fished a little box out of his pocket.

"This is from *pappou* and me," he said, taking a silver bracelet with a small pomegranate out of the box. He fastened it on her wrist and said, "No matter what you decide about the house, you have two friends here." He placed his hand on her knee casually. "This is to wish you good luck. Cypriots believe pomegranates bring luck."

"Thank you," Lucy said, touched by the openness and warmth with which they had received her. They had made her feel like a part of the family.

Throwing judgement out the window, she cupped his face in her hands and kissed him lightly on the lips. Michael responded more ardently. She kissed him back, losing herself in the kiss.

A motorbike parked next to them, and Lucy broke away. She mumbled her thanks and got out of the car, feeling his eyes on her back. She took a few steps, stopped, and turned around. "Your polo shirt!" she cried out.

He shook his head, amused. "Keep it!"

He watched her disappear through the entrance, caressing his lips with his fingers as if to prolong the sensation of their kiss. When she was out of sight, he drove into the night.

23

1300

The last day of the year, the eve of Saint Basil's feast day, was chilly and bracing, full of excitement and commotion. Everyone in the Provence *casale* was invited to the New Year's Eve feast. There would be singing and dancing and plenty to eat and drink. No one would go to bed hungry tonight. It took two men to carry the boar that Provence had shot with an arrow that forenoon.

Gathered around the crackling fire, serfs took turns praying to Saint Basil to tell them if the one they loved also loved them back. They cut a slit in the middle of an olive tree leaf and placed another leaf in it, forming a cross and tossing it into the fire. If it leaped, their love was reciprocated. If it burned, alas, it was not!

Lois waited anxiously for her turn, but Emilia said she needed help with the *vasilopitta,* Saint Basil's pie. Lois followed her into the kitchen, wondering if she would find the silver coin in the pie that would bring her good luck for the whole year.

The chapel bell chimed, and everyone gathered at the table. They bowed their heads, and Provence said grace. He raised his chalice to make a toast, but he was distracted by the sound of a horseman arriving. "It's Master Nicholas!" a disembodied voice shrieked, and the evening was filled with a cacophony of whispers. Lois' heart missed a beat, as she glanced at Nicholas' silhouette.

While everyone's attention was turned to the young master, Lois cast a cross of olive leaves into the fire. Her heart beat fiercely as she watched it leap high; not once, but twice! She searched for his eyes, but he was in his parents' arms. Everyone around the table wanted to welcome him, too.

Provence raised his chalice again and said, "Let us rejoice and thank the Lord, for He has brought me back my son!"

"To Nicholas!" Kontostephanos said, thrusting a wine cup in the young man's hand.

"I thank you all! It's good to be back," Nicholas said, looking around the table. At the sight of Lois, he broke into a grin that she gladly returned. His gaze lingered a second longer on her face. Two years can change the looks of a girl. Seeing her again in the flesh, she was more charming than she was in his memory.

"How was it, Nicholas?" Eloise asked. She had lost count of the sleepless nights of worry she had spent waiting for his return. Everyone huddled around him, their collective curiosity piqued, their necks craned, their appetite for news from faraway places insatiable.

"We sailed for the Holy Land in November, along with the Templars, the Hospitallers, and the Teutonic knights," Nicholas began his narration. "The weather was mild and we had a safe crossing. It took just a day to reach Tortosa, sailing with the wind. We took the Saracens unawares, attacking in the dead of night when they least expected it. We literally caught them in their sleep. We laid siege, and indeed, under Amaury's deft command, we succeeded in recapturing the fortress and the town. And then we waited. For twenty-five whole days, we just waited for Gazan and his Mongols to join us, but they did not come."

He refrained from exposing the pillage, the rapes, and the whoring that took place in those twenty-five days. "In the meantime, hordes of Saracens began gathering outside Tortosa. We could not take up the fight against so many of them, so we retreated to Arwad, a small island about half a league away. We had little choice but to come back home. Only some Templars remained."

The brief account was not what his intrigued audience had expected. They would rather have exciting narrations, entwining facts and fiction. But Nicholas no longer found anything gallant in killing and was not inclined to indulge them by spinning stories on the spur of the moment.

"How many men did we lose?" Provence demanded.

"Quite a few," Nicholas replied grimly; the images of the battle-field turning into a graveyard for the unburied made him queasy.

Provence nodded slowly and said, "Let us take a moment to mark the passing of those who are no longer with us!" he said, and heads bowed in gloomy silence.

*

When the Christian ships had returned from Arwad, Nicholas spent some time in Famagusta with Albert and Guilhelm. They had been overjoyed to see him again. They felt beholden to him beyond words and had tried to persuade him to stay and take over the second galley they had purchased, but Nicholas had other plans for the future.

He was convinced that he was destined to do greater things, and he'd had time to consider what exactly in those long twenty-five days. He wanted to serve Henry. He shared the king's vision for commercial prosperity and religious peace between the Catholic and the Orthodox Church that would lead to harmonious coexistence with the locals.

But for the moment, he needed to erase the brutality of the battle images from his mind and to unwind. He went for a stroll, swishing a stick through the weeds along the riverbank, enjoying the familiar sight of the landscape he had grown up with. The reflection of the full moon on the water seemed to him to dance to a mystical rhythm. A cold wind blew down the river, but Nicholas took no notice.

At the sound of light footsteps, he looked over his shoulder and saw Lois. She shuddered with cold.

"You're freezing!" he said, taking his mantle off. He put it around her shoulders and rubbed her arms.

"Thank you," she whispered.

"Cannot sleep, *pichòt?*"

"No, not yet." She wished he would stop calling her that. She was a bairn no longer.

"So, I hear they call you the 'nose' now," he teased gently, brushing his forefinger on the tip of her nose. "I can see why!"

"What do you mean?"

"It is a rather... distinguished nose," he said.

"What?"

"A bit longer than most girls' noses."

She caught a telltale grin and knew he was teasing. "Who says I'm like most girls?" she said, sticking her nose up in the air.

Nicholas smiled generously. "No, you are not."

"Besides, I'm almost a woman now."

He shook his head in mock disbelief. "Indeed, *pichòt?*" She was still little Lois to him. Though he had noticed the habitual unkempt mop on her head was now replaced by two braids, brought from the nape of the neck and crossed over the top of her head and tied together. He plucked an orchid and jeweled her hair.

"You have been away and had no way of knowing, but Gregory, the baker's son, has sent the matchmaker to *pappou*," she said complacently.

Nicholas was aware that his mouth was open. "And?"

"And nothing. I'm still too young, *pappou* said. Perhaps next year. I still have a lot of things to learn. I have no time for marriage."

"But you like him, the baker's son?" He had no inkling why that mattered.

She shrugged. "He's a good boy, God-fearing and all."

"But do you *want* to marry him?"

She took a moment to think. "No."

Nicholas realized he had been holding his breath.

"It is foolhardy, dangerous even, to wed below my rank. *Pappou* has explained that if I marry a serf, not only will I need the bishop's consent, but my children will lose my rights as *lefteri*. He says he will arrange a marriage with another *lefteros*, but there is no one in our *casale*, so he will have to seek one out in the nearby *casalia*. Anyway, now that you are here, I would rather spend my time with you."

He held her gaze. "You know I will not be here for long," he said gently, watching a cloud cross her face.

She sensed a deeper sobriety in his voice and manner. She might have taken the news with equanimity, but she obeyed a sudden impulse. "Why? The war is over!"

"I know. Father is well-acquainted with the king's uncle, Philip of Ibelin. I will ask him to try and arrange a post for me in the palace in Nicosia. His secretary is old. He will be retiring soon from what I hear."

Lois stepped away from him, but he grabbed one arm, turning her around to face him. "I shall come and visit at Easter or in the summer."

That was, of course, not what she wanted to hear.

"You can write to me if you like; tell me about the things you learn, the *casale*, and the new wine. Would you like that?"

She nodded. She even managed a wan smile. Nicholas sensed that this time a gift would not suffice to cheer her up.

"Would you like to see the capital? Perhaps we could arrange for your grandfather and you to come and visit one day," he suggested, though they both knew it was next to impossible.

Lois gave a small noncommittal smile. "I think I should go back now. *Pappou* is probably wondering where I am." She was proud her voice was steady. She squared her shoulders and turned with blundering haste away from him.

This had been the first time Nicholas failed to swing her mood, and he found it hard to accept.

*

The door in the chamber she shared with Kontostephanos creaked as Lois closed it gently behind her.

"Lois?" Her grandfather's voice startled her.

"Yes, *pappou*?" She had hoped he would be asleep.

"Come and sit with me. It's late. Where have you been?" he asked gently.

"By the river."

"With Nicholas?" She nodded. "He's very dear to you?" It was more of a statement rather than a question. Lois nodded again. "Well, you cannot meet with him in the evenings alone anymore, Lois. You are a child no longer."

Everyone could see she was a child no longer, she thought; everyone but Nicholas.

Kontostephanos gazed at her sad face with sympathy. "Whether we like it or not, this is the way things are. Do you really want to give your heart away to a man who cannot love you back?"

Too late for that, Lois thought. She was already badly smitten with Nicholas.

"Do you want to live your life in pain and misery?" Kontostephanos went on.

Lois shook her head. "Oh, *pappou*, life is not fair," she said, resting her head on his shoulder.

Kontostephanos patted her back. "Life is what it is, and we must make the most of it. Trust in the Almighty to help you find a way to make it meaningful. As you grow older, you will see that every moment is a blessing."

*

Zabel's head was pillowed in Amaury's shoulder, her jet-black hair spread on his chest. He ran his fingers through it playfully. Their coupling earlier had been filled with urgency, and now they needed to catch their breath.

"It is good to share my bed with you again, beloved."

His infidelities when they were apart did not matter. Neither did his ephemeral harlots. Amaury had always been discreet. Not once had he embarrassed her by bringing them under their roof or parading them as trophies in front of his friends. No, he loved her too much for that.

"It is good to be home, Zabel." He planted a kiss on the top of her head.

"Victorious as well!" she added with immense pride.

"Not quite. We did retake Tortosa, but we had to abandon it when the Mongols did not show."

"Still, you recovered it. If there is fault to be found, it lies with the Mongols. Not with you... At the very least, you established a foothold at Arwad. It was high time Henry entrusted you the command."

"It was only a matter of time."

"Shall I now tell you what happened at court in your absence?" She had tried to tell him earlier, but Amaury had been more interested in getting her into bed first.

"I was counting on it," he said teasingly. Zabel had yet to learn to curb her impatience.

"Well, while you were risking your life for Christendom and country, your brother, the king, was stricken with this disease no physician understands or knows how to treat. Needless to say that all those present were shocked," she said with just enough venom to emphasize the nobles' displeasure but without sounding disrespectful. Amaury was sensitive when it came to his brother, and she needed to broach the subject with care.

"Poor Henry," he offered noncommittally.

"You would be such a fine king, beloved! A much better king than Henry."

Amaury looked into her beautiful, big, almond-shaped eyes with the dense eyelashes. They had been married for eight years, but he still had to tire of her. "Ah, the vagaries of fate! He had to be born before me," he made a comical gesture, but Zabel was not amused.

"You are jesting, but half his court think the same. I wager even more so now after your victory." Amaury lay still in contemplative silence. Zabel rolled onto her side to look at him. "It seems that the Seneschal is urging Henry to wed."

His lips broke into a knowing smile. "I would not fret about that."

Her brows shot up. "How can you say that?" she said, resting on her elbow. "How do you expect the prophecy to come true?"

"His queen will give him no child," he said with infuriating confidence, refraining from elaborating further.

Zabel's eyes widened, and her pupils grew bigger. "You sound as if you know something I do not. What is it?"

Amaury chuckled. "I do not think Henry's seed will quicken any woman's womb. One day, I will be his heir."

Zabel was not tempted with the prospect. Henry was young; only two years older than Amaury. She studied him closely. His statement produced no enlightenment, only puzzlement.

"What do you mean?"

"Let it lie, Zabel! No man would be proud if his sister-in-law were privy to such matters," he said soberly.

Zabel struggled with herself. She did not want to anger him, but she had to know. "You do not need to tell me embarrassing details, beloved. But for the love of God, take pity on me. Put my mind at ease. How can you be so sure?" she asked in a triumph of curiosity over conscience.

Amaury let out a sigh. "Can you not be contented if I tell you he cannot? Do you not trust my judgment?"

"Of course, I trust your judgment, beloved." Zabel had long ago learned that her husband's pride was unpredictable, easily affronted. She kissed him full on the mouth, her fingers sliding down his torso, reaching between his thighs. It took only a few strokes before his breath became shallow. She brought her lips to his ear. "But I wish you would tell me," she whispered, her warm breath tickling his ear, sending new thrills down his body.

Amaury came on top of her, restraining her arms above her head, immobilizing her with his weight and claiming her lips harshly. "He had a riding accident in his boyhood," he said, penetrating her forcefully, as if punishing her for the power she exerted over him, a power she knew only too well how to wield; punishing himself for the weakness he felt in her arms.

"Oh, yes, Amaury; yes, beloved!" Her hips matched his, thrust for thrust until their cries mingled loudly.

*

Doing Kontostephanos' bidding and not meeting with Nicholas alone by the river in the evenings turned out to be a lot easier than Lois had expected. Nicholas spent most of his time in the capital in his effort to secure a place at the palace.

It was a hot afternoon early in July when Lois came back from overseeing the last of sheep shearing for the season. She swung from the saddle and led the docile mare back to the stables when she suddenly stopped in her tracks. That was Roland! She greeted Nicholas' stallion with affection.

"Ah, *pichòt,* there you are!"

She turned around slowly. He seemed happy to see her. He gave her a smile that caught at her heart, so loving was it.

"Welcome home, Nicholas." She sounded more reseved than she had intended, and Nicholas had a gift at picking up subtle nuances in her expression.

"Thank you, *pichòt.* It's good to be home. I hope you will not shy away from me again."

So, he had noticed; she flushed crimson red. "*Pappou* is getting older. He needs my help more these days. But I will try," she said evasively.

"You will try?" he asked, raising an eyebrow. In the space of a heart-beat, he covered the distance between them, lifted her up, and swirled her around until she cried out, "I surrender!" In that moment, nothing had changed between them.

He put her down and let her catch her breath. "I have something for you," he said.

"Really? What?" Her eyes were luminous, aglitter with sudden excitement.

"Ah, but I will not give it to you yet lest you avoid me again."

She looked at him, stunned and disappointed. It was only when he could contain his laughter no longer that she realized she had been hoodwinked. She joined in the laughter.

He took colorful hair ribbons out of his saddlebag and gave them to her. "They are beautiful! Thank you, Nicholas," she said and gave him a quick kiss on the cheek.

He smiled fondly at her. "I'm glad you approve. I have to find Father, now. I will see you later?" he said, about to leave.

She dreaded to ask but did anyway, "How long are staying this time?"

He gave a regretful smile. "Just a few days, *pichòt*. There has been a new call to arms. We will be sailing in a fortnight."

"I see." Her voice was composed. "I will be praying for your safe return."

"Thank you, *pichòt*," he said and walked away.

24

2013

Lucy let her gaze glide around the living room. She had not imagined she would sell the apartment so fast. But it was in a sought-after neighborhood and in very good condition.

She was in a bittersweet mood: eager to move on to the next chapter in her life and sad about closing this one in equal measure. She had been happy in London, a successful career and a classy boyfriend, but those days were gone.

Despite the frivolous night with Michael – and that was all it was she reminded herself, the man was still pining over his runaway bride – she missed William and the cosmopolitan life they enjoyed. She had found herself fighting back the temptation to call him several times these last couple of weeks.

Yet she could not explain why she was wearing Michael's polo shirt as a pajama top since she was not over William yet. Perfunctorily, she played with the bracelet with the pomegranate on her wrist. She shook her head as if to dispel these confusing thoughts. She had more pressing matters to consider.

She loved cooking passionately, but she did not want to go back to the stressful life of Michelin-starred restaurants. 'Med Cuisine' had been the perfect way out. All those exciting new places and flavors; if only it didn't have to end! Perhaps it could start again. If not in London, then maybe somewhere else?

Declan Gallagher, a friend from her days in Dublin, sprang to mind. A quick search on Facebook reassured her he was still working at TV3. Lucy quickly typed a program proposal for 'My Cuisine in the Sun' to avoid any conflict with UKTV, which owned the rights to her previous program, and emailed Declan.

Her cell phone warbled, startling her.

"Hello, sweetie! Welcome home! How's the house? Are you really going to move? What are you going to do with your apartment?" Brian's voice was cheerful, as he bombarded her with questions.

"Oh, Brian, it's a dream house!" She gave him all the details but not the part about Michael. She also told him about the quick sale.

"If you need a place to crash, you know where I live... Well then, since you're seriously thinking about leaving, you won't mind that the beast has found himself a new beauty," Brian blurted out.

Lucy held her breath.

"Lucy? Are you still there?"

"Yes, I'm still here. It didn't take him long," she said resentfully, forgetting for the moment that she, too, had jumped into bed with Michael.

"You want me to come over?"

"No, it's all right. Let's do dinner if you're not working."

"I'll arrange it. Good night, Luce," Brian said and ended the call.

Lucy buried her head in her hands and let out a muffled cry. "Damn you, William!"

*

The days after Lucy had left were hectic for Michael. He moved all his personal belongings to *pappou's* house, and with Lucy's advance payment, he got down to work. His days were filled with appointments from early in the morning until late in the evening.

He needed to have his new company registered, find space to rent and an architect to draw the plans to be submitted to the Town-Planning-Housing authority. He also had to apply for permits and licenses to half a dozen more authorities, find suppliers for equipment and service utensils, and technicians to implement the architectural drawings, and he needed to hire staff.

Michael needed to think out the menu, the equipment, and the configuration. He would have to evaluate food suppliers he had worked with in the past and negotiate new terms of payment in the light of the recent financial circumstances. And he had not begun considering promoting the business yet. When he had started drafting his business plan, he thought he would have time and money. Now he was short of both.

Michael was worn out at the end of each day, but *pappou* was content to see his grandson's optimism and zest for life had returned. *Pappou* was also looking forward to Lucy's return.

25

1301-2

Nicholas did not leave for Nicosia until the fall. Already on his first day at the palace, he found himself thrown in at the deep end. Philip's old secretary had little time and patience for the young man's inexperience, and Nicholas burned the midnight oil, learning the protocol, the procedures, and the names of those nobles who customarily moved through the palace.

Since the archbishopric was only a short walk from the palace, Nicholas had been hoping to spend some time with Peyre, but he had just moved to Famagusta to work together with the famous architect Jean Landois on the design and construction of the Saint Nicholas Cathedral.

At the end of January, Nicholas was on his own with his duties, as the old secretary retired to his home estate, earlier than planned, after falling down the stairs and breaking a hip. Come February, the Seneschal of the realm died. In his place, Henry appointed Philip of Ibelin, and Nicholas often went home just to sleep.

*

Provence watched the grass sway in a late fall gust of wind. The leaves scattered, as he walked away from the alehouse on the palace square and into the shaded streets of the capital. Now that he had been relieved of his duties at the court due to his age, he had no reason to come to Nicosia other than to visit Nicholas and a few old friends. He did not want to admit it to himself, but he missed the times when he was at the center of events, witnessing history being made.

He sensed a movement in the shadows and settled his hand on the hilt of his sword.

"Hello, Provence," he heard Roussillon's familiar grating voice, coming out of the shadows.

"Roussillon," he said gingerly. He had not heard from him for some time.

"When justice is done, it brings joy to the righteous," Roussillon quoted Proverbs with a gleeful smirk.

Provence stared at him, puzzled. And then, in the space of a moment, he knew. Roussillon had been behind Albert's arrest. *God rot your misbegotten soul!* Hot rage possessed Provence, and he itched to get his hands around Roussillon's throat and choke the life out of him.

He did not know what held him back. If it was St. Peter's preaching about not returning evil for evil, or the calm grasping that nothing good would come out of it. He stared at Roussillon long and hard. "But terror to evildoers," he completed the quote. "The Lord will judge His people."

Provence made a snap decision not to seek revenge. Although he could not accept what the man had done, Roussillon had already been punished with his unmarried daughters. He had no sons to carry on his name. It would die with him. That was penance enough. He even pitied him.

"Goodbye, Roussillon," he said and walked away with an inexplicable sense of calmness. They were even. Their long unsettled dispute was resolved, or so he thought.

Roussillon stared at him in outraged astonishment, chocking anew on his hatred. He swore that he would see Provence broken, or he would die trying.

*

Comfortably seated by the fireplace, Provence asked Nicholas about his work at the palace. His voice did not reveal his concern for him. Nicholas had lost weight, and the circles around his eyes told of a man who did not sleep enough.

"Enthralling; exhausting! Ever since Philip became the Seneschal, he has the world on his shoulders." He downed his wine and explained, "As if running a kingdom for his nephew is not enough, he has pressure from the Templars to start a new expedition, and he has to contend with the pirate assaults. And now, the Pope has ratified the Peace of Caltabellotta, which raises the possibility of an Aragonese prince on the throne of Cyprus. There is so much to do and so little time!"

A hint of worry sat on Provence's brow. "The Aragonese have a claim to the throne of Cyprus?"

"Sicily will pass to the Angevins when Frederick of Aragon dies. Until then they have to pay a tribute of 100,000 ounces of gold, unless the Pope agrees to allow Frederick to conquer either Sardinia or Cyprus."

Provence cursed under his breath at the arrogance of might toward small realms like Cyprus and Sardinia. The thought that such a conquest would be carried out with the blessings of the Pope, the representative of God on earth, made him nauseous. Provence doubted that there was anything divine in this settlement; it seemed more diabolic to him. Perhaps the Orthodox Church was not wrong in questioning the Pope's infallibility.

"What is Henry going to do?" he focused on the issue at hand. The last thing they needed was another war.

Nicholas shrugged. "I'm not privy to his thoughts. When Philip asked my opinion, I suggested doing nothing."

"Nothing?" Provence looked over the brim of his cup.

"Well, it is clear that the Sicilian nobles support Frederick. They insist that only a descendant of his can ever rule Sicily after he dies.

What is more, Sardinia is larger than Cyprus, closer to Sicily, and has no king."

This made sense, Provence thought, marveling at his son's political acumen. Nicholas seemed to watch events avidly and to grasp European political intricacies more profoundly than Provence ever had.

Nicholas had spoken with self-possession, Provence noticed. At the age of nineteen, Nicholas had been the youngest knight in the service of the king. At twenty-one, he had already amassed a little fortune as a merchant, and at twenty-two he was the youngest scribe in the palace, the Seneschal's right-hand man. What more could a father ask?

"I think we should be more worried about the malcontent nobles," Nicholas went on.

Provence nodded thoughtfully. The capital simmered with rumors that Henry's illness had brought the realm to a terrible impasse. They were after blood, he thought. It did not matter that it was because of Henry's inspired moves that Cyprus stood strong when a swarm of fleeing Christians came to the island; or that he had forged ties to deter the Saracen threat, or that the dispute between the Catholic and the Orthodox Church was quiescent.

"We can only hope that Henry will get better soon. Tell me, Nicholas, do you think he solicits important advice without Philip's involvement?"

"No, on the contrary; I would say he fobs off the others in his retinue." The young man noticed Provence's lips form a grim line. Was Philip's strength also his weakness? "Do you think they are envious?"

"Is it inconceivable?"

"I see what you mean. It is a matter of trust. The king knows he can rely on Philip; apparently, less on others."

The two men sat in contemplative silence for a while.

"You know that Genoese pirates raided the *casale* of our neighbor, the Count of Jaffa." Provence said. "They killed all his servants, carried off the count and his wife, his eldest son, and daughter, and robbed the house."

"Yes, I know. It was Molay, the Templar Grand Master, who acted as an intermediary when they demanded ransom."

"Even in our own homes we are not safe from the plague of the pirates," Provence said. He frowned and paused for a moment as he tried to unscramble his thoughts. "Your mother sends you her love and this." He indicated with a jerk of his head a basket with meats preserved in wine, cheese, nuts, and dried fruits. "She wishes you could come home for a visit soon. It has been a whole year." It was stated neutrally, but Nicholas sensed the longing nonetheless.

"It seems unlikely any time soon," he said ruefully, a touch of nostalgia in his voice. "How is Mother? And everyone?"

"She has her good days. Emilia's remedies seem to work most of the time. Kontostephanos and I still play chess in the evenings. He is getting old, just like me."

"And Lois? Has Kontostephanos found a *lefteros* for her?" In his long absence, he'd hardly had the time to think of her or anything else other than work.

"No, not yet. I think he is in no rush. He got it into his head to teach her everything he knows. This can take a while," he said lightly, and both men laughed.

Provence's face suddenly became serious.

"Is something the matter?" Nicholas asked.

"It's probably nothing. Some of the serfs on the estate have not paid their taxes yet."

"Surely, Konstostefanos will handle it."

"I hope so. They've been complaining that they need to work on their fields an extra day a week; that the drought has been disastrous for their crops; that it takes them an awful lot of time to carry water from the river."

The latter was a serious problem, not necessarily one to solve with negotiations that Kontostephanos was good at, Nicholas thought, but he had no solution to offer.

"If it does not rain again this winter, it will be a very long summer," Provence predicted with a faint pricking of unease. He paused briefly. "Uh, it's probably nothing. Serfs always complain when there is drought," Provence said and broodingly helped himself to some more wine.

*

Amaury let out an agonizing cry, his heart pounding with an adrenaline rush. Zabel put a placating hand on his arm.

"I'm right here, beloved. It's all right; it was just a bad dream."

He was sweating profusely, and she threw open the shutters and let in fresh air and moonlight. She filled a cup with wine and offered it to him. He drank thirstily and regained his wits with some effort. She replenished his cup, but he placed it on the floor without drinking.

"Do you want to talk about it?" Zabel ventured.

He shook his head.

"Passing strange that you had a nightmare just now," she said.

He gave her an inquiring sidelong glance.

"Right before that, I was having a dream. I dreamed of how you could be rid of these dreadful nightmares." She stopped talking deliberately.

"How?" His voice was hoarse.

"The fulfillment of the prophecy you received as a child."

She had long puzzled over it, drinking on delusions. It was her husband's destiny to be king; hence, hers to be queen. Amaury seemed content to be the Lord of Tyre, but Zabel had tired of Henry's disease and whims. A weakling like him did not deserve to be king, but Amaury was so stubbornly loyal to him. He did not share her vision to see what could be his for the taking if only he dared. What other means could she resort to in order to make him see reason other than God-sent dreams?

"What do you mean?"

"The nightmares will stop when you come to rule over the people of this island."

"Are you out of your senses? You, of all people, know what happens to usurpers. Your own brother placed your other two brothers in custody when they tried to dethrone him! Besides, I cannot do this to Henry; I will not!"

"Your stubbornness can put a mule to shame," she said coolly.

"Use your brain, woman! What do you think Henry would do to me?"

"That would depend on who will wear the crown at the end of the day, would it not?" He looked at her wordlessly, a look that burned between them. Zabel averted her gaze in feigned submission.

Amaury picked up the cup and downed the wine, deliberating over Zabel's words. Was God telling him what to do through his wife's dream?

26

2013

Lucy ended the call with Declan, wearing a pensive expression. He had found the idea about 'My Cuisine in the Sun' interesting and said he would spy out the lie of the land, but he could not make any promises. That was good enough, Lucy knew.

She wondered if it made sense to move to Cyprus if this went through. She could perhaps keep the house as a holiday destination – or not. She would only lose the advance payment. At least, it would be money well spent. Michael was worth every penny.

Lucy felt guilty, nonetheless, for she knew that the advance was only a small fraction of the startup capital he needed, and he was counting on receiving the entire amount soon. She did not even want to begin considering how he would come up with the rest if she backed down.

Had she inadvertently messed up his life – again? Perhaps she could find another way to help him, she thought, pushing all worries to the back of her mind. The universe would send her a sign. Mentally, she set the end of the month as a deadline. If she heard nothing from Declan before then, she would know what to do. Besides, Brian would be picking her up soon. She had to get ready.

*

An hour later, Brian was ushering Lucy down the hallway of his apartment building.

"So, you're cooking for me tonight!" She flashed a smile at him. "What a treat!"

"Always a pleasure," Brian said, pulling a set of keys from his pocket. He threw open the door and turned the light on.

"Surprise!"

Lucy stood astounded, staring at her gathered friends' smiling faces and the big banner on the wall: 'Have a wonderful life, Lucy! We'll be there for a visit soon!'

Brian put a glass in her hand. He raised his and said, "To Lucy and her new life in the Mediterranean sun!"

"To Lucy!"

*

In the privacy of his study in his three-story Notting Hill lavish mansion, seven bays wide, with a pair of service wings flanking a front courtyard, Sinclair poured himself an XO from the liquor cabinet and lit his pipe. The room was filled with the exquisite blend of Burley, Cavendish, and Virginia.

He grabbed his cell phone and sank into a dark brown leather arm-chair. He cast a perfunctory glance at the bookshelves that were filled to bursting with leather bound books; some of which were original first editions, waiting for his call to be put through.

"Yes?" the familiar voice said on the other end of the line.

"If I'm right, the "X" marks the land that used to belong entirely to a man by the name of Michael Costa. It seems that recently he kept only a small part for himself and sold the rest to a Lucy Hernandez, my ex-girlfriend I believe," he added reluctantly.

"Perhaps it's time you rekindled the relationship, professor," the voice suggested, and the line was disconnected.

Easier said than done, Sinclair thought. If Lucy did not return his calls, he would have to surprise her on her doorstep. But that would have to wait. Cynthia would be there any moment now.

27

1303

On the day of the feast of the Transfiguration, Lois awoke excited. It was the annual fair at Episkopia, and Kontostephanos had promised to take her with him this year. It was about an hour's walk from the Provence *casale*. The road was busy with drays nose to tail.

Lois had never seen so many people gathered in one place before. Peddlers and merchants from the nearby *casalia* and beyond had come with all kinds of goods for sale, from spices to rugs, but Lois' attention was caught by the dazzling jugglers. They moved through the crowds, tossing oranges skyward as they sauntered past.

She stopped at a booth filled with fragrant perfume vials of *eau de chypre* and was instantly enraptured by the aroma. She indulged herself in a moment of fanciful whimsy: she was a lady and could afford wearing perfumes and colorful dresses. She smiled and walked on to the next stall.

There was enough *soutzoukos*, almonds threaded onto strings and dipped in a mixture of must and flour, to satisfy the greediest sweet tooth. Adjacent to the stall, a magician performed the cups and balls trick whilst his captivated audience stared in awe at the ball penetrating the cup.

Kontostephanos had given Lois a *gros petit* to spend on whatever her heart desired, and she meant to spend it well. She wandered from stall to stall but soon realized that most items for sale were expensive and only nobles and knights could afford them. At noon, the stalls selling pies were the most sought after, and Lois made a mental note for next year. She could set up a pie stall. She felt confident that she could talk *pappou* into it.

A young man shoved her as he passed by and Lois almost lost her footing. She was about to protest when she noticed the young man strain his neck behind a throng of people. They were blocking her way and it took some effort to get a closer look. They had gathered around a man demonstrating a Y-shaped twig. Lucy could not quite hear what he was saying, but she was intrigued and waited for the crowd to dissolve to have a chance to talk to him.

"What is this strange twig you are holding?"

"This, my fair lady," the man said, giving her his most fetching smile, "is a divining rod. It helps me locate groundwater, so I can tell people where to dig a well."

Lois' eyes widened; not just because this was the first time anyone had called her 'fair lady'. A well was exactly what they needed at the Provence *casale*! She had no idea how hard it was or how long it would take to dig one, but she figured it should not be all that bad since the *casale* bordered the river. A well would ease the tension between the serfs and Provence and make her grandfather's task easier.

"How much for your trouble?"

"A bezant," he replied.

"That is a lot of money," Lois said, shaking her head. She was about to go away when curiosity got the better of her. "How does it work?"

"I will come to your estate, walk around, and tell you if and where there is groundwater."

"So, I may pay you a bezant for nothing if there is no groundwater!"

No one had asked him that before. She was sassy, but he liked that about her. He looked at her from head to toe. She was not stunningly beautiful, but she was fair to look upon, a glint of mocking intelligence in her chestnut eyes.

"How about that: if there is groundwater, you will pay me a bezant; if not, you will pay me half."

Lois looked him up and down. "Will you stay until we find it?"

"Oh, no! I'm a wanderer. I never stay in a place that long."

Lois had never heard of wanderers. "And your master allows that?"

"I have no master! I'm *lefteros*, free to come and go as I please." His lips formed an alluring smile.

Lois squared her shoulders. "I'll make you a deal. If there is groundwater, I will give you two bezants if you stay until we find it. I can even give you a place to sleep and a warm meal a day if you help in the construction of the well."

"You can offer me two bezants, a place to sleep, and a meal a day! What would your master say?"

It was Lois' turn to smile smugly. "Like you, I have no master. I'm *lefteri*. I'm the bailiff's granddaughter, and I help him with his duties."

The stranger looked at her with renewed interest. He had never met a girl so quick-witted and sure-footed before. He took a liking to her from the very first. "It's a deal," he said, stretching out an arm.

Lois shook his hand. "What do I call you?"

"Theodore. What do I call you?"

"Lois."

"A beautiful name for a beautiful girl," he said, but his honeyed words did not elicit the coquettish smile from her that he had anticipated.

*

As the night wore on, Emilia made her way upstairs to light the candles in her mistress' chamber. She was not surprised to find the master kneeling by her side, holding her hand. Eloise had stopped responding to treatment. There was nothing more anyone could do. It was in God's hands now. Provence had already sent word to his sons that morning. He hoped there would be enough time for Eloise to bid them goodbye.

It hurt Emilia to see her mistress like this. Even more, it hurt to see Provence, a proud man, unafraid to defy the entire world if he had to, powerless by her side. She shared his desperation. She had lost her husband many years ago. It was the hardest thing to do, to watch your loved one fade away when there was nothing you could do to help, nothing to ease the pain. Emilia knew.

When her husband died, Emilia's life was in ruins. She needed a man to protect her, but she did not want to marry again. Provence had been kind enough to take her in as his cook, and she had been grateful for his kindness ever since. A lesser man would have made her beg or demand repayment of one kind or another, but not Provence.

"Master, shall I bring you your supper here?"

"No, Emilia, thank you. I'm not hungry."

He did not need to be strong in her presence. She understood and that was a relief. Emilia nodded and left the room quietly.

In the lambent candlelight, Provence observed Eloise's ashen face and colorless lips, her hair in disarray. His mind wandered back to the first time they had met. "I do not know how you do it, Eloise, but you are as beautiful as the first day I laid eyes on you."

"That is because your hawk's vision is no longer what it used to be." She made an effort to open her eyes and gave him a faint smile.

"Ah, but the eyes of my soul are in perfect shape, woman, and I'm telling you, your beauty is like good red wine."

Provence stroked her hair gently and planted a kiss on her forehead. He remained by her side all night long, oblivious to time or any human need.

Eloise did not wake up the next morning.

*

In his slanting Italic script, Nicholas was laboriously composing the letters Philip had assigned him. So absorbed was he that he gave a start at the sound of his name, ink spattering on the parchment. He cursed under his breath and lifted his head.

"Monsieur Provence, this is for you." The messenger handed him a parchment and took his leave.

Nicholas recognized his family crest at once, a poppy, Eloise's favorite flower. Slipping a finger under the edge, he broke the wax seal. He unrolled the scroll and read the message with shaking hands. He read it once more, unable to accept the news. He took a moment to compose himself and went off in search of the Seneschal.

Within the hour, Nicholas was leaving the outskirts of the capital behind. He had often dreamed of the day he would be going back, but nothing had prepared him for the reason he was returning.

28

2013

Lucy came back to Cyprus just in time to have her things delivered to her new house. In the days that followed, she gave the place her personal touch. Wanting to add color to her new living space in the sun, she chose corn and peach for the first floor; ocean blue and grassy green for the spare bedrooms upstairs. For the master bedroom, she went for magnolia white, violet curtains and matching upholstered bed, pillows, and covers.

Despite his long hours at work, Michael was always willing to lend a helping hand when he could. Then they would relax on the couch and discuss the menu, the equipment and the service accessories, his progress with the bureaucracy and a plenitude of business possibilities over a glass of good wine, sometimes till the wee hours. Lucy was careful not to speak about partnership yet, but she was thrilled to be part of the shaping of a new enterprise. She was flattered by the way Michael listened to her ideas and embraced them, though he would sometimes modify them to suit the reality of Cyprus better.

That evening, Michael was so beat that he dozed off on her couch. Lucy took his shoes off carefully, helped him lie down properly, and placed a cushion under his head. She covered him with a blanket, staring at the shadow of a beard that accentuated his masculinity. She planted a goodnight kiss on his forehead and went upstairs. When she woke up the next morning, she felt strangely disappointed he had already left.

Pappou proved to be a great help, too. He had magic hands with the plants. After his morning swim, Lucy and he would spend a couple of hours every day working in the garden.

"You know, you can use the swimming pool whenever you like," Lucy suggested one morning.

"Thank you, Lucy. This is very kind, but I'm a sea person." A pause. Then, "I bet London's changed a lot since I was there," he said, digging holes to plant the camellias he had bought for her.

"You've been to London?"

"A very long time ago, during the war."

"The Second World War?"

Pappou nodded. "Back then Cyprus was a colony of the crown. The British had promised *enosis,* unification, with Greece if we helped them in the war. Well, not in so many words. We were naïve then and perhaps heard what we wanted to hear, certainly naïve to believe *enosis* was feasible. Some thirty thousand volunteers fought alongside the British; quite a few if you consider that the island's population was roughly four hundred thousand at the time."

Lucy nodded. "How old were you then?"

"Not yet sixteen, but I took my elder brother's papers to the recruiting sergeant. I remember he looked at me from head to toe twice, but he stamped my papers all the same. After the initial training, I was shipped off to London."

"So, you're a war hero!"

"Far from it. When the squadron leader noticed me, he put me on cooking detail; although I did some flying later... That's when I met Mustafa. We always said that if we made it back alive, we'd open a fish tavern together in Pente Mili, the village I come from."

"Mustafa? A Turk?"

"Turkish Cypriot."

"But why would a Turkish Cypriot fight for the unification of Cyprus with Greece?"

"You're right, of course. Turkish Cypriots wanted either unification with Turkey or independence." *Pappou* chuckled. "But Mustafa couldn't care less about politics. He just needed an excuse to leave his mean wife in Limassol – or so he said."

"I see. And you both came home? After the war, I mean."

"We both came back to Cyprus. But Mustafa never went home. He came to Pente Mili with me instead, and we opened the fish tavern we'd always talked about. Our friendship wasn't easy, not with some pigheaded rogues on both sides. It only takes a few brainless rascals to destroy everything. We got beaten up several times."

"Has there always been tension between Greek and Turkish Cypriots?"

"History has a way of repeating itself. The worst could have been avoided, but the peace loving people kept quiet, minding their own business; never expecting things to get out of control. Cyprus became independent in 1960, but the Constitution was inadequate – to say the least. It caused uproar. The situation escalated, the Turkish Cypriots seceded, and the United Nations sent a peace-keeping force. Cyprus was a nation in a state of insanity where people were either 'patriots' or 'traitors'! The coup followed and then the invasion, and now we have to live with the consequences.

"Mustafa often joked about me saving his life from his wicked wife – never met the woman – but it was, in fact, *he* who saved us when the Turks invaded in '74. We took the boat out for fishing that night. It was the first time I'd taken Michael with me. By the time we came back, the Turks had landed."

He stopped for a moment, reliving every second of that dreadful day as if it were yesterday, and Lucy waited patiently for him to proceed with the story.

156

29
1303

Despite the early August stifling heat, Eloise's funeral was widely attended. Provence was a highly respected man. Along with the family and the entire *casale*, nobles and knights from nearby *casalia* had come to pay their last respects.

Standing behind them, Kontostephanos broke out in a cold sweat, nauseated. He felt discomfort in his chest and mopped his forehead with his sleeve, lightheaded. He grimaced and shifted his weight, breathing heavily. His knees began to tremble.

"*Pappou*, are you all right?" Lois asked, but he did not respond. The priest's chanting and the women's keening filled the hot, humid air, as Kontostephanos fought for breath. Lois had never seen him like this. She stared at him with apprehension. "*Pappou, do you want to sit down?*"

Kontostephanos' eyes looked at her without recognition. He squeezed his right palm on his chest to ease the pain – in vain. Abruptly, he collapsed.

"*Pappou! Pappou!*" Lois let out an anguished cry that made everyone hush and turn their head around.

Nicholas was only seconds faster than Theodore in kneeling by Kontostephanos' side. He untied the ribbons of the unfortunate man's chemise and searched for a pulse, finding none. He placed his ear against Kontostephanos' chest to listen for the slightest sound of life; to no avail.

He raised his eyes to hers. "I'm so sorry, Lois," he said, his voice hoarse with emotion. She stared at him uncomprehendingly. "He's at peace now, beyond all earthly concerns," he added.

Despite the sun's sultry heat, a cold chill ran down her spine. *Pap-*

pou was dead? Impossible! Lois shook her head in disbelief. "No, no! *Pappou! Pappou!*" She shook the lifeless body desperately. "*Pappou!* No, *pappou!* Don't leave me!"

Emilia came to kneel by her side, placing a placating hand on her shoulder. Time seemed to freeze as Lois stared numbly at Kontostephanos' ashen face. As in a dream, she heard people murmuring their sympathy. Mute, she looked at them without seeing them.

Eventually, the priest resumed the chant. Some serfs helped Theodore move Kontostephanos' body to the shade, while Emilia helped Lois back to the manor.

She made some poppy tea with honey and put a cup in the young woman's hand, worried about her vacant stare. She stayed with her all through the day and all through the night, until Lois began reluctantly to accept the truth. A stream of hot tears rolled down her cheeks that soon turned into uncontrollable sobs. She was devastated by a sudden sense of abandonment; the feeling of unbearable loss. Emilia hugged her and whispered gentle words in her ears.

The first streak of dawn found Lois huddled in Emilia's arms, calmer but exhausted after a night of sleepless grief.

*

It was late in the evening, a couple of days after the funeral, when Nicholas found Lois at their secret place raking tears off her cheeks with the back of her hand. Her haunted eyes upset him. He wanted to see her cheerful again.

She cupped both hands over her mouth and nose and sobbed harder. He took her in his arms, waiting patiently for her sobs to subside. Fighting for breath, she hid her face in his shoulder. The warmth of his body was mollifying and solacing. He stroked her back and pressed a kiss on the top of her head.

Calmer now, Lois broke off his embrace and dropped down on the ground. She sat with her hands together and her shoulders sagging.

For a while she was quiet, subdued, and mournful as she stared into nothingness and deliberated a bleak future.

"What am I going to do, Nicholas? I'm all alone now," she said, sounding so forlorn that he wished he could shield her from her burdens.

"No, you are not. Everyone in the *casale* loves you."

"Your father will find another bailiff, and I shall have to leave or marry a serf." Her voice quavered and her eyes moistened again.

Nicholas' face was thoughtful. "Maybe not." She met his gaze. "I will speak to Father. He does not need another bailiff. He has you! You can read and count. The peasants look up to you, *pichòt,* especially after your ingenious idea about the well! Now that Kontostephanos has passed, they will need a familiar face more than ever. I'm certain that Father will agree with me."

His words fell like balm on her wounded soul. "Let's see if we find water first." A pause. Then, "How is it possible that you believe I could be bailiff when you still think of me as a bairn?"

"You will always be a *pichòt* to me, I guess; the little sister I've never had. When you're a grown-up, I won't be able to tease you. Where is the fun in that?" He smiled at her fondly.

"I wish you didn't have to leave in the morning," she said, unable to shake the sadness out of her voice. It seemed that one by one the people she loved either died or abandoned her.

"My life is in Nicosia now," he said gently.

A sigh escaped her lips. "I know." He caressed her moist cheek gently. She had so missed that! She had missed him and the blithe days of their childhood.

"It's getting late. Come on," he said and helped her up. They walked back in silent companionship.

*

The earth trembled in the dead of night, miles and miles away, but it was felt all over the island. In Nicosia, the tremors damaged the pride of the city, Santa Sophia Cathedral. In the Provence *casale,* the earthquake startled the inhabitants out of their sleep. The walls of the manor moved but did not crack, though some dry soil fell to the ground. Even the peasants' mud-brick houses stood the test.

Nicholas' first thought was to check on Provence and Lois. He found his father helping the servants out.

"We are fine here. Check on Lois. She hasn't come out yet," Provence said.

The tremors had stopped by the time Nicholas reached Lois' chamber. He found her standing with her back against the wall. He stroked her arms, tilting his head down to look at her more closely. "Are you hurt?" She looked like a scared and helpless little bird.

She shook her head and hid herself in the safety of his brawny arms. "Thank God you are here," she whispered.

"It's all right now. It's over," he said. He could hear the erratic hammering of her heart and patted her gently on the back. He did not know how long they remained locked in each other's embrace. They might have been killed, but God had spared their lives for a reason. It felt good to be alive.

When she was calm again, she lifted her chin up and stared into his eyes. Nicholas was acutely aware of her physical presence, aware of the moist, red mouth. Her gaze made an emotion stir inside him, closely akin to desire. He found himself leaning down, taking her lips. He felt her cling to him, and he wanted to hold her forever.

"Lois!" They heard Theodore's voice as he was coming up the stairs, and Nicholas broke away. "There you are! God be praised; you are unharmed!" Theodore said, reaching the doorway.

*

Confused by his reprehensible behavior the previous night, Nicholas did his best to avoid being alone with Lois the next morning. He was relieved that he was leaving. Distance and time would set things straight until they met again.

When he walked into the stables, Roland whickered a greeting, and Nicholas nuzzled his neck.

"You are leaving without saying goodbye?"

Nicholas' muscles tensed at the sound of Lois' voice. He looked over his shoulder. For an unguarded moment, his face showed sudden unease. "I thought I did in the manor," he said, offering a small smile.

Lois groaned inwardly. He seemed uncharacteristically reluctant to look her in the eye. She studied his face but found none of the signs she had been hoping for. All night long, her thoughts had kept turning of their own volition to how his lips had touched hers. Their first kiss! Her heart would not be still, and the fluttering had kept her awake till the sun came up.

A brief, strangled silence settled over them, fraught with all that they dared not say.

"Yes, of course, you did... Well, Godspeed!" Lois said eventually, a lackluster smile on her lips. How foolhardy to believe that he had lost his sleep, too!

The desolation on her face was so dangerously disarming that he almost moved to take her in his arms and console her. He made as if to say something, but then he just bid her goodbye, mounted Roland, and urged him on.

Lois stood numb as she watched him disappear into the distance, wondering if that kiss had been a figment of her fevered imagination.

*

It was a cold day, and the leaves had turned gold and red. Lois walked toward the river, the wind on her face. The long summer was suddenly followed by a frigid wind, but it carried with it no rain, yet again. It would be another year of drought. Kontostephanos' last vaticination of the stars had been unerringly accurate.

Ensuring sustenance for everyone in the *casale* was a daunting responsibility. Lois would have to be strong and ingenious. It was unheard of for a sixteen-year-old girl to be bailiff, but Provence had agreed to it willingly. His only condition had been that Lois should assist Emilia with the daily chores when she had time, a condition that Lois accepted gladly.

At least, the well digging progressed without much difficulty. The men were now building a dividing wall to provide diggers with fresh air. Gaps had to be stuffed with straw and pitch. Theodore was optimistic. They would not have to dig deep, he had said. They were lucky they were so close to the river. Nevertheless, the construction was expected to last at least a year.

Lois was surprised Theodore had stayed. She oftentimes wondered why he had accepted the deal in the first place and why he was still holding up his end. Indicating the location of groundwater was much more lucrative compared to digging a well.

She sat by the tall reeds and stared at the flute in her hands. She began to play, wondering if there was a celestial way for Nicholas to hear her music and be reminded of their kiss.

*

Theodore was tired of the hard labor and missed being on the road. Yet he had begun to appreciate the dry pallet bed for him and the straw for Julius, his mule, and a warm meal each day. Even more, he enjoyed Lois' company. He could tell that she liked him too by the way she looked at him when she thought he was not looking.

Dusk was descending over the *casale* when Theodore came to the river in the hope of bumping into Lois, but she was not there. With a sense of disappointment, he took his clothes off and waded into the water. It felt cool in the chilly fall, but Theodore did not mind.

From behind the reeds, Lois watched his muscular body and his male anatomy. She blushed, although she knew he could not see her. She grabbed her flute and rushed back to the manor as noiselessly as she possibly could.

*

Lois was startled out of sleep that night. She had dreamed that she was watching Theodore naked in the river from behind the reeds. As he came out of the water, Nicholas suddenly emerged to the surface to catch his breath.

30

2013

Pappou caressed the leaves of the camellias in his hand perfunctorily and went on with his narration, "It was Mustafa who saw the Turkish ships in the distance first. 'I'll swim ashore,' he said. 'Keep rowing and don't look back.' But I couldn't do that. My daughter and my son-in-law, Michael's parents, were there."

"What did you do?'

"We reached the shore at a nearby jetty. I told Michael to be silent no matter what he saw or heard. We went back to the village from the dunes. When we were close enough, I saw everything."

A painful grimace spread across his face. "The Turks had rounded up everyone they could find in the village square. They separated the women from the men and then made the men watch as they raped their women. I saw my own daughter being raped, and I didn't help her. There was nothing I could do for her; I could only try and save Michael." His voice broke. The secret of shame and humiliation was finally out. He stared at the ground, his shoulders sagging. He suddenly looked very old.

Lucy shut her eyes for a moment. "I had never imagined –. Never thought that –. Oh my God! This is appalling! And Michael? Did he see all this?"

"No. When I realized what was happening, we went back, but he heard the screams and the shots. He asked me about it later, and I tried to be as vague as I could. Luckily, the memories of a two-year old fade away quickly. I can't say I didn't envy him."

"So, he's got nothing of his parents?"

"Nothing; we ran for our lives."

"I'm so sorry, *pappou!*" She could not begin to fathom the agony this man had endured, fleeing with a two-year old, and then bring-ing him up all by himself. "How did you get away?"

"By the time we got back to the boat, Mustafa had brought my old jeep with some water and bread, a few tins and a couple of blan-kets. 'Save yourselves. I'm staying. I've nowhere else to go. They won't harm me,' he said. We embraced and parted. I drove all the way to Agios Sergios, a village just outside Famagusta, making sure I stayed away from main roads. My wife, God rest her soul, had relatives there."

He fell silent for a moment, drowned in memories. "War brings out the worst in people," he went on. "While we were in Agios Sergios, we heard that in retaliation for what'd happened in Pente Mili, EOKA B' fascists slaughtered women and children in a small Turkish Cypriot community while retreating. To complete the vi-cious circle, when the advancing Turkish troops spotted their mass grave, they committed even more atrocities." He shook his head sadly. "A story without end... So, you see, Mustafa saved us."

"I see. But isn't Famagusta also in the North?"

"Famagusta is also occupied, yes. We had to flee again three weeks later when the Turkish troops advanced."

"Oh, my God! You had to escape twice! What did you do?"

"We came to Limassol. One out of three Greek Cypriots became a refugee that summer. There was not enough housing, so we spent the first few months in tents in refugee camps, surviving on food rations from the Red Cross; God bless them. There were no jobs, of course. We had nothing. But slowly things got better."

"Michael's lucky to have you," Lucy said.

"Well, at least he had me, but the truth is I was lucky to have him, a reason to stay alive." He lifted his dreamy eyes to the horizon. "He was such a good a boy, loveable. Never once did he give me a hard time, even when I had to leave him alone to go to work, sometimes two jobs if I could manage. He never got into trouble. He'd always do his homework, tidy up, fix broken things; cook. We'd have starved otherwise. No wonder he became a chef." He chuckled.

How like Michael that was, Lucy thought, kind-hearted and reliable! His disciplined, practical turn of mind made sense to her now.

"The day we reached the Red Cross camp I made a deal with God," *pappou* said. "I'd do anything I could to live a healthy life if He could spare my life for as long as Michael needed me. So far, we've both kept our end of the bargain. I gave up smoking and sugar that same day. Wine is my only vice, but they say a glass a day keeps the doctor away."

There had been a moment during his chemotherapy, some twenty years earlier, when he thought his time had come, but it seemed the good Lord had other plans; not that he complained.

Lucy and *pappou* worked silently side by side for a while before *pappou* asked the question he had meant to ask from the start, "How come you made such a bold decision to come and live in another country?" *all by yourself.*

"I don't know if it's so bold. I needed a change, I guess. My contract wasn't renewed and my boyfriend turned out to be married – still. So, I guess there was not much to hold me there." Then she added in a lighter tone, "Aren't you happy I'm here?"

"Oh Lucy, I'm very happy you're here. You've brought the smile back to Michael's face."

"Thank you, *pappou!* I'm glad I'm here, too."

31

1304

Lois sat by the river, immersed in private thoughts. Theodore would usually walk her home after Mass, but today he had pretended not to see her. She was stung, for he had walked home with Maria and her younger sister, Christina, instead. He was not as handsome as Nicholas, Lois contemplated. But he was able to bedazzle when he so chose and the two young women had giggled all the way home.

It had been six months since Nicholas' last visit for his mother's funeral. He had not come home for Christmas, and Lois wondered if he ever thought of her and their kiss. She sighed, plucking a daisy absentmindedly. She picked the petals off slowly. *He loves me. He loves me not.*

Out of nowhere, Theodore materialized from behind the reeds. "I'm sorry. I did not mean to startle you," he said affably. He was charming again.

He saw her crumbling the flower in her hand and assumed that the daisy was for him. He smothered a grin. She was cross with him, so she must be jealous, he inferred, delighted.

He picked up a flat stone and sent it skimming across the water. "Can you skip stones?" Lois picked up a stone and matched his throw. "Whoever taught you to do that has taught you well," he said, stunned.

Lois remained taciturn.

"You are a mystery, Lois! I bet you are the kind of girl who would enjoy a wanderer's life."

"What's it like?" she said at last. Curiosity got the better of her.

"It's freedom. I'm slave to no one; no master, not tied to the land.

I go where the road takes me. There is hardly a town or a *casale* I have not been to."

Lois was startled at how fascinated she was by the mystic laws of freedom of the wanderers. "Do you have a home? Where do you come from?"

"I grew up in Anogyra, a beautiful little village, perched on a hill, overlooking the Salt Lake of Cape Akrotiri; the Episkopia bay and the Akrotiri bay, left and right of the cape. I was born a serf. My master set me free in exchange for finding groundwater on his estates." *And because he found pleasure in my mother's bed, and I was becoming too unruly to accept it.* "I was a beardless boy then. I have been on the road ever since and I have enjoyed every moment. How many Cypriots can say that about their lives?"

"But how do you live? Where do you sleep? Does your divining rod provide you with food and lodging every day?"

"Sleeping under the stars in the summer is amazing, watching shooting stars. When it gets cold and rainy, there is always lodging somewhere. I have done all right."

She looked at him thoughtfully. "Is it not dangerous? Traveling alone?"

He shrugged. "Not really. I have heard stories about the perils of traveling alone in faraway places, but Cyprus is a safe place. It's just a rock amidst the waves."

"It sounds like a lonely life to me."

"I wish I had a traveling companion," he took a cue from her, looking at her meaningfully. He cleared his throat. "Lois, I know you are still young, but you're a *lefteri* and so am I, and that is rare, and I..." He paused searching for the right words. "I guess what I'm trying to say is that I would like you to be my wife."

Lois' jaw dropped. "I'm too young to marry!"

"I know, and I suspect I'm old enough to be your father." He deliberately let a pause develop before he went on, "Lois, I can wait for you if I know you will consider me."

She tilted her head to the side, weighing his words. "Do you think it safe to have children on the road?" It was utterly absurd, yet having this conversation felt like she was betraying Nicholas.

Theodore took her hand in his. "Oh, Lois! You are young, yet so wise; and beautiful! Lovely like a lemon blossom… Here's what we will do. I'll ask you again when the construction of the well is over. You had better say 'yes'. I'm only staying for you, you know." He gave her a beguiling smile.

He did not commit to staying here after the wedding, Lois noticed. "We'll see."

*

Paul of Nimes was a merchant of high esteem, dealing mainly with linen, garters, cloth of gold, and French cloths. He supplied most of the nobility and high-ranking members of the clergy, beginning with the king himself and the archbishop. Although he was dumpy and fat, he was always impeccably dressed.

A flash heralded the sudden breaking of the storm. Nimes stood in front of the blazing logs in the fireplace in his manor in the capital, rubbing his hands. He had the reputation of a calm and fair man, but now he was enraged, imprecating the weather for his misfortune. He had just received the devastating news about the sinking of the galley carrying a consignment of precious cloth from Marseille.

Nimes had been trying to arrange a marriage for Antoinette, his only surviving child, to a baron or at least a castellan and needed money for her marriage portion. And now, he would have to borrow money to get back on his feet! He had ordered his bailiff to collect all taxes due, but the man had failed once again. Flogging did not help this time, he had said. The prolonged drought had brought serfs to the verge of famine, and the sudden storms had even washed away some of their huts.

At the sound of Lucile's, his wife's, determined strides, Nimes looked over his shoulder as she marched into the great hall, her long dress trailing behind her.

"Paul, I believe we should talk," Lucile said, her tone of voice unusually peremptory.

"I'm listening, my dear," he said. He had postponed telling her about their misfortune until he had figured out a solution.

"I pray, ere you fly into a rage, we need to keep a cool head and reach a decision this instant," she said with subdued urgency.

He nodded. He did not usually fly into a rage. That was her faculty. Nimes could not fathom what she could possibly tell him that would upset him so. "What is it?"

"Antoinette is with child," Lucile blurted out. "It is not showing yet, but we need to find her a husband at once!" She heard the tone of panic in her voice and paused for breath.

Nimes looked at her thunderstruck. "Are you sure?"

"Of course, I'm sure!"

"What about the father?" Nimes feared to hear the answer.

Lucile shook her head. "He is married," she said, raising a palm as if to fend off any protest.

Nimes' face turned red. "That little…"

"That little… is your daughter, your responsibility!"

"She can forget marrying into nobility now. I'm not selling anyone damaged goods. I have a reputation to uphold." He threw his pudgy hands into the air.

"Then how about a knight? Or a wealthy merchant at least? You know everyone. Surely, you will find someone!"

Nimes swallowed the vile words that came into his mind. Instead, he began thinking of eligible bachelors.

*

It was already evening when Nicholas put his quill down and rubbed the knuckles of his tired, stiff fingers. He placed some scrolls under his arm to take home for further study and wished Philip good night.

The cold air hit him, and he pulled the hood over his ears, raising his gaze to the gray clouds hanging low in the sky. It would be spring soon, but it felt like it would snow, he thought, glancing at the almond trees. They were in full blossom, dressed with white and pale pink flowers, like lace on a bridal dress.

In long, brisk strides, Nicholas crossed the palace gardens. He heard someone call his name and stopped reluctantly. He would rather be having hot soup in the alehouse than standing here in the cold.

"Provence, I'm glad I caught up with you. Let's have some ale, shall we?" Nimes said, patting him on the shoulder, registering the young man's surprise. Nicholas could not imagine what Nimes might want to discuss with him.

*

A servant let Nicholas in and showed him into the great hall. Nimes rose to his feet, shook hands with the young man, and introduced him to his wife and daughter.

Her blue velvet dress with a lace-up front closure exaggerated the color of her eyes. With her soft white skin and rich clusters of blonde curls protruding from beneath her loose wimple, Antoinette looked like an angel on earth. Her silky voice sounded like music to Nicholas' ears who was instantly dazzled by her pulchritude. He had yet to take his eyes off of her, and Nimes and Lucile exchanged a conspiratorial grin.

Lucile had exerted herself that evening. She had gone to great pains to present a festive meal on such short notice. Roasted moufflon with raisins, honey, and walnuts were served to impress.

Over dinner, Nicholas caught Antoinette's shy sideways glances and the fluttering of her eyelashes, the thickest and longest he had ever seen. Each time he spoke to her, her eyes opened wide enough and deep enough to drown a man in their rehearsed innocence. She seemed so vulnerable that Nicholas felt the need to protect her. Her small smile was sweet and inviting, and he felt attracted to her like a butterfly to the light.

After dinner, the men were left alone to discuss the bride's dowry over a glass of sweet wine. Nicholas was not moved by the marriage portion, and Nimes threw in his Strovolos manor that bordered Amaury's estates, his nest egg, as an additional lagniappe to ensnare the unsuspecting young man. He was inwardly infuriated with his daughter's stupidity that led to this situation, but he was also aware that time was a luxury he could not afford.

*

The wedding ensued within a fortnight, respecting Nimes' 'dying' wife's wish to see her only child wed before she passed. It was a settlement that pleased everyone. The Nimes had avoided the scandal, and Nicholas, in his ignorance of Antoinette's condition, was content that his young wife came with a good dowry and the looks of an angel.

Nimes went to great lengths to put on a lavish wedding, one the town talked about for weeks. The archbishop officiated at the wedding, and all the nobility of the capital attended. The king himself came to wish the newly-wed couple well.

Lucile's health improved miraculously in the days after the wedding. Nimes ascribed this to the overwhelming joy of seeing her only child so fortunately wed, and Nicholas was too preoccupied with the new wave of pirate assaults and the affairs of the realm to give the matter more thought.

32

2013

Lucy helped *pappou* carry the shopping bags from the trunk of the car into the house. She placed them on the kitchen counter, and *pappou* began to fill the fridge and store dry food in the cupboards.

"Oh, Lucy, can you take this to Michael's room while I make us coffee?" he said, handing her one of the bags.

"Sure. That's…"

"The second door on the left," *pappou* said, filling the *briki* with water.

Lucy was aware that she was entering Michael's room for the first time, a discreet suggestion of his cologne in the air. She left the shopping bag on the table, taking a peek into his private life. The room seemed too small for him, shelves filled to overflowing, stacks of boxes. But it was tidy and clean.

Her gaze came to rest on a wooden box under the bed. She did not know why she pulled it out and opened it. That was out of character, but there she was, staring at its content, photos of a tall and statuesque woman and Michael. She had no idea why she was irritated that Michael still kept these. Yet of course she knew. It was because Michael always listened to Lucy raptly, as if her words were vital, as if she were the most beautiful girl in the world.

"Coffee's ready," *pappou* shouted from the kitchen.

"Coming!" Lucy said startled, putting the box back in its place.

*

Sinclair consulted the academic calendar. The spring break was just a breath away. He hoped the vacation would be sufficient time to see his mission through. If not, he could have his assistant replace him for the revision week and the invigilation of the exams the following week.

He booked a one-way first-class ticket to Larnaca online and a suite in a luxury hotel in Limassol. Then he searched for a car rental. Unable to find an Aston Martin, his favorite brand, he settled for a Jaguar. That was the easy part.

Now he would have to tell Cynthia that he needed to leave for an unforeseeable length of time. He could hardly take her with him. He leaned back in his seat and thought of Lucy and of the likelihood of getting back together again. A part of him welcomed the possibility. He had tried to call her, but she never answered. At first, he had toyed with the idea to surprise her at home, but his ego forbade that. And then he met Cynthia.

Sinclair passed by Lucy's apartment when he had been given the green light for the trip to Cyprus, but she was no longer there. A neighbor said that the apartment had been sold. His search at UKTV had been equally fruitless. He would have to come up with a good excuse for showing up on her doorstep in Cyprus, but he was not worried about that. He never lacked imagination.

He still needed to deal with Cynthia though. Perhaps he could tell her the truth; or part of it: he was following a new lead in his research into the Order of the Knights of the Temple.

*

Adriana's contract in the United Arab Emirates was over. So was the sheikh's interest in her, and she was running alarmingly short of money. She flung herself onto the bed, considering her miserable options. Staying was pointless; there seemed to be no prospect of work any time soon.

Going back to Romania was not an option. The day she had left, chasing the dream of a prosperous life, she had sworn never to go back and never to be poor again. She secured a visa to go and work as a dancer in Cyprus as soon as she had turned eighteen and never looked back since.

The trip down memory lane made her mouth twist in a derisive smirk. She did not want to think back to the agonizing nights she cried herself to sleep. She had never been comfortable with the things the club owner asked of her, so she charmed the first unsuspecting boy she came across.

Sweet little Marios had been her ticket out. He had fallen madly in love with her, and his father, who worked for the immigration office, pulled some strings and helped her leave the club without too much difficulty. She had felt relieved when Marios finished his military service and left Cyprus to study abroad. Drifting apart was inevitable, though she suspected that his father might have had a hand in this. Adriana needed a new employer to secure her stay. With her looks, modeling was the natural choice.

But what was she going to do now? Her parents still lived there, but she could never return to that dreadful farm in that godforsaken village in the middle of nowhere. She lit a cigarette and sighed, disheartened. Where could she go? What could she do? She poured herself a generous glass of vodka and downed it.

She wondered if she had burned all her bridges when she left Cyprus. She missed Michael now and the security she had felt with him. If only he hadn't lost everything! She had looked to a comfortable life with him, and he had let her down. But Michael was resilient. For the sake of curiosity, she searched for his Facebook page and was intrigued to find out that he was about to open a new business.

Adriana wondered if he had found anyone else in the meantime. Knowing Michael, that was rather unlikely. It had only been a few weeks since she left him. It took Michael a long time to commit to a new relationship, Adriana recalled all too well. She contemplated calling him but thought better of it and put her cell phone back down.

33

1304

Nicholas peered at Antoinette's beautiful, albeit white and unsettled, face as the carriage approached slowly the Provence *casale*.

Antoinette's ill health did not allow her to share his bed after their first evening as husband and wife. Nicholas' long hours at the palace did not help either. He was hoping that spending time away from the capital would help them find the way to each other. They owed it to themselves and to their child. He wanted her to see his childhood world and show her off in the *casale*.

She had made it clear she did not want to make this perilous journey in her condition. Her mother had agreed vehemently with her, but Nicholas did not want to wait for two more years until the baby was born and fit to travel. The midwife thought it was best to postpone the trip, but if they had to travel, they should do so with plenty of intervals for her to rest. And so, indeed, they did.

Nicholas looked at her staring out the window and making no effort to meet his gaze. Her pregnancy so early in the marriage did not bring them closer. Neither had Nicholas' sampling of the most disreputable delights the capital had to offer. But that was only after she had feigned ill health evening after evening, he eased his conscience.

*

Lois was not shocked to see Emilia leave Provence's bedchamber at dawn. Solitude can dry out the soul. It had been several months since Eloise's death. Emilia had lost her husband long before that.

Catching Lois' gaze, she asked her to join her in the pantry and Lois followed obediently. Emilia and Provence were the people closest to her since her grandfather had passed.

"How are you and Theodore getting along," Emilia asked, making anise tea.

Lois contemplated her answer for a moment. "He is patient and kind, but I do not know if he's happy here. Sometimes, I think he would be happier on the road."

Emilia nodded. "It is not an easy change. But he's been here for several months now." She poured some tea into two cups and gave one to Lois. "The master has received news of Nicholas."

Emilia knew that Lois had adored Nicholas as a child, but since his last visit, something had changed. She was worried that Lois had not taken the news of the young master's wedding well.

"How is he? And his wife?" Lois asked with a semblance of indifference.

"Lois," Emilia waited until the young woman stopped fidgeting and raised her eyes to look at her. "They are coming home today."

"Oh!" With trembling hands, Lois placed her cup on her lap. His marriage so far away seemed like a bad dream. But if they came here, it would be real. And Lois did not know how to cope with that.

She stared out the window. The pomegranate trees were in full blossom, dressed with fiery red flowers. How could they be so cheerful when she felt so miserable? She thanked Emilia for the tea, murmured something about going for her rounds, and forced herself not to run as she left through the back door, avoiding passing by the construction of the well.

Lois was not there when Nicholas brought his wife to the manor, but the talk of his impending fatherhood followed her everywhere in the *casale*.

*

Lois watched the sun dipping and knew she could not stay away forever. When she came back, she found Theodore waiting for her on the kitchen porch.

"Are you all right?" He peered at her with a worried frown.

"Yes, just fatigued. It's been a long day," she said, shaking off her sadness with a determined effort.

"Anything I can do?"

"No, but thank you." She took a step toward the door.

"Wait!" he said, showing her the three lemons in his hands. "I have a new trick for you; watch!" He began throwing the lemons in the air and catching them.

Lois' worries dissolved and she was tempted to ask him to teach her the trick, but her relief was only ephemeral. "That is really nice, Theodore. Perhaps you can show me how to do it one day, but now I have to help Emilia serve dinner."

"Meet me at the swing after dinner. I'll cheer you up," he said with a confident smile.

"That is a tempting thought, but I expect this to be a long dinner. The master has not seen his son in a long time. Some other time," she said and left him standing there.

Under Emilia's vigilant, albeit discreet, gaze, Lois took a moment in the pantry to summon her courage. She picked up the platter with the partridges and a carafe of wine and marched into the great hall.

"Ah, Lois, there you are!" Provence said.

"You have asked for me, my lord? I was out, making my rounds," she delivered the response she had rehearsed, keeping her eyes on the partridges as she placed the platter on the table.

"Yes, yes, I know. As you can see, Antoinette here, Nicholas' wife, is with child, and I would like you to assist her during her sojourn in the *casale*."

Lois wanted to shout that this was not a bailiff's duty. The words hovered on her lips, died there. "Of course, my lord," she said instead. She began to serve the wine, not finding the courage yet to look anyone in the eye.

"Is there no one else?" Antoinette protested to Provence's and Nicholas' disapproving astonishment. Startled, Lois kept her eyes on the carafe in her hand.

"You have not had the chance to get to know her yet. Lois is our bailiff. She's good at everything," Nicholas said, coming to Lois' defense, to Antoinette's resentment, and to Lois' surprise.

"She's consorting with the devil!" Antoinette cried out, and Nicholas cocked a brow in warning. "Look at her! She is left-handed," Antoinette insisted, pointing a stubby forefinger at Lois who was serving the wine with the left hand. Aggrieved, Lois drew in a sharp breath, biting the inside of her cheek so as not to respond to this unjust accusation.

"What arrant nonsense! Lois does nothing of the kind," Nicholas snarled, glaring at his wife. Antoinette never talked much, and Nicholas could not fathom the cause of this blatant outburst tonight.

Antoinette shot him a glance like thunder. "How dare you speak to me like that in front of a serf?" she cried out indignantly. She stuck up her nose in the air and walked with exaggerated dignity out of the room. The two men barely stood up.

Nicholas considered going after her, but only briefly. He shook his head, confounded. "I'm sorry, Lois," he said, locking eyes with her. In the strained silence that followed, Lois made a quick escape.

"That's what you get when your wife is close to giving birth," Provence said, trying to make light of what had just happened.

"Close to birth?" Nicholas said almost to himself.

"Yes. It's the impatience pregnant women have when the time for childbirth draws near. Frankly, I was surprised she made so venturesome a journey in the first place." He cast his gaze at the goblet in his hand and went on dreamily, "I still remember Eloise's moods as if it were only yesterday. She would not even let me touch her." He chuckled.

"She does not let me touch her either," Nicholas said and paused suddenly. 'It cannot be."

"Well, you coaxed her into your bed before wedding her," Provence said with laughter in his eyes.

"That's the point. I did not!"

*

Nicholas was too upset to sleep or lie down by Antoinette's side. He was trapped in his own mind, a whirlpool of thoughts. A man who had valued his accomplishments he saw now how God was punishing him for his pride. Nimes had tricked him, and Antoinette had made a fool of him. And he had allowed it. How could he have been so blind? He clenched his fists and darted out of the manor, heels grinding gravel.

His steps brought him to their secret place. Slowly, he understood that he wanted Lois to be there; being with her soothed his soul. He wanted to apologize for Antoinette's behavior. Lois had done nothing to deserve that. But she was not there. He sat on the ground and rested his back against the trunk of a hawthorn tree. He was trying to find a way out of the labyrinth of his muddled thoughts and to decide what to do with Antoinette when he registered movement from the corner of his eye.

He turned his head and saw Lois testing the water with her feet, the star light caressing her naked body. He leaned forward, bringing to mind that kiss, sweet as honey, on the day of the earthquake. He became aware that he was gaping, thoroughly captivated. He fought hard to suppress the desire to join her in the water. Intent upon listening to reason, he leaped to his feet and went back to his wife.

*

In the blink of an eye, Theodore was certain about two things. He knew why Lois had been so flustered earlier. The young master had not come to this particular spot by the river by chance. At least, he had the decency to walk away when he saw Lois naked. This reassured Theodore that nothing had happened between them.

He also became aware of how desperately besotted he was with this girl. He was aflame with desire; not sure he could wait for her until the well was finished. He had to have her! But tonight was not the right time; not when the young master was so close. Soon, he promised himself. With patience, he could sway her. If only patience were one of his virtues!

*

Antoinette was staring out of the window when Nicholas came into the room.

"Antoinette, I believe we should talk," he said, but she did not move. "Come and sit with me!" He sat on the bed, patting the space next to him.

Antoinette steeled her nerves and did as he had said. How she wished she could be anywhere else but there!

"I have not found the way to your heart, have I?" Nicholas said.

She raised her bewildered eyes to him.

"And that is because your heart belongs to someone else."

Antoinette did not like his line of reasoning.

"You are not denying it, so I shall take that as a 'yes'. No wonder you do not want to share my bed… How far along are you?"

Her eyes widened as a feeling of panic began to creep over her.

He stared at her; a hard, knowing stare. "The child is certainly not mine. I suppose you could not marry the father." He thought he saw a flicker of surprise and recognition in her eyes. "Is he dead? Married? Abroad? A member of the clergy?"

She gave a squeal of fright.

"You understand that this discovery changes everything?"

"What are you going to do?" Her small voice was unsteady and her shoulders slumped.

Nicholas had been right, but he derived little consolation from that. "Rest now! We are cutting our stay short. We are leaving in the morning. I am taking you back to your parents," he said quietly and walked out of the room.

Antoinette did not sleep that night. She was sure she would die of mortification.

*

It was a long and uncomfortable ride back to the capital. The wheels of the carriage rattled, struggling over the rough terrain. Nicholas stared into nothingness, mulling over how best to deal with the situation. He could, of course, keep quiet about it, but he could not live with himself if he did. Or he could try and have the marriage declared null and void. The latter seemed more appealing the longer he pondered on it.

The truth was that he had slept with Antoinette only once, on their wedding night. He wished now that he had confronted Nimes when there had been no trace of blood on the bed sheets. At the time, he had thought it was tasteless. He had hoped then that Antoinette would warm up to him.

Perhaps he could still talk to Nimes and see if they could reach a gentlemen's agreement. Neither of them could afford a scandal. After all, Nimes must have known that his daughter was with child when he tried to rush him into marrying her.

Antoinette shifted uncomfortably in her seat. Nicholas glanced at her and was alerted by her chalk-white face. "How are you feeling?" he asked. His concern was genuine.

"Not well… I feel," her voice broke for a moment, "so weak."

"Antoinette, is there anything I can do to make you feel better?"

She closed her languorous eyes and opened them again with some effort. "I think… I think I'm losing blood," she managed.

Nicholas looked but saw nothing. "The next village is about two hours from here," he said, his forehead puckered, frustration crinkling his eyes. "Should we stop for you to rest before then?"

"I need a physician or a midwife," her voice was not more than a whisper.

Nicholas' eyebrows plunged into a frown. The tiny village ahead was not more than a row of dilapidated huts, and he doubted that there was a physician. They would be lucky to find a midwife.

Now, he could see the blood flowing over Antoinette's ankles. Would she make it to the next village? He had no idea how he could stop the bleeding. With the sleeve of his chemise, he dried the beads of sweat on her forehead. He caressed her hair with gentle fingers.

The carriage seemed to move more slowly than a garden snail. The journey was long, pure agony. His stomach was in knots. It had been his idea to drug her to the *casale* and then to cut their stay short. What if something bad befell her? His mouth felt suddenly dry, and his heart beat fast and irregularly. He found himself drowning in guilt.

"I'm cold," she said, her voice barely audible.

He used his mantle to cover her and rubbed her arms to keep her warm. The wheel of the carriage banged on a spiky stone, and Antoinette clutched her belly, letting out a howl of pain. Helpless and clueless, Nicholas put a protective arm around her shoulders. He tried not to look at the pool of blood at her feet. He whispered words of comfort in her ear. Seeing her suffer was torture. All he could do was pray.

But his prayer never reached heaven. Half-way to the next village, Antoinette drew her last breath in his arms. Her pale face stayed with him long afterward. He could not lie to himself: he had killed her.

34

2013

"So, where are we going?" Lucy asked when Michael took the Agios Silas exit.

"You'll see," he said, an enigmatic smile crossing his face. A few minutes later he pulled over in front of a two-story building. Lucy looked around.

"What is this place?"

"Patience is not one of your virtues, is it?" he said, amused, fishing a set of keys out of his pocket. She made a funny face at him. "That was scary. Please, don't do it again," he teased her.

"Close your eyes," he instructed her as he was about to open the door. She did as she was told, and he took her by the arm and towed her inside. "You can open them now," he said, barely containing his excitement.

Lucy opened her eyes. It was a kitchen with work tables located in zones by operation, cutting, cleaning, baking and so on. It was a smart configuration which prevented collisions, tension, and chaos. She walked around, paying attention to detail. The kitchen had modern equipment and good ventilation and seemed energy efficient.

Michael realized he was holding his breath. "Well?"

"Still looking for a partner?" She grinned cheekily.

He fixed her with his gaze. "I am."

"Make me an offer I can't refuse." She flashed a brazen smile at him.

"You bet."

His gaze was intense, and Lucy glanced away. "You've thought of everything. When did you do all this?"

He shrugged unassumingly, yet furtively enjoying her admiring look. "It was a lot of work, and there's still a lot to be done. The hassle was mainly with the plumber and the electrician, but it's almost there now," he said. "I've also contacted several friends to let them know what I'm doing. In fact, I already have the first order," he added.

"Wow! Someone's been busy!"

"You can say that again. And I've talked to some people in the media I know. I should get some coverage for the opening… Now, I need to make time for the interviews! Once the staff's in place, I can breathe more easily."

"I could help. We might even end up being partners after all," she reminded him playfully.

He grinned. "I'd love that."

"Well, let's discuss partnership after the opening," she said, opening a drawer. "What about cutlery and stuff?"

"This afternoon, they said. I'm expecting their call for the delivery time." He glanced at his watch. "In fact, they should've called by now."

"A lot of work," Lucy murmured, glancing around. She had not expected anything less of him though. Michael would either do something right or not at all.

He took a step closer and stood behind her, taking in the scent of magnolia in her hair. She did not move, and he put his arms around her. She leaned her head back against his shoulder, and he kissed the top of her head, squeezing her gently. He pushed the hair from her neck. His moist, hot kiss gave her shivers. She closed her eyes, her breath becoming shorter.

His cell phone rang.

A sigh escaped Michael's lips. "I'm sorry. It's the cutlery supplier."

The moment he ended the call, his cell rattled again. He gestured an apology to her and kept the telephone call brief, but the moment was gone. "Look, it seems I have to be here for a couple of hours. Why don't I call you a taxi? I'll make it up to you with dinner and dancing somewhere nice tonight."

He was trying so hard, Lucy thought, smiling inwardly. "Why don't you try and come home early and we can make dinner together?"

"It's a date then."

"Dinner," she corrected him.

"So long as it's with you, it's fine by me." He gave her a charming smile.

He had a gift for putting people at ease, Lucy thought. He must have gotten that from *pappou*.

*

"You're home early," *pappou* said, turning the television down. "I'll heat up the *kleftiko*."

"No need. I'm not staying," Michael said, heading for the shower. *Pappou* turned his attention to the quiz show he was watching.

Fifteen minutes later, Michael got a brut rosé Nicholas Feuillatte and a confectionery box from the fridge. "I'm off," he said, planting a kiss on *pappou's* top of the head and walked to the door, leaving a trace of perfume behind him.

"Aren't you forgetting something?" *pappou* asked.

Michael stopped in his tracks, looking about him. "What?"

"Your car key?"

"I don't need it tonight."

"You have a date with Lucy!" *pappou* said, approvingly.

"Dinner," Michael said, smothering a smile.

"Champagne dinner for two!" *Pappou* nodded slowly. "Have fun!"

Michael walked the few steps to Lucy's house and let himself in through the unlocked kitchen door. He found her wearing one of her sexy cute summer dresses and matching high heels.

He came up from behind her, wrapped one arm around her waist, while placing the champagne and the confectionery box on the counter. He pulled her close, kissed her neck, and said, "Hi, beautiful."

"You have to stop doing that," Lucy said, lifting the knife in the air playfully.

"What's that?"

"Kissing me on the neck." He stared at her in baffled amusement. "I won't be responsible for what happens next," she said teasingly.

Now, that was just the Lucy he remembered twenty years ago. "Is this a promise or a threat?" he quipped.

"That's for me to know and you to find out. But first things first. Put the champagne on ice until I'm done here."

Michael did as she had said, noticing the oysters on ice and the final touches she was adding to the citrus cured salmon with avocado purée and caviar. "Wow! I think this might be the most aphrodisiac dinner I've ever had."

"Mm, the night is young," she said playfully.

"Indeed!" Michael said; the exhaustion of the day forgotten in an instant.

He helped her carry the ice bucket and the dishes to the dining room. Soft music was already playing, the lights were dimmed, the candles lit, roses in the vase, and the table set. If this wasn't a romantic dinner, Michael didn't know what was.

He opened the bottle, and the effervescent sound of the champagne filled them with anticipation. They drank to the success of Michael's business, and he complimented her on the delicious meal. Throughout dinner, Lucy returned Michael's teasing gaze, and he was excited that she was finally ready to take this, whatever this was, to the next level.

When the main course was over, Michael helped Lucy clear the table. She had hardly placed the plates in the sink when Michael told her to close her eyes. Lucy did, wondering what he might have thought of this time.

"Open your mouth!" he said, and she did.

The next moment, she savored a sweet explosion. "Mm," she opened her eyes. "What an interesting combination. Exquisite Belgian chocolate..." Her taste buds were at work while she struggled to identify all the flavors. "Butter and cream and... Is that Greek yogurt?"

"It is!"

"What's the alcohol in it?"

"Commandaria," he offered helpfully.

"Yes, mm. Delectable!"

"I need to see for myself," he said, savoring her lips, his kiss deepening.

Lucy ignored her buzzing cell phone, relishing the kiss. But it buzzed again. And again. "Let's have the pralines with the rest of the champagne," she suggested, checking her calls.

Michael carried the pralines to the table. Lucy hesitated for a moment, but then said, "It's a friend from London. Do you mind?"

He gestured for her to take the call, thinking she could have ignored her cell this evening. But Michael was a patient man.

"Hello, Brian!" she said.

"Check the entrance door," Brian said.

"What?"

"Go on; check the entrance door!"

Lucy shrugged, gesturing that she had no idea what this was about and opened the door.

"Hello, Luce!" Brian said, standing in the doorway. Lucy looked at him flabbergasted. "Well, are you going to let me in?" He gave her a hug and let himself in. Lucy closed the door and followed him at a loss of words.

"Oh, I'm sorry. I should've called first," Brain said, his eyes resting on Michael. "How stupid of me to think that you might need my strong arms with the house or my shoulder to cry on! Hello, arms and shoulder, I'm Brian, just a friend," he said, stretching an arm.

"Michael," he introduced himself, shaking Brian's hand. "Please join us." He pointed at an empty seat at the table. The evening was ruined, but he concealed his disappointment behind good manners.

"Mm, champagne dinner; nice. Just a glass for me, love. I'm not hungry." He took a seat at the table. "Well, are you going to speak to me?" Brian asked, turning to Lucy when Michael got up to bring a glass.

"Well, you've always known how to make an entrance." *Your timing could have been better!*

"Mm, nice butt," Brian said in a low voice, and Michael pretended he did not hear. He filled a glass and gave it to Brian.

"Welcome to Cyprus," Lucy said.

"Thank you, it's good to be here!" They touched glasses and sipped their champagne.

"So, Michael, what do you do for a living?"

"I cook," Michael said plainly. The notion that Brian was testing him to see if he was a good match for Lucy was both funny and annoying, but he played along congenially – for her sake.

"Michael's starting a gourmet catering business. He's a chef," Lucy put in.

"So, you're one of us." A pause, then, "You're not married or in the process of getting a divorce by any chance?"

Michael shook his head. "None of the above."

"Well, it's nice to meet you, Michael!"

"Same here." Apparently, he had passed Brian's test, he thought, faintly amused.

"Well," Brian turned to face Lucy, "I hope you can put me up for the night. Tomorrow I'll rent a bike and drive around, do some sightseeing."

"You don't have to leave so soon," Lucy said.

"Thanks, Luce, but I'm only staying for a few days, and I'd like to see a bit of the island while I'm here. Perhaps you could join me?" he suggested, and Michael wondered what she would do.

"Aw, I'd love that, but the opening's just around the corner, and there's still so much to be done," she said ruefully.

"Right! I take it that you're helping Michael."

"That's right," she said, and Michael smiled to himself.

"Well, Michael, perhaps you could give me some pointers on places to visit while I'm here," Brian said, and Michael did just that.

35
1305

When Nicholas broke the news to Antoinette's parents, he had half expected them to accuse him of her death. But all he encountered was sorrow and guilty silence. It would have been pointless to tell them that he knew the truth, so he held his tongue.

It had been several months now, but Antoinette's cold, white face as she died in his arms still deprived him of sleep, and Nicholas searched for peace in the daily routine of his duties. Fortunately, his work was absorbing and challenging.

Seated at his desk, he checked the day's calendar. The next audience was with the new Templar Marshal, Aimo of Oiselay, who had already arrived and was waiting in the antechamber. Nicholas studied him stealthily as he opened the door to the Seneschal's office to announce him. Oiselay's sullen face told of a single-minded, willful man who would achieve his goals by hook or by crook.

"Thank you for this audience, Seneschal." Their eyes locked, and the two men tried to take each other's measure.

"State your business, Oiselay."

"I am here to discuss a new expedition to reclaim the Holy Land."

"Indeed? It is my understanding that the Pope has issued no such bull. I see no other Christian leaders gathering armies."

After the deadly blow the Christians had sustained at Acre, the holy cause of reconquering Jerusalem seemed like a fading dream, as the Christian rulers were preoccupied with fighting one another.

"It is time we initiated one," the Marshall said, undaunted. "We have devised a new battle plan we wish to discuss with His Grace, but I understand he is indisposed." *Again.* "After all, the Saracens are in close proximity to Cyprus."

The Seneschal's lips stretched into a smile, but it did not reach his eyes. Did Oiselay really think that Henry needed to be reminded of this? He ignored the part about Henry's illness.

"My memory must be pitifully short. I have no recollection of His Majesty's consent for a new expedition," Philip said with a shrug, one of dismissal.

"The king's illness is preventing him from fulfilling his Christian duty to liberate the birthplace of our Lord Jesus Christ," the Marshal persisted, keeping his temper at bay. "It is sad, really, that he's not more like his brother Amaury. Healthy, I mean, and strong like the brave Lord of Tyre."

The Marshall seemed to be taken with his own importance, and Philip did his utmost to conceal his spontaneous revulsion for the man. "I would be more careful if I were you, my lord. That sounded almost like an insult! You should best remember His Majesty's generosity so long as you are guests in his realm."

The Templar swallowed a protest. "Indeed, very generous," he conceded.

"Thank you for your suggestions, my lord. I will forward them to his Majesty," Philip said coolly, his remote, inward look veiling his thoughts.

Oiselay opened his mouth as if to press the issue further but changed his mind. They were clearly deadlocked. Time for deeds, not words, he decided, and took his leave unceremoniously.

Philip waited until the door closed behind the Marshal. "What do you make of that, Nicholas?"

"I'm not sure I understand why the Templar Marshal felt the need to compare the king to his brother. It was insulting the way he praised the Lord of Tyre for his courage and fortitude."

"A flagrant offence," Philip said more to himself.

"It was almost as if —" Nicholas stopped abruptly, his brows drawing together.

"As if?"

"As if he would rather have Amaury on the throne," Nicholas articulated Philip's fears.

"You are right. I did not like it either. Although he has only just arrived on the island, he's been aggressively campaigning for a new expedition and he's launched a scathing attack on Henry." He rubbed his chin. "Nicholas, invite the Hospitaller Grand Master to the palace."

"I hear he is very sick, dying."

Philip seemed distracted. The recent death of his nephew Guy, Henry's brother and Constable of the Kingdom, had been sudden and overwhelming. Henry appointed Aimery, his younger brother, as the new constable. Philip had his reservations about Aimery but no better candidate to propose. Aimery was young and very impressionable.

"Then we shall have to wait."

*

In the Provence *casale,* the Orthodox serfs had gathered for the Paschal Vigil. At midnight, all the candles were blown out, and the priest lit the Holy Flame and passed it throughout the congregation, chanting, "Come receive the light!" Everyone lit a candle and wished each other *Christos Anesti!* Christ has risen! The youngsters lit the fire in the yard and burned the effigy of Judas.

It was not until the wee morning hours when the priest, standing in the church yard, knocked on the closed door of the church, chanting, "Open to me the gates of repentance," Lois' favorite part. Soon after that, the members of the congregation took their lit candles home and made the sign of a cross in the doorway of their homes with the charcoal from the burnt wick before entering.

Everyone was looking forward to cracking the red dyed eggs, symbolizing the color of the blood of our Lord Jesus Christ, and breaking the Lenten fast after fifty long days. Theodore grabbed a red egg from the basket and dared Lois.

"All right," she took up the challenge. "What does the winner get?"

The yearning she saw in his gaze was of such intensity that she felt flustered. No man had ever looked at her like that before. Her face turned crimson.

"If I win, you marry me now," he said. "The well is nearly finished anyway."

Lois gathered her wits and gave him an enigmatic smile. "We'll see about that," she said. "And if *I* win?"

"Ask me anything!"

"You fix the hen house," she said and stretched out the hand with the egg. "You first!"

"Christos Anesti!" Theodore said.

"Alithos Anesti!" Indeed He has risen, Lois replied.

Theodore tapped the end of his egg against the end of her egg, but it was his egg that cracked. "The other end!" he said eagerly.

Lois watched the tension on his face as he tapped the other end of the egg. His egg cracked again. Theodore pouted for a moment, then smiled warmly at her and said, "I would have fixed the hen house for you anyway."

36

2013

Lucy dried her hands with a towel and noticed the tears rolling down on the new intern's cheeks, as Michael walked into the kitchen. Inconspicuously, she moved closer to the young man and said in a low voice only he could hear, "Wipe those pretty eyes of yours. You don't want the chef to see you crying now, do you?" Though Lucy did not think Michael would mind, she'd had first-hand experience with chefs mocking young trainees if they caught them crying while peeling and chopping onions.

The young intern raised his bemused eyes to her and did as she had said, murmuring, "I'm sorry, chef. This is my first day."

"What's your name?" she asked kindly.

"John, chef."

"Well, John, watch, learn, do what you're told, and you'll be just fine. If you're not sure about something, come to me." She flashed a smile at him and winked.

"Thank you, chef!" John said, lit up like a Christmas tree.

Lucy nodded and went back to her place while Michael stopped at each station, supervising and exchanging a few words with his staff. Lucy felt the cell phone vibrate in her pocket and fished it out.

"Hello, Luce!" Brian said brightly.

A smile blossomed on her lips, belying her fatigue. "Hey! How's sightseeing?"

"Great! Wish I had more time. I think I'll be back soon; take you with me next time."

"I'd love that. Just let me know in advance…Oh, Brian?"

"Yes, darling?"

"The opening's next Saturday."

"Oh, Luce, I'm sorry. I'm cutting my stay short. Brett Grahm just called. I'm starting work at the Ledbury on Thursday! I wanted you to be the first to know."

"Wow! The Ledbury! Congrats, Brian!"

"Yes, I just got lucky, I guess. Well, I wish Michael the best of luck with his new business. Gotta go now. Bye, love!"

Lucy put the cell phone back in her pocket and rubbed her neck. It had been a long day. Michael materialized behind her, giving her a quick massage on the shoulders.

"Mm, that feels good," she said, closing her eyes.

"Why don't you go home and fill the bathtub? I'll come and join you soon," he whispered in her ear, giving her goosebumps. Lucy hesitated. "Go! Get some rest. I need you relaxed and refreshed when I come home. Now, go!" he insisted, rotating her toward the door and giving her a gentle push.

"I won't argue with that!" she said, taking off her uniform.

*

When Lucy got home, she had a quick cup of cocoa with pappou and took grateful Lola out for a walk. As she was climbing up the short flight of steps to her kitchen, she heard Michael's car in the driveway and checked the time. He had come unusually early.

"Everything all right?" she called out.

Michael locked the car and took a step closer. "Oh, fair Lucy! When you left, you took the light with you," he said, spreading his arms in a theatrical gesture.

"What?"

"The lights went out. Blackout. The electrician's not picking up, so

I gave everyone the rest of the shift off. I hope this doesn't happen next Saturday," he said lightly, but Lucy could tell that he was worried. "I'll check on *pappou,* and I'll be right over. Did you fill the bath tub?" he asked saucily.

"I'm on it," Lucy said, with a quiver of anticipation. She got in and turned on the tap. A moment later, her cell rang.

"Lucy," Michael said, "I'm taking *pappou* to the clinic. He's slipped in the shower." His voice was practical but concerned.

"Oh my God! Wait for me! I'm coming with you!"

*

The next morning Michael made breakfast for *pappou* and took it to him.

"An early start?" *pappou* asked, sitting up in bed and glancing at the clock on the bedside table.

"Yes! How are you feeling?"

"As good as new," *pappou* said, hiding his embarrassment over last night's fall. He had suffered a mild concussion the doctor said.

"Look, *pappou,* I have to go now, but Lucy will be over soon. She'll stay home today, so if you need anything…"

"I'm all right. You can both go about your business as usual. Don't worry about me. I'll read in bed all day. I promise. Now go!" *pappou* said.

"Lucy's staying home anyway." Michael planted a kiss on his head. "I'm off now."

*

It wasn't until about an hour later when Michael realized that he had forgotten his cell phone at home. On a side street, just off the busy Makarios Avenue, he turned the car around.

At the same time, Lucy was closing *pappou's* bedroom door, letting him take a nap. Since she was staying home, she would prune the rose bushes in the back garden to be closer to *pappou's* house. She put her garden gloves on and began from the base of the plant, wondering how the evening might have turned out if it hadn't been for *pappou's* fall.

A taxi stopped in front of the driveway. A tall, slender woman got out of the car and walked to the entrance, getting a set of keys out of her bag.

"Can I help you?" Lucy asked, taking a closer look. She knew who the woman was, she thought, feeling her muscles stiffen. She looked like a cover page in her mini cloche skirt and tiny blouse, clinging to her voluptuous body.

"Who are you?" Adriana asked, a tinge of irk in her voice.

"I'm the owner of the house. And you are?" Lucy knew but asked anyway.

"The owner?" Adriana was not quick on the uptake. "What do you mean? Where's Michael?" She did nothing to conceal her growing exasperation.

"I'm sorry. I didn't quite catch your name," Lucy persisted, mainly to irritate her.

"I'm Michael's fiancée," Adriana said, raising her chin a notch, as Michael pulled into the driveway.

The two women stood, looking with firm and unwavering expression into each other's eyes. Michael killed the engine, astounded, and hurried toward them, wondering what the hell Adriana was doing here.

The young model was relieved to see him. "Darling!" she said in a high-pitched voice of pure delight, throwing herself into his arms and ignoring Lucy completely.

Michael took a step back, and her arms fell by her side. "What are you doing here?"

Adriana stared at his unsmiling face but was not discouraged. She caressed his cheek playfully. "Oh, darling! It's such a long story. Let's go home and I'll tell you all about it."

Michael wondered if he cared to find out. He noticed Lucy's face harden in resentment as she attacked the rose bushes with the pruning scisors. These last couple of days had come as a pleasant surprise, but he didn't properly know where he stood with her; if she was over Mr. Perfect.

"Come on, Michael! Let's have some coffee," Adriana simpered, but Michael did not move. "I've come such a long way just to see you!" she said plaintively.

"Seriously? You just up and leave and think you can show up for coffee?"

"Michael, I'm pregnant!"

There was a moment of stunned silence and immobility. Lucy straightened her back, lifted her chin, and got into the house. She had heard enough; there was no way she could compete with that!

*

Lucy was furious with herself. All this time, she'd had the illusion that she was calling the shots in her relationship with Michael. Now she was confronted with the dawning realization that she had deluded herself into thinking the choice was hers to make. Michael would not sit around waiting for her to make up her mind.

She remembered how he used to talk twenty years ago about having a house full of children. Seeing him so close to *pappou,* she could imagine how important family was to him. But would he fall for Adriana's ploy when she had dumped him at the first sight of trouble? Would he take her back just because she was pregnant? Her mouth twisted in a bitter smile. It would not be so hard to imagine. Michael was responsible, one of the qualities Lucy loved about him.

She washed her hands and caught herself wondering what they might be saying to each other. She hurled the towel onto the kitchen counter. This was beneath her and not helping. Michael could do as he pleased, and so could she.

Lucy suddenly remembered that Adriana still had the key to the house and called into town. She wanted the lock changed as soon as possible. The locksmith said he would come by later in the afternoon. Too wired to sit still, she grabbed her keys and her bag. It was such a glorious day, and a stroll at the beach would work wonders on her mood.

*

Determined not to think about Michael and Adriana, Lucy reminded herself that she needed to set her priorities in order. She slogged through the sand with the warmth of the spring sun and the fresh breeze in her face, feeling the tension slide away slowly. She wondered how many people had sauntered in this timeless place before her and what their problems might have been.

Her woolgathering was interrupted by her ringing cell phone. "Hello, Declan! Any news?" She tried to sound cheerful.

"Yes! They want to have a meeting with you; yesterday if possible. I've already made the arrangements for Wednesday. Tell me you can be here," Declan cut to the chase.

"Wednesday? As in the day after tomorrow?" Lucy asked, her adrenaline spiking, thinking of all the things she would have to do to make it happen.

"Yes, and?" Declan could see no problem there. "You can fly out tomorrow, have the meeting on Wednesday, and go back to your precious new house on Thursday."

Put like that, it sounded less complicated. Lucy heard herself agree.

"Great, I'll see you on Wednesday morning, at eleven. If you don't have any plans for the evening, perhaps we could have dinner together?"

"That'd be great," Lucy said and ended the call.

She walked back to the car and drove home, thinking of the twists of fate and the possibilities ahead.

*

Michael heard Lucy park in the driveway and dashed out of the house. "Hey! Everything all right?" he asked. She had seemed upset with Adriana's news. In fact, so was he.

Lucy shrugged. "Sure."

Michael studied her closely. She had been ruffled earlier. Going for a drive had calmed her down. That was good. There was just that look on her face he could not exactly decipher. "Is there anything you want to ask me?"

"Is there anything you want to tell me?"

"Listen, Lucy! I don't know if Adriana *is* pregnant or if the baby's mine. I need to see the results of her medical tests. I told her that if this is the case, I'll acknowledge the baby and help her financially and with the upbringing. But I also made it clear that there's no way we'll get together again."

Lucy stared at him, too stunned to say anything.

"Would that be a problem?" *If we were together?*

She looked at him bewildered. Why would it be a problem if he wanted to be there for his own child? "It's good to see you both know where you stand," she said, measuring her words.

Lucy still had feelings for William locked up at the back of her mind. Surely, Michael must have feelings for Adriana, too, she thought. The baby would inevitably bring them close again.

That was not exactly the response Michael had been anticipating. Why did she seem distant? What more could he have done?

There was one more thing. He wasn't sure how to say it, so he just said it, "There's a snag: she'll be staying with me until she has the results."

Lucy's brows furrowed. *And if the child's yours, probably longer.* "Oh!" she uttered.

"It's not what you think. She has no money and nowhere to go. If she's carrying my child, I can't turn her away."

Lucy nodded. "I see."

"Any chance I might use your couch until then?" he added lightly.

"Um, listen, Michael! I need to get inside. I have some packing to do."

"Packing?" His brows set in a scowl.

"Yes, I'm leaving tomorrow."

"You're leaving!" His lips pinched into a thin, grim line. She nodded silently. "Where are you going, Lucy?" he demanded, spreading his arms in a helpless gesture. Technically, it was none of his business, but he had to ask.

Lucy had been single for too long, and in her short relationships she never had to explain her actions; Michael's honest concern startled her.

"Dublin. I'm having a meeting on Wednesday with TV3 about an

idea for a cooking program I proposed to them before I came out."
Why was she telling him this? She sounded defensive, and it irritated her.

Michael stared at her in disbelief. Her words felt like a punch in
the stomach. "So, you might not be staying here after all." Where
did that leave him?

"I don't know yet. A lot will depend on how the meeting goes on
Wednesday," she said, glancing away. *And how things between you and
Adriana finally work out.*

Michael did not want her to leave, but he had no right to say that.
"Is this your understanding of a partnership?" he said eventually.

"Can we have this conversation when I come back? Things are a bit
blurry right now – for both of us."

"You can speak for yourself. Things are crystal clear to me both
personally and professionally."

How could he be so self-assured when she was assailed by doubt?
She sighed.

"How long will you be gone?"

"I don't know that either." That was true. Why did he make her feel
like she was in the wrong?

"Tell me the time and I'll drive you to the airport," he broke the
barbed silence.

Lucy looked away and then back to him. "You don't have to. You're
so busy."

"I want to," he said plainly.

"All right. I'll check the time and let you know."

*

Lucy stared out the porthole at the fluffy clouds in the endless sky.

The thought of Adriana moving in with Michael, heaven knew for how long, left a bitter taste in her mouth. Mentally, she wished them well, but she did not want any part in this. She even considered selling the house and moving to Dublin if she were offered a contract.

She'd never had that kind of mess with William. So far, she had not returned his calls. But if he called again, not that she thought he would, she'd take the call.

37

1305

Oiselay cantered by oceans of golden wheat fields immersed in private thoughts. If Amaury was half as ambitious as Molay had said, he would rise to the bait. The Templar Marshal had yet to meet a man thirsty for power who would not seize it when the opportunity arose, no matter at whose expense.

When he reached Amaury's estates in Strovolos, the guards informed him that the Lord of Tyre was hunting in the forest and stepped aside for him to pass. Oiselay rode on and saw Amaury's hunting party in the distance.

He reigned in as Amaury was about to take a shot at a woodpigeon. The bird stopped in midair and came down with a thump. Amaury chortled with satisfaction, and his entourage gave a cheer. "Fetch!" the servants called out to the dogs, and they obeyed instantly. Oiselay moved closer.

"Oiselay, welcome! Will you join us?" Amaury said.

"It is kind of you, my lord," Oiselay replied, dismounting. He took the bow and the arrow a servant offered him, aimed at a turtle dove, and shot it with withering accuracy.

"Well done," Amaury exclaimed.

He was in a good mood, Oiselay noticed. "I was hoping we could talk," he said. His blank face betrayed none of his thoughts.

"Let us ride back to the house," Amaury said, and they mounted their horses and rode away. "I'm listening."

"You know I'm not a man to mince my words," Oiselay said. "I will get straight to the point. The Templars are not happy with Henry's condition. Almost the entire court is equally dissatisfied, but I believe you are aware of this." He paused for a moment, giving Amaury a chance to protest.

"He is the king to you, Oiselay," Amaury said gravely.

"His illness leaves him far too often incapacitated. Cases are not discussed; audiences are constantly postponed. The affairs of the realm are not dealt with. This has been going on for too long. Something must be done!"

"You are exaggerating. It is true that Henry is often unwell, but I would be very careful about accusing him openly of neglecting his duties. You have sworn an oath of obedience and so have the other nobles and knights; do not forget that!"

"Am I really exaggerating? Then so are most of the members of the court. There is clearly a problem. It is no use denying it. It will not vanish on its own."

"Am I right in thinking that you might have some sort of a remedy?" Amaury asked circumspectly. Surely, the Marshal had not come all the way just to complain.

"You!" Oiselay said quietly. "You are King Hugh's son as much as Henry."

Amaury gave him a blank stare. He recalled the seer's prophecy. When his brother John died a year after ascending the throne, no one had suspected that Amaury had assisted Henry in poisoning him. Was the blood the soothsayer foresaw on his hands not only John's? Amaury flinched inwardly. He would not relive such a nightmare. Ever! He was done killing brothers. John's ghost still called on him unbidden, depriving him of sleep and equanimity. No, Amaury wanted no more of that.

"My brethren speak highly of your courage when you retook Tortosa," the Templar Marshal went on. "It is you who should be sitting on the throne, my lord. People look up to you. They trust you. You inspire them with your valor."

"Perhaps, but it is unlikely to happen," Amaury said.

"Sometimes even young people die. Look at what happened to your brother John."

Amaury, a man haunted by his past and plagued by his future, shot him a bleak glance, wondering if the Templar Marshal knew. But that was not possible. "This should not happen to Henry."

"Perhaps there is another way." Oiselay hesitated for a moment. Amaury's expression was sincere. "Overthrow him."

Amaury shook his head. "I could not do that; there would be a revolt. There must be a peaceful way."

Oiselay breathed in and reminded himself to be patient. "If there were a way that would not cause an uprising, would you rule over your people? Would you lead your army to a new expedition when the time comes?"

Amaury shivered inwardly. Those were the exact words the seer had said: that he would 'rule over the people of this island'. She had never said that he would be king. "If there were a peaceful way," he consented at last. Would his destiny finally be fulfilled? Was that the Lord's bidding?

Everyone was entitled to a change of heart, Oiselay thought, barely concealing his sneer. "I shall have to think of a way then."

"Let us discuss this further while supping. Zabel would want to hear what you have to say," Amaury said. "You will find that she is of the same mind."

*

In the Grand Commandery, Le Rat, the Hospitaller Marshal, knocked on the new Grand Master's door.

"Come in!"

"You have sent for me, my lord," he said, closing the door behind him.

"Yes, take a seat," Villaret said and placed his hands in a steeple. "The meeting with Molay did not end quite as I had hoped."

A long pause. Le Rat did not press. He seemed content to wait for Villaret to go on.

"Molay wants twelve to fifteen thousand horses and forty to fifty thousand infantry. He is right, of course. The Saracens could meet anything smaller on equal terms. We also agree that a fleet should clear the seas in its path."

"On what do we disagree?" Le Rat asked after another long silence.

Villaret exhaled audibly. "Molay wants an all-out surprise attack. I believe it is wiser to blockade their coast; prevent any ship from going in or out. When they are half-starved and their troops are wearied by being drawn from one place to another, then we can attack. What also worries me is that Molay wants Amaury on the throne. I fear this will only complicate matters."

Another long pause.

"I think the time has come to move the Order to Rhodes. In the meantime, I need to understand where the Seneschal stands."

"We could invite him for hunting," Le Rat suggested.

"Good idea. See to it," Villaret said.

*

Nicholas had not been at the *casale* since Antoinette's death. He was elated now that he was going back after a whole year. Villaret had extended an invitation to the Seneschal, and Philip seized the opportunity for a meeting beyond the reach of prying eyes. He had suggested that Nicholas ride with him, not only because his father's *casale* bordered the Hospitaller's estates and he could pay him a visit, but simply because he enjoyed the young man's company.

Nicholas came home on the last day of harvest, in time to celebrate the pressing of the grapes, a major event in the life of the *casale*. To the sound of a lute and a flute, accompanying local songs about wine, the women took turns in the watts, crushing the grapes with their feet. With the hem of their dress raised to the knees, they danced on the grapes to the delight of the men standing around, clapping to the rhythm, and singing along.

It had been a good year. There would be plenty of wine. The tedious work of bringing the crops in was done, and everyone was looking forward to the evening feast. The air was filled with the collective pride that comes from a job well done.

Nicholas' gaze lingered on Lois, her calves and knees showing, her hips moving to the rhythm. But he was not the only one gawking. No wonder. She was pretty, eighteen, and unmarried. Lois was educated, the bailiff, and *lefteri,* the ideal bride for every Cypriot in the *casale* and beyond.

One man, in particular, seemed to have eyes only for Lois, Nicholas noticed, experiencing an unexpected sense of possessiveness. He seemed vaguely familiar. Nicholas asked the serf standing next to him about that man.

"That? That is Theodore! We owe the well to him; he's the one who showed us where the groundwater is!"

"And he's still here?" Nicholas wondered out loud.

The man chuckled. "I don't think he will be leaving any time soon. He has proposed to Lois," he said with a knowing smile.

Unwilling to witness the suitor's interest any longer, Nicholas went away in search of his father. In the manor, Emilia said that the master had not come back from hunting yet. Disinclined to stay indoors, Nicholas sauntered down the slope and along the river. Images of Lois swaying her hips in the watt mingled with the image of her naked in the dim light of the silver crescent moon, and he was filled with sudden desire. He had no right to think of her this way, he chided himself. He needed distraction.

Hastily, he got undressed and waded into the river, enjoying the freshness of the water. He hardly had any time for himself any more, not since he had moved to Nicosia. Although he found his work engrossing, he missed the simple life of the *casale*.

*

Nicholas' fingers were wrinkled when he looked at the sun moving to the west. His father would be home soon. He moved toward the bank but heard the sound of women teasing and laughing. They had come to the river to wash their feet.

There was no time to reach his clothes and put them back on. Instinctively, Nicholas hid himself behind a boulder. He heard the splashes and caught a glimpse of the women frolicking and giggling in the shallow water under a clear cerulean sky. Suddenly, Maria grabbed Christina's scarf, rolled it into a ball, and hurled it onto the boulder that Nicholas was hiding behind.

"Why did you do that? Mother will kill me if I go back without my scarf," Christina complained. Some of the women laughed and then there was a louder murmur of disapproval. "Bring it back to me!" Christina wailed.

"I will fetch it for you," Lois volunteered.

When she reached the rock, she thought she saw a shadow in the water and looked closer, dazed to see Nicholas there. He quickly brought his index finger to his lips to hush her. She nodded, flashed a conspiratorial grin at him, grabbed the scarf from the rock, and returned it to thankful Christina.

Refreshed, the women got out of the water and went back to prepare the feast, singing and jesting all the way. Relieved, Nicholas climbed onto the bank and put his clothes back on.

*

Dusk had fallen when the denizens of the *casale* gathered for the feast. Nicholas joined them in the yard where Lois was giving some last minute instructions. Their eyes caught and held before he took a seat by his father's side. He wanted to talk to her, but he would have to wait for a more opportune moment.

Nicholas focused on the conversation with his father, casting covert glances in Lois' direction. When he saw her heading for the kitchen, he excused himself and got up to follow, but Theodore shared the same intention; only, he was closer and faster. Nicholas watched him monopolize Lois' attention, and his muscles flexed of their own will. He wondered if he should insert himself between them, but he decided to see her reaction.

Casually, Theodore leaned into her, whispering something in her ear. In that moment, Lois looked over Theodore's shoulder and caught Nicholas' eye. For a fleeting, unguarded moment, she thought she saw a flicker of jealousy in his eyes. She took a side step, putting some distance between her and Theodore. Yet the enigmatic smile she gave her suitor drove Nicholas crazy; Theodore as well from what Nicholas could tell.

This was maddening, and Nicholas did not trust himself to witness any more of this. He had to walk it off. He turned around and started pacing. The sound of music and laughter dissipated slowly, until it eventually ceased.

His steps brought him to the river. Their secret place reminded him of the buoyant days of his childhood. Not surprisingly, Lois was in almost every single one of his memories at the *casale*. He picked up a flat stone, threw it across the water, and counted the times it leaped. His lips quirked upward in a smile when he remembered little Lois' frustration when her stone would not skip; not at first. He had never met a more persistent girl. She would try over and over again till she got it right; same with making the bird call sound or whistling with her fingers.

He dropped a pebble into the river and watched the ripples widen out in overlapping circles. He sat on the ground and rested his chin on his hand, reminiscing, staring into the darkness for what seemed like an eternity. It was not until Lois repeated his name that he brought his thoughts back to the here and now.

"Still thinking about the women in the river?" she said brightly, sliding behind him.

He cast his gaze to the ground, smothering a triumphant smile. She had come to him! "You have a remedy for that? Some of Emilia's herbs perhaps?"

"I do," she replied, taking his teasing in stride. "Come with me!" She began to walk back to the manor without waiting for him.

He jumped to his feet agilely and rapidly covered the distance between them. "Where are we going?"

"You'll see," she said with a mischievous grin. He liked that side of her character.

By the time they got back to the manor, the candles had been extinguished, and the inmates of the *casale* were already abed. Lois unlocked the cellar door and threw it open while Nicholas plucked a primrose from the closest bush and presented it to her with self-mocking gallantry. She gave a mock curtsy and thanked him, taking in its scent.

"Welcome to my kingdom," she said, lighting a candle. She placed the candle holder on a cask and drew a cup of wine from a barrel for him and one for her.

*

Theodore's nostrils flared by an unfamiliar, corrosive jealousy. He was not a fool. In a flash, he had seen it all. Not only had Lois run after the young master, but she had also invited him to the cellar where the two of them could be alone and undisturbed. She had never done the same for him.

*

"*Santat*," Lois said, and Nicholas matched her toast. She raised her cup and her eyes to the ceiling. "Here's to You, oh Lord, for giving us a taste of heaven on earth."

The candle flame illuminated her face. There was a freedom in her expression and in the fluid movements of her body that had not been there before, he noticed.

"I hope you do not talk like that in public! They will call you a blasphemer, a heretic!"

Lois made a noncommittal sound, gazing into the candle flame, then at him. "You know when wine tastes best?" she said, ignoring his teasing.

"No. When?"

"When the carriage is gone."

"The carriage?"

"Aye. The carriage that carries our pain and human worries away, and all that's left is bliss. You are on earth, but you're in heaven. Do you understand?"

He nodded slowly, his eyes fixed on hers. "You have grown."

"No longer a *pichòt?*" she asked challengingly.

"No, no longer," he admitted, his eyes registering every nuance in her expression.

"Well, life goes on even when you are not around, Nicholas of Provence."

"I shall have to think of a new nickname for you," he said, amused.

"Heaven forbid!"

She finished her wine and licked her lips, noticing his eyes all over her. Nicholas leaned into her as if to kiss her. Instead, he took a step away from her.

Lois bit her lower lip. "Did I say something wrong?"

Nicholas gazed at her. How could he make her understand? This sudden flame inside of him that should not be. That threatened to consume him. That only she could put out. No, some things were best left unsaid.

"I should leave you to lock up," he said decisively, heading for the door.

"Why?"

He stopped in his tracks and turned to look at her. "Because —" He paused. "I might do something we will both regret."

When he looked at her so intensely, with his green eyes and wry smile, she was helpless. "Regret?"

He slipped his fingers through his wavy black hair, taking a deep breath and letting out a loud sigh. "Lois, you don't understand. I want to —" *ravish you*, was the word that came to mind, but that would frighten her. He struggled to find the right words. "Do things to you... Things that only a husband should do to his wife and you are betrothed now."

"No, I'm not." Her heart was galloping. This was the first time he had confessed his attraction to her.

"Spoken for; same thing."

"I'm not," she said softly.

He stared at her. "Everyone else seems to think you are."

"Theodore has proposed to me, and I said, 'We'll see.'"

"Lois!" His voice was husky. "He is a *lefteros*, a good match for you. Do not throw that away," he said and summoned up enough strength to walk away.

38

2013

"Lucy, what a surprise!" William's astonishment was genuine. She was finally returning his call.

"It's been a while. How are you, William?" she asked guardedly.

"I'm fine, considering. And you?"

"Fine. I've moved away."

"I know! Your apartment's been sold." He was careful not to ask any direct questions.

She was impressed he knew that. "Yes, I've bought a house in Cyprus."

"What a coincidence! I'm flying there tomorrow to do some research on the Templars."

Was this a sign? "Perhaps we could get together next week for a coffee. I'm in Dublin at the moment."

"What's in Dublin?" Sinclair ventured.

"Oh, I'm looking into the possibility of having a TV cooking program here."

Sinclair smiled. She was opening up to him again. "That's great! I'll keep my fingers crossed."

"Thank you, William… So, I'll see you in Cyprus then?"

"I'd love that. I miss you, Lucy."

A brief pause.

"I'll see you soon."

*

Michael had not expected to see the lights on in Lucy's house when he got home that evening. With a rush of excitement, he jogged up the short flight of stairs and rang the bell.

"Hello, Michael," she greeted him in the doorway.

"Hi! Can I come in?"

She stepped aside. "Sure. How's *pappou?*"

"Fine… I don't know how you do it."

She looked at him, uncertain. "Do what?"

"You're even more beautiful now than you were twenty years ago."

She thanked him but did not glow with pleasure as Michael thought she would.

"How was your trip?"

"All right."

"Will you have your TV program?" he tried again.

"It seems so."

Michael studied her impassive face. "Adriana's not pregnant. It was all a lie."

Lucy stared at him for a moment or two. "I don't know what to say, Michael. Is this good or bad?"

He was taken aback. "You don't know?"

She shrugged.

"That's great news!" he said with feeling. She had that inscrutable look on her face again, and that irked him. "Lucy, what's wrong?"

"Nothing."

Michael took a breath to calm the impatience growing inside him. "It doesn't look like nothing."

She looked away uncomfortably.

"I could swear that if Brian hadn't shown up that evening the other day…"

"Perhaps," she interrupted him. "Anyway, that was then. A lot's happened since."

"Like what? Adriana's lie? Am I to be held responsible for that?"

"It broke the spell." *And William's coming to Cyprus.*

"You're not serious," he said, dubious.

"I'm tired, Michael. It was a long flight."

Was she shooing him away? "Tell me what *I've* done to deserve this!" He controlled his temper with intense effort.

Lucy experienced a twinge of guilt. "Nothing, Michael. You've done everything right." She ran her fingers through her hair.

"Then help me understand this, Lucy!"

"I don't know, Michael. I can't explain this. Something broke when you took Adriana back."

"I never did!"

"Let's just be friends, all right? Can we do that?" It was the sensible thing to do. It would give them time to think. Why then did she feel so wrong-footed?

Michael cast his gaze down, gathering his pride. He raised his eyes to her again. "Sure! We can do that. Good night, Lucy!"

*

"Hello, *pappou!*" Lucy said when the old man opened the door the next morning.

"Lucy, my sweet girl, you're back!" he said, giving her a warm hug. "Come on in!"

"These are for you," she said, stepping inside and handing him a pair of Irish leather gloves.

"Thank you. They're beautiful, but that wasn't necessary. How are you?"

"I'm fine," she said but did not sound convincing. *Pappou* gazed at her face, waiting. "Maybe not so fine," she confessed eventually.

"This calls for coffee." He got to his feet, giving her time to collect her thoughts.

"I think Michael's upset with me."

"Does he have a reason to be?" he asked, placing the cups on the table and taking a seat.

"This is all so confusing!"

"Sometimes life is simpler than we think."

She sighed. "One day we kiss, and the next day Adriana shows up, saying she's pregnant."

"Well, she's not. And why should Michael be upset with you if she lied about that?"

Lucy stared at the coffee in her hands. "I told him I want us to be just friends."

"Am I missing something?"

She kept her gaze on the cup. "I've been offered a job in Dublin. And my ex is coming to Cyprus for his research," she said at last.

Pappou nodded slowly. "I see."

"It's not that I want to get back together with him, but perhaps this is a good moment to clear some things: how I feel about William; how I feel about Michael; what I want to do with my life! I could go back to Dublin, or I could stay here and do some traveling. I don't know…"

"Does Michael know that William's coming?"

"I haven't told him yet. The discussion last night was tense enough as it was."

"I just hope William's coming after the opening party," *pappou* said. "Michael's stressed out at the moment. There's been some delay. I heard him say so on the phone. He never shares his business problems with me; he doesn't want me to worry. I bet he could use a friend right now."

*

Lucy finished her coffee and drove to Michael's kitchen. The team was preparing some new recipes while Michael was in his office, arguing with the plumber. She put on her chef's uniform and got to work.

If he was surprised to see her when he came to check on his team, he did not show it. He merely acknowledged her with a nod.

*

In her mother's Camden apartment, Cynthia stared at the cell phone in her hand as if she could find the answers to her questions there. William was off to Cyprus for his research and was not sure when he was coming back. That was not what she had planned for Easter. He could have asked her to go with him. But he hadn't.

She grabbed a beer out of the fridge and eased herself into a chair. She rocked back and flung her feet on the table. Was he really going to Cyprus for his research? Would he be alone? Why did he not want her there with him? Was he telling her that their relationship was over? In the mirror, she saw the worry lines on her gorgeous features and reminded herself not to frown; it causes wrinkles.

Raised in the rough part of Camden by an unmarried and more often than not unemployed mother, Cynthia had learned early in life to be a fighter, though her beauty sometimes mitigated the need for confrontation. Her mother had insisted that she finish school. A drop-out herself, she had given birth to Cynthia at the age of sixteen. She had hoped her little girl would study and become whatever she wanted in life. Cynthia, however, had other plans.

Early on, she had noticed the way boys and men looked at her, and she resolved not to waste her time and looks on studying – or on some poor student. She set her sights on a wealthy husband. She was not particularly picky. She simply wanted to live the good life as much as possible and as long as possible.

Sitting around idly increased the risk of losing William. She considered her options. Her white Persian cat leaped onto her lap, purring, and Cynthia stroked its thick fur absentmindedly. Suddenly, her eyes glittered with enlightenment. If William was really going to Limassol, he would be staying at a luxury hotel. How many could there be?

39

1305

"Christina, go and ask Theodore to come and give us a hand with the cart, will you?"

The young woman winced. "You haven't heard?"

"Heard what?"

"He's gone," Christina said in a small voice.

"Gone? Where?"

Christina shrugged. "I don't know. He's left; taken the divining rod with him."

Lois stared at her in incomprehension. They were planning a feast for the completion of the construction of the well. Did he change his mind about marrying and settling down? And how did she feel about it?

*

"My dear Philip, how nice to see you again," Provence greeted the Seneschal amiably.

"Ramon, it is always a pleasure. Nicholas," he acknowledged the young man with a nod.

They shook hands and exchanged pleasantries for a few minutes. Then Provence led the way to the great hall.

"I have told Lois to bring the best wine from the cellar."

Philip looked over the top of his spectacles. "You have a woman for a butler?"

"Lois is my bailiff, my right-hand man; or should I say, my right-hand woman?" He chuckled. "And she has an exceptional nose for wines," he added, as they sat at the trestle table.

Praise came out of Provence's lips quite naturally, Philip noted. "Then you are a lucky man."

Moments later Lois brought a flagon of wine, served, and left quietly. She loitered in the corridor, considering the man that Nicholas worked for. His eyes revealed little, missed even less. Nicholas was very formal in Philip's presence, but he had been ruffled earlier when he offered her his sympathy over Theodore's unexpected departure. Words were left unsaid between them, and Lois was certain he would seek her out later.

In the great hall, the three men drank to the king's health.

"As Nicholas must have told you, I paid Villaret a visit," Philip got straight to the point. "There are rumors that the Templars are trying to convince Amaury to usurp the throne."

A stunned silence greeted this revelation.

"And you think there is some truth in that," Nicholas said, studying Philip's face. Only rarely did the telltale slight twitch of the right upper lip betrayed the Seneschal's anxiety.

"I will hope to God it will not come to that. Brother against brother is an ugly feud. I believe Amaury may well be up to something, but we have no way of knowing what exactly, how, where or when."

"What is the Hospitallers' position?" Provence asked.

"They made it clear that they have no intention to support Amaury," Philip said. "I was left with the impression that they wanted to warn me and see where I stand. I do not think they wish to get enmeshed in our affairs. They did not, however, conceal their concern for Henry's lack of enthusiasm to launch a new expedition. And they are losing patience with his illness."

"Now that the new Pope has asked for the grand masters' advice on a new campaign, one might assume that they would rather have warlike Amaury on the throne than Henry." Nicholas could see the pawns moving on the political chessboard now that Clement V had succeeded Benedict XI and was considering issuing a new Bull.

"You are probably right," Philip said matter-of-factly. He loved both his nephews. He had felt torn by his split loyalties for a long time and wished there were a way to bridge the gap between his sister's two sons. But he feared the time had come to take sides, and it was clear as daylight in his mind on whose side he would be.

"We must hope for the best, but ready ourselves for the worst." Philip paused and sipped some wine. "I wish I could say that Amaury was not malleable and that he would never plot against his own brother," he went on, rubbing his chin. "We need to find out what he is conniving, but I do not see how."

"I know his new steward," Nicholas put in reluctantly, aware of the need to chart the undercurrents. "We fought together in Nephin, but he is Amaury's sworn man."

In the corridor, Lois listened intently to the strained quiet that settled over the great hall. Her heart leaped with hope. Could this be her chance to be close to Nicholas and be venturesome? She smoothed her hair with a trembling hand and took a deep breath to steady herself. She straightened her back, schooling her face in an expression of self-possession, and walked into the great hall.

"Excuse me, my lords," she said; her heartbeat racing.

The three men raised their gaze and stared at her.

"What is it, Lois?" Provence asked, vexed by the interruption.

For a moment, some of her confidence began to falter, but she gathered enough nerve to speak. "I think I might have a solution to your predicament."

"You have been eavesdropping?" Nicholas said in a voice that mixed surprise with disapproval.

"I have not, my lord! I was passing by in the corridor and could not help overhearing your conversation."

"So, Lois," Philip said calmly, his darting eyes observing the intensity between the young woman and his scribe. "What is the solution that you say you have?"

She took heart by the Seneschal's interest. "You could place *me* in lord Amaury's service."

Nicholas stared at her in mingled disbelief, apprehension, and admiration. "That is too dangerous," he discarded the notion.

"Will you just think about it for a moment, my lord?" Lois persisted. "If I were a ewerer, for instance, I would be able to see who visits him and report his conversations. No one pays attention to serfs. No one expects them to speak *lenga d'òc*. They will speak freely in my presence. I will be invisible to them. We just need to think of a way for me to pass the information to you. I can do this. I'm certain!"

"And how could we do that? Place you in Amaury's service," Philip asked expectantly, but Lois had not thought that far.

"Nicholas, you said you know Amaury's steward. Who is he?" Provence asked.

"Poitou."

"The man whose life you saved at Nephin?" Provence said, and Philip and Lois looked at Nicholas with high regard.

Nicholas shrugged. "It just happened."

"And I just happened to hear about it in the palace corridors!" He paused. "I presume that Poitou must feel in your debt. Perhaps you should look him up. Lois might be right, Nicholas." Provence disliked putting Lois in danger, but in the task of saving the king, one was obliged to use the tools that came to hand. "No one would suspect a serf; let alone a woman. I cannot think of anyone better.

She is young and pretty, attributes that Amaury appreciates from what I hear. Lois is smart. She can fend for herself. If anyone can do this, she can."

Lois was fascinated despite her fear.

"Can we place her in Amaury's service without raising suspicion?" Philip asked.

Nicholas wanted to protest, but Lois had outmaneuvered him. "I could ask Poitou to take her in on some pretext," he said, fearing that they were treading an unmarked road.

"It is settled then," Philip said.

*

Dawn the next morning found Nicholas choosing the mellowest mare for Lois for their journey to Nicosia. Although he had taught her to ride when they were children, she had never ridden farther than the fields of the *casale*.

"I'm ready!" Lois announced brightly, entering the stables.

One look at her beaming face and Nicholas felt his own face soften, but he was not ready to give in just yet. "What were you thinking!" he asked, throwing his hands in the air.

"Come on, Nicholas!" she said in a reconciliatory tone of voice. "Both your father and the Seneschal think this might work. Besides, I need a change."

Nicholas gave her a searching look. Did losing Theodore cause such recklessness? "At what price? This is not a game, Lois. These people are ruthless. If they suspect anything, I might never find out where they have dumped your body."

She blenched inwardly but gathered her nerve. "I will be careful."

Satisfied that he had scared her enough, he asked, "Did you take your black dress?"

"Of course, I did. I only have three: one for work, one for church and feasts, and one for mourning."

"Make sure you wear that one when you are there." His voice was solemn.

"Why?"

"Because you were wrong."

"About what?"

"About being invisible. It is not just Amaury who likes pretty young servants."

She gave him a skeptical glance; then her eyes glinted with mischief. "Are you jealous?"

"Worried," he said. "Worried for you."

For a while, they rode silently side by side until Nicholas broke the silence. He explained in words as simple as possible what was going on in the capital. Lois listened attentively and tried to commit to memory all the names he mentioned.

"Help me understand this," she said. "The king is often sick, but his brother is healthy, strong, ambitious and successful on the battlefield. Yet you believe he's not fit to rule?"

"He may or may not be fit to rule, but this is not the point. We need order. Without order, there is chaos. The king rules and all his brothers and vassals need to support him. Ruling a realm, even in times of peace, is a grave task. A king should not be distracted away from his duties. Henry has already achieved a lot in terms of religious peace and prosperity. He may not be a perfect ruler, but even imperfect rulers can improve people's lives. In any event, overthrowing a king means tearing the realm asunder. It costs lives and wreaks destruction. And who is to tell if Amaury is really better suited to be king or that he will not become a tyrant?"

Nicholas became aware of how much he had missed their conversations. Lois had always been wise beyond her years and would not easily take arguments at face value. He found her unconventional way of thinking, part of Kontostephanos' legacy, challenging.

"Perhaps there would be no reason for such animosity if the queen mother ruled," Lois said musingly.

"In theory maybe, but kings have to make tough decisions; go to war. Women are not cut out for this."

Lois was not convinced. "I am certain Empress Irene of the Byzantine Empire would disagree with you. And that is just one case in point," she said, bringing to mind her grandfather's teachings.

"I'm talking about the rule, not the exceptions."

"So, what you are saying is that women cannot be bailiffs either," she said with ponderous aplomb. "Surely, bailiffs make less important decisions, but they can sometimes be tough. And if a woman cannot do something herself because her body is weak, can she not ask the serfs on the estates to do it? If the queen mother cannot fight on the battlefield herself, can she not make the decision whether to send her men to war or not? Do all kings fight? Even when they are ill or old?"

"That might be true, but a bailiff's worries do not compare to a king's!"

Lois thought he was prevaricating, and perhaps he sounded a bit condescending, but at that moment she could not come up with a better argument.

*

As the evening was falling, Nicholas looked for lodging in the next village along the way, but all they were offered was a place in the barn attic, a windowless structure that had a patched and half-derelict look. Grateful that they had at least a roof over their head, they made themselves comfortable on the dry straw.

After a frugal meal, Nicholas said, "I'm sorry about Theodore."

Lois shrugged. "It's better this way. He is what he is: a wanderer. I had my doubts if he could stay in one place long enough. It is clear that he cannot, and I'm glad I have found out now."

"Is it because of him you wanted to leave the *casale?*"

Was he jealous? She offered an enigmatic smile but no reply. "It's been a long day. We should get some rest."

Nicholas watched her loosen her primly coiled braids and wondered if she had an inkling of how inviting this gesture was. She rubbed her tense neck. Instinctively, he moved closer and began to massage her shoulders. Lois' heart was pounding.

It would be easy for him to take her there and then, but that would be unseemly. She was vulnerable and at his mercy. He gathered every morsel of self-control he possessed and moved away from her. "Get some rest. I will go for a walk."

Bewildered, Lois watched him leave. The night before, his excuse had been Theodore. What was his excuse now?

40

2013

Sinclair got out of the car, smoothed his hair in a way that made most of his female students sigh, and walked through the garden. He climbed the short flight of stairs to the porch and rang the bell.

"Hello, William!" Lucy greeted him guardedly. He looked as handsome and elegant as ever.

"Hello, Lucy!" he said, wearing his most beguiling smile. "These are for you, a little housewarming gift." He presented her with a bouquet of long-stemmed red roses and a Château Laffite Rothschild.

She thanked him and put the flowers in a vase. She filled two cups with coffee, and they made themselves comfortable on the sofa.

"Lucy, I've been itching to tell you on the phone, but I think it's best if you see for yourself." He produced a document from the inside pocket of his jacket.

"What is it?"

He handed her the document. "My divorce papers. I knew you wouldn't be convinced of my feelings for you otherwise."

She quickly scanned the document. So, he had not lied to her. But what about that beauty Brian had mentioned? "You're divorced!" she said incredulously and handed him back the document.

He took her hand in his. "Yes, and I hope I can date you again," he said lightly. His face became more serious when he added, "Lucy, I can't begin to tell you what you mean to me. Being without you all these weeks is something I don't want to go through again. I miss you, Lucy. In every sense of the word. I hope that now you have no doubts about my love for you."

Lucy looked at him perplexed. Where did this come from? Not

once in the six months they had dated had he expressed his feelings for her in a manner even remotely similar. He was the kind of man who could have any woman. Why would he try so hard to win her back? Yet here he was, sitting in her living room with his divorce papers in his hands, proof of his sincerity. A few weeks back, she would have been packing her bags to follow him already; no questions asked. But now she felt ambushed, backed into a corner.

"It's all happening so fast," she said, finding her voice again.

"There's no rush. Take your time; anything you need. I'm staying at the Amathus. Let's have dinner and talk a bit more; tomorrow maybe?"

"One of these days," Lucy said.

He nodded, reminding himself to be patient.

*

The moment Sinclair was out the door, he took a good look around, bringing the riddle to mind once more.

> 'You shall find your faith
> In Lorraine,
> On the tree whose seeds
> Weigh gold,
> Facing Ursa,
> Taking as many strides
> As Judas' pieces of silver.'

The second half of the riddle was easy to break. Taking as many strides as Judas' pieces of silver meant taking thirty strides. He could also tell in which direction. Facing Ursa meant facing north. And he knew that the tree whose seeds weigh gold is the carob tree.

What he could not figure out was the first part: You shall find your faith in Lorraine. Lorraine as in Lorraine, France? If that were the case, what would the map of Cyprus be useful for? Unless there was a clue in Lorraine somewhere, but he had no idea where to begin looking for it. Or was it Lorraine as in a girl's name? Again, Lorraine who?

All of a sudden, a small beagle ran up to him, barking furiously. Michael did nothing to stop Lola. Sinclair stretched out a hand for her to sniff, but she would not stop barking.

Lucy stepped outside, wondering what the commotion was all about. The scene would have looked comical if it weren't for Michael's solemn demeanor and William's shocked expression. If she found it strange that William was still there, she hid it well.

Since Michael was not willing to calm Lola down, she would have to do that, Lucy thought, and walked over to her. "It's all right, Lola. William was just leaving," she said gently, caressing her behind the ears, and the beagle was quiet. Lucy rose to her feet and made the introductions. The two men shook hands, measuring each other up.

"So, you're a friend of Lucy's?" Michael said.

"Maybe more than just a friend," Sinclair replied smoothly, and Michael felt his muscles tense. "And you are?" Sinclair asked.

Michael gave Lucy a penetrating look, but she averted her gaze. "Just a neighbor," he said at last.

"Well, it was a pleasure to meet you, Michael." Sinclair turned all his attention to Lucy. "Goodbye, darling," he said in a warm, mellow voice. Before Lucy could react, Sinclair slid his arms around her waist, giving her a quick kiss on the lips. Out of the corner of his eye, he caught Michael's pursed lips and knew he had hit home. He gave Lucy his most seductive smile, ignored Michael completely, got into his Jaguar, and drove off.

"Really? William? The William who forgot to mention he's married?"

That stung, but Lucy refused the bait. "The very same," she said.

Michael's unrelenting stare made her feel ill at ease; unasked questions hung in the air.

"It's been a long day. I think I should better go inside. Goodnight, Michael."

He responded with disapproving silence, and Lucy felt that she owed him an explanation. Lost in the labyrinth of her thoughts, however, she had none to offer.

Michael watched her walk away with a sense of frustration. He took Lola back home and stood by the kitchen window, staring silently into the darkness.

"Have you met Lucy's visitor?" *pappou* asked casually, recognizing that jutted chin on his grandson's face.

"Her 'close to perfect' friend or 'maybe more than just a friend'? Yes, I've met him," he said with a mirthless smile.

"Oh? Just a friend from London she told me." *Pappou's* tone was reassuring.

"I guess we'll see about that."

Michael had not mentioned Lucy's wish to remain friends to *pappou*. Deep down he had hoped it was just a phase, her way of dealing with Adriana's predicament, but her cocky ex-boyfriend's visit changed everything.

*

Sitting comfortably in the Amathus lobby, Sinclair was enjoying a *negroni sbagliato* before dinner while listening to the soft music floating across from the bar. He cast a desultory glance at the tropical gardens and the view of the Mediterranean. He was preoccupied by Lucy's puzzling attitude. He had thought she would fall into his arms when he showed her his divorce papers, but he had evidently misjudged the situation. It must have been because of that neighbor – Michael. His manner had been peculiarly possessive.

Sinclair detested the prospect of going through another briefing session with the Grand Master without any tangible progress to report. It was time for a more drastic plan. He resolved to call his lawyer first thing in the morning and instruct him to contact the real estate agency and have them make an exceptionally generous offer on the house. He would also have them make an offer on Michael's house. The map could possibly refer to the second property.

41

1305

"Thyme, oregano, and many an herb," a young lad shouted over Nicholas' shoulder at the Saturday farmers market. The boy walked through the crowd, carrying a sack laden with fresh mountain herbs.

The palace square bristled with people: moving, gesturing, arguing. Finding Poitou would take some effort, and Nicholas willed himself to be patient. On market days, the number of people in the capital doubled, as peasants brought their produce from the countryside. Dressed in knee-length woolen tunics, they led sheep around carts loaded with poultry. Women with their heads covered in wimples mingled with merchants in colorful *cotehardies*.

The bailiff walked around with an air of authority. He approached a rich and rotund merchant and reminded him that he could not let his horse stand there on market days. Grudgingly, the man led his horse away.

"Eggs! Fresh eggs! Who will buy my fresh eggs today?" a girl with a pock-marked face cried out to passers-by. Next to her, a juggler vied for the crowd's attention.

Nicholas wandered from stall to stall, indifferent to the plenitude of merchandise, looking for any sign of Poitou. He strolled past a knight's valet in a short tunic who was energetically haggling over the price of candlesticks. The valet opened his purse, hanging from a thong attached to his belt, and took out a *gros petit*. "Take it or leave it!" he said firmly, and the salesman elected to take it.

The market was a noisy meeting point and a place for drinking ale. Nicholas strode to the alehouse at the far end of the square, passing by sacks of wheat and barley, stacks of apples and pears, and makeshift enclosures holding goats and pigs.

He reached the tavern, walked in, and looked around unobtrusively. Luck was on his side. Poitou was enjoying a tankard of ale with some friends. Nicholas slid into a seat at the next table. The alehouse keeper's wife, a stocky and rather intimidating woman, came and took his order.

Recognizing his voice, Poitou looked over his shoulder. "Provence!" he cried out and came over. He clapped Nicholas on the shoulder heartily.

"Poitou!" Nicholas feigned surprise. "How are you?"

"I cannot complain! And how's yourself?" His face became more serious when he added, "I've heard about your wife. I'm sorry for your loss."

"Thank you!"

Nicholas felt relieved to hear Poitou say, "I'm in your debt, Provence." It made things easier. "It has been a while since Nephin, but I will never forget!"

"That's all right. You would have done the same." Nicholas dropped his gaze to his hands on the table.

"You seem concerned," Poitou observed.

"The truth is that something is worrying me," Nicholas conceded.

"What is it, my friend?"

"Well, a promise to a dying man is sacred," he started carefully.

"Indeed!" Poitou nodded in agreement.

"Our bailiff died in my hands, and I promised him I would see to it that his granddaughter, a *lefteri*, marries a *lefteros,* but I do not know how to do that. I do not have the time for this, and I'm stuck with her until then."

"Perhaps I could help," Poitou ventured, rubbing his chin. "It is the least I can do for the man who saved my life!"

"That would be a weight off my shoulders. What did you have in mind?"

"Bring her to Amaury's estate tomorrow, and I will see what I can do. I'm certain we can use an extra pair of hands," Poitou said confidently.

42

2013

Sinclair's lawyer got off the phone with his client and called *Dream Homes*. If the realtor found it unusual that he wanted to double the offer while the real-estate sector was collapsing, he did not say so. Mentally calculating his own commission, he jotted down the details and made the call right away.

"Ms. Hernandez?" He introduced himself and went on, "This may come as a surprise to you, but we have a foreign client who's interested in your property. I was hoping we could meet some time later today to discuss his very attractive offer."

"I've just bought the house; I'm not interested in selling. So, really, it would be a waste of time," Lucy said, placing a tray of tartlets in the oven.

"I think you'd find his offer most generous." He said a figure twice as high as Michael's original asking price.

Lucy hesitated. "I'm busy right now. Perhaps you could call again next week?"

The real estate agent said he would call on Monday, and Lucy got back to her baking without giving the matter a second thought.

*

Sinclair leaned on the twin balcony balustrade of his exquisite Amathuntia suite on the top floor of the hotel and took in the perfumed manicured gardens and the lush lawns. He sipped his chilled *Pouilly Fuissé*, assessing the situation. The early fourteenth century map might lead to a significant discovery about the Order, and Fortune dictated that he was the one chosen to make such a discovery. Yet Lucy's reserved attitude toward him and her reluctance to sell the house were impediments he had not foreseen. This aggravated him.

He went back into the room and placed the empty glass on the table, looking dejectedly at his cell phone. It was time for the progress briefing, and he disliked having so little to report.

"Tell me the good news," a familiar voice said on the other end of the line a few minutes later.

"The meeting with the real estate agent has been scheduled for next week." There was a pause, and Sinclair sensed disappointment.

"I'm confident you'll find a way to convince them, professor."

"I'll handle it."

*

Sinclair rubbed his chin and dialed Lucy's number. A nice relaxing dinner would help.

"I'm sorry, William," Lucy declined the dinner invitation. "Tonight's Michael's launch party and I promised I'll drive *pappou* there."

"Who?"

"His grandfather."

"Another day then,' Sinclair said and ended the call.

So, all three of them would be out for the evening, he thought; that might work just as well. He made several calls until he had tracked down a name and a number.

"A friend suggested you might be able to assist me with something I need," Sinclair said.

"Which friend?"

"A mutual friend who speaks highly of you."

A pause. "You know Limassol?"

"I'm sure I can find a place."

"Mexico Pub," the voice said and gave him the address. "I'll be sitting at the bar. I'll know who you are."

*

About an hour later, Sinclair parked his rental outside the pub. It was a run-down place, its wall sign battered, the paint peeled off the walls. He walked in and took a seat at the bar. He ordered a draught beer and waited, casually observing the people who walked in and out.

"I believe we have a mutual friend," a man said, taking the seat next to him.

"Indeed, we do."

Sinclair glanced at the man. A scarred face was half covered by an unkempt beard. A greasy, dark curly ponytail protruded from the back of a black leather baseball cap, pulled down low over the eyes. A large silver cross hung from one ear. His black motorcycle vest was worn over an old Harley Davidson T-shirt that smelled as if it had not been washed in weeks.

*

The last item on Michael's to-do-list was the dry cleaner's; he had to pick up his suit for the launch party. He drove by the store, tapping his fingers on the steering wheel nervously.

One of the challenges fast growing cities face is the shortage of parking lots, and Limassol is no exception. Michael drove around the block once, and then once more, desperately looking for a parking space. He was pressed for time.

As luck would have it, there was just enough space in front of a run-down pub, adjacent to the dry cleaner's.

*

Inside the pub, the stocky frame next to Sinclair asked, "So, what do you need help with?" He lifted an arm, blacked out by tattoos, and ordered a pint.

In that moment, Sinclair felt that he was crossing a line, a point of no return. He felt strangely exhilarated. He took a folded piece of paper out of his pocket and left it on the counter.

The bartender placed the pint next to the piece of paper, and the man chugged some beer. He belched and Sinclair was surprised to hear him ask to be excused. The man casually unfolded the sheet of paper and glanced at the address that was scribbled on it.

*

Michael parked between a red Jaguar and a classic Harley David-son in front of the pub. He locked the Audi and cast a quick glance through the tinted window to make sure no one would complain, his eyes suddenly widening. Was that Lucy's ex?

*

"The tenants will be out tonight," Sinclair said, avoiding eye con-tact. "Wreck the place. I want them frightened off the premises."

This was not the time to think about how Lucy would feel when she got back home, he told himself. He had given her the chance to get back together, and she did not take it. That was a bad decision. Now, she had to suffer the consequences.

Throughout the years, Sinclair had been single-minded in ascend-ing through the Order's hierarchy. He had even made substantial contributions to that end. In his wildest fantasy, he was the next Grand Master. There was no room for failure. Success was the only option.

He slipped an envelope from the inside pocket of his jacket and left it on the counter. The man took another long pull and reached for the envelope. Sinclair got up and left without noticing Michael.

43

1305

At the gate to Amaury's estate, Nicholas drew the reins and stated his business to the guards while Lois trailed behind on foot. One of the guards inspected her with lascivious insolence. Out of the corner of her eye, Lois noticed Nicholas clench his fists. She cast her gaze to the ground, hoping the moment would pass.

"New merchandise," the guard said, loudly enough for everyone to hear, as Nicholas and Lois went through. His laughter made Lois' hair stand on the back of her neck. Nicholas gritted his teeth; his eyes narrowed. He was tempted to turn around and leave, taking Lois with him. He let her catch up.

"This is madness!" he hissed.

"We are here now. We cannot go back," she said quietly.

He studied her face for a moment before spurring Roland again. His heart was filled with dread. He felt as though he was leading a lamb to the wolves, and her feigned self-assurance did nothing to assuage his anxiety.

When they arrived at the manor, Nicholas was asked to wait in the great hall while Lois was shown into the kitchen. Her heart was thudding, and she took deep breaths to compose herself. The other serfs ignored her, going about their business. After a while she began to breathe normally again and took a look around.

The kitchen was at least five times larger than the one in Provence's manor; the stone tile flooring so much cleaner than the earthen floor in Emilia's pantry. Here, the shelves were filled to bursting with pots and pans and ladles. The air was heavy with the scent of rabbits being stewed with cinnamon and almonds in the iron cauldron, hanging over the fire on a hook and chain. Half a dozen servants walked in and out. Lois observed one of the cooks pick up a broom and chase a rat.

"So, you are the girl from the Provence *casale*," Poitou's voice made her jump. That was not a question, and Lois remained silent. Amaury's steward scrutinized her from head to toe. "What is your name?" he asked, walking around her.

"Lois, Sir," her gaze still on the ground.

"Lois! A pretty name for a pretty girl! Finding you a husband should not be hard!"

Husband? This was Lois' first intimation of the understanding Nicholas and Poitou had reached.

"Nicholas has told me of your exceptional nose," Poitou went on, and Lois wondered if he was jesting. "But we already have a butler. Who has ever heard of a woman butler anyway! The best I can do for you is a place in the kitchen and cupbearer duties at meals."

Perfect! Her spirits lifted. "Thank you, my lord," she said, still avoiding meeting his eye. "You are most kind."

To her disappointment, she was assigned chores outside the house the moment Poitou left the kitchen. She was eager to find her bearings in the house and locate the places where she might listen discreetly. But, for the moment, she must simply do as she was told. She picked up the pails and fetched water from the well in the yard, fed the pigs, the hens, and the geese, and then cleaned the pen.

As suppertime was approaching, Lois thought she would be given tasks inside the house, but she was sent to pick lemons from the tree in the back yard. Lois stood in front of the tree, staring at the fruit hanging from the highest branches. The lemons from the lower branches had already been picked.

She noticed the other girls in the kitchen observing her from the window, giggling, and thought that this was probably a game they played on newcomers. She took no umbrage. Instead, she straightened her shoulders and lifted her dress. With steady, nimble movements, she climbed to the top branches. Tree climbing had been one of her favorite childhood pastimes.

She had almost filled her basket when she heard voices. Looking down, she saw two men: a knight and a noble.

"It's time, Amaury," the knight said. "You need to begin gathering support if you are to become regent without bloodshed. Start with the ones that are unhappiest with Henry. When some of them come over to you, it will be easier to convince others. We need to move quickly and in secrecy."

Lois watched Amaury closely. There was a sternness about his countenance, a hard-eyed ruthlessness that frightened her.

"What about the Hospitallers, Oiselay?"

"Let me worry about them. Focus on the nobles and knights!"

"All right. I know whom to approach first." Amaury had clearly given the matter some serious thought. "Hugh of Peristerona and Simon of Montolif. I shall send for them first thing in the morning." A brief pause. Then, "Zabel has given instructions for a festive meal."

"My apologies to your fair wife, but I must return to the Order at once. Send word of the progress you make."

"Zabel is thinking of hosting a banquet, an excuse to invite people who think it is time for change," Amaury apprised him.

"Your wife is both beautiful and clever," the Marshal said admiringly. "You are a lucky man, my lord!"

*

Lois lay still in the kitchen, waiting for the house to go quiet and for the serfs lying next to her to fall into deep sleep. When she was certain that no one was awake, she tiptoed out of the room.

In Amaury's chamber, the Great Dane drifted out of sleep, raised one ear for an instant, and then relaxed on the floor by his master's bed again.

Lois avoided the main gate where the guards played dice. She made her way through the groves, protected by the moonless night. She lifted her dress and climbed over the stone wall, checked that the road was clear, and leaped down to the ground. She took a moment to collect herself and find her way in the dim light.

Earlier in the evening, she had felt a surge of eager anticipation at the prospect of seeing Nicholas again. She was proud that her proposal to enter Amaury's service had borne fruit on the very first day. Now, she looked at the trees that had taken on unfamiliar and menacing shapes and felt the first stirrings of fear.

She stumbled up the hill, tripping over roots and stubbing her toes on stones. She glanced up at the dark sky and then whirled around, unable to decide which way to go. All paths looked alike. Assailed by doubt, she prayed for guidance and tried to remember the signs that Nicholas had shown her. If she could reach the brook, she was confident she could find her way from there. But everything was different in the murk.

Had she made a terrible mistake? Getting lost would jeopardize everything. She cupped her face with her hands. The plangent howl of wolves off in the distance made the blood freeze in her veins for several harrowing moments.

She broke into a run in the opposite direction and did not stop until she was completely out of breath. Just then she heard the sound of running water. The brook! She could find her way now. Thankful for the sign, she cut through the wheat fields and scampered to Nicholas' house.

Not wanting to alert his old manservant, she picked up some cobblestones and aimed at Nicholas' window. She missed the first couple of times but hit it with the third stone. His head appeared through the open window seconds later. His heart quickened at the sight of her. She gestured to him to come down. Moments later the door opened, and he scurried across the courtyard, beckoning to her to follow him to the stable.

"What is a regent?" she asked before even saying hello, breathing in ragged gasps.

One dark brow lifted in silent query as he explained, "Someone who governs when the king is too young, absent, or ill. Why?" The mere mention of such a prospect was in and of itself alarming.

She drew a deep breath and shoved the hair off her face. "Amaury had a visitor today," she said. "His name is Oiselay." The Templar Marshal, Nicholas thought and nodded. "He told Amaury to start gathering support if he wants to become regent without bloodshed."

Nicholas' senses were alert. "What did Amaury say?"

"That he will start with Simon of Montolif and Hugh of Peristerona. And Zabel will have a banquet to gain support for Amaury."

Nicholas grabbed her gently by the arms and said, "Well done, Lois!" Obeying a sudden impulse, he bent down and kissed her. Then, with a kind of brutal attention to the business at hand, he said, "Let me take you back lest you be missed."

Lois stood dazed. He had kissed her!

*

When they reached Amaury's estate, Nicholas watched Lois climb over the fence before turning his horse around. She walked charily in the pale starlight and slipped back into the kitchen.

"From now on, you will be doing my chores, or I shall tell the master you sneaked out," Anastasia, one of the servants, whispered in Lois' ear as soon as she lay down.

Lois' eyes widened in the gloom; "You can tell the master whatever you want, and I might do just the same."

"What do you mean?"

"Tell the master, and you shall find out soon enough," Lois said sternly. Would the young woman call her bluff?

She did not. Disconcerted, Anastasia lay down again, wondering what the new girl might have on her. Had she seen her stealing the ham from the cellar?

Lois lay still, hoping Anastasia could not hear her heart beat like a drum.

*

Nicholas had not been sleeping well lately. He had not heard from Lois since her first day in Amaury's service. An imp of anxiety at the back of his mind whispered that something was amiss, but he tried to ignore it, telling himself that she was all right. That her silence only meant that she had nothing new to report. This was disquieting, too. Without her reports, they were in the dark. But mostly, he missed her. He missed kissing those full, moist lips. His longing for a sight of her was like an ache.

He got up restlessly and went to the open window. He looked wistfully across the stable yard to the outline of the orgival arch of the Santa Sophia Cathedral. In that moment, a horseman rode through the gate. Looking closer, Nicholas saw Poitou dismounting and hurried down the stairs, suppressing the fear that some tragedy might have befallen Lois.

"Poitou, to what do I owe this visit?"

"I have news for you, my friend!" Poitou's grin spread from ear to ear.

"You have my undivided attention," Nicholas assured him.

"I have found a *lefteros* for Lois!" Poitou announced. "So, you get to keep your promise to her dying grandfather."

Nicholas swallowed nervously; his stomach flexed. "You have!"

"I thought you would be pleased."

"I am. It just happened… so fast, rather unexpectedly. And thank you, of course," he said, gathering his wits.

"It was rather by chance," Poitou said with a reluctant smile.

He was lying. He had searched high and low. He did not quite trust the girl for no apparent reason, just a gut feeling, or maybe because of the shrewd alertness in her eyes that had made him uneasy. In any event, with everything going on in Amaury's estate, he could not be vigilant enough. He feared he was surrounded by invisible enemies and spies. He had been in young Provence's debt, but he was the Seneschal's right-hand man, and the Seneschal was the king's most trusted counselor. Finding a husband for the girl, as he had promised, meant killing two birds with one stone.

"I accepted on your behalf. It is all settled," Poitou went on with an air of finality.

His words hit Nicholas like a kick in the teeth. "Settled?"

"Yes, the wedding has been arranged for Sunday. Lois has been so good around the house that Amaury is even going to give her a small dowry."

He was convincing, and he was lying again. Amaury ignored Lois' existence. It was a lagniappe Poitou had thought of to encourage the first *lefteros* that came across.

"Next Sunday?" *So soon?* He had not anticipated Poitou to be so efficient.

"Well, this *lefteros* is in Nicosia only for the Saturday market, but he will have to wait a day longer as we are not expecting the priest before Sunday."

Nicholas had to think; find a way to get Lois out or he would lose her forever. Suffering moments of private doubt and inner uncertainties, he wondered if this arrangement might be the best for her. "What did Lois say?"

"Lois?" Poitou raised a brow. "It did not cross my mind to ask her; I thought I should tell *you!*"

"Yes, of course! Thank you, Poitou. I appreciate everything you have done." Nicholas had to speak to her as soon as possible.

"Well, I should be going now."

"Poitou," Nicholas called out, as he reached the door.

"Yes?"

"Could you tell Lois that her dog has had seven puppies?"

Poitou looked at him baffled. He threw open the door and repeated, "Seven puppies. Right; I shall make sure to pass on the message."

Nicholas' face was set in a grimace of anxiety. He could only hope that Poitou would not forget. Seven would be the right time to meet after vespers.

Where did this turn of events leave them? In peril, obviously. He would need to come up with a plan to get her out of Amaury's estate without raising suspicion – unless she chose to marry this *lefteros*. The thought made him queasy.

44

2013

Clean shaven, dressed in black jeans and a white shirt, the man Sinclair had met at the pub checked the address on the little piece of paper one more time and drove his gray Hyundai Azera slowly in front of Lucy's house, calculating the best point of entry. In his rear-view mirror, he saw her get into her jeep and drive off.

He turned left, parked on a side street, and walked casually to the back door, his eyes scanning for a security system and finding none. That made it almost too easy, he thought, smirking. He had even doubled the regular fee since it was such a short-notice assignment.

Hidden behind the curtain, *pappou* observed the bulky figure on Lucy's kitchen porch. He was about to call the police when the stranger walked away. False alarm, *pappou* decided, patting Lola's head to quiet her down. He glanced at his watch. Lucy would be back soon, and he had to get ready for Michael's party.

*

On the other side of Limassol, Cynthia walked into the Amathus Hotel. She only had to wait a few moments for her turn at the reception to ask for Professor William Sinclair. The receptionist made the call, but there was no answer.

Cynthia resolved to have a coffee in the lobby and wait for him. She marveled at the indigo of the Mediterranean spreading in front of her, wondering what his reaction would be when he saw her.

*

Pappou waited patiently for Lucy to settle on what to wear. Punctuality had always been one of his virtues, but he was not annoyed that he was kept waiting. If anything, he was amused by Lucy's effort to look her best. She had already changed her mind twice. *Pappou* had been a little worried when her ex showed up and she and Michael stopped spending time in the evenings together, but the way she was fussing about how she looked at such an important event for Michael was comforting.

"Stunning!" he reassured her when she finally showed up in the living room, glowing in her white cocktail dress. She thanked him with a bright smile.

By the time they arrived at the inauguration party, the place was packed with people. It only took Lucy a few seconds to spot Michael who was giving the floor to the President of the Cyprus Chefs Association. Michael looked exceptionally smart in his charcoal slim-fit suit, standing at ease, with his hands interlocked in front of him. When the brief speech was over, he invited his guests to the cocktail reception. His energy and ready smile reflected his enthusiasm for a new start.

With a glass of *prosecco* in her hand, Lucy made polite conversation with Dino and Tony, two of Michael's friends. Her eyes followed Michael furtively across the room, while she was waiting patiently for everyone to have a short word with him, congratulate him for this daring initiative in such difficult times, and wish him well. She admired the ease with which he shifted his attention from one guest to the next, smiling broadly.

And then he saw her, easy on the eye, dressed in her white cocktail dress, looking like a princess. He chuckled when he noticed his two friends vying for her attention, squaring their shoulders, like peacocks fanning their plumage. He quickly excused himself from the elderly couple he was speaking to and walked over to her.

"Congratulations!" Lucy said, giving him her undivided attention, and Dino and Tony took this as their exit cue. They shook hands with Michael, exchanged a few words, and moved on to the next woman standing by herself.

"You've worked so hard to see this through; I'm so proud of you!"

"Like Phoenix, rising from his ashes," he replied self-mockingly. "I wouldn't have done it without you," he said, eliciting a satisfied smile from her.

The effect of Adriana's little gimmick was suddenly dissolved, and William seemed rather distant. Slowly, Michael placed a hand on Lucy's slim waist. He leaned closer and whispered in her ear, "Wow, you take my breath away!" Damn him if he were to lose her again without a fight.

"I could say the same about you." She looked up through her lashes, offering him an enticing smile. He knew that look well, and it thrilled him.

"Michael!" More people wanted to talk to him.

This was neither the time nor the place; later, he thought. They had the whole night to themselves.

*

Sinclair walked through the hotel sliding doors with a haughty smile on his lips. He had to admit that for a brief moment when he had seen the man in the pub, he would rather have been anywhere else but there; yet he had rolled the dice, and now he simply needed to sit tight and wait.

He was about to step onto the elevator but stopped in his tracks at the sound of a familiar voice calling his name. He looked over his shoulder.

Cynthia materialized out of nowhere and fell into his arms. "Surprise!" she cried out excitedly.

What on earth was she doing there? His cold expression made the smile freeze on her lips.

"You're not happy to see me?"

He regretted the way he had to treat her, but there was no room for her here and now. "Cynthia, what are you doing here?"

"I came here to be with you." *What else would I be doing here?*

"Well, I don't know what you were thinking! I'm not here on holidays. In fact, I'm rather busy. I thought I'd made that perfectly clear."

Cynthia searched for some warmth in his face and found none. She looked at him through the blur of tears.

He cast a cursory glance around. He could do without a scene. "What I'm saying is that I'd like to take you on proper holidays when I have the time to enjoy your company. Somewhere romantic! Paris or Venice maybe. Would you like that?"

"Are you asking me to leave?" she asked in disbelief, her bottom lip quivering.

Sinclair drew a quick breath. Pushing thoughts of guilt to the back of his mind, he said softly, "I'm here to work, Cynthia. I don't like mixing work with pleasure. I hope I can still see you when I'm back in London?"

"When are you coming back?"

"Soon. I'll call you as soon as I know."

"Don't send me away, William! I won't be in your way. You can wander off and do what you have to do all day long, and I'll wait for you to come back in the evening. I'll make it worth your while," she said playfully.

It was a tempting prospect, and Sinclair cursed silently, for he had to lure Lucy to his suite tonight. "It seems we're not on the same page. That's too bad. I wanted to pick up from where we left off in London. I see now this is not going to happen."

She looked at him terrified. He was serious! "No, no. We can do that," she said, barely able to control her voice. "Take your time with your research. I'll go back to London and wait for you there."

"Since you're such a good girl, we could have an early dinner before I drive you to the airport if you like. I'll take care of your return ticket."

"Thanks, I guess."

"Would you like to wash before that?" He still had time to kill.

"That'd be great," she said, hoping to change his mind in bed.

*

Sinclair's man drew deeply on his cigarette as he drove by Lucy's house. The tenants were out, just as his client had said. The small house adjacent to the rear garden was also dark. Like taking candy from a baby, he thought smugly.

He drove round the corner, parked the sedan, and slunk through the darkness to the back door. Breaking into the house was simple. He stepped inside, closed the door, and glanced around. It was a nice place. Too bad he had to tear it apart, but business was business. He heard a dog barking. Probably from the house at the back, he thought, and got down to work.

When he was satisfied with his masterpiece of destruction, he walked out of the house, closing the door behind him. He got into his car, making sure he was leaving unnoticed. He turned left onto the main road and took the cell phone out of his pocket.

*

Perched on the beach, the Amathus Hotel seemed like a piece of paradise with its tropical gardens. Cynthia looked out at the breathtaking view of the Mediterranean, sitting across from Sinclair in the Grill Room and enjoying the wagyu steak that he had chosen for her.

She wished he would let her stay. What a magic time they could have together on the island of the goddess of beauty and love! But he was adamant: she had to leave and wait for him in London.

Though a part of her wanted to defy him, she dreaded infuriating him. She had too much to lose.

His ringing cell interrupted her thoughts. She watched him pick up.

"It's done," a voice said, and the line went dead.

Sinclair smiled contentedly and took a sip of his *amarone,* allowing a warm sense of triumph to suffuse his senses. He turned his attention to the gorgeous woman accompanying him. It was a shame to be deprived of that sensual body, but he did not want to take any risks.

45

1306

Oblivious to the cold, Nicholas waited in jittery anticipation outside the chapel of Santa Anna shortly after seven. Mass was over,
and the evening was filled with the sound of metal hinges as the
priests bolted and barred the heavy oak doors.

She was late. Had Poitou failed to pass on the message? It was a
simple code. If they needed to meet, they should do so outside the
chapel. The number of puppies signified the time.

What if she did not show up? He was weighing his options when
he made out her silhouette in the distance. He breathed a sigh
of relief. Moments later he was leading her behind the trunk of
a century-old golden oak tree. She was shivering. Alerted by her
pale, shocked face, he brought her frozen hands to his mouth and
warmed them with his breath.

"What's wrong?"

"Something… Something's going to happen – soon."

"What do you mean?" Nicholas put aside for a moment the reason
why he had asked to meet her.

"People walk in and out of the estate all the time. Amaury spends
hours with them, locked in the great hall."

"Do you know who they are?"

"I heard the names of some of them, but there are more, of course."

He gave her a rapid nod. "Who are they?"

"Aimery –"

"The constable?" he asked, thinking that Philip had been right to
suspect him.

Lois shrugged. "I would not know, but I heard that he is the king's brother."

Nicholas nodded again. "That is the one. Go on!"

"A few Ibelins. Let me see if I have the names right. There is Balian – Do not interrupt me or I will forget!" She held up a hand to silence him.

"I'm sorry. Please!" He gestured for her to go on.

"Baldwin, Albert, Philip, and Hugh," Lois continued. Nicholas' brows furrowed, but he managed to hold his tongue this time. "And then there are several knights. You know about Hugh of Peristerona and Simon of Montolif already. Sir Albert Le Tor came to visit. And Sir Hugh of F... something."

"Four?" he prodded helpfully.

"Yes, that's the one. At least a dozen more, but I did not quite catch their names. Someone mentioned the Bishop of Limassol, too, though I did not see him."

"Blessed Virgin Mary," he said, more to himself. That was worse than their worst nightmare. He must inform the Seneschal at once. The king must be warned!

"I couldn't have done better myself. I'm very proud of you." She glowed at his praise.

He placed his hands on her shoulders and looked at her grimly. "There is something you need to know. Poitou has found a *lefteros* for you." Lois looked at him aghast. "The wedding is to take place on Sunday."

She was momentarily speechless. She looked down, breathed in, and regained control.

"My wedding? This Sunday?"

He nodded his head yes. Lois thought of her grandfather. He would have gone down on his knees and thanked the Lord Almighty for such a convenient arrangement. She should consider herself lucky she was not being married off to a serf.

"Lois, this is the best for you," he said, without conviction.

"Is it?" she asked, unable to conceal the bitterness in her voice.

"Lois," his voice was hoarse. "*Lefteroi* do not grow on trees."

"Please, do not marry me off! He could be old, ugly, hairy, rude; violent!" she protested, striking a nerve. "Please, Nicholas! I do not want to go away with a stranger; not when I have the chance to do something as important as I'm doing now." *Not when I can be with you!* "We do not know yet how or when Amaury will make his move!"

She was right.

"I cannot protect you in there," he said, agitated.

She knew this only too well. It was pure luck that she had escaped from the hands of that hideous guard the other day. Luck would not last forever.

"Do not fret about me. No one pays heed to me."

"That is the problem. I cannot stop worrying about you!" he blurted out. "Besides, what will you do about the wedding?"

Lois shrugged. "I shall thank Poitou and explain that I'm still in mourning. My husband-to-be will have to wait for me until next month. If he is a *lefteros*, he will not find another *lefteri* easily, so the wedding can be postponed until then. What is a month in a lifetime?" she brushed his qualms aside.

He could see that she was being more sensible than he. Though still troubled, he smiled inwardly at her resourcefulness.

*

In the privacy of the king's solar, Philip reached the conclusion of his report, fixing Henry with his gaze. "So, you see, my liege, all this time they have been professing loyalty to their king, but in fact, they have been preparing insurrection!"

"And how have you found out that my own brother, *your* nephew, and most of my court are conniving against me?" Henry stared at his uncle's careworn face, but he could not bring himself to accept that there was merit to the allegations. He had worked assiduously every single day since he ascended the throne, and this was how the people closest to him repaid him? It was absurd.

"We have placed a servant in Amaury's manor," Philip explained.

Henry's eyebrows furrowed at the extent of his uncle's shrewdness. Like wrapping a viper around Amaury's wrist, he thought. "Who?"

"Provence's bailiff."

"I thought you said he died last summer."

"He has a new bailiff; or rather had, since she's in Amaury's service now."

"She? *She?* You want me to believe a woman's gossip! A serf?" Henry said indignantly.

"My liege," Philip said, but Henry cut him off.

"Enough!" He pushed himself to his feet exasperated, thinking that these were no more than rumors and unfounded accusations. "I will not have you speak ill of my brother and my court in my hearing. Not until you find some irrefutable proof!" Henry turned his back on Philip and stared out of the oriel window.

Unaccustomed, yet impervious to Henry's dismissiveness, Philip bridled his chagrin. Rejecting the report was easier than accepting it, he thought, taking his leave.

Henry had not taken the threat seriously, but Philip knew better.

Time was of the essence. He bustled through the draughty corridors of the palace to his sister's chambers.

"My lady, might I have a word? In private."

"Of course," the queen mother said, and the ladies in waiting left the chamber discreetly. "You look worried, Philip," Isabelle said when they were alone.

"Isabelle, I'm afraid the tidings I'm bearing are anything but joyous," he said and gave her a succinct account of the situation.

A pragmatist by nature, Isabelle knew at once what had to be done. "Philip, you must intercede for Henry. Go and see Amaury. Tell him you know everything and advise him to desist. Tell him that this news has grieved me profoundly. If it comes to that, remind him that I have already lost two sons, and I do not wish to lose another. And tell him that there is no doubt in my mind about who the rightful king is. Go now, before it is too late!"

Brother turning against brother was a mother's worst nightmare. Worse still, such a discord would tear the realm asunder. Her poise suddenly deserted her, and Philip watched her composure shred like a flower under pressure. When he closed the door behind him, Isabelle dropped her chin into her palms, thinking that only fools believe that power brings happiness.

*

At the sight of the man standing in Amaury's kitchen, Lois almost dropped the pails she was carrying, swashing the water around.

"Theodore?"

"Lois!" he said with a spurious smile.

She put the pails down and looked him up and down. He seemed to have done well for himself. He could easily pass for a merchant. She met his eyes. There was so much she wanted to ask him.

"Ah, Lois!" Poitou's voice came from the corridor behind her. "I see you have already met your husband-to-be."

Lois froze for a moment. Self-preservation kicking in, she switched into practical mode. She could not claim to be mourning still. Theodore had been there when her grandfather died; he had even helped dig his grave! She tried hard to think of a plausible reason to postpone the wedding but came up with nothing.

"Yes, we have," Theodore said at last.

"All right then! Lois, go get ready. The priest should be here any moment now."

Lois looked at Poitou alarmed. "Now?" There was no way to notify Nicholas!

"Yes, he has come back earlier than expected. Talk to Anastasia! I think there is a nice dress for you somewhere. Theodore, come with me," Poitou said.

Lois looked at Theodore's impenetrable expression as he went past her. The thought of fleeing right here and now was tempting. But that would be unwise.

*

"Get your things; we are leaving," Theodore enjoined Lois when the few bystanders had congratulated them after the wedding.

Lois' brows furrowed. "What? Right away?"

"Yes, woman, right away!" Theodore said rather curtly.

She looked startled for a moment or two before she could compose herself. There was an air of authority about him that had not been there before. Although it would take her a while to accept, he had every right over her from now on. He was her husband. She looked at him in silent defiance and did his bidding.

She followed him to the stables, acquiescing for the moment. Theodore mounted Julius, his mule, and kicked in without uttering a word. Lois walked alongside the mule toward the estate gate, trying to make sense of what was happening.

"Are you going to speak to me or are we to spend the rest of our lives in silence?" she asked, trying to make light of the situation.

He was stung but did not reply. Lois decided she would keep trying anyway. When he was cross enough, he would finally say something, and that would be a start.

"Tell me, Theodore, why did you leave the Provence *casale* without so much as a goodbye? Did you get cold feet about the wedding?" she goaded him, but he kept his mouth shut. "You said that when the well was finished, you would ask me to marry you; remember?"

She raised her eyes and looked at him. Never before had she seen his face distorted with fury and she was staggered.

"You have the nerve to ask?" his voice tight and controlled but seething with a barely concealed anger.

"*I* have the nerve to ask! *You* are the one who vanished from the face of the earth!" Her eyes flashed mutiny.

He reined in his mule, jumped down, took her by the arms, and shook her. "I waited for you for over a year. I was your fool. Never once did you let me kiss you. And then the young master shows up and you invite him to the cellar in the middle of the night! What would you have me do, Lois? Watch you go to his bed?"

Like I watched my mother? He clammed up. He had been only a child when the master would summon his mother whenever he pleased or had guests to entertain. His father's shame, chiseled on his face, was an image imprinted in little Theodore's mind, a wound that refused to heal, that kept on festering.

Lois shook her head, absorbing what he had said. "Nothing happened, Theodore. Not then, not before, not later." *Almost nothing. A kiss is still a kiss.*

She saw doubt cross his face, and then his expression hardened again. "Why was Poitou in such a hurry to get rid of you? Did *he* have his way with you?"

Lois shook her head. "No!" she said forcefully.

"A master can do as he pleases with his servants, so do not pretend to be indignant. Why would a master care if his serfs get married or not, let alone provide a dowry for them!"

Lois' head was spinning. Poitou had provided a dowry for her? "It seems that Nicholas saved his life once, and he was returning a favor."

"So, the young master is Nicholas to you? And why would he care if you get married or not, let alone bring you all the way to Nicosia and involve Poitou in this?"

Lois wondered if she could trust Theodore with the truth. She decided she had little choice. In as few words as possible, she let him in on the plan to spy on Amaury.

Theodore stared at her in disbelief. "And why is this *your* fight, Lois?"

She blinked. That was a good question. "It's not... I thought it would be my chance to see a bit of the world after you had left." This was not quite a lie, just not the whole truth.

He gave her a long, hard, searching look. "Is this what you want?" His voice was gentle now, hopeful, and Lois breathed more easily.

"For now. I would like to settle down and have children one day," she said. With Nicholas, but this was not going to happen.

Theodore cupped her face in his hands. "There is nothing I want more than to father your children and show you the world." If that was what God had planned for him, he vowed never to miss another Sunday Mass.

Absorbed in the moment, they did not take notice of the four men emerging from behind the bushes and closing in on them.

*

Awakened by the banging on the door in the dead of night, Nicholas hastened downstairs. Jacob, his manservant, answered the door, and Nicholas' heart stopped at the pitiful sight of Lois. He stared aghast, hardly recognizing her with her cheek so puffed up that her eye was almost closed. He glanced at her torn dress, a square of cloth dangling, and her hair in disarray. She was shaking.

In two long-legged strides, he reached her, lifted her up, and went up the stairs, calling out to Jacob, "Bring water to wash her wounds! And some food and wine!"

When he lay her down on his bed, he sat by her side and carefully brushed the hair from her face. "What happened?" he asked, appalled.

Lois was not sure where to begin. "I got married," she said.

Nicholas' jaw dropped. "You got... *married?* When? To whom? Did *he* do this to you? Where is he now?" Rage surged slowly through him, white hot and volatile, and he struggled to maintain control.

"The day after we met at the chapel, Theodore came to Amaury's estates. *He* is the *lefteros* Poitou found for me. He would have known I was lying if I had insisted on still grieving for my loss, and that might have made Poitou suspicious."

"So, you married him!" Nicholas said in astonished indignation, forgetting for the moment that the suggestion had been his.

"Do not look at me like that! This was *your* understanding with Poitou in the first place!"

He heard a dangerous note in her voice and suppressed a retort. His pride was hurt; hence his ire. He waited until he was sure his anger abated. "What happened?"

She took a moment to collect her thoughts. "Everything had already been arranged."

"Did he…?" Nicholas faltered and cleared his throat. "Did he force himself on you?"

Lois shook her head and the headache returned. She writhed in pain. "No, no!" She went quiet when Jacob appeared in the doorway.

"Leave everything on the table. You can go to bed now. I will not need you any more tonight," Nicholas said, eager to have the room to themselves. Jacob wished them good night and closed the door behind him, keeping his thoughts to himself.

"Who did this to you?" Nicholas asked, washing her wounds gently.

"Four men attacked us shortly after we had left the estate. It was as if they had known we would be carrying my dowry with us. Theodore tried to protect me, but he could not take it up against four men."

Tears rolled down her cheeks, and Nicholas kissed them away. "It's all right now. You are here with me. You are safe."

He put his arms around her and let her cry until she had no more tears to shed. He did not ask about Theodore. He could guess what had happened to him. She would tell him the details later in her own good time.

*

Lois awoke from a restless sleep and was startled to see Nicholas lying beside her. It took her a moment to get her bearings, and then it all came back to her.

"Run, Lois," Theodore had said, but she could not leave him. She kicked, bit, and scratched. But they were outnumbered. She had fought like a wild animal until someone's fist landed in her face so hard that she lost her footing. She had fallen to the ground, her head landing on a spiky stone. The darkness had enveloped her and she had passed out.

When she had come to, there was no sign of the four men or of Theodore. She had no way of knowing what had befallen him, but she was certain of one thing: if he were alive, he would not have left her there. Her guess was that the four men had robbed them of everything and left them there to die. Theodore, wounded most likely, tried to get help, but Lois feared he never made it to the next village.

She felt Nicholas stir and looked thoughtfully at his handsome face.

"Good morning!" he murmured. His lips broke into a sleepy smile. He put his arms over his head and gave a good stretch. "How are you feeling?" he asked, kissing the top of her head.

"As if I have just run into a stone wall!"

He ran a fond eye over her. "Did you get any sleep?"

"A bit."

A pause. Then, "Lois?"

"Mm?"

"Have you thought about what you want to do? You cannot go back to Amaury's estate," he stated the obvious. "You can stay here, of course, but what do *you* want to do?"

Lois was not sure that was an invitation, so she said, "Could I stay until I'm fit enough to travel?"

Nicholas did not know what he had expected to hear, but that was not it. "Of course! You can stay for as long as you like."

46
2013

After the party, Michael followed Lucy and *pappou* home in his convertible, that familiar look under her lashes vivid in his mind. He could hardly wait to be alone with her. He longed to feel her, taste her; caress her. The mere thought aroused him. He opened the window and let the late evening breeze cool him down.

But when they pulled over outside the house, they were in for a big surprise. Two police cars were parked in the driveway. Some neighbors had gathered around. Others peeped out their windows.

Michael got out of the car and strode over to the men in uniform. Lucy and *pappou* followed suit.

"What's going on?" Michael asked an officer, and the latter wanted to know who they were. "The owners," Michael said, curbing his impatience.

"There seems to have been a burglary," the officer said. "Perhaps you could check what's missing."

Michael translated quickly, and Lucy walked to the house. In the doorway, she stopped in her tracks, gasping for air at the sight of the shattered windows, broken vases, and overturned furniture. She shut her eyes and remembered to breathe. She trudged through the debris, her stomach tight, and went up the stairs reluctantly. The sound of Michael's and *pappou's* voices talking to the police was reassuring amidst the violation of her private life.

Her bedroom was wrecked: a hodgepodge of clothes, jewelry, make-up, and shoes, thrown on the floor and trampled on. The cupboard doors were open and the drawers had been pulled out, their contents strewn all over the place. Her suits had been slashed. The pillows had not been spared. They had been cut open, and their cotton stuffing had been scattered around.

A quick check confirmed that all the rooms had been ransacked. Yet, as far as she could tell, nothing was missing. She sat on the bedroom floor with her back against the wall, hugging her knees, shaking her head in disbelief. Tears of anger and despair pricked her eyelids, but she bravely fought them back. There was a hushed sound of footsteps on the carpet coming up the stairs.

"Hey, come here!" Michael knelt beside her, folding his arms around her, crooning soft words to her. "It's all right. I'm here; I'll help you take care of this." The tenderness in his voice was overwhelming. Lucy rested her head on his shoulder.

He gave her a moment to compose herself, smoothed the hair from her face, and reminded her gently that the police were waiting downstairs. She nodded and he helped her to her feet, took her arm, and steered her out of the room and down the stairs.

"There's nothing missing. But a lot of my things have been ruined," Lucy informed the officers.

She slid into a kitchen chair, and Michael put a cup of tea in her hand. For the next twenty minutes, Lucy answered the officers' questions as fully as she could. When they were satisfied with the statement, they got ready to leave.

"So, what happens now?" Michael asked.

"If the place is insured, I'd call the underwriter," an officer suggested.

"I haven't got around to that yet," Lucy said. "Wait a minute!"

"You remember something?" the officer asked.

"Yes. I received a call yesterday; some real estate agent. Something about a foreign client who wanted to buy the house."

"Do you remember the agent's name?"

Lucy opened her mouth and shut it again. Her mind was blank.

"If you do remember later or if there's anything else you might want to tell us, here's my card," the officer said.

"Do you have any leads?" Michael asked.

"Not much I'm afraid."

"Didn't anyone see anything?"

The officer shook his head.

*

When the police had left, Michael took Lucy gently in his arms and stroked her back.

"Who would do something like that, Michael? Why? They took nothing, so why? They broke in for fun? Just to smash everything up? It doesn't make sense."

"I don't know, Lucy. But I think you shouldn't be alone tonight. Why don't you come and sleep in the small house? You can have my bed. I'll take the couch. I'll help you tidy up in the morning."

Lucy broke away from his embrace reluctantly, picked up her bag, and fished out her ringing cell phone.

"How was the party?" Sinclair asked brightly.

"Fine," she said, without conviction.

"Something wrong?" His concern, like his enthusiasm, was somehow pronounced.

"Oh, William, someone's broken into my house and wrecked the place entirely!" She sighed.

"What? I'll be right there!" He had already left Cynthia at the airport with a boarding pass for the next flight to London in her hand and was now driving into the Limassol suburbs.

"No, really; it's all right."

"I'm on my way already," he said decisively and ended the call.

Lucy looked at Michael. "That was William. He's coming over."

"Lucy, let me tell you something weird about him," Michael said. "I saw his rental parked outside a dodgy pub this afternoon. When I looked inside, he was giving an envelope to a thug; you know... lots of leather and earrings and tattoos and –"

"Not everyone with a tattoo is a thug!"

"I think I know that. I happen to have one myself; remember?"

Lucy lowered her gaze at the thought of the evening they had spent together.

"Lucy," he said more softly now. "*Pappou* saw a man on your kitchen porch this afternoon. He, too, had tattoos and earrings."

"He might have had the wrong address. Besides, you don't know it was William. It might have been someone that looks like him. And anyway, I'm sure there's more than just one red Jaguar on the island. William would never do something like that. Why would he? It makes no sense."

"I just thought that it was weird that he was there in the first place, and I also think that it's a weird coincidence that your place was ransacked on the same day... Not to mention the sudden interest of a foreigner to buy this house."

Lucy shook her head. It was preposterous! Why would William travel two thousand miles to come and show her his divorce papers in an attempt to win her back and then have her place ransacked? She decided not to share this thought with Michael. She understood, of course, why he would say things like that, but it wasn't fair to William. And he wasn't even there to defend himself!

"You don't know the first thing about William." The tone was harsh, even in her ears, and she regretted it instantly.

Michael's eyes flashed with anger. "I only know what you told me: he's close to perfect and still married."

"Divorced," she corrected him softly. "He's shown me his divorce papers."

Michael stared at her, processing this new development. Then he turned practical. "I'll get a broom."

Silently, they began sweeping shards of glass.

47

1306

By the time Lois had finished sewing her new dress with the woolen cloth Nicholas had bought for her, her face looked as fresh as ever. Alone in his chamber, she tried it on and brushed her long hair.

She looked at herself in the mirror, bringing to mind last night's dinner: the way his gaze lingered on her and how his hand brushed against hers when they both reached for the loaf of bread or how his leg casually touched hers under the table. Her lips curved into a smile. She sighed. What was she thinking? She would have to leave any day now.

"It's beautiful," Nicholas said, standing in the doorway and marveling at the dark curls cascading over her shoulders.

Lois whirled around, blushing as if he could read her mind. "Thank you... How long have you been standing there?"

"Long enough." There was an amused quirk to his mouth. He took a step closer, lifted her chin with one finger, and turned her face to the side gently. "Your wounds have healed."

Their eyes met, held. "Yes, my face does not hurt any more. I should be going back to the *casale* soon."

"What's the rush?" His voice was low and beguiling.

What she saw in his eyes was a yearning so strong it might have broken her heart. Her senses warned her that she was going down a treacherous path, but she was unable to stop herself. "What's the point of delaying?"

He grabbed her arms gently; his mouth dry, his breath shallow. "I do not want you to go!"

Her heart quickened. He gave her a moment to refuse him, but she was lost in those green eyes. Slowly, he brought her hand to his lips and his tongue circled her palm. He put a finger in his mouth and sucked a little before moving on to the next one. He was tempted to take her there and then, but only briefly. He could resist and wait, though it was not easy.

Her breasts, rising and falling, looked inviting. He slanted his mouth over hers, outlining her lips. Lois had often wondered what it would feel like to be loved by him, and now it was all so real! Gently, he breathed on her neck. His lips moved lightly around her cheeks and under her chin. She felt his tongue in the corner of her lips, her lips parting eagerly, his lips on hers. His tongue penetrated her mouth slowly; teasingly. He deepened his kiss.

He pulled away gently. In her eyes, he saw her need for more. He closed the door and came back to her. His hands squeezed her softly around the waist and drew her close to him. His hot lips on her neck ended any prospect of reason. She wrapped her arms around his neck and returned his kisses with abandon.

He untied the knot of her girdle deftly and took off his tunic and shirt. Lois explored his strong torso with the tips of her fingers, and he helped her out of her dress and chemise. Her heart was pounding. She let her hair fall in front of her breasts, but he pulled it back, taking in every single detail of her firm young body.

"You're beautiful!" he whispered.

He took off his hose and put his arms around her again. She felt him aroused where their bodies touched, and she was filled with a frisson excitement of the unknown and jolts of desire. Her hands moved away from his neck and caressed his strong back. He touched her breasts and contoured them with his palms. "So mesmerizingly beautiful," he whispered and let his fingers slide between them.

He cupped her breasts and felt her nipples draw up tight under his touch. He bent down and kissed the silky smooth skin of her neck and her throat, his tongue teasing, his teeth biting gently. His hands slid down her back while his lips and tongue savored her throat, down to her nipples. He heard her gasp with pleasure and could wait no longer.

"Lois, oh Lois!"

He cupped her buttocks, squeezing, his lips traveling all the way down to her stomach. Lois felt her body awakening; she was alive in a way she had never been before. He lay her down on the bed, caressed her thighs, and buried his face between them. She was afire; her shivering and her moans, thrilling.

He pulled back for a moment; then his tongue teased out softly again, and she thought she would go mad. It was torture, what he was doing to her, but he wanted to drive her dizzy with need. When he stopped again, her fingers tightened in his hair, pulling his head toward her. His lips curved in a smile. The sensation she experienced now surpassed her wildest dreams.

Her body was ready for him, and he moved on top of her. He penetrated her just a little and pulled back again. It had taken all his self-discipline, for he wanted to thrust himself inside her, be one with her, find relief inside her. She was in a frenzy and that aroused him even more. He pushed harder but felt a resistance. He pulled back.

"You're a virgin!" he said short of breath.

Was that surprise or rejection in his voice? She did not want him to stop, but she was too mortified to say it. She arched her body to meet his, and he took it as a sign of consent. He kissed her as he moved gently inside her until something gave way. Lois gasped.

"Are you all right?"

"Yes," she whispered.

He moved inside her again, slowly at first, with tender moves. Instinctively, she began to move in rhythm with him. His moves became faster and harder, and each move was matched by a sigh from her. He kept pushing in and out of her, his breathing very rapid. A moment of clarity followed that felt as if he had been struck by lightning; his moans mingled with hers.

*

With her soft cries of rapture still ringing in his ears, he fought for breath as he lay on top of her. He kissed her lips again and rolled on his side. He took her in his arms, stroking her hair.

All those horror stories she had heard about a woman's first time meant nothing now, Lois thought, grateful for Nicholas' tenderness.

"Do you know what the best sound in the world is?" he asked.

Lois thought for a moment and shook her head. "No, I do not think I do."

"Your little cries of delight when I'm inside you."

"Like that?" She feigned those sounds, blushing.

Nicholas gazed at her, pleasantly surprised. He marveled at how comfortable she felt with herself, with her body, with him. Whores were professionals, of course, and did not count, but all the other women he had known intimately had been too shy or unimaginative.

He took her lips in a demanding kiss. "If you do this again, I'll have to ravish you," he teased. Then, remembering that it had been her first time, he asked, "Are you sore?"

"A little."

"It will be better the next time. We can try again later."

"Does it get any better than this?"

He grinned. "Oh, yes, it does," he said self-assuredly.

She turned on her side, her lips on his ear, and breathed one of her little cries.

"What are you doing?"

Was it possible? Was she urging him to take her again? He had never thought that a virgin would enjoy the first time so much. He wondered how wild her imagination could get with some guidance.

"Testing if you really get horny."

He had not realized she knew such words, let alone use them. It was strangely arousing. He should teach her a few more.

"Do that again, and I won't be responsible if you get really sore," he warned her.

She breathed in his ear again. This time he rolled her on top of him.

*

When they were done, they lay in each other's embrace. He took her lips in a lingering kiss. "Sweet Lois, I shall treasure these moments forever," he said, blissfully exhausted.

Cuddled close, she lifted her head from the crook of his shoulder, and he ran a hand softly down her back. She pushed up onto an elbow, looking into his eyes.

"I think you know this already, but I will tell you anyway. You have held my heart my entire life. My guess is you always will. In my dreams we have made love a thousand times. Now, I know what it's like to feel you inside me, to be one with you. And now we can have that forever!" She kissed him lightly on the lips, wearing a beatific expression.

Forever? For a moment, Nicholas found himself struggling with conflicting emotions. For a man who believed that a kind falsehood was sometimes better than a hurtful truth, he could not lie to her.

"Lois," his voice was husky. "I know how you feel. In a way, I feel the same, but I —" He swallowed hard. "I could never marry you," he said, taking the air out of the room.

"I know," she said quietly. *If wishes were horses, beggars would ride.*

A flicker of disappointment flashed across her face as she got out of bed. He noticed her chin rise a fraction and her body stiffen, and he knew that she was gathering the shreds of her pride. He watched her get dressed.

"Lois, don't be angry! You are my ray of sunshine in this dismal city," he tried to appease her. "In fact, this will be your new nick-name: *solelh*. Without your light and your warmth, my life is dark and cold."

He had always been honey-tongued, but these were not the words Lois had longed to hear. She looked at him reticent, and he knew her silence was an ill omen. She turned away from him and walked to the door.

"Lois, don't go!" he cried out, sitting up. But she needed to be alone with her thoughts. He watched her open the door in disbe-lief. "Lois, come back here!" he shouted, but she was already rush-ing down the stairs.

He drew a quick breath and slammed his palm down onto the bed. Disgruntled, he leaped to his feet and put his clothes hastily on. He dashed downstairs and caught up with her in the parlor. His breath was rapid and shallow.

"Did you just walk away from me?"

Like most men when they are in the wrong, Nicholas focused on her reaction rather than on his action.

Lois squared her shoulders and held his gaze steadily. "What if I did?" she countered.

Out of the corner of his eye, Nicholas noticed his manservant watching from the kitchen with acute interest. "Jacob, go busy yourself in the stable!" he said tersely, his eyes never leaving hers for a moment.

"Yes, my lord," Jacob murmured and disappeared through the kitchen door.

"Since when do you run away from an argument just because it's not to your liking?"

For a moment of eternity, they stood still, staring at each other. It was Lois who broke the silence in the end.

"I know what you said is true, but it does not mean it hurts any less," she said in all honesty, lowering her eyes, and he was instantly deflated.

"Oh, Lois! Come here," he said tenderly, stretching out both arms. He could not stand seeing her sad, especially when he was the cause of her pain.

She raised her eyes to meet his. She wanted to run to him but hesitated. The knock on the door put an end to Nicholas' efforts for reconciliation. He sighed and gestured for her to answer the door.

*

"Lois, you're here!" Provence's eyebrows shot up. He had no way of knowing Lois was no longer in Amaury's service. Her unbraided, unkempt hair did not go unnoticed.

"Yes, my lord," she said, letting him in, finding a small smile for him.

"Father!" Nicholas said. "Come on in. You must be tired."

"Indeed!" The two men shook hands and patted each other on the arm. Provence did not comment on his son's disheveled looks.

Nicholas asked Lois to bring some wine and to tell Jacob to make them supper. "Of course, my lord," she said and disappeared into the pantry. Soon afterward, she returned with wine, olives, and some bread.

Provence made himself comfortable and took the chalice she offered him. He noted the way Nicholas tried to catch her eye when she served him. There was an undeniable tension, an undertone of passion, between them.

As the afternoon light was beginning to fade and the parlor was growing dim, Lois lit the candles and returned to the pantry to help Jacob.

"*Santat, pare!*" Nicholas raised his chalice, wishing his father had come a little later.

"*Santat, fill!*" Provence matched the toast. He looked at Nicholas, a frown of inquiry on his face. "So, you are sharing Lois' bed now?"

Nicholas' lips went up in a half smile. "Little escapes you, Father."

"I hope you know what you are doing," Provence said quietly.

"Not much different than you sharing Emilia's bed," Nicholas said, keeping his tone light.

"Not quite the same, my boy." His voice was not stern, but concerned. "Dallying with a widow serf at my age does not compare with you sleeping with a young, unmarried *lefteri.*"

"Widow, most likely," Nicholas corrected him. Provence looked at him, mystified, and Nicholas gave him a brief account of the events of the last few days.

"Well, she is still very young. She should marry again," Provence said.

He was right. They both knew it. The underlying question was: what would Nicholas do about it? It was not that he lacked the moral rectitude to assume responsibility for his actions. He just wanted to postpone marrying her off for as long as he could.

Provence sensed his discomfiture. "Tell me the news about Amaury."

"I'm afraid the situation may now be beyond control," Nicholas said gravely, yet relieved to change the subject.

"Oh?"

Lois returned with more wine, and Jacob brought chicken in lemon and oregano sauce and began to serve supper.

"Lois, join us and tell Father here what you have found out in Amaury's service."

"Thank you, my lord," she said, still a bit shaken up, yet pleased he had granted her a seat at the table in his father's presence. She swept onto the bench and gave Provence a detailed account of Amaury's actions. The longer she was allowed to be part of the discussion, the less tense she felt.

Nicholas' leg touched hers unobtrusively, but she casually shifted away from him. He knew she had never been one to hold grudges, and she forgave easily. But she had not been one to forget either.

Lois focused her attention on the old knight's face as she spoke. He seemed to have expected some of the names she mentioned, but others came as a complete surprise. Nicholas noted his father's admiration for her as she recounted her tale and smiled inwardly; it was easy to be taken by her wit and grit.

"How long will you be staying this time, Father?" he asked and shoveled a piece of bread into his mouth.

"A couple of days. I intend to pay Philip a visit. Then I will go to Famagusta to discuss Amaury's moves with Peyre. He is close to the bishop. I would like to hear how he assesses the situation. And, of course, I will spend a few days with Albert and Guilhelm. I have not seen them since your mother's funeral."

48
2013

They both knew who it was when the bell rang. Lucy rose to her feet and answered the door, feeling Michael's disapproving stare on her back.

"Lucy! Are you all right?" Sinclair asked with a tone of rehearsed apprehension in his voice.

"Yes, thank you," she said, guardedly. Unable to disregard Michael's concerns completely, Lucy wondered if William might have some involvement in this mess. But that was insane, she decided.

"Come here, sweetie!" Sinclair said, taking her in his arms.

Aware of Michael's eyes glued on her, Lucy broke away almost instantly. Michael shifted in his seat, making his presence known.

"Oh, hello, Martin," Sinclair pretended he had forgotten his name.

"Michael," he corrected him dryly.

"Right," Sinclair said and cast a cursory glance at the ransacked place. He shook his head, experiencing a farrago of exultation at how easy it had been to trample on someone's life and guilt for what Lucy was going through because of him. It was collateral damage, he tried to convince himself. This was not the time for self-doubt.

For the second time that evening Lucy was told that she could not stay in her house. "Come to the hotel with me. I can book another room for you if you don't want to share my suite," Sinclair said, with the air of a man accustomed to having things done his way. A quick mental calculation assured him that Cynthia was on board by now.

"Thank you, William. It was kind of you to come in the middle of the night to check on me, but I think I just need to clear my head." She turned away from him a little and spoke into the room. "Thank you both for your concern, but I need to be alone tonight. I'm sorry."

The two men hesitated, each waiting for the other to make the first move. Lucy resolved the dilemma; she held the door open and wished them good night.

*

When Lucy woke up the next morning, Michael was mowing the lawn in his garden. "Morning! There's fresh coffee in the coffee maker," she called out to him in a sprightly tone.

He looked at her but did not move. "Is that an invitation?"

"It is."

"In that case," he said, leaving his sentence unfinished. He secured the lawn mower and went over.

"How come you're not at work? I thought you had this last-minute order."

"Already taken care of. Just some final touches left. I'll deal with that later."

In so many ways, Michael put her first on his priority list. He deserved better than last night's cold shoulder, she rebuked herself.

"When did you do all that?"

"Last night. After you so kindly kicked me out." He said that lightly, but it was clear it hadn't gone down well with him.

"I'm sorry. There was too much tension," she said, shaking her head ruefully.

He nodded. "Come on! We have a lot of work to do. This place is a mess!"

"But if you were up all night, you should go and get some sleep!"

"That's all right. You can show me your gratitude later; any way you like." He offered a mischievous grin.

"All right then. Let's get to work," she said.

*

When the place looked habitable again, they collapsed on the sofa, tired, but satisfied with the result of their work.

"Thank you, Michael!" Lucy said.

"Anything for you!"

He stretched his arm on the sofa behind her neck and gently pulled her to him. His lips teased hers, and he ran his fingers through her hair. Lucy closed her eyes but did not allow herself to get carried away. She had to clear her feelings and thoughts about William once and for all.

"I can't do this, Michael," she whispered, disengaging herself.

"You can't or you won't?"

"I need some time to think."

"You do that." He nodded slowly. "You know I'm a patient man, Lucy, but even my patience has limits. Don't let it take you too long."

Lucy nodded in understanding.

49

1306

Now that her face had healed, Lois decided it was time she saw a bit of the capital. When Nicholas had left for the palace that morning, she made her way to the square. It was at least six times as large as the market square at Episkopia. The sheer size of the massive cathedral and the sight of the crowd made her slightly dizzy. Never had she seen so many gathered in one place.

The bells of Santa Sophia rang, a loud peal, and Lois was intrigued to take a peek inside. She was not supposed to. It was a Catholic church, but it looked so majestic that she could not resist.

She took a seat on one of the benches at the back and looked around in silent wonderment. It was different from the Orthodox churches, not just the size, but also the stained glass and the statues of the Virgin Mary and the saints; even the icons looked different. It was strange that she found such unalloyed serenity in a Catholic church, but it was, after all, one of God's dwellings, she pondered. It was where Nicholas prayed.

Lois mused long on the situation she was in and on what she should best do. For the first time in her life, she felt that she had a choice. It was up to her if she would stay with Nicholas or go back to the *casale;* or if she would try and make some money for herself, perhaps by selling pies at the market. She settled on finding out right away what it would take to set up her own stall and when the next market day was. She could have used Jacob's assistance, but he had gone to visit his sick sister.

Lois walked out of the cathedral with a newfound sense of power to determine her own life. The capital seemed filled with opportunity, and she was suddenly overwhelmed with optimism and exhilaration.

*

It was already dark when Nicholas left the palace, worried and exhausted. For the second time in a row, Amaury had avoided meeting with the Seneschal on some pretext. Something was in the wind. There was tension in the palace. Everyone looked over their shoulder with alert wariness; even the walls seemed to have ears. Philip had assigned Nicholas to give a clandestine order for more weapons and the guard leader to enlist more men. It was a costly, albeit requisite, bane. The only pleasant thought on Nicholas' mind those days was Lois.

It was a crisp early spring evening, and he quickened his step. He threw open the front door and was pleased to see that the fire had been lit and the parlor was warm. Lois rushed to him. His grin belied his agitation and fatigue.

"You look cold. Come and sit by the fire!"

Nicholas' heart beat faster at the sight of her hair worn down and the surmise that he had been forgiven. He did as she had said, and she gently massaged his scalp. He closed his eyes, thinking he must have done something right to deserve this, though he did not know what that was. No matter; he enjoyed her attention all the same.

"Does this meet your approval, my lord?" she asked playfully.

"Everything you do meets with my approval." It was not less than the truth, although he did not know how to reassure her of that without putting her hopes up too high. He was still in quandary after their last argument. He was swept by tenderness, a new and somewhat unsettling emotion for him.

When she finished, he had her sit on his lap and folded his arms around her, burying his face in her lavender-scented curls. Lois closed her eyes and relished the warmth of his embrace, slipping a hand in his chemise and entwining his soft chest hair around her fingers.

"I think I like '*solelh*', *amor meu*," she said and planted a quick kiss on his lips.

"Where is Jacob?"

"You gave him permission to visit his sick sister," she reminded him. "He will be back on the morrow."

"Take your clothes off!" he said in a husky whisper.

"What? Here?" she asked, intrigued.

"Yes, *solelh,* in front of the fireplace."

She rose to her feet and did just that.

"Turn around!"

She did – slowly. He watched the soft glow to her smooth skin, brought by the luminous flames, and longed to feel her body close to his.

"You dazzle me!"

She licked her lips the way she knew he liked it and got excited by that familiar look on his face. He rose to his feet and undressed himself, his swelling groin proof of the urgency of his need for her.

"Already? You can't hide it," she teased him.

"Who wants to hide?" he said, grabbing her backside, squeezing. She felt his inviting stiffness against her belly, and a wave of heat surged through her.

"I want us to try something new," he said.

"What's that?"

He whispered his fantasy in her ear and saw her amazed amusement.

"You would like that?" Lois asked.

Shyness was an alien emotion to Nicholas, yet he found himself ensnared by it now – for a brief moment. "I think we both will."

"Will it hurt?"

He cupped her face in his hands and looked deeply into her eyes. "Lois, I would never hurt you."

"I know." She smiled at him.

He made love to her ardently that evening, then once more, gently. Inside her, all his worries disappeared. There was only bliss.

When he rolled onto his side on the rashes on the floor, she moved away from him.

"I will fetch some wine," she said, but he looped her hair around his hand, slowly pulled it taut, until she laughed and rolled back into his arms.

He locked eyes with her and asked, "Does this mean you are staying here with me?"

She smiled and nodded yes. Earlier in the afternoon, while sitting in the cathedral, she had made her peace with God to live in sin with him.

He drew her to him and kissed her again, a lingering and tender kiss.

"Nicholas?" she said when she finally caught her breath.

"Yes?"

"Might I borrow a silver *gros?*"

"Need you ask?" he said without inquiring what she needed the money for and took her lips once more.

*

When Nicholas left for the palace that Saturday morning, Lois asked Jacob to help her carry the pies to the market. They set up a makeshift stall in the space she had rented with the silver *gros.*

It was a slow morning, but as noon drew close, more and more people stopped at Lois' stall, and she made sure she saved a piece for Nicholas and sent Jacob to the palace with it.

"My lord," Jacob said when he was shown into his master's office, "Lois sends you this pie."

The mere thought of her brought a smile to his lips. "Thank you, Jacob." The old man would not move. "Is there something else?" Nicholas asked.

"I just thought you might want to know that she's here," Jacob apprised him. Although he had been reserved at first, the old servant grew fonder of Lois with each passing day.

"She's *here?* Where? In the palace? "

"On the square, my lord."

Nicholas pushed away from his desk and got to his feet. He exchanged a few words with another clerk before turning to Jacob again. "Right, take me to her!"

"There she is," Jacob said a few minutes later, pointing at her stall.

"I cannot see her. Where?" All Nicholas saw were people passing by.

"There, by the pie stall."

Nicholas looked more closely. Eventually, he spotted the familiar petite figure behind hungry customers. A smile sprouted from his lips. Of all the women he knew, only Lois could go through what she had gone through and get back on her feet in a new place so quickly. His Lois!

*

Behind closed doors, Oiselay and Zabel listened to Amaury's account of the Seneschal's visit attentively. Amaury rubbed his stiff neck and shifted in his seat restively, waiting for the Templar Marshal to speak.

"We need to act at once and find out who the rat is among your supporters. We can kill two birds with one stone," Oiselay said in an unwavering tone.

"How?" Amaury asked.

"Have Hugh of Peristerona summon everyone: knights, vassals, retainers, burgesses, lieges, whoever can be found today. Give orders that no one who enters the house is allowed to leave. Have everyone take an oath to guard you, the Lord of Tyre."

"But would that not mean breaking their oath of fealty to Henry, my lord? Will they not resist such an oath?" Zabel asked, concerned.

"Good point, my lady," Oiselay said and was thoughtful for a moment. The Marshal was not a man who let obstacles obscure his goals. "Very well then. They should guard you, the Lord of Tyre, as much as they are bound to guard the king against the face of every man except against the person of the king, to whom they are bound by oath."

Amaury stared at Oiselay in admiring silence. Amaury had long ago realized that his own imagination was rooted in barren soil, but the man across from him could teach a fox about slyness. The oath would give Amaury a special pledge to which he had no real claim unless and until he became regent, and at the same time it preserved the appearance of personal loyalty to the king.

"And if anyone refuses to take the oath, we will know that he is the one who warned my uncle," Amaury concluded.

*

Lois gave Nicholas back the silver *gros* she had borrowed, wearing an exuberant smile. "Go ahead! Ask me where I have the money from!"

"Where do you have the money from?" he humored her. She had

had her hands full at noon, and he had decided to merely watch her from a distance.

"I sold my pies at the market today!" she said with an immense sense of accomplishment.

"I know, *solelh*. I was there. You looked quite busy."

"You were there?" Her eyes glistened at the thought that he had witnessed it all. He nodded. "It was a good day. Better than I had expected," she went on with a glowing smile.

"What do you want to do with your little fortune?"

She lowered her eyes momentarily. "Promise not to laugh?"

"No, but I can try," he said, amused and intrigued at the same time.

"I know this is going to take a long time, but I would like to build a home for orphans one day," she said earnestly. Nicholas did not laugh; he was bedazzled. This woman never ceased to amaze him. Heartened, she went on, "You know, when my parents died, I would have ended up in a cloister if it had not been for *pappou*."

"I would have ended up in a cloister, too, if it hadn't been for Provence," he said, sympathizing. "You will have to sell a lot of pies to do that though."

"At first, yes." He looked at her, puzzled. "I think there's more profit in olive oil soap, but I need to save some money first to buy olive oil. I could make soap the way Emilia taught me and sell that at the market."

"You're serious!" he said admiringly, and Lois nodded, beaming.

50

2013

With a steaming mug in his hand, the real estate agent took a seat at his desk on Monday morning and cast a glance at his unusually short to-do list. Since March the property sector had frozen and, unless a miracle happened soon, he was facing ruin. All his money was tied up in properties that no one wanted to buy and in shares. The decline of ninety-eight percent of the stock exchange was in and of itself a massacre. The thought of taking his own life had crossed his mind – more than once. He glanced at the photo of his smiling little girl on his desk and shook his head to dispel the thought. He drained his coffee and dialed Lucy's number, the most promising item on his list.

"Good morning, Ms. Hernandez. I'm calling from *Dream Homes* with regard to the interest of a foreign client of ours about your house. We spoke on the phone last week and you asked me to call you back again on Monday."

Lucy moved away from the men installing the new windows and jotted down the company name. "Ah, yes, good morning. What's your client's name again?" She tapped the pencil on the kitchen counter.

"I'm afraid he wishes to remain anonymous."

"But *you* know who he is?"

"In actual fact, we don't. We've been contacted through his lawyer." A brief pause. "All legal, of course," he rushed to add.

Lucy informed him that she was not interested in selling the house and that her decision was final. When she got off the phone, she searched for the card the police officer had given her. This might or might not be related to the burglary, but that was for the police to decide. When she ended the call, she made coffee for the workmen and waited for the police officer to contact the realtor and call her back.

It took him a couple of hours before he did. There seemed to be nothing suspicious in the correspondence with the lawyer in London, he said. She should consider herself lucky that someone was willing to pay above market price in this time of uncertainty.

Lucy put the cell down, feeling no wiser. She needed answers. It was not like Michael to blow things out of proportion, but at the same time she could not find it in her heart to believe that worldly William was capable of machinating such a brutal violation. She could not see what he could possibly gain out of it. There was perhaps a way to find out.

*

Some forty-five minutes later, Lucy was letting Sinclair into the living room.

"Wow! The place looks as good as new," he marveled.

"I had some help," she said, and Sinclair refrained from commenting on that. "Come and sit with me!" She took him by the hand and led him to the sofa. "I need to ask you something."

"All right." He flashed a smile at her, revealing perfect white teeth.

"Do you know a pub here by the name of 'Mexico'?" Her eyes were glued on his face, registering the slightest nuance in his expression.

"I don't think so," he said, without blinking.

"Never been there?"

He had no idea how Lucy had found out about the pub, but he suspected that she did not know much. "No! Would you like me to take you there?"

Lucy interlocked her fingers. He was either telling the truth, or he was a great liar. But why would Michael come up with such a grotesque story? None of this made sense. "No, I don't... I just can't accept what happened on Saturday."

"Lucy, I know this is all too much to take in right now, but have you thought about selling the house and coming back to London with me? Even if you choose not to be with me, I respect that, but I truly think you shouldn't live here all by yourself. It doesn't seem safe. Or you might want to go to Dublin for your TV program." *Anywhere else but in this house!*

His handsome face looked sincere. A long pause. "Go out with me tonight!" She hesitated. "Come on, Lucy! I've come thousands of miles for you. Just one dinner. If you don't feel comfortable with me, I won't ask you again."

Lucy did not see how she could decline.

*

Michael got back home early that evening, as *pappou* was hanging up the phone, wearing a puzzled look on his face.

"Bad news?"

"That was the real estate agency again. They just made a better offer on the house," *pappou* said.

"Which agency is that?"

"It's all jotted down." *Pappou* handed him a piece of paper.

Michael glanced at the figure on the paper, bug-eyed. "That's a lot of money. What do you want to do?"

"What do *you* want to do? I don't mind either way. But I have a feeling that you might want to be close to Lucy. You know I'm very fond of her; she's a keeper. The decision is yours," *pappou* said quietly.

"I'll give them a call and let them know we're not interested," Michael said, placing the note in the back pocket of his jeans. "I won't be staying for dinner," he said, taking his shirt off and heading for the shower.

"You're leaving?"

"I'll be at Lucy's if you need me. I thought of surprising her with a new recipe I came across."

"I won't need you. Have fun!"

51

1306

Lois raked the leaves from the porch, allowing herself a moment to take in the sweet scent of orange blossoms. She had a busy day ahead and she had planned it with care, the day she would tell Nicholas she was with child. Another moon had passed with no trace of her flux. She placed her palms on her still flat belly gently. She would tell him at supper tonight. She had given Jacob permission to visit his sister so that they could have the place entirely to themselves.

A reminiscing smile sprouted on her lips. Nicholas only needed to look at her from the far end of the room with that familiar gaze to trigger stirring sensations, almost unbearable in their intensity.

She could hardly wait until he came back home. She imagined how he would take her in his arms and kiss her tenderly, the mother of his child. Then he would make love to her gently; men thought women were fragile when they were carrying.

Soon, Amaury's plot against the king would change the world around her. But until then, she could be happy.

*

Philip of Ibelin had cancelled that morning's audiences. The meeting with Amaury turned out worse than he had feared. The Seneschal's face was usually unfathomable, but today it attested to the burdens weighing down upon him. Nicholas had never seen him so fretful.

Philip confided in Nicholas that Amaury's words had frightened him, for he truly seemed to believe that he was doing God's work, and a man of divine mission was a menace.

"If that is how he eases his conscience, he is a man much in need of absolution," Nicholas said and opened the door to the antechamber to announce the cancellation of the day's audiences.

Buenaventura, a wealthy Catalan merchant, was not intimidated by the announcement. When everyone else had left, he insisted that he had a very lucrative proposition, and Philip decided to see him after all.

"My lord, thank you for granting me this audience. I know how precious your time is, so it behooves me to be very brief. I am seeking a suitable husband for my daughter," he said, producing a small picture of an attractive young woman and placing it in the Seneschal's hands.

"Beautiful, indeed," Philip said, concealing his astonishment at this unorthodox request, waiting to hear about the lucrative proposition.

Buenaventura cleared his throat and continued, "As a token of my gratitude for your assistance, I shall donate one hundred bezants to the realm."

Nicholas' brows furrowed. It was a large sum, an unexpected gift. Henry was bleeding financially.

"My good man," Philip said, "we gladly accept your offer. In fact, Nicholas here," he pointed vaguely toward him, "is not only my scribe, but also a knight, young and handsome as you can see."

Was Philip insinuating that *he* should marry Buenaventura's daughter? Nicholas was unnerved by the intensity of his sudden rage, by the realization of how close he was to losing control of his temper, his tongue.

"Perhaps you could pay him a visit this afternoon to discuss this further?" Philip went on. "You can bring your generous contribution on the morrow."

"I will, my lord. Thank you." Buenaventura bowed and took his leave.

The moment the door closed behind the Catalan, Nicholas gave Philip a look of incomprehension. He failed to see why Philip had decided that he should marry the girl; perhaps because he happened to be present at that moment?

"Seneschal —"

"Nicholas," Philip interrupted him, speaking with heavy authority, "The king needs you now more than ever, my boy." Nicholas opened his mouth to protest, but Philip cut him short. "What? Lois? As extraordinary as she may be, she is no match for you." The young man stared at him nonplussed; his outrage barely tempered by common sense. "You think I'm too old to notice how you look at her or how your face lights up when you speak of her?" Philip went on.

There was no way of disobeying the Seneschal and the king without being impudent. Nicholas would have to come up with a sound argument. He had to think this through — and quickly.

"These are unsettled times, Nicholas," Philip said. "We need Buenaventura's contribution. You can at least discuss with the man. Heaven knows what will happen on the morrow. Besides, I can imagine that the marriage portion he provides is appealing. Meet the girl; you have nothing to lose."

Nothing but Lois.

With his last words, Philip turned his attention to his scrolls, hastening to forestall any entreaties. Nicholas stared at him, feeling caught up in currents beyond his control.

*

Nicholas came home to a parlor steamy and larded with the cloying smell of wild roses. The hall was warm and the fire lit; the flames, amber and gold, dancing in the fireplace. The bathtub had already been filled, and fresh clothes were folded on a stool. The scent coming from the pantry, a medley of thyme and oranges, filled the room.

Lois heard the door being unlatched and the clump of his feet. She gave the stew one last stir and bounced out of the room. "You are home! Let's have a bath; together!" she said with a gleaming smile.

Nicholas had always been pleased when she initiated their love making, especially when she came up with a fresh angle. But now was not a good moment. "Later. Let's just sit here for a while," he said and sat by the fireplace, conscience-stricken over the news he was bearing.

Lois sat on his lap, and he wrapped his arms around her. She sensed him tense and woebegone. "What is it, *amor meu?*"

"Lois," Nicholas had always been careful not to use the word 'love' when he spoke to her, "there is something I need to tell you."

But the tap at the door put an end to this thought. Nicholas cursed under his breath. He wished he had time to prepare her for what would follow. He grabbed her arms. "Whatever happens, promise me you will not jump to conclusions!" Lois stared at him, baffled. "All right?" He waited until she nodded and walked to the door. With swift movements, she pinned her hair up and reached for her headscarf, crestfallen. Today of all days, Nicholas had to have guests!

The door opened and a wealthy couple accompanied by the most beautiful woman Lois had ever seen came in. Her head was held high on a long graceful neck. With her rich ebony hair, turquoise eyes, and skin of milk, she looked like one of the paintings on Amaury's walls, Lois thought.

Nicholas asked them to have a seat and told Lois to bring some wine and lemonade. Lois sensed more than saw Nicholas' abashment and had an uneasy suspicion about this visit. She did his bidding and kept an eye on them from the kitchen.

Cognizant of her formidable looks, the young woman seemed

schooled in the art of flirting, Lois noticed. The way Nicholas studied her when he thought Lois was not looking made her morning sickness return.

Dusk was setting over the capital when the men moved onto the veranda to discuss serious matters while the women remained seated in the parlor, sipping lemonade. Lois lit the candles and carried a jug of *commandaria* to replenish their chalices. She did not like the barrel-chested, bull-necked man. He was loud and self-important.

"So, what do you think of the Seneschal's suggestion for a marriage between you and my daughter?" Buenaventura asked, and Nicholas almost choked on his wine.

Lois gasped and held her breath. She tried to steady her shaking hand but spilled some wine on Nicholas' hose all the same. She felt the veranda spinning and murmured words no one could make out. Buenaventura made a throaty noise of contempt.

She suddenly looked vulnerable, and Nicholas' heart lurched. "That would be all," he said, endeavoring to meet her eye, but she would not raise her gaze. She moved out of sight yet remained within earshot.

"Why do you bother with a left-handed serf when there are so many good servants out there? Once you have settled down with Sofia, I will send you a couple to look after my daughter and the house."

It did not sound as if he was suggesting, Nicholas noticed. Lois wanted to hear Nicholas' response, but his guest noticed she was still there and gave her a cold-eyed stare. Lois had little choice but to step inside.

"Please, excuse me a moment," Nicholas said, rising to his feet and following her to the pantry.

"Lois, please! Don't be so sad! This is what I wanted to tell you before they showed up," he said with compunction. "Let us talk when they have left! I need to go back now. Will you be all right?"

Despite the misgivings that clutched at her heart, she nodded bravely and watched him go out on the porch again. She stood listening to him long after he had finished speaking, pondering his words.

*

The sentry had strict orders from Amaury not to let anyone in or out of the manor once everyone had gathered, but he could hardly deny entry to the queen mother and the Seneschal when they insisted upon seeing the Lord of Tyre. Grudgingly, he led them to the assembly in the great hall.

At the sight of Isabelle, all voices hushed. Everyone bowed as she entered the room, wearing the face of a queen mother in the midst of an unspeakable nightmare. She took her time, her gaze penetrating. She could determine who had taken the oath unwillingly by the embarrassment on their faces. *Lord, give me the right words to say*, she prayed. When she spoke, it was with authority.

"So, it is true!" Some had the decency to lower their heads sheepishly. "Look at you! Like a pack of ravening hounds that have smelled blood. You, and you, and you," she said, pointing a bony finger. "You all have sworn allegiance to your king. Is this how you defend him? By conspiring against him? Shame on you!" Tears of rage brimmed in her eyes.

Amaury sensed the men wavering and knew he had to intervene. The mere presence of the queen mother inspired awe, but his uncle was an easier target. "Tell us, Seneschal, how many times have you covered for the king's inability to perform his duties? Is it not true that complaints are piling up because he is so often impaired?" His tone was barbed; each word carried a separate sting.

"The realm and its people are thriving. Is this not just a cheap excuse to usurp the throne? Kings are entitled to the respect due them as God's Anointed," Philip said in his authoritative voice.

Isabelle's eyes flicked from face to face. Her gaze rested on Aimery, her younger son. She looked at him long and hard. The young man flinched inwardly but held her gaze.

"You are wrong, uncle," Amaury said. "We shall be rid of an absent king, a sick king who did not protect us from the Genoese pirates or from famine; a king who did not protect Armenia from the Saracens," he said, enunciating each word with chill precision.

Vague accusations and no solutions, Philip thought. How could they all be so blind?

"Hear, hear!" Amaury's strongest supporters cried out, Aimery amongst them.

"Mother, perhaps you should go back now," Amaury said. It sounded more like an order rather than a suggestion.

It is over, Philip thought, despondent by their unnerving gall. He had failed to protect the king. He stared at their faces, fearing that Aeolus' goatskin bags had just been opened.

*

It was nightfall by the time Peyre's coach reached the outskirts of Nicosia. For a moment, he struggled between going to Nicholas' house or straight to the archbishopric, but he finally settled on arriving at the archbishopric before supper. He would pay Nicholas a visit at the palace first thing in the morning. The two brothers had much to discuss in these ill-starred times.

He rubbed his chin, wondering if the Bishop of Famagusta had been exaggerating with the rumors of uprising. He shook his head in dismay. Brother turning against brother was vile and contemptible. How was it possible that they did not see that?

52

2013

Sinclair was pleased. Lucy had finally agreed to go out with him. He was confident that he would find a way to sway her and make her give up the bloody house. He might even consider picking up from where they had left off if she came back to London. He was not prepared to give up Cynthia, not yet anyway, but Lucy did not need to know about her.

He was walking back to his rental when a faded cross of Lorraine carved on an ancient carob tree caught his eye. The trunk had cracked in places, but the cross was there all right. His pupils dilating, he examined it more closely and then, facing north, he began to pace, counting; the adrenaline spiking. He took twenty-one steps and stopped right in front of Michael's garden gate. He had the location!

Exultant, he strode back to the car. He no longer needed to try so hard at charming Lucy, nor did he have to make her give up her house. He had suffered a pang of guilt when he had seen at first hand the depredation he had caused, but he quickly reminded himself that the end justified the means.

Now, he needed to focus on Michael. It did not surprise him that the realtor reported that Michael had refused to sell. He wanted to be close to Lucy, especially with her ex in town. Perhaps, Sinclair thought, Michael needed an incentive. He took his cell and called a number.

"I have a new assignment for you."

"Same place, same time," the voice said on the other end of the line.

*

Sinclair could hardly contain himself until it was time to call and report on his progress.

"I have the location of the 'X' mark," he said on the phone, later that evening.

"You broke the riddle!" the elderly man said contently, like a master expecting only success from his best student.

"Yes!" Sinclair said, making an effort to keep the triumph out of his voice. 'You shall find your faith in Lorraine' refers to the cross of Lorraine carved on a carob tree, 'the tree whose seeds weigh gold'. I turned north, 'facing Ursa,' and took twenty-one strides."

"Not thirty? Like 'Judas' pieces of silver'?"

"At twenty-one, I had to stop in front of Michael Costa's gate. The 'X' mark is under his house."

"Good! See this through! We will spare no expense to retrieve our history."

"Thank you, I will!"

*

"Lucy?" Michael knocked on the kitchen door. It was unlocked and he let himself in, eager to give her the little gift he had found for her in the open-air market, a fortunate stroke of serendipity. "Lucy?" he called again, climbing the stairs two steps at a time.

"I'm upstairs," Lucy cried out, taking a long open back black dress out of the closet and laying it on the bed, still wrapped in a towel after a shower. "I'll be down in –"

Michael reached the doorway and stopped in his tracks. He smiled widely. "Wow!" he said, letting his tender gaze slide from top to bottom. "You look beautiful! And I have something for you."

He opened a little jewelry box and took out a small silver-plated butterfly, adorned with blue topaz stones, hanging on a matching neck chain. He took a step closer and stood behind her in front of the mirror. With gentle fingers, he removed the hair from her neck and fastened the chain. Locking eyes with her in the mirror, he planted a kiss on the curve of her neck but felt her stiffen.

"You were so excited about the blue butterflies that day in Akamas. I thought you'd like it."

Lucy took the butterfly in her hand and stroked it. "It's beautiful."

"Then what?" He noticed the dress on the bed. "I take it you're not wearing that for me tonight," a touch of acrimony in his voice. "You're going out with him?"

It was almost frightening how he could read her mind. She turned around to look at him. "I'm sorry, Michael. Please, try to understand. I need to do this – for us."

"For *us*? If there's an *us*, why do you need to go out with him?"

"To make sure that *us* is the real thing."

His first inclination was to grab her and kiss her, but the resolve in her eyes held him back. He stared at her in disbelief.

"Don't you know that?" They might not be sharing the same bed, but they had the intimacy that only couples share. They were a perfect match! How could she deny that?

"Please, Michael. Don't make this any harder than it already is. All my life, I've tried to face my problems rather than hide from them. If William might be a problem for us, I need to know this *now*, and I think you do, too."

"I know everything *I* need to know, Lucy. Too bad you don't," he insisted with infuriating certainty. Then, "You say you're doing this for us. Does he know about us?"

Lucy stood still in stunned silence. His gaze became too hard to hold, and she looked away.

"It figures," he said and bolted from the room.

She watched him leave, open-mouthed, feeling wrong-footed.

53
1306

Nicholas said his goodbyes to the Buenaventuras at the gate, wishing he had more time to think before he spoke to Lois. His legs felt like iron as he slogged back into the house.

To his surprise, Lois was not there waiting for him. She was not in the pantry either. He went upstairs and found her in his bedchamber throwing her few belongings into a satchel.

Lois had heard the sound of his footsteps on the battered wooden staircase but did not stop to meet his eye when he came into the room.

"What are you doing?" he asked quietly.

"You know what I'm doing," she said, tying the final knot.

He sensed her anger and did his best to ignore it. "Why?"

"Why are you asking me questions you already know the answers to? You are going to marry this girl!"

Caught in an outburst of helpless rage, he grabbed her by the arms and made her look at him. "I never said that."

Lois squared her shoulders and looked him straight in the eye. "Tell me that you will not marry her then."

A sigh escaped his lips, and he let go of her. "The truth is I do not see how I can go against the king's and the Seneschal's wishes." Lois' stomach heaved. "Look, Lois. It all happened so fast. I need to think how to deal with this. I have never made promises. I have always been honest with you."

Brutally so, she recollected but did not interrupt him. He was at war with himself. A part of her felt sorry for him.

"I care for you deeply," he went on. "You know that. But I also need an heir for the estates and the family name. Neither Peyre nor Albert are going to have children. Father is counting on me. You of all people should understand that."

"What?"

"It was all right for you not to marry the baker's son, so that your children inherit your rights as *lefteri*, but it is not all right for me to consider that my children will lose my rights if I marry below my rank?"

She absorbed his words with more composure than she knew she had. She even managed to see his point of view. Put like that, he was right. She nodded, a bitter smile settling on her lips.

"Do you love me?" she asked softly. He had never said the words. He had told her so many other things, but not that.

He gazed at her, too stunned to respond.

"Well?" She needed to hear the words, even if just once.

"Lois, this is not leading anywhere."

Lois felt like her world was crumbling down around her. "Oh, Nicholas, I gave you my heart and you broke it!"

"Lois!" he said, a lump in his throat. He knew she was miserable and that made him angry as well as sad.

She turned her back on him and drew a deep breath, fighting back tears. Kontostephanos' panacea for all difficulties came to mind: 'This too shall pass.'

Nicholas had never felt so torn inside. He longed to take her in his arms and kiss her tears away, but what would he tell the Seneschal in the morning?

Slowly, she turned around to face him again.

"You are right; this is not leading anywhere… It is true that you have made no promises, and I have made my peace with God to live in sin with you since there is no way for us to be married. But you... marrying this girl... It changes everything! I will not add adultery to the long list of my sins."

Her voice broke, but she carried on. "And quite frankly, I do not know how I could sleep alone in a cold bed when she warms yours. So, the only thing left for me to do is to leave."

Nicholas' jaw sagged; deep furrows appeared on his forehead. He wanted to say something in his own defense, but there were no words. She had spoken out of love. There had been only anguish in her voice.

"You are not going anywhere. I forbid you to!"

She gave him a doleful smile. "I'm neither your wife nor your serf; I'm a *lefteri*," she reminded him.

Pain was etched on his face. He stood helplessly, both arms outstretched as if stunned. "I don't want to lose you! I don't want you to go; wait till the morning! I will think of something. I will find a way!" That would be against all odds, and they both knew it. He tried a different tactic. "Besides, it is dark outside. It is not a good idea to leave now. Please, do not put yourself in harm's way; wait until the morning!"

The apprehension she read on his face was so profound that she heard herself agree. "All right, but you will sleep alone tonight."

*

Under the cloak of night, Amaury and a cohort of supporters descended on the palace, taking the guards unawares. Their inside men gave them access to the solar upstairs from where they charged into the king's chamber.

Henry, bedridden, remained calm. He sat up with some effort. One by one, he registered the traitors. Philip had been right about each and every one of them. "And you, too, are among them!" he said, recognizing his erstwhile dearly beloved Baldwin of Ibelin.

He had refused to believe Philip's reports, and now he felt a part of him dying inside at this treason. It was penance enough to have to humble his pride before Amaury. It seemed he would have a chamber full of witnesses, too.

He swallowed words of condemnation that sprang to mind and looked them in the eye. They would suck the very blood from his veins if they could. Until that moment, he had been slow to see the magnitude of his mistake not to heed his uncle's warnings.

Baldwin read out their proclamation; bombast and hyperbole in abundance. All the while, Amaury was watching Henry in poorly conceded triumph. Amaury was proclaimed regent that night and promised that all the king's needs would be honorably and liberally supplied; a magnanimous, albeit ephemeral, gesture from the victor to the vanquished.

*

In the stillness of the night, Lois found it impossible to rest. How different the day turned out than what she had planned! The secret hopes of a life together with him, even in sin, were utterly shattered. Nicholas' choice was obvious, and she did not have the stomach to wait till the morning to find out that he was intent upon marrying that woman after all. She should best spare him – and herself – the mortification of such a conversation.

With a sense of impending doom, she got out of bed, got dressed, and picked up the satchel she had prepared earlier. Overwhelmed with emotion, she cast a last glance around before slipping away. She headed to the stable in a headlong rush. She ran her fingers through the mare's mane to greet her, lifted herself into the saddle, and disappeared into the darkness.

*

Nicholas' breathing became heavier as he drifted into a restless sleep only to be awakened by the howling wind. He could not lie still. He missed her soft body close to his.

He got out of bed and threw open the shutters to let in air and clear his head. Why was Buenaventura willing to offer this excessive amount for a husband for his daughter? Why was he in such a rush? Was Sofia a second Antoinette? Philip should not force him to marry for a second time a woman who was carrying someone else's child. He would have to look for another groom.

Nicholas needed to think of the right words to say when he talked to Philip on the morrow. A plan was slowly firming in his mind. He resisted the temptation to tell Lois here and now. She had been pale lately. He should best let her rest and tell her first thing in the morning. He closed the shutters and got back to bed calmer, rehearsing in his mind what he would tell Philip.

He did not know how long he had been lying in bed when his head jerked up, warned as much by instinct as by the sound of approaching galloping horses. He darted out of bed, as four silhouettes rode through the gate. His first thought was to look for Lois. But she was nowhere to be found. She had left him!

A loud banging on the door demanded Nicholas' immediate attention. He opened the door, a shiver of foreboding creeping down his spine.

"Nicholas of Provence?" the group leader asked.

"Yes?"

"In the name of the law, you will come with us," he said brusquely.

Nicholas noticed that the men did not have the royal guard's insignia on their tunics. It was happening already. "On whose authority?"

"The regent's."

Nicholas followed them outside. He was not particularly surprised to see that Enric of Roussillon was amongst them. He had never made a secret of where his sympathies lay. Nicholas' eyes glinted with remembered rage at what the man had done to Albert and Guilhelm.

54

2013

Michael bolted from Lucy's kitchen and walked back to the small house. He stood by the kitchen window, hoping against hope that Lois might change her mind and cancel her date. The sound of the engine in the driveway, however, shattered the last shreds of hope. He slammed his fist against the door then flexed his fingers to ease the pain.

Pappou looked over the book he was reading and observed his grandson's bleak face without comment. Lola took a hesitant step toward Michael, saw that he had no interest in her, and waddled back to her basket.

Michael opened the fridge door and closed it again, more resoundingly than he had intended. He did the same with the dry food cupboard before he sank in an armchair and grabbed the remote, clenching his jaw. He switched channels faster than he could register what was on. With a heavy sigh, Michael turned the television off, lurched upward, and snatched his keys from the coffee table.

"You're leaving?" *pappou* asked.

"Yes, don't wait up for me." He patted Lola on the head goodbye.

"Everything all right, Michael?" *Pappou* put his book down.

"No! Everything's *not* all right. And I need to clear my head. Will you be okay on your own? I have no idea what time I'll be back – if tonight at all."

"That bad, hah?" *pappou* asked with the patience of old age.

Michael was almost out the door but veered around and took a couple of steps closer to him. "You know where Lucy is right now?"

"No! Where?" *Pappou's* voice was devoid of all expression. The man was perpetually calm.

"She's at some fancy restaurant, having dinner with her ex; despite everything!"

"So, you really love her?" *pappou* said quietly.

"You know I do."

"Have you told her that?"

"Not in so many words." *But she should know.*

"I see," *pappou* said, picking up his book.

Michael looked at him gimlet-eyed. "Please, tell me what you see because I don't know what I see. One moment I think she's my girl, and the next, she goes out with her ex!"

Pappou lowered his book again. "I see that you're too proud to open up your heart and tell her how you feel about her, and in the confusing situation she's in, she's decided to go out with her ex, who swears he loves her and has even brought his divorce papers along to prove it!"

"So, it's my fault now?" Michael stretched his arms in front of him in disbelief.

"Is that how you feel?"

Michael shook his head. "I'm off now. Don't wait up for me!"

"We'll be here when you come back. Isn't that right, Lola?" *pappou* said. Lola came over to him, and he patted her. He hated to see Michael leave like this, but he understood that he had to let off steam.

*

Lucy parked the car close to the hotel entrance. For a moment, she contemplated leaving again, but she had come for a reason, she reminded herself. She walked through the sliding glass door and found William waiting for her in the lobby. He looked handsome and sophisticated, but her heart did not beat faster at the sight of him, as it used to.

"You look dazzling," he said, looking at her from head to toe. She thanked him. "How about a pre-dinner drink?"

Lucy nodded and he signaled the waitress. She came to their table and William ordered two glasses of champagne.

"Let's get married tonight," Lucy ambushed him. It wasn't planned. The words slipped out before she could think.

"Tonight? Is it even possible?" His lips twisted into a half-hearted smile.

"Yes, it is. I checked," she lied. "Let's get married right away."

The waitress returned with their drinks, giving Sinclair a moment to breathe. He blinked. Now that he knew that the treasure was not buried under Lucy's house, he did not have to play this game any longer. But keeping Lucy onside might still be convenient.

"Wouldn't you like to plan the wedding?"

She cast her gaze down at her hands and then looked him in the eye. "It's all right, William. You can breathe now. I was only teasing." She watched the taut muscles on his face relax. He downed his drink. "There's just one thing," she said.

"What's that?"

"While you were weighing your answer, I caught myself wishing you'd say 'no'." She paused for a moment and then added, "I think this is where I say 'goodbye, William. I wish you the best.' Now, if you'll excuse me, there's somewhere I need to be."

"Michael?" he guessed.

"Yes," she replied with a radian confidence. She stood up and he followed suit. She planted a kiss on his cheek. "Goodbye, William!"

He held her gaze a moment longer before saying, "Goodbye, Lucy!" He watched her walk out of the hotel.

*

Michael had no idea how long he had been driving around aimlessly before he found himself parking outside his kitchen in Agios Silas. He went into his office and took a bottle of *pinot noir* out of the wine cooler and poured himself a glass. He took a generous swallow, poured himself some more, and inserted a Pavarotti CD in the CD player.

In the company of *nessun dorma*, he enjoyed the wine. He closed his eyes, concentrating on his other senses, but Lucy's smiling face disturbed his ephemeral tranquility. The thought of losing her – again – before he'd even had a chance to fight for her, left a bitter taste in his mouth.

His relationship with Lucy was like a *Château Pétrus* served at the wrong temperature, he decided: rare and exquisite but not thoroughly enjoyable. They were perfect for each other but hadn't found a way to pure gratification yet. He poured himself one more glass and turned the music up. The tenor's *vincerò* soared through the room while Michael sang along.

He jumped to his feet. The combination of Pavarotti and good wine had always had an inspiring effect on him. The new order that had come in that afternoon asked for new recipes based on local ingredients. What if he used *hiromeri*, *halloumi*, and dried figs dipped in *commandaria* in small pouches of *phylo* pastry, tied with chive leaves? He would call that *amuse bouche* 'Adonis and Aphrodite'.

His lips twisted in a mirthless smile as he remembered their day out at Aphrodite's Baths. He put the thought from his mind with some effort and grabbed his uniform, intending upon being creative.

*

Seated in his Hyundai Azera, hidden in the shadows of the night, a bulky man covered in tattoos waited patiently for Michael to finish his experiments so that he could begin his work.

55

1306

Right after the Morning Prayer, Peyre scurried to the palace. Already from the distance, he sensed trouble brewing. There were more guards than usual, edgy and alarmed, working in tandem, as if watching each other's back. They searched every single cart and looked through all the baskets that were carried through the gate. The bishop had not exaggerated after all, Peyre thought, standing in line. He did not like the way the guards pestered the peasants but thought it wiser to hold his tongue.

"State your name and business," one of the guards asked the barrel-chested man in front of Peyre.

"Buenaventura. I have come to see the Seneschal." The guards exchanged a glance, and the elder of the two said that the Seneschal was not there. Buenaventura was reluctant to leave. "What about his scribe?" he asked, and Peyre strained his ears.

"If he hasn't been hanged already, good luck finding him in the dungeons," the younger guard said and cackled. Dread hit Peyre in the gut. He said a quick, silent prayer, hoping he had not come too late.

Buenaventura settled prudently on walking away. He did not know what had happened in the course of the night, but it did not matter. It was not his fight. He was relieved he was still in possession of the hundred bezants, but incensed that his efforts at finding a husband for his pregnant daughter had been muddled.

*

A warder gripped a torch and escorted Peyre down the cold, humid, dark aisle. Pain had long vanquished prisoners' pride and their groans of agony and cries for mercy washed over Peyre in chilling waves, but the warder seemed to take no notice. The light was dim, and Peyre paused for a moment to adjust his eyesight accordingly. It seemed as though half the town was locked up. The overcrowded cells did not compare to the privacy Albert and Guilhelm had enjoyed in the empty dungeons in Famagusta.

"Peyre!" Nicholas moved closer to the door. The two brothers touched hands fleetingly.

"Stay clear of the door," the warder bellowed, and they pulled back.

"Nicholas, what are you accused of?" Peyre asked aware of the brief time allotted to him with his brother.

"Nothing yet. They said the regent needs to ask me some questions, but no one has asked me anything yet. It was just a pretext to drag me here – not just me apparently." He jerked his head to the other inmates.

Peyre observed his brother's calm self-possession. "We will do everything we can to get you out," he promised.

"I know... Peyre, I need you to find Lois. Tell her I know I have failed her and I regret that."

Peyre was not surprised. During his last visit, Father had told him about their affair. "Nicholas, you have been kind to her all your life. It cannot all go to waste because of a mistake you may have made."

"I would die for her," he blurted out, more to himself.

"Better you should live for her," Peyre said.

"Time is up!" the warder cried out.

"Courage, brother! Find strength in prayer until we get you out of here!"

Peyre left the dungeons, wading into the gathered crowd, women and children, desperately seeking their loved ones. The entire realm was torn asunder, losing its soul. It was the devil's work. Peyre sought to vanquish the fear for his brother's life, finding respite in prayer. He resolved to return to Famagusta at once and speak with the bishop, the only bishop who had not taken sides. Peyre believed the time had come for a neutral man of God to intervene.

*

The regent's supporters made sure the news of his seizing power reached every corner of the island. To stoke fear and discourage resistance, the news was spiced with the threat that all those who did not display loyalty to the regent would be judged to be against him. Hanging was the reward for disloyalty, and all of the regent's loyal supporters were expected to attend. Dissidents whom Amaury considered still useful were stripped of power and thrown into the dungeons. Some were under house arrest or deported to Armenia.

Amaury sat in the oriel window in the solar and looked out at his guards performing their duties painstakingly. He knew that the arrests caused an outcry, but he was resolved to hold his course till the furor died down. He took a deep breath. The island was being cleansed of the plague of his brother's supporters. The air already tasted purer.

*

Kontostephanos' sister had changed her name to Eleni when she made her religious vows. She was very old now, waiting for the Lord to take her. She had readied herself for that. A childhood accident had left her with a stiff right leg and a limp that only got worse as time went by. Leaning heavily on a cane, she passed by a row of praying nuns; sibilant voices and burning incense wafting through the air.

In the quiet anteroom, Lois poured out her heart to her. The nun ran a compassionate eye over her. "So, you are with child and he is to marry one of his own?" Lois nodded. "Your fault is human, and frailty is in our nature. You are not the first woman to bear a child out of wedlock," she remarked calmly. "You are welcome to stay here with us for as long as you like."

"Thank you!" Lois said.

Eleni discerned there was more that Lois did not feel ready to reveal. "Have you ever thought of this love child you are carrying as a blessing?" Lois raised her befogged eyes to her. "The ways of the Almighty are beyond our understanding, and although we only see the knots at the back of the tapestry He is embroidering for us up there, rest assured He loves all His children. He may test us, but he would never forsake us. The ones He tests most are dearest to Him."

Lois wondered if she preferred to be less dear to Him and less tormented but held her tongue.

"It is vain to think that we can plan our lives. We do not know what the future holds. This child might bring you immeasurable happiness."

"Or misery; an unmarried mother with a bastard in her arms," she blurted out.

"Who is to say that if you take the child's life, your life will be happier?"

"Maybe not happier, but easier," she said, yet in her heart she knew the nun was right. She could never hurt her baby.

"Then let us pray together to discover the will of God."

*

At the Grand Commandery, which Amaury had taken from the Hospitallers and granted to the Templars as a token of his appreciation for their support in overthrowing his brother, Albert and Guilhelm waited patiently for Pierre of Montpellier, the Templar knight Nicholas had dealt with in the past, to come to the gate. In a few words, they briefed him about Nicholas' incarceration and asked for help. Montpellier was not optimistic but promised to see what he could do.

They thanked him and rode back to the manor, worried not only about Nicholas but also about Provence. Nicholas' imprisonment and this fluid situation fraught with uncertainty were wearing him out.

*

Lois had resolved to take Eleni up on her offer and stay at the convent until the baby was born. The nuns provided food and shelter, and Lois helped out any way she could. She was not the only unmarried mother there, but she kept to herself, despite other women's overtures.

She was collecting herbs when a messenger came to the nunnery, wreaking havoc with the news of the hanged supporters of the king. Lois thought her heart stopped; she could not breathe or hear any more of this. She needed to mourn in private. It had only been a few days since she had meant to tell Nicholas that she was with child; his child. She had been so happy then, an eternity ago.

How was it possible? Why had God allowed all this to happen? No matter how she turned things over in her mind, nothing made sense. Her head was spinning. An iron grip of a sharp pain burned inside her, tearing her apart; suffocating her. She bent over and retched.

As if in a trance, she trudged through the dusty land, oblivious to the heat and the thorns scratching her feet and calves, tearing her dress. She could not accept that Nicholas was dead, though the messenger had made it clear that no dissident's life had been spared.

Mad with sorrow and frustration, Lois wandered for as long as her legs could carry her. It was dark when she dropped with exhaustion on the gravel of the wasteland abutting the nunnery, taking no notice of her thirst or her sun-scorched skin.

"Nicholas! Oh Lord, no, not Nicholas!" She let out a loud, pro-longed, mournful cry that scared away a murder of crows. All her sorrow washed away in hot, salty tears. She fought for breath, her whole body shaking uncontrollably. Would the pain ever go away?

Now she knew what misery and loneliness felt like. Her only hope was the child growing inside her. For this, she felt deeply grateful. How could she have doubted God? How vain she had been! In that instant, she knew beyond doubt that she would bring his child into this world, raise him and care for him. She would make sure to tell him how great his father had been. She was convinced that she was carrying his son.

She wept and wept until she cried herself into a fitful sleep that brought no rest with it. In her dream, thick fog started to clear very slowly. In the moonless night, she made out a gloomy, stooped figure in the distance, but she was not afraid. She moved closer, till she could see him clearly. It was Nicholas! His handsome face looked sorrowful and tormented. He lifted his head and called out her name, his arms spread out as if trying to reach her. "*Amor meu! What have they done to you?*" she murmured. He called her name again, so loudly that she was startled out of sleep.

In a moment of insight, Lois knew that she should return to the *casale* if for no other reason than Provence had the right to know about his grandchild.

*

Lois reached the Provence *casale* bone-tired, travel-stained, and saddle sore. In the manor, there was only Emilia, busying herself with supper.

"Lois! Is that really you?" Emilia said, throwing her arms around her. "You look so pale! Are you ill?" She scrutinized the young woman's face with a worried frown.

"Just tired," Lois said, thinking that Provence should be the first to know the news about Nicholas' baby.

"Come! I'll make you some tea and something to eat."

"Thank you, Emilia… The master's not here?" she asked, taking a seat at the table.

"He is at the grain warehouse, trying to find a way to keep the grain thieves away."

"Grain thieves?"

"Yes, they emptied the grain warehouse of the Count of Jaffa at Episkopia last night. They could strike here tonight for all we know, so everyone is alert… This is the last thing the master needs right now. He was going to meet with the count to discuss…" Emilia clamped abruptly, drawing a sharp breath. "Have you heard about Nicholas?"

Lois nodded, tears forming on her eyelashes. She was too exhausted to try and hold them back.

"It's terrible that Nicholas is languishing in the dungeons, but his father and brothers are doing everything they can to get him out. It's hard though. No one seems to want to madden Amaury."

Lois jerked her head around. *Dungeons?* "You mean … Nicholas is alive?"

"If you can call this a life," Emilia said.

"I thought he was dead!" Lois said, smiling with hope for the first time in a long time. "People say that Amaury has hanged *all* dissidents," she added, dismayed.

"Not Nicholas." *Not yet.*

"I have to go to him!"

"You will never get there the way you are. Eat, rest tonight, and if you feel better in the morning, you can go." Emilia's voice was authoritative.

There was a knock on the kitchen door.

"Come in!" Emilia said, and the door opened slowly. "Theodore!" she cried out, astonished.

"Hello, Emilia!" Theodore said. "What? No hug for me?" he asked playfully, spreading his arms in front of him.

"A spank is what you should get, vanishing into the blue," Emilia replied with feigned annoyance but hugged him all the same.

"It's a long story," Theodore said, his eyes resting on Lois. "How about a hug from my wife?"

Emilia's brows furrowed. "Your *wife?*"

"Another long story," Theodore said, his eyes lingering on Lois' pale face. He sat beside her and took her hand in his. "I hoped I would find you here," he said quietly.

"I need to check the hen house for eggs," Emilia said, leaving discreetly.

Theodore waited until she had closed the door behind her. "You look as if you have seen a ghost. Not that I fault you."

"What... What happened that day?" Lois found her voice again at last.

"I knew the men who attacked us. Many years ago, when I first started going from village to village with my divining rod, I showed them the location of groundwater on their father's estate. Apparently, they did not find any. It was rotten luck that we ran into them, especially on our wedding day. They wanted to teach me a lesson, I guess." He shrugged.

Lois found his insouciance maddening. "I thought they beat you to death or that you died while trying to get help!"

"I'm sorry you had to go through this suffering." He sounded contrite, but she was not entirely mollified. "You are not so wrong though. They nigh sent me to my grave. They only stopped when I told them I could search for groundwater again, so they dragged me to their estate. They kept everything we had for good measure; everything but Julius. He can be stubborn when he wants to," he said with a mirthful smile.

She shook her head in disbelief. "Did you even wonder if I was dead or alive?"

That stung, but Theodore managed an affable smile. "They said you were alive, but they did not want to take you with us. I could only hope that you would make it back to the estate when you came round or that some Good Samaritan would pass by," he said. He caressed her hair. "There was nothing I could do then, Lois. But I have come for you now; to take you with me."

"And go where, Theodore?" There was an edge to her voice.

He narrowed his brow. "If my memory serves, last time we spoke, you wanted to see a bit of the world."

"That was before we were battered." She saw his eyes flash with anger and bit her lip. It was stupid to antagonize him.

But then he smiled at her. "It will not happen again."

"How can you be so sure?"

"Because I am now involved in other things."

"What things?"

He cast a cursory glance around, made sure there was no one within earshot, leaned into her, and said almost in a whisper, "Now that the regent's and the king's men are busy butchering one another, now is our opportunity!"

Lois tried to conceal her involuntary shudder at the thought of Nicholas being butchered and tried to focus on what Theodore was saying. "Opportunity for what?" she asked as Emilia came back with a basket full of eggs.

"All in good time; go get ready now. We are leaving!"

Emilia noticed a shadow of panic crossing over Lois' face. "Leaving? You are not going anywhere! Lois has just come home and she's not well enough to travel. And anyway, I was going to make you something to eat." Emilia spoke in a do-not-argue-with-me tone of voice, and Theodore knew better than to contradict her.

He flashed a wide smile at her and rose to his feet. "The truth is I'm famished. Tell me how I can help!"

56

2013

Michael had not come back yet when Lucy parked the jeep in the driveway. She checked the time. It was only ten. He could be anywhere. She was itching to call him but decided it was better to talk face to face. She would wait for him at home; or perhaps at his place? Ten was usually *pappou's* bedtime. Would she be waking him up? Lola's barking resolved this dilemma.

Lucy noticed *pappou* peering through the window and waved to him. He opened the door, and Lola came out to greet her. Lucy rewarded her with a huge cuddle.

"*Kalispera, pappou!* You're still up?" *Perfect!*

"*Kalispera*, Lucy! Look at you; don't you look wonderful tonight!"

"Thank you!" She flashed a smile at him.

"I'm having cocoa. Want some?"

"Sounds great! If it's not too much trouble that is."

"No trouble at all," *pappou* said and took to making a cup for her while she let Lola in and closed the door behind her. "How was your date?" he asked, handing her a mug.

Lucy let out a sigh. "It was not a date, *pappou*," she said, wondering what Michael had told him.

"You could have fooled me with that dress," he smiled kindly. "But what does an old guy like me know?"

"A lot, for sure! *Pappou*, I only went out with William to test myself, to see how I feel around him."

"And? How do you feel around him?" There was no judgment or mockery in his voice.

"Nothing special; not like when I'm with Michael."

"I see. Does Michael know that?"

"Not yet, but I'm going to tell him when he comes home," she said coyly. *Pappou* nodded, smiling kindly.

The corners of her lips suddenly twitched. "I tried to explain to him earlier why I had to do that, but he wouldn't listen. It was as if I had to choose right there and then! Do you know what I mean?" It was important for her that *pappou* would see her point of view.

"I do understand, my sweet girl, but maybe you should try and understand him, too. It's only been a couple of months since his bride ran away, and now this. It's going to take him some time to trust again."

"But I didn't run away. I only made sure that I really want to do this with all my heart; that there won't be any 'what ifs'."

"I know. I know. Give him some time. He'll come around. He'll come back when he's ready. Men sometimes need to be by themselves when there are things on their minds."

She took a sip. "What did he say?"

"Not much. I've never seen him like this before, so wound up, so tense. He said he had some thinking to do."

"Can I wait for him here if you don't mind?"

"Sure. It might take a while though. Why don't you take his bed? It's more comfortable than the little sofa."

She smiled. "Thank you! Thank you for everything!"

"There's nothing to thank me for."

Lucy finished her cocoa and made herself comfortable in Michael's bed, mentally rehearsing what she would tell him when he came back.

57

1306

Lois thanked Emilia for the meal, said she would go for a walk, and asked Theodore to join her. He was about to disagree, but the unwavering look in her eyes made him change his mind.

"Whatever my wife desires," he said, rising to his feet.

"I suppose there's a reason why you are procrastinating?" he asked as they walked through the vineyards.

"Theodore, a lot has happened since our wedding day," she said, choosing her words with care. "When I came to that day, I looked for you but you were not there. I waited for you, but you never came back for me." Theodore opened his mouth to protest, but Lois went on with resolve, "I thought you were dead. I could not walk all the way back home to the *casale*. Neither could I go back to Amaury's estates. The only thing left for me to do was to go to Nicholas."

Theodore stopped walking. She never called Nicholas the 'master', and it riled him profoundly. He drew a deep breath to calm himself. Quarreling would get them nowhere. He looked at her winsome face and those beautiful chestnut eyes that had kept him captive since the market day at Episkopia.

There was something in the way she lowered her gaze that made his stomach muscles contract. "Did I ... lose you?" The words tasted foul in his mouth.

Lois raised her gaze to look at him. "How can you lose someone you never had?"

"You are *my wife!*" he reminded her.

"Only for a couple of hours. And not even in every sense of the word."

Theodore looked away and then back at her. He would not lose her again. "We will forget about what happened. You are still my wife."

"I do not know if we can forget about it. I'm with child."

Theodore's heart stopped. He reminded himself to breathe. He turned his back on her, bringing both hands to his head, cursing under his breath. The barbarians, he thought bitterly, they take a woman just because they can. And they call themselves noble! His own mother had given birth to a boy that was the spitting image of the master. He turned to face Lois again.

"Well, you are not the first one to carry a foreigner's bastard," he said sourly and saw the hurt look on her face. He snorted, shaking his head in disbelief. "You want to keep it?"

"Yes!"

He was startled by the intensity of her monosyllabic reply. She was about to tell him that she had to go and find Nicholas in the dungeons in the capital, but she feared that it would be more than he could handle for one day. After all, she was his wife in the eyes of God and the law, and she must obey him.

Theodore realized he must make a snap decision: either leave her behind or accept her circumstances. Was she worth it? No doubt about it!

"Very well then; keep it. No one needs to know the baby's not mine." He summoned the resolute smile of a gracious looser. "I will take care of both of you. Just be nice to me. Are we in agreement?"

"You are a good man, Theodore," Lois said dutifully, lowering her gaze. Theodore might have mistaken this for submission if he had been foolish enough. But he was not a fool.

"Now, let us leave this place," he said, eager to be on the road again.

*

They bid Emilia goodbye, and she gave them a satchel for the road.
Lois was thankful that Theodore let her ride Julius. The mule was
traveling at no more than a sedate walk, and Theodore fell into
step with it.

"Tell me when you need to rest," he said and was quiet after that.

His silence gave her time to think her own thoughts. Thoughts of
how her life would be from now: a life with Theodore; without
Nicholas. Her mind was filled with poignant memories of happier
days. At least, she would have his baby if God willed it. She had
heard stories of how easy it was to lose a baby or die at birth. She
brought her palm to her belly, lifting her gaze to the sky. *Thy will
be done!*

They had been on the road for a couple of hours when Lois found
the nerve to ask, "Where are we going?"

"Psimolophou first; Potamia after that."

"What are we doing in Psimolophou?"

"Meeting two friends."

"And in Potamia? Where is Potamia anyway?"

"Potamia is a village just before Nicosia," Theodore said, and Lois'
heart leaped. She wondered whether there was a way she could see
Nicholas one last time.

"What's in Potamia?" she asked, trying to maintain an indifferent
tone of voice.

Theodore locked eyes with her and said, "A grain warehouse."

Lois' eyes widened. "The grain warehouse?" Emilia's chatter about
the grain thieves sprang to mind. She could hardly picture carefree
Theodore as a grain thief.

"Now that all these foreigners are at each other's throats, it is our
chance to take back what is rightfully ours." There was no doubt in

Theodore's mind that nothing served Cypriot interest more than Frankish discord.

Lois gasped. "What are you saying, Theodore? Are you going to start a rebellion?"

"We are not ready for a rebellion yet, but we can cause the Franks some damage and profit from it at the same time. When was the last time you looked around you, Lois? People are starving. We can begin by feeding them. We did it last night in Episkopia. God willing, we will do it again in Psimolophou. My friends have already prepared the ground for that. There is no greater reward than the grateful look of a hungry child being fed."

He spoke with fervor, and Lois could only imagine how he enchanted simple peasants. "I daresay I have never seen you in this light." There was a touch of admiration in her voice that made him feel good about himself.

"It is you actually who gave me the idea when you spoke of Amaury's plans. If a brother can turn against his own brother, why should we not turn against our oppressors? Fight for our rights — our land?"

Lois felt torn inside. It was as if she could hear her grandfather speak. What Theodore said made perfect sense to her, but that made Nicholas, the father of her child, the enemy, and that was too much to bear.

"But how are you going to fight? You have no weapons!"

"We have our brains. We know we are no match for their knights if it comes to a confrontation. We will ambush them. They do not expect simple peasants to have a plan. We choose our targets carefully; never in the same area or direction. So they have no inkling where we might strike next. It is called the element of surprise!"

Theodore pulled in the reins on Julius and helped her down. He let the mule graze by the river and filled his goatskin bottle with fresh water. "Here, you must be thirsty," he said.

She thanked him and took a sip. As she gave it back to him, he held her hand in his a while longer. He slid his arms around her waist and drew her to him, but she pulled herself gently back.

"It is Wednesday today."

"And?"

"It is a fasting day."

He nodded and let go of her grudgingly.

*

Nicholas was now in complete solitude, with no company but his own thoughts. He had been moved to a tiny dark cell, barely larger than the size of a straw pallet. Once a day a warder threw a piece of stale bread and a cup of water into his cell. Nicholas kept track of his days in confinement by making marks on the wall, thirty-seven so far. For these last thirty-seven days, his life had been suspended.

Isolation had insidiously begun to take its toll, eating away at his soul, spirit, and brain. He sometimes caught himself speaking to himself and tried hard to keep despair at bay. He was deprived of sunlight. That was almost worse than torture.

The dungeons were permeated with a sense of finality; you were left to rot. Relief only came when the warder came to take you to the gallows. Nicholas slapped his face as if to awaken from a nightmare. He had to banish morbid thoughts. He was certain that his father and brothers were talking to anyone who might help. Yet in his dark and cold cell, his only consolation was the memory of Lois.

In his lonely torment, her image kept him company. He recalled every treasured moment they had spent together, from the day she arrived at the *casale* after her parents' death until the dreadful evening of his arrest. How he wished he could turn time back to the moment he had decided to talk to Philip. He would have confessed his love for her then. If he were to be hanged this instant, this would be his only regret.

He shivered at the memory of her in his arms, of how uninhibitedly she relished their love making, almost as much as he did; initiated it even. Of how she let him experiment with her body, driving his imagination wild. He jumped to his feet and took the two strides from one side of the cell to the other and back. He had to stay alive – for her.

He vowed that if by a miracle he survived, he would ask her to marry him. In these thirty-seven days, he'd had time to think. He dared to dream that he had even found a way to make things right by her if only he were given a second chance.

58

2013

It was well past midnight when Michael turned the key and opened the house door. He took his jacket off, threw it over the back of a chair, and padded to his room. He turned the light on and was surprised to find Lucy sleeping in his bed. Though he was still not happy about the way she had handled things, he could not help grinning with satisfaction at the thought that she had come home to him.

He watched her breathing steadily. She looked so peaceful and beautiful in her sleep. He stroked her hair gently, and she opened her heavy eyelids.

"What are you doing here?" he whispered.

Lucy got out of bed while Michael stared at the daring décolletage. She smoothed the hair from her face. "Waiting to see that you're home all right. There's something I need to tell you," she said, straightening her shoulders.

Michael's gaze lingered a moment longer on her breasts before he met her eyes.

"Look! We may agree to disagree about the dinner thing tonight, but I don't believe I made a mistake." She brought her hand to her heart. "I'm sure beyond doubt now," she spoke slowly, drawing her words out for emphasis, "that you're the one for me. Now, I don't want to waste another day without you, but if you need time to think, I understand. You know where to find me."

She grabbed her bag and walked out of the room with her head held high. Michael did not stop her. He could have kissed her right there, but he wanted to leave room for anticipation. He heard the house door close behind her.

Pappou appeared in the hallway. "Are you done thinking yet?"

"I am," Michael said, smothering a smile.

"Then what are you still doing here?"

"Thank you for keeping an eye on her," he said.

"No problem. Go now!" *pappou* said, but Michael was already grabbing his jacket on his way out.

Moments later Lucy answered the door, her heart thudding. Michael was propping up the doorpost with his jacket suspended over the index finger of his left hand; a freshly cut rose in his right hand. He let her take in its scent, locked eyes with her, and caressed her cheek with the rose. His nostrils flared as he let his fervent gaze linger on her from top to bottom.

"Have I told you how irresistible you look in that dress?"

Lucy draped her arms around his neck, claiming his lips. Michael stepped inside, wrapping his arms around her and closing the door with one leg.

*

Michael's cell rang in Lucy's bedroom in the small hours. Disoriented, he groped on the bedside table for his cell phone.

"Mr. Costa?" an unknown voice asked.

"Yes?' Michael turned on the light and checked the time. It was past three. Lucy sat up beside him, frowning.

"Mr. Costa, are you the owner of *Gourmet Catering MC?*"

"Who's this?"

"This is inspector Alexandrou. Sorry to wake you up at this ungodly hour. I'm afraid I have some bad news. There's been a fire. We're looking into it as we speak. I was wondering whether you might be able to come here. We have a few questions we'd like to ask you."

Michael held his breath, his mind racing. "Sure. I can be there in twenty minutes." He ended the call and jumped out of bed.

"Who was that?" Lucy asked, springing to her feet.

"The police. There's been a fire," he said, pulling his pants up and grabbing his shirt.

"Oh my God! I'm coming with you."

59

1306

The sun was almost in mid-sky when Theodore and his entourage reached Potamia, drunk on a recently gained sense of dignity and self-esteem. They had wagered the impossible and came back invincible. The word of their arrival spread in the small village in no time, and all the serfs assembled outside the tiny Orthodox chapel to welcome their heroes.

Theodore reined in Julius, his gaze scanning the small crowd for Lois. Their eyes met, and he reached her in two long-legged strides. She smiled widely, relieved he was unharmed, and his heart leaped with hope.

The gathered peasants around them celebrated with collective pride and euphoria. "Kiss her! Kiss her!" some of the men teased them.

Theodore was not sure he could read Lois' face and planted a quick kiss on her lips. He had looked forward to a more feverish first kiss, but that would have to suffice for the moment. The people around them clapped and whistled, and Lois blushed.

"I see you're glad I'm back," he said cheerfully, eliciting a timid smile from her. He squeezed her hand gently.

Then he turned to the peasants and cried out, "Help yourselves to the grains, courtesy of the knight of Potamia."

His words were followed by a new round of cheers and laughter. Theodore's men began sharing out the grains. Within minutes, the cart was empty. Not before long, the villagers came back, bringing whatever food and ale they had, and a spontaneous feast ensued with singing and dancing.

"To our heroes!" someone cried out, and they all raised their cups.

"To Theodore! Next time, we will come with you," another man said. "Yes, and we can help ourselves to more than just the grains!" someone else called out.

Laughter rippled through the small crowd, followed by more praise for the leader of the rebellion and bold statements for future attacks, fused with constant toasts and the refilling of cups.

Theodore had not seen Lois so relaxed since the harvest feast at the Provence *casale* and dared to hope that he was gradually winning her over. He casually leaned into her. "Will you dance with me?" he whispered in her ear, a soft kiss brushing her temple.

Lois would have loved to allow herself to feel carefree, but caution won out. For anyone who might be watching, she flashed a smile at him and whispered in his ear, "I do not think it would be good for the baby. There will be plenty of time for dancing later."

"That's right. We have a whole life ahead of us!" he said, cupping her hand.

"But you can go ahead and dance," she encouraged him.

"I know. I would rather sit here and talk with you."

His gaze was too intense to hold, and Lois looked away at the serfs dancing.

*

It was dark when the feast slowly came to an end. Theodore and Lois wished the serfs good night and headed for the hut where they were being put up for the night. Theodore reeled backward several times, and Lois put his arm around her shoulders and supported him by the waist. With some difficulty, she managed to throw open the door and helped him lie down.

"Come lie with me," he said eagerly.

"You're drunk!" she replied, keeping her tone of voice light.

Theodore stared at her sadly. "This is the third time you have refused to lie with me. If it is not a fasting day, you are unwell or I'm drunk. You should be careful, Lois. I might not ask you again. You might have to come to me of your own accord. Pray that when you need a man's touch, I will still want you."

Lois was thunderstruck. She knew she could not go on making excuses forever, but she had not expected such a warning.

*

When Lois awoke the next morning, the hut was empty. She searched for Theodore in the village and then in the adjacent fields. Eventually, she saw him sprawling cross-legged in the grass in the shade of an old walnut tree with his men. She walked over to them and heard them burst into laughter; the unsteady, exultant laughter of those who had dared against all odds and somehow won. She felt strangely excluded.

Theodore and his companions looked as invigorated as ever, and Lois sensed last night's self-worth turning into conceit as she listened to their conversation about where to strike next and when. She wanted to caution them against recklessness, but it was not a woman's place to interrupt men.

All the time she had been standing there, not once did Theodore cast a glance in her direction. She did not know why she felt exasperated by the way he ignored her completely. Had she become so vain that she loved the father of her child, but sought her husband's attention? The irony dawned on her.

When the discussion seemed to cease, Lois seized the moment. "Husband," she said, aware that she was addressing him this way for the first time. "I need to show you something when you are finished here."

She did not. She merely wanted to rouse his curiosity, but he regarded her with polite disinterest. It stung, and she walked away irked.

*

It was in the gloaming when Theodore finally deigned to put in an appearance. "What is it you wanted to show me?" he asked nonchalantly when they sat down to have supper.

Lois repressed the urge to scold him for disregarding her all day long, but only with considerable effort. "Theodore, what you are planning is madness!" she blurted out and bit her lip. Antagonizing him would be pointless.

A sardonic smile touched his mouth. "You have a better stratagem to suggest?"

Oblivious to his sarcasm, Lois went on, "I thank God you succeeded yesterday, but do you really believe your luck can last forever? You want to attack the palace grain warehouse, but you are hopelessly outnumbered!"

He snorted. "Why are you so troubled, Lois? If I live, I will look after you. If I die, you can go back to your precious Nicholas."

She shook her head. With an intense effort of will, she sought to keep her temper in check. "Do you really think I do not care about what happens to you? Do you?" She spoke emphatically.

Theodore blinked.

"I will not rest until you have come back." Her eyes bored into his. "If you survive this, I will feel relief. And if you die, I will grieve. Whatever the case, I cannot go back to my precious Nicholas. Even if he is still alive, he is locked up in the dungeons." She fought for breath. Why did she feel so livid?

Theodore looked at her long and hard. When he spoke, his voice was bitter and barely audible. "All this time, you have been refusing my bed for a man condemned to death."

Lois lowered her eyes for just a moment. Then she squared her shoulders and looked him straight in the eye. "What did you expect, Theodore? I have known him all my life, loved him all my life, and then you show up at the *casale* and speak of marriage. Then, all of a sudden, you vanish off the face of the world without a word. Chance has it that we get wed for an hour or two and, because of you, we are attacked, and you abandon me."

He opened his mouth to protest, but she raised a hand to silence him and went on, "There I am, in the middle of nowhere, thinking you are dead, having nowhere to go to but to Nicholas. Things happen, and I now I carry his child. I cannot change any of this, but that does not mean I do not care if you live or die. It does not mean I cannot learn to love you one day if you are patient with me. God knows how I look up to you for living your life by your own rules, for carrying out this rebellion almost single-handedly. But breaking into the palace grain warehouse is pure madness, and I cannot, will not, be silent. All I have are my words to try and talk you out of this."

She felt her cheeks flush crimson red and was surprised at the fervor in her voice. His hand closed over hers. "You are such a remarkable woman, Lois! If God wills it, we will be one, you and I. But this is my destiny. This is the moment when simple serfs have the guts to fight for themselves. I cannot take that away from them! I cannot let their hopes falter and crumble."

"Theodore —"

He ran a thumb over her bottom lip. "If I come back alive, will you lie with me?" He looked at her so intensely, as if his life depended upon her answer. Lois could hardly breathe.

"Will you not go if I do?" she whispered.

He lowered his head slowly and savored her lips. "Don't do it out of pity! Do it because you want me in your arms! I have waited so long. What's one more day?"

*

Day had not broken yet when Theodore pulled the reins on Julius at the palace gateway. For the sake of the cause, the poor creature drew a cart laden with rebels, hidden in butts, and a keg of ale.

"You're too early," one of the guards said. "We cannot let anyone in before sunrise."

"Of course, I understand. It's just that my wife is close to giving birth, and if I do not deliver this ale at the alehouse, they will not order from me again, and I cannot afford to lose my best customer." His voice was pleading. It was Lois' pregnancy that had sparked the idea.

The guards exchanged a meaningful look. "Ale, you said?"

"Aye, good ale. I have brought an extra keg in case I could make the delivery so early," Theodore played along.

"Why not leave the extra keg here with us?" one of the guards said.

"Thank you, my lord," Theodore said and waited for the guards to unload the keg.

As he rode on, he heard them call their colleagues to join them. So far so good, Theodore thought, and led Julius behind the alehouse and in front of the grain warehouse. He checked the deserted streets. Everyone was abed at this ungodly hour. He gave the signal, and the covers of the butts opened noiselessly in the stillness of the night. The rebels skulked to the warehouse, forced the lock easily, and began to carry sacks of grain to the cart briskly. No sooner had the last sack been loaded than Theodore covered the cargo and drove off.

At the gateway, he slowed down and waved at the merry guards who hardly paid heed to him.

*

Lois opened her eyes languidly. She was surprised Theodore was not by her side. The entire village had celebrated the rebels' latest success until late at night, and Lois thought Theodore would sleep all through the day.

She had recoiled from his touch the night before, and he had been gentle and patient with her until she could bear it. But Theodore was not Nicholas. She doubted she would ever enjoy making love again. She pushed the bed cover aside and the thought to the back of her mind. She was Theodore's wife; her body belonged to him now.

She got dressed and searched for him, unable to shake off a nagging suspicion that something was amiss. One of the women in the fields said that Theodore had gone to the palace together with all the village men. They had come up with a new plan.

Lois was filled with apprehension. She could not fathom what had made him change his strategy of never hitting twice at the same place. There was nothing she could do now, but wait and pray.

60

2013

Michael and Lucy took the Agios Silas exit with a sick, worried feeling in the pit of their stomachs. The smoke rising in the distance made the fire real. They drove in dreadful deafening silence.

Fire engines and police cars parked haphazardly attested to the devastating catastrophe. The firefighters were pumping water into the building. Flames were still shooting out of the window, and smoke was billowing out of the eaves.

Michael and Lucy looked about them utterly shocked. She shook her head in disbelief. "Oh, Michael, I'm so sorry! Is there anything I can do?"

"Help me clean up the mess when they let us in?" he said lightly, but Lucy sensed the strain behind his smile.

"Mr. Costa?" A man in civilian clothes approached them.

"Yes?"

He introduced himself as the inspector who had notified them. "This is an unusually clear case of arson; as if someone is sending you a message. It looks like the fire began due to the explosion of a propane tank over there in that corner," he explained, pointing in that direction. "We need to know if you have any enemies. Is there anyone who might want to harm you? A competitor perhaps? Anyone you owe money to?" *A jealous husband or boyfriend?*

Michael shook his head. "No. I have no enemies; I don't owe anyone anything, other than the bank, and I don't believe that my competitors would ever do anything like this."

"Is the place insured? I'm afraid all the furniture and equipment's been destroyed."

Michael nodded slowly. He had insured the place for about half of what it was worth in order to save on the insurance premium, he explained. Good luck with getting any money out of the insurance company if this was arson anyway, he thought.

"Here's my card. They'll want to get in touch with me," the inspector said, taking the ringing cell phone out of his pocket and taking a few steps away from them.

Michael turned to Lucy. "Any chance you might have a few hundred thousand Euros lying around?" he asked jokingly.

"Oh, Michael," she said, stroking his arm. "We'll figure this out somehow."

*

Lucy and Michael had drifted in and out of sleep for a couple of hours before Lucy's alarm rang. They had a busy day ahead of them, and the sooner they dealt with this the better. She got out of bed and made coffee, letting him doze for a few more minutes.

He was ending a call when she came back with two steaming mugs. "Who was that?" she asked, getting under the covers.

He took a sip from the mug she offered him and placed his cell phone on the bedside table. "That was the realtor. They've just made a new offer, three times the market price." They exchanged an incredulous look.

"They must want that little house very badly," Lucy remarked. "I wonder if the arson might have anything to do with it."

"I've asked myself that same question."

"What did you tell them?" She took a sip.

"Well, I told them that the house is for sale on one condition: that *pappou* can go on living there for as long as he lives."

"Did they accept?"

"That's the strange part. They did. I still don't understand why they would want it so badly. And if they do, how come they're willing to wait? It doesn't make sense. They'll draft the contract today."

"Today already? Who are these people?"

"That's just it. They want to remain anonymous."

"Is this even legal?"

"So it seems. Anyway, my lawyer will look at the contract before I sign it."

Lucy nodded in agreement. Michael took a sip and placed his mug next to his cell. "I guess this means we don't have to worry about finding the money to start over again."

"Mm, so it seems." She smiled.

"And it seems we're not in a hurry to leave either," he said playfully, caressing her thigh under the cover.

*

Sinclair waited anxiously for the Grand Master to pick up. "They've accepted on the one condition that the old man goes on living there until his death," he reported. "But old men die in their sleep all the time," he added, holding his breath.

There was a long silence as the elderly man on the other end of the line considered his words. Eventually, he said, "We are patient people, Professor. We have waited for centuries. A few more years won't make any difference. Congratulations on a job well done."

61

1306

Determined to have their moment in history, all the male serfs of Potamia between fifteen and fifty followed Theodore to the capital; most of them losing their life in the attack on the treasury. The rest were incarcerated, waiting for the gallows to be set up. The Orthodox Archbishop appealed for the enforcement of the common theft penalty, the cutting off of the right hand at the wrist, but Amaury, deaf to reason and adamant about seeing all of them hanged, extinguished the peasants' last flickers of hope. He wanted to set an example of zero tolerance for rebels.

Dressed in black, the women of Potamia had walked to Nicosia to bid their loved ones a last farewell. When the guards refused them a visit in the dungeons, there was nothing else to do but to wait.

At sunrise, the capital prepared for the hangings in front of Santa Sophia Cathedral and before God. The first spectators appeared in the square. The Potamia women positioned themselves right in front of the gallows. They had to be strong for their men. There would be ample time to grieve later.

Slowly, a small crowd filled the square. The guards brought the rebels up from the dungeons below the palace, hands tied behind their backs. Being the leader, Theodore was the first to be hanged. He walked upright, his pale face defiant, fearless. The crowd jeered at him and cursed him, but he seemed not to see them.

"Theodore!" Lois cried out. He looked around as if coming out of a reverie. Their eyes met and held. He found a tender, mirthless smile for her. His lips formed the words, 'I love you'. Instinctively, she responded in the same way, and he nodded in understanding.

Lois cringed at the site of the rope being placed over his head, but she was determined to look steadily into his eyes until the bitter end. His gaze fastened on hers. In those last minutes of his life, he was not alone. Her face was a beacon, guiding him to the afterlife with a sense of dignity.

It was a cruel way to die, and Lois felt nauseated. The noose tightened around Theodore's neck. His body was dropped, but his neck did not break. As his body was suspended, strangulation was inflicted gruelingly slowly for the next harrowing twenty minutes. He writhed and kicked on the noose until he went limp. Theodore drew his last breath, vowing to wait for her until Judgment Day. When his eyes closed, Lois bent over and threw up.

One by one, the rebels were hanged. The lamentation of the women around Lois was mingled together with the crowd's cheers. The execution was the spectacle of the day. Nipping the serfs' rebellion in the bud gave the nobles and burgesses a false sense of safety in those troubled times.

When the last rebel breathed no longer, the women were mercifully permitted to collect the bodies. Lois grieved quietly for this extraordinary man who had loved her so much. Yesterday's hero, Theodore had turned into today's scapegoat. Though the women did not say it in so many words, Lois could see it in their eyes: it was Theodore who had led their men to their demise.

When they took the road to Potamia, Lois did not go with them. There was no one and nothing waiting for her there. Her thoughts turned to Nicholas. She was still reeling from the shock. Her knees were trembling with exhaustion, but she found the strength to walk the short distance to his house. Dare she hope that he might still be alive? Jacob would know, but he was not there. Lois had no idea if Jacob had died, or if, in the absence of his master, he had set himself free. She hoped it was the latter.

*

Provence's heart ached and his breathing was labored as he walked out of the dungeons. Watching Nicholas become a shadow of his former self was a sharp dagger twisted in his gut. He was filled with this same sense of powerlessness the evening before Eloise had passed away. She, at least, had lived a full life.

Nicholas was still so young, so talented! It seemed unfair. Provence had sought respite from pain in prayer, but it availed him little. His faith was shaken; an affront to God. It was simply beyond his strength to accept what he could not change.

Amaury had not granted Provence an audience. No one in his entourage would, and Provence was shattered by the dawned realization that he might not be able to save his boy. If only he could swap places with Nicholas! Beset with a father's misgivings, he trudged into the alehouse and took a seat in a quiet corner.

"Provence!"

He shivered inwardly with revulsion at the sound of the familiar abrasive voice. He had not heard from Roussillon for a long time, but that was a voice he would never forget. He gave him the briefest nod of acknowledgement.

Roussillon invited himself to Provence's table. "Your boy is rotting in the dungeons, and I bet you know why." He made no effort to hide the malice in his voice.

Provence wanted to strangle him, but he did not allow himself to be blinded by pride. The irony was not wasted on him that Roussillon was the only one of Amaury's supporters Provence could still speak to. "Was this your doing as well?"

Roussillon shrugged. "You may not believe this, but I feel for you, Provence. I would like to help you."

"I'm listening," Provence said, certain he was about to strike a deal with the devil himself.

"It is quite simple actually: your boy for the *casale*."

Provence was not surprised. He wouldn't have expected anything else from Roussillon. The *casale* had been the core dispute from the start, and Roussillon had been nursing a grudge ever since. "On the day my boy is free, the *casale* is yours," Provence said without hesitation. He stretched out an arm to seal the deal.

Roussillon shook his hand, saying. "You will hear from me soon."

*

Provence came out of the alehouse and drew in a breath of fresh air to clear his head. Roussillon's offer had been a bitter brew to swallow, but he would do it again if it meant giving his boy back his life.

Out of the corner of his eye, he noticed a familiar figure scurrying past him. "Lois?"

The young woman stopped abruptly and looked over her shoulder. "My lord," she said, startled.

He took a step closer. She looked pale and rattled. "Are you all right? Where have you been?" Nicholas had asked about her each and every time.

Lois recounted her tale, giving him an abridged account, bracing herself for his disapproval, but Provence had lived long enough, heard and seen too much, to be scandalized. Nicholas' baby was the best news he'd had these last few months.

"You need to take care of yourself and my grandchild," he said, pressing some silver coins in her palm. Lois was about to protest, but he silenced her with a slight shaking of his head. "Are you going to see Nicholas?"

"Yes, my lord — if the guards let me. I hope they like wine," she said, lifting the hem of the cover from her basket.

"Luckily, they do." There was a suggestion of a smile of approbation on his lips. For a young woman who had never left the boundaries of the *casale* until a few months ago, she had proven to be streetwise. Provence's face looked grave when he said her name again.

"Yes, my lord?"

"I would not tell Nicholas about Theodore just yet."

Lois nodded in understanding.

"Tell him, his brothers and I may have found a way to set his freedom in motion. Hopefully, next time I see him will be to take him home. Soon, very soon," he added as an afterthought.

The prospect lifted Lois' heart. "Oh, my lord, that would be a miracle!"

*

Nicholas heard the clink of the key in the iron door and sat up. "Lois!" he cried out as if the sun suddenly shone in his dark cell. He sprang to his feet. The sheer sight of her made his soul sing.

Lois placed the basket on the earthen floor, casting her gaze to the ground, reeling from Nicholas' gaunt countenance. Her heart bled for her guiltless darling, whose only crime had been his loyalty to his king. She raised her eyes to look at him, caught up in a whirlwind of emotion.

Becoming pragmatic, she dismissed all thoughts from her head. She would deal with them later. Right now, she was here with him. He was alive; nothing else mattered! She threw her arms around him.

He wanted to ask her where she had been all this time, but her body clinging on to his so tightly told him everything he needed to know.

"They spread rumors that they killed everyone who did not support them," she said, horror coloring her voice.

"They may have for all I know. It is a wonder I'm still alive," he said, caressing her cheek. He closed his eyes and inhaled the scent of her. In a flash, he became aware of how filthy he must be and took a step back, but Lois took a step closer, taking his face in her hands.

"I only have a few moments, *amor meu.* Your father and brothers will get you out of here. Soon! They have found a way. You have to believe that; do you hear me?"

"Oh, Lois!" his voice broke. He squeezed her tight, kissing the top of her head.

"Listen, Nicholas! There is something I must tell you before I go." There was so much to say and not enough time in which to say it.

He relaxed his embrace to look at her. "What?"

"You need to be strong for the three of us," she said, taking his hands and placing his palms on her belly.

"Three?"

She nodded. As if to confirm, the baby kicked in her womb for the first time. Nicholas' eyes widened, his mouth gaping.

"*Solelh,* you are with child!" He was filled with a farrago of happiness, sadness, and guilt. "How far along are you?"

"Almost five months now. I meant to tell you on the day I left…"

Nicholas had a sudden flashback to the day of Buenaventura's visit. "Oh, my love," he whispered, abashed. "I'm so sorry I hurt you!"

She put her finger to his lips in a shushing gesture. "I love you, Nicholas. I always have and always will." She sealed his lips with a kiss. He did not need to know about Theodore in here, she reminded herself.

They broke their embrace at the sound of the guard's approaching steps. "I will try to come back again tomorrow if the guards let me. Eat now and stay strong for us. We need you!"

"You have to leave now," the guard said curtly, and Lois gave Nicholas a quick kiss on the lips before parting.

*

Provence's heart beat fiercely as the guard unlocked the iron door to Nicholas' cell to announce his freedom. Roussillon had moved heaven and earth to get his hands on the *casale*. Provence was not surprised that it had only taken him a couple of days to have Nicholas released. If anything, he was utterly grateful and relieved.

Nicholas stared at the guard as though he might not have heard correctly, but then he saw his father and brothers and Guilhelm standing in the tenebrous corridor. Their smiling faces was all the confirmation he needed.

"How did you manage this?" he asked, overwhelmed by emotion.

"Well, the Bishop of Famagusta intervened between the king and the regent, and they signed an agreement to wait for the Pope's response before any more blood is shed, so the moment was favorable," Provence said in the neutral tones he used whenever he was making a conscious effort not to lie. He prided himself on never lying – almost never. Technically, this was not a lie, just not the whole truth.

"Thank you!" Nicholas whispered, the words sticking in his throat. Grateful, he said a quick, silent prayer. This was no less than a miracle. The Lord had granted him a second chance, and he meant to make the most of it.

"Let's go now. Lois is waiting," Albert said lightly, and they supported him down the dark aisle and up the stairs. Unaccustomed to the sunlight, Nicholas staggered, slamming his eyes shut. He allowed himself a moment to take in the air of freedom.

"Are you going to tarry all day?" Guilhelm teased him, and Nicholas exerted himself to walk faster; Lois was waiting!

*

Lois had prepared a festive welcome for Nicholas' return. It was a joyous, yet quick meal, for as soon it was over, Provence excused himself. He had to thank someone for Nicholas' release, he said, without going into detail. Peyre, Albert, and Guilhelm did the same moments later.

When everyone had left, Lois cut Nicholas' hair, gave him a bath, and shaved him. There was so much to say, but they did not know where to start. In the end, they let their bodies talk, long and gently. They made love tenderly, as though time had stood still. Then, they lay clasped in each other's arms, reassured that the fire of their love was still burning white hot.

Nicholas caressed her belly softly, planting small kisses and whispering kindly to his child growing inside her, filled with joy and hope for the future. Suddenly, anything seemed possible.

He rested on his elbow and smoothed the hair from her face. "I should have told you a long time ago. Lois, you hold my heart."

Lois experienced a pang of guilt. She barely stopped herself short from telling him about Theodore. This was not the right moment; Nicholas had been bereft of joy and hope for so long. She sealed his lips with a kiss instead, thinking that they still belonged in two different worlds. That had not changed.

*

After leaving Nicholas in Lois' care, Provence went straight to the notary's. The contract had already been drafted; Roussillon had seen to that.

The quill pen the notary handed him felt unusually heavy in his hand. He dipped it in ink.

"In the end, everyone gets what they deserve," Roussillon said spitefully, catching Provence in mid-movement.

"That can only be judged after one's death, Roussillon. May the Lord have mercy on your soul!" Provence signed with a steady hand and walked out of the room with his head held high.

Once on the street, he turned south and walked back to Nicholas' house. Now he could tell him about the arrangement. Then, he would get Emilia and go and live in Famagusta to be close to his two sons and not far from the third one.

62

2014

Lucy got out of bed, casting a glance at Michael. Satisfied he was asleep, she tiptoed to the bathroom. With slightly trembling fingers, she took the pregnancy test out of the cupboard and stared at it for a while, dreading the result. She had recently turned forty and her chances at getting pregnant were slimmer as time went by. She wanted to have a baby, Michael's child!

On her birthday, a few days earlier, he had implied marriage, but Lucy had been evasive. She had never felt comfortable with commitment. Yet it was the natural thing to do. They had been living together for several months now. Deep down, she wanted to; she just needed time to get used to the idea.

With her eyes glued to the window of the test, Lucy watched the two lines become darker. She froze for a moment, suddenly uncertain of so many things. *That is insane!* Everything will be all right she tried to convince herself and got back into bed.

Michael turned and cuddled her in spooning. He nuzzled his face into her neck, his breath warm on her skin, giving her goosebumps. She turned around to him and their foreheads touched. "Good morning," she said.

"Mm, it's always a good morning when I wake up by your side," he said and gave her a sleepy kiss on the lips.

She rested on her back and was silently thoughtful for a while. "Michael?"

"Mm?" His hand rested on her stomach, caressing her leisurely.

"If I asked you for something that's yours, would you share it with me?"

"You need to ask? What do you need?" His lips traveled on her throat and down between her breasts.

"Guess!"

He stopped for a moment and then his lips moved down to her belly. "I hope you will say 'my bed'." He kneeled before her, taking one of her toes into his mouth.

"That, I'm sharing already. More than that!"

"More?" His lips moved to the arch of her foot. "Any help from the audience?"

"Something that's yours that I can't have otherwise."

He locked eyes with her. "Did you just propose to me?"

"I did!"

He moved on top of her and kissed her full on the lips. "The answer is 'yes;' anytime, anywhere." He kissed her again, but then pulled back, looking at her quizzically. "You did not quite jump at the idea the other day. What made you change your mind?"

She gave him a mischievous grin. "Oh, I don't know. I think it's better for the baby."

His eyes widened. "You're pregnant!" She smiled widely, and he kissed her again, the tenderness welling inside him.

63

1306

The sky was aflame when Christina set the table for Nicholas and Lois in the manor in the capital. Though she missed her family, she was glad that they had taken her in and she no longer had to live in the *casale* under the horrid new master.

Lois had fallen asleep after a soothing bath when Christina knocked gently on the door to let her know that the master had come back from Limassol and that dinner was ready. Lois thanked her and got out of bed slowly. She walked down the stairs, minding her steps; she was getting heavier by the day.

When she came to the table, Nicholas rose to his feet and kissed her hand. He pulled out a chair for her, and she thanked him with a broad smile.

"I could get used to that, my lord."

"You will!" he assured her.

Christina came in with a platter of goose with honey, almonds, and figs and a carafe of wine, a festive dinner as Nicholas had instructed before leaving.

"How was your trip to Limassol?" Lois asked when they had the room to themselves.

"Useful. I paid a visit to James Mara, the Venetian *baiulo*. As of today, *solelh*, you are a White Venetian," he said, producing a document out of his pocket.

"I'm what?" Lois knew who the Venetians were, but White Venetians?

"Although this is a right usually passed on to Venetians' bastard children in the Outremer, I have managed to secure this right for you. They laughed at me at first, but they took me more seriously when I told them I was willing to pay for it." Not deeming it necessary to go into detail about the amount, he said, "You're now officially under the protection of the _Serenissima_, the Republic of Venice."

Lois stared at the document in her hands and then back at him. "Nicholas, this must have cost a fortune!" she said in a small voice.

"Indeed! But we can earn it back. White Venetians are mainly involved in trade. I have already made some inquiries. There seems to be increasing demand for olive oil soap. This is what you once said that you wanted to do. Remember? So this is what we're going to do... on one condition."

"What's that?"

Nicholas stood up and came to stand in front of her. He got down on one knee and took a ring out of his pocket. "Will you be my wife?"

Lois' mouth fell open. She felt a stir in her womb and placed her hands gently under her stomach. "But what about your title and the estates?" Could she be so lucky?

"That is the beauty of it! I can pass them on to our children now that you are a White Venetian. But you have not answered my question yet: will you marry me?"

Her smile faltered. "Nicholas, there's something I have to tell you." She knew she would have to tell him one day, but she had not thought that day would come so soon. She understood now that she had been waiting for the birth of the baby before telling him the truth. She was ill-prepared she contemplated, fighting down the panic.

He rose to his feet, bemused. He would have expected her to fall into his arms, elated. Had he misjudged the situation? "I'm listening." His tone was casual. His scrutiny was not.

"When I left you that evening, I was convinced you would be marrying that girl. Then, I heard about Amaury seizing power and about all the hangings in the capital and thought you were dead. I only found out you were alive when I went back to the *casale*."

Nicholas listened with mounting impatience. He knew all that already. She paused, searching for the right words. He could see, watching her face, that a struggle was going on inside her and he waited.

"On that same day, Theodore showed up at the *casale*."

Nicholas felt as if he had been knocked down by a charging bull. "Theodore? He's alive? Oh my God!" He ran his fingers through his hair. "You cannot marry me; you are married already!" The epiphany stung like a whip.

Lois stood up, shaking her head. "Please, let me explain. It is important that you understand."

Her eyes pleaded with anguished eloquence. Nicholas was not sure there was much she could explain, but he gestured for her to go on.

"I had no choice that day. I had to follow Theodore, my husband — through no choice of mine if I may remind you."

His face hardened. It seemed he would live long enough to regret this suggestion to Poitou.

Lois shrugged off his embittered disapproval with equanimity. "You were imprisoned, so you could not have heard of the grain thieves. It was an attempt at a rebellion. Theodore was the leader. They caught them and hanged them all the day I came to visit you in the dungeons."

He snorted bitterly. "You know what kept me sane all these endless days and nights in the dungeons?"

Instinct kept her silent.

"It was the thought of you, how I had hurt you, and how I might one day make it up to you," he went on. "And all this time, you were sharing his bed!" His green eyes burned in accusation.

"Just once, on the evening before he was hanged," she muttered. There! She had said it. For good or ill, she had gotten it off her chest.

He raised a palm to stop her speaking, struggling to quell the fury flaring up inside him, but it was a losing battle.

She saw his jaw muscles so tightly clenched that she yearned to reach out and caress away those signs of strain, but the enraged look in his eyes held her back.

He took a step closer, towering over her. "Do you have any idea where the money came from to pay the *baiulo* so I could marry you?"

Lois stared at him silently. It would have been easier to keep quiet about Theodore, but how could she square that with her conscience?

"I exchanged the manor in Strovolos for the favor." There was an alarming edge to his voice.

This was the day Lois should have felt like the happiest and most fortunate woman on earth. Nicholas had done the impossible: he had proposed. Yet she felt as though they were saying goodbye. She was walking on thin ice and was not sure which words would appease him.

"Oh, Nicholas, you did this for me!" she said at last.

"I did it for us. And you lay with him!" he said, throwing his hands up in the air, consciously trying to block images of her in another man's arms.

Lois endured the wave of nausea sweeping over her, holding her nerve with an effort. She did her best to ignore his anger and accusatory tone. He was carried away by emotions, not that she faulted him. Perhaps appealing to reason might placate him.

"Tell me, Nicholas, did you not sleep with your wife?" The question was mild in tone, conciliatory in intent.

"It is not the same thing!" he protested vehemently.

This was so unfair! She drew in a strangled breath.

"How so? Because you're a man and I'm a mere woman? Or is it because you are highborn, and I'm but a commoner? Of course, you may be right. You married her of your own accord, whereas I had *no* choice!" Once their rage was unleashed, she feared they would say things they would later regret.

"Nothing could be further from the truth." His voice was now low and controlled as he enunciated each word. She stared at him nonplussed. "That was before I lay with you. That is why it is not the same thing! Unlike you, there has been no one else since I lay with you."

Lois hated to admit that she was losing ground in the argument, but she was not ready to give up yet; too much was at stake.

"But you were contemplating marrying the Buenaventura girl *after* you had lain with me."

"Contemplating; correct! I was given an order and was trying to talk my way out of the marriage when you ran away from me in the dead of night."

He stared at her, steely-eyed, and Lois sensed that he had gone where she could not follow, and it frightened her. Nicholas could no longer stand looking at her and turned his back on her. Not only had she been unfaithful, she had deceived him! All this time, she had kept it a secret. He felt as though he was suffocating.

"I need to be alone," he said and stalked from the room. Lois lapsed into a chastened silence.

A few minutes later, she heard him rush down the wooden staircase. She moved to the bottom of the stairs and stared at the saddlebag in his hand. She wanted to say something, but the words got caught in her throat. She had been tested and found wanting.

Nicholas did not meet her eye as he passed her by, heading for the stable. His leaving sent her spirits plummeting, and her poise deserted her. Weak at the knees, Lois dropped down on the staircase. As he left the room, he took the air with him, and she felt faint.

In a headlong rush, Nicholas reached the stable, tearing rage accumulating inside him; a rage that was blind to consequences, to common sense. He buckled the saddle girth and was taken aback when he saw Christina.

She dried her palms on the skirt of her dress and mustered up her courage. "Pardon me, my lord," she said in a shaky voice. "I've only been here for a few days, and I do not know my way around. Should anything happen in your absence is there a midwife I could get?"

Nicholas did not move a muscle; he had not thought of that. But Christina had noticed Lois' pale face and was sick with worry.

"Fetch me! I'll be staying at the inn behind the cathedral," he said at length. Then he lifted himself into the saddle and disappeared into the night.

*

Christina was doing her best to comfort Lois while Nicholas was emptying a tankard of ale at the alehouse. Unwilling to talk to anyone and unable to stand the noise and the laughter any longer, he decided to go back to the inn.

He mounted the stairs in a dark mood and locked the door of his tiny room. He sat on the straw bed and leaned back against the wall, propping a pillow behind him. The arrogance of his class and his lacerated male pride were at war with the voice of reason and his love for her.

He had spent every morsel of his mental and physical strength, trying to find a way to accomplish the unachievable, to offer her the stars. He had exerted himself to overcome the problem of her ignoble birth and find a way to marry her, a way that cost him an estate many would kill for, only to find out that she had not waited for him. She had slept with another man while he was rotting away in the dungeons. He willed her to be utterly devoted to him, pledged to him body and soul, even if he were dead.

He was too incensed to think that the man she had bedded was her husband, a marriage that he himself had engineered; that a woman had the obligation to fulfill her marital duty. He chose not to consider that for some time she thought he had been dead or that when she had found out that he was incarcerated, he had been more dead than alive.

He did not know if he could ever forgive her.

64

2015

Michael checked the blinis in the oven, the last batch for delivery to the inauguration party for the Limassol Boat Show at the marina, the most jet set event on the island. He calculated mentally the time and felt confident that he could deliver before the deadline.

His cell phone rang.

"Michael, it's time!" Lucy made an effort to sound casual.

"Time for what?" he said, noticing how one of the young interns was stingy with the caviar on the blinis. Without a word, he grabbed a teaspoon and demonstrated the required quantity.

"My water's broken! It's time!" she insisted, getting the packed bag.

Michael put the teaspoon down, experiencing an adrenaline rush. "But the Caesarean's scheduled for tomorrow," he said, uncertain.

"Michael, you need to come, now! I must get to the clinic right away!"

"All right, all right, I'm coming!" he said, already reaching for his keys. "George," he called to his sous-chef, "You're in charge of the delivery."

His sous-chef met his eye, terrified. That was their largest order ever.

"I'm having a baby!" Michael went on gleefully. The staff clapped and cheered, wishing Lucy well. Still on the phone, Michael dashed to the car. "Did you hear that?"

"Yes! Ouch!"

He frowned. "Is *pappou* with you?"

"Yes, he's here. Now, hurry, but be careful!"

"On my way already. Hold on, hon! I'm coming." he said, reaching the highway and moving into the fast lane.

*

By the time Michael got home, Lucy had already notified the clinic and the necessary arrangements for the Caesarean section had been made. A wheelchair was waiting for her at the entrance when they arrived, and she was swiftly prepared for surgery.

When a nurse asked Michael to wait in the waiting room, he squeezed Lucy's hand and planted a kiss on her forehead. "It'll be all right. I'll be right here. I love you," he said encouragingly, determined not to let his anxiety show and even managed a reassuring smile.

Lucy nodded. "I love you too," she said, fighting back the panic about the anesthesia and consciously dispelling uninvited premonitions.

The last thing she remembered before closing her eyes was the doctor asking her to count backwards from one hundred.

*

"*Pappou*, meet Alexander, your grandson," Michael said proudly, placing the newborn in the old man's arms. He sat by Lucy's bed and took her hand in his, watching *pappou* gape at the little bundle in awe.

Little Alex looked so tiny and fragile, and *pappou* felt an instant surge of affection and the need to protect him. He was overwhelmed.

On the day Michael and Lucy had married, *pappou* thought he was the happiest man alive, but the teensy-weensy hand of this little creature, his great-grandson, curled around his index finger was a wonder, a miracle! And he had lived long enough to see it. He was profoundly grateful.

"Isn't he beautiful?" Lucy asked, and *pappou* nodded.

He cleared his throat and found his voice again. "He's the most beautiful baby I've ever seen. So perfect!"

Lucy and Michael exchanged a tender glance. It had been a difficult pregnancy and an even more difficult birth. There had been a moment when the baby's survival was in the balance, but little Alex had fought bravely for his life. Lucy was also recovering fast although she had lost a lot of blood. When the doctor had explained that they might not be able to have another child, Lucy and Michael decided to focus on the bright side. They felt blessed they had Alex at least.

65
1306

It had been a scant few days now since Nicholas had taken up lodging at the inn, but he already detested eating and sleeping alone. In the solitude of his room, his only company was a carafe of wine. He downed the last cup. The wine warmed his heart and made him feel mellow.

He missed Lois, her company, loving her; his baby growing inside her, a life sprung from his seed. When he caught himself half wishing that Christina would show up to fetch him, he knew that he had forgiven her.

He sprang to his feet, excited about going back home. Hastily, he threw his few belongings into the saddle bag, paid the inn keeper, and strode to the stables. He had barely swung in the saddle when he noticed Christina dashing to the inn, the muscles of his stomach contracting. Had he inadvertently challenged fate? He spurred Roland and reached her within moments.

"A midwife" was all she managed to say. Her breath came in ragged gasps.

"Go back to your mistress. I'll fetch the midwife." He was about to spur Roland again when she caught her breath and said, "A physician too." Nicholas frowned. Childbirth was women's business. Physicians attended only under the most extreme circumstances. "All right; I'll see to that. Go now," he said with a sense of dark foreboding.

*

Hour after hour outside the closed door of the childbirth chamber, Nicholas prayed to Saint Margaret. The physician had been neither particularly enlightening nor optimistic. The child's position worried him, and the midwife had not been able to turn it right. There was nothing he could do that the midwife was not already doing, he had said and left.

In those endless hours, Nicholas blamed himself for what Lois was going through. If only he had not let his male pride blind him. If only he had not left her alone when she needed him the most! If only he could turn back time.

At the sound of the door opening, Nicholas span around. Christina came out of the room to fetch more water, and he grabbed her by the arm. "Tell me the truth! How is she? It's been a whole night! The sun will be up soon."

"We need to wait a while longer, my lord. The midwife is still hopeful she can turn the baby around," she said for the fourth time that evening. Even in her own ears, she sounded less convincing each time.

Nicholas tightened his grip around her arm. "Do not lie to me! Tell me the truth, or I will go mad!"

Christina glanced at his wrinkled forehead. His skin was gray and there were black circles around his eyes. "She has lost a lot of her strength, my lord. She is weak, but she has not given up yet. She so wants to give you a son! The midwife has given her opiates and herbs to relieve her of pain."

Just how effective were these opiates and herbs, he wondered? How many hours of pain could Lois endure? Nicholas never knew what moved him. Men had no place in the female sanctum of the childbirth chamber. But he flung the door open and walked in, despite Christina's and the midwife's protests and warnings.

"I need to see her. I need to be with her. I'm sure she needs me by her side," he fobbed them off.

Nicholas was not prepared for the small pool of blood under the birthing stool, and he felt weak at his knees. He noticed the hastily scrubbed blood stains on the outer fringes. She had obviously lost more blood earlier.

He closed the distance between them in two strides, grabbed a chair, and sat by her side. Lois was wearing amber on the birth girdle. Nicholas had heard that it eased the pain. At least, it eased his mind to think that the midwife had thought of everything.

He took her hand in his and felt the crucifix she was holding. He wiped the sweat from her forehead and planted a kiss on her cheek. She opened her languorous eyes. They were vacant at first, but then there was recognition. With immense effort, she gave him a wan smile then closed her eyes again.

Nicholas was taken aback by her chalk-white face that reminded him of Antoinette's last hour. *Oh, merciful God!* Was he being punished for Antoinette's and her unborn baby's death? A life for a life? No, the Lord was not vengeful. Or was He? Why did Lois have to suffer for his sins?

"Since you are here, you might as well make yourself useful," the midwife's practical tone of voice interrupted his troubled thoughts. She still had not forgiven his intrusion.

"Tell me what I can do," he said, grateful he could do something – anything.

"You can rub her lower back gently," she said and resumed chanting.

It was comforting to be able to offer Lois some relief from her pain. He whispered gentle words in her ears. Her eyelids moved, and he knew she could hear him.

He glanced around the room. Only then did he notice the tapestry hanging over the window. The shutter was open ajar to let in some fresh air. The room was scented with purifying herbs; a mystic atmosphere.

When Lois was coaxed into pushing one more time, she moaned, cried, screamed, and swore, and when Nicholas saw her bloodshot eyes and her vagina tear, he slowly began to comprehend why men were not allowed into the childbirth chamber. Lois was utterly exhausted, bathed in sweat. Nicholas feared that she would faint; worse still, that she might not regain consciousness.

The midwife gave Lois a potion to imbibe and rubbed more herbs on her belly, chanting. Christina came back with more water and cleaned Lois and the blood from the floor. Nicholas remembered that each time Christina had come out of the room was to fetch water. She had come out four times. Jesus! How much more blood could Lois lose?

Morning had broken when he had the answer. The midwife had made one last effort to turn the baby around but failed. Lois barely breathed from fatigue and the loss of blood.

The midwife beckoned Nicholas to follow her to the window. "If she loses any more blood, we will lose her," she said in her matter-of-fact tone of voice.

"There must be something you can do!"

There was a strange brilliance in his eyes, bordering madness, the midwife noticed, but she had no time to worry about him. She cast her gaze to her hands then met his gaze again. "There is something, but there is no guarantee."

"Anything! Can't you see she is —" He clammed up. He was not sure if Lois was sleeping or lying there with her eyes closed. "Weak," he added.

In a low voice only he could hear, the midwife said, "This is something I have seen done only on cows. You need to understand that it is very likely that they will both die anyway."

Nicholas swallowed hard. Hearing her say his fears out loud was like a blow with a club in the gut. He gathered his wits. "What did you have in mind?"

"We can try and slit her belly open, but it is dangerous," she warned him again.

Caught between Scylla and Charybdis, Nicholas glanced at Lois fading away. "Do it!" he said resolutely.

*

The next few months were a labyrinth of torture. Nicholas had convinced himself that the death of their infant had been God-sent punishment for Antoinette's death, a guilt he did not deem necessary to burden Lois with. But he had to come to terms with more than just his own guilt. Lois had fallen into a deep melancholy, and he feared he might not be able to drag her out of it. Day after day, he watched her withdraw to a place inside herself where he could not reach her. No matter what he said; no matter what he did.

There was a moment when he thought she had returned to him. She had said that they could have another baby. Nicholas did not share with her the midwife's admonition, "Get her with child again, and you will be hammering the nails on her coffin!" But she must have read the apprehension on his face. She had withdrawn to that inward look after that, seeing without looking.

It had already been several months now, and Nicholas was beginning to lose heart. He would not admit it, not even to himself, but he could not coax her from the shadows back to the light.

Pray seemed to be all Lois did. She would only get out of the house to go to church. Then, she would come home and pray in solitude.

After mass that Sunday morning, Lois asked Nicholas to take her for a walk by the river, and his heart leaped with hope. They strolled leisurely to Pedieos River in the heart of the capital. Apart from a couple sauntering, the area was deserted. Nicholas picked a secluded spot and sat on the grass, resting his back on the trunk of an old plane tree. Lois sat between his legs, leaning back on his chest, enjoying silently the serenity of the place for a while.

It was Lois who spoke first. She had thought long and hard for days and this was a conversation they had to have. "Nicholas, I am to blame for losing the baby. It was God's punishment, and I will spend the rest of my life regretting that when I thought you would be marrying that girl, I wished —" Her voice broke, but she found the strength to go on, "I wished I had never conceived. I cannot expect you to ever forgive me —"

"Lois, there is nothing to forgive! Besides, we do not know God's will. We do not know why He took our little boy. All this time I've been blaming myself, too. I thought it was punishment for the death of Antoinette and her baby. But the truth is that sometimes babies or mothers do not survive birthing. And that is just the way things are."

"That may well be, but Nicholas, you still need an heir for your estates, and since we are not married —"

"Don't!" In an instant, he knew where she was going with this. Was this what had tormented her all this time, what had kept them apart? He tilted his head to the side to be able to read her eyes. "I will arrange for our wedding right away," he said decisively.

"But Nicholas —"

"What? You don't love me anymore?"

"I love you more than I love my own life, but —"

"I did not survive the dungeons, give up the Strovolos manor, and outlive the fright you gave me to lose you now. Is that clear?"

She cupped his face in her hands, hot tears of relief coursing unashamedly down her cheeks. "Oh, *amor meu!*" She kissed him tenderly, and he lay her down on the grass.

"*Solelh!* It is so good to have you back."

"Do you not mind my ugly scar?" she finally found the nerve to ask. Would he not think it revulsive?

His lips traced the length of her scar over her dress. "I love everything about you. Your scar most of all because it reminds me of how close I came to losing you." A brief pause. Then, "But I do mind one thing," he said playfully.

"What's that?"

He raised his eyes to hers. "That I won't be able to come inside you anymore. So, you will have to make it up to me in whichever way you see fit. I'm not picky. I will take whatever you are offering," he said and savored her lips.

66

2018

It was a beautiful, sunny afternoon in May, the day of the flower festival. Michael lifted little Alex out of the bathtub, and Lucy began to dry him.

"Are you sure we did not forget anything for tonight?" she asked Michael for the second time. More than just the flower festival, it was also *pappou's* ninety-first birthday, and they were organizing a surprise party for him.

"You want me to go through the list again?" he asked, more amused than annoyed. She was a little perfectionist, and he had long ago come to terms with it. He carried Alex to his room where Lucy had already picked out a nice suit for him.

"Did you call his friends to remind them that it's tonight?" She buttoned up Alex's shirt, and Michael made a knot in the tie around the boy's neck. He could see why she was worried. *Pappou's* few surviving friends were over ninety and likely to forget.

"Oh, damn! I completely forgot about that."

"Oh, damn!" Alex said and laughed.

"Michael!" Lucy glared at him.

He did his best to wipe the grin off his face and sound serious when he spoke. "Now, Alex, this is not a nice word. Daddy shouldn't have said it and neither should you," he tried to patch things up, but without much success.

"Oh, damn," Alex said again, enjoying the sound of it.

Michael looked at Lucy apologetically. "I'm sorry, hon. I'll try to be more careful in the future, but he's bound to use language you don't approve of at some point."

"That point didn't have to be today," she replied matter-of-factly, combing the boy's hair. A pause. "You did call them, didn't you? You were just teasing me," she said, seeking reassurance.

"Me? Teasing you?" he said with a mirthful smile.

"Now, why would I think that?" she played along congenially. Then, "Have you checked that they delivered the flowers and the balloons to the restaurant?"

He slid his arms around her growing waist. "Lucy, I said I'll take care of everything," he said tenderly.

"I know," she said, and her lips touched his.

"Hug," Alex said, embracing their thighs. Michael lifted him up, and Alex found himself squeezed between the two of them, enjoying their kisses. When he had enough, he wanted to be put down. "Flower festival," he reminded them.

A few minutes later, the three of them were knocking on *pappou's* door. *Pappou* loved flowers, and this was his favorite festival. Michael knocked again, but there was no response. Having a sudden premonition, he fumbled in his pocket for the key.

"Lucy, take Alex and wait in the house, will you?" Lucy nodded and did as he had asked. "*Pappou!*" Michael cried out, throwing open the door, his eyes anxiously scanning the living room, but there was no sign of him.

Michael checked the other rooms. He found *pappou* lying in bed motionless, the color drained from his face. "*Pappou!*" Michael called out again, feeling for his pulse, finding none. *Pappou* was already cold.

*

Lucy and Michael felt relieved when the last guests at the funeral reception had finally left, and they could grieve in private for the loss of a great man. *Pappou* had been the only constant in Michael's life, and Lucy loved him dearly.

Michael had held *pappou's* dead body for a long time before he allowed himself to be persuaded to let go. He still had not been able to cry. He had a sudden flashback. When he was a little boy, he had once asked *pappou* what would happen to him if *pappou* ever died. *Pappou* had smiled reassuringly and said, 'I'll be here for as long as you need me, Michael.' And he had kept his promise – to the utmost.

They dropped on the sofa, exhausted. Michael hid his face on her shoulder and felt his eyes sting with tears. Lucy hugged him, sobbing. They remained entwined in the solace of each other's embrace for a long time.

"I'll check on Alex," she said eventually and rose to her feet. Alex had fallen asleep during the reception, and he might wake up any moment now.

A sudden pandemonium broke out, startling them. It seemed to come from outside. They rushed to the kitchen porch. It took them a few moments to understand what they were looking at. Hydraulic excavators, bulldozers, backhoes, and dump trucks were busy tearing the little house down.

Lucy slid her hand into Michael's. They stood there with their fingers entwined, staring in stunned silence.

*

In the next few days nothing was left standing of *pappou's* house. Lucy looked with sadness out the kitchen window at the men digging. The tearing down of the little house felt like sacrilege.

Suddenly, one of the men caught her eye. She could only see his back, but that smoothing of the hair was all too familiar. He seemed to be giving orders with the air of authority. Lucy stepped onto the porch and looked more closely.

"William?" she cried out, and he turned around. He exchanged a few words with the foreman and walked over to her.

"Lucy, you're still here!"

"Well, it's my house," she reminded him, wondering what on earth he was doing there.

"Of course, it is," he said and looked down at little Alex who was half concealed behind his mom's legs. "And who is this?"

Lucy ruffled the little boy's hair. "This is Alex, my son. Say 'hello', Alex," she encouraged him.

"Hello," he said, stretching out his little arm.

Sinclair smiled and shook hands with him. "Hello, Alex. I'm William," he said, amused by the boy's good manners. He gave Lucy an inquisitive look.

"Michael and I got married," she explained. "What are you doing here?"

"I'm in charge of the excavation," he replied vaguely.

So, that's what this is. "You're here with the university?"

"No, this is a private excavation. I was hired to manage the project." He didn't offer any further explanation.

What were the odds, Lucy wondered as the foreman jogged over to them.

"Professor, we've found something. I think you should see this."

Sinclair turned to Lucy. "Um, it was great seeing you again, Lucy, but I have to get back to work now. Tell Michael he's a lucky guy," he said and gave her a peck on the cheek.

Lucy stared at him as he went back, wondering what else this might be if not a coincidence.

67

1307

Amaury's priorities as regent revolved around repairing Henry's strained relations with Venice and Genoa. His rule was popular at first, but his suspicious mind soon saw only threat everywhere. Despite his assurances, Henry was exiled to Armenia. Soon, Amaury would earn the dubious immortality conferred upon him by Dante who referred to him in *Paradiso* as a 'beast' for his irrefutable cruelty.

That was the year when the whole of Europe was shocked as the Templars were rounded up and tortured until they confessed that they had engaged in heresy and had been guilty of depravities.

When Amaury sent his men to arrest the Templars and confiscate their possessions, Oiselay made a bold counter-offer. They would not surrender, but they would withdraw to one of their estates and stay there in the custody of secular knights, who had strong sympathies with the Order, until the Pope pronounced judgment. The Templar Marshal knew that Amaury would not accept this, but it would buy him valuable time.

That very same evening, Oiselay supervised the loading of the Order's possessions onto *Falconus*. With Molay captive in France, the brethren looked to him for leadership. It was a heavy responsibility, but Oiselay accepted it without complaint.

Although the signs had been there for some time, he had not expected the once almighty 'Soldiers of Christ', prosperous merchants, and money-lenders for the Crown and Church to be on their knees. Oiselay reined in his anger at Philip the Fair, a man with a history of seizing property and persons when it suited his needs, as well as at his puppet, the Pope, and ordered what remained of the Order's wealth to be buried in various different locations. He also had maps drawn with the precise treasure locations for all Templar estates in Kolossi, Yermasoyia, Gastria, and Khirokitia. If unearthing the treasure were not possible within their lifetime, then it could be done by their successors, even if it took a thousand years.

"Marshal, we are ready to set sail," one of the brethren announced.

"Even if all is lost, save these maps," Oiselay said. "Do not let them fall into the wrong hands."

"I understand", the knight replied, taking the parchments. "I hope I can give them back to you on Rhodes."

"Godspeed!"

*

Simon Le Rat finished his prayers, crossed himself, and rose to his feet. The tide was turning. The vulnerability of the Templars was a lesson to all Orders, but Le Rat had always believed that there was opportunity in any danger.

The Templars had thought that supporting Amaury would have been a safety guarantee, but the new Pope's delegate had changed everything. Amaury was forced to hand over his allies. At the same time, this signified his independence from the Templars. Le Rat thought: opportunity in danger. One only needed to be flexible and choose the right side.

He stroked his long beard, wondering what opportunity there could be for the Hospitallers. Though they had moved their command post to Rhodes, perhaps they could reclaim the Grand Commandery that Amaury had unashamedly taken away from them and given to the Templars.

That was perhaps too bold, but could they find a way to supervise the entire collection of Templar possessions on the island? That would give the Hospitallers great power and wealth. Amaury would not agree to it, Le Rat knew, but the regent's days were numbered. Amaury had become paranoid and had turned against his supporters. Fearing his own shadow, he had imprisoned many of them. Nicosia simmered with plans for his assassination and plots to restore Henry to the throne.

Henry, of course! The Hospitallers would have to find a way to end his exile. Le Rat resolved to speak to the prior at once.

*

Despite the Templars' public confession of faith, they were arrested. Whatever riches Amaury might have expected to find, his men retrieved only arms, food supplies, and a hundred and twenty thousand bezants. The Templars were interrogated, but Amaury was none the wiser as to what had happened to their legendary treasure.

68

2018

"Mommy, daddy! Come and see!" Alex cried out, storming into Michael and Lucy's bedroom. Unwillingly, Michael opened his eyes. The little boy pulled at his sleeve. "Daddy, come!"

"All right! All right!" he said, stifling a yawn. "Let mommy sleep," he added protectively, casting a glance at Lucy. When she had given birth to Alex, the doctor had not been particularly optimistic about their chances of having a second child, and they were glad she was proven wrong.

"Too late for that," Lucy said, sitting up slowly.

"Are you all right?"

"Go ahead, I'll join you in a minute," she said, and Michael picked up Alex.

"Where are we going?"

"The porch," Alex said.

A few minutes later, the three of them were watching the road roller compact the soil where *pappou's* house had once stood. They were sad because of its destruction, but at the same time relieved it would be over soon. They watched one of the men drive a post with the sign 'For Sale' into the ground.

"Why would someone pay so much money for a house they don't need, spend a fortune on an excavation, and sell it a while later?" Michael wondered.

"A hidden treasure maybe?" Lucy ventured.

"Good luck with that! Cyprus is full of legends about buried treasures."

"Who's to tell if they failed to report what they unearthed to the Department of Antiquities?"

"They wouldn't be the first ones," Michael remarked, placing an arm around her.

*

Sinclair stood gleefully in the center of the labyrinth at Chartres Cathedral with a wooden chest at his feet as four men in dark suits walked in and sat in the shadows.

69

1310

Lois asked the serfs to pack the olive oil soap bars from the stall at the Saturday market and take them back to the cart while she carried the box with the day's sales. She had a knack for trade, and the business kept growing.

Nicholas was supervising the safe loading of the soap when she reached him. "How was trade this time, Madame Provence?" he asked, placing an arm around her waist.

She liked it when he called her that. "Better than last week, Monsieur Provence," she replied. "If business goes on like this, we might be able to start building the home for orphans when spring comes."

Although it had never been said in so many words, it had become their common goal in life, so important that Nicholas declined to lead a team to subvert Amaury and restore Henry to the throne. Sympathetic though to the cause, he contributed financially.

"A dream come true," he said, smiling proudly.

"Indeed! I feel as though I have been blessed. Marrying you was like a dream come true and now a home for orphans, God willing."

They never spoke about losing their baby, about almost losing her; about never being able to have a baby of their own. Some things were best left unsaid.

Nicholas gazed at her for a moment before breaking the news. "Amaury's dead; murdered," he said casually, as if talking about the vagaries of the winter weather.

"He deserved no better," Lois remarked. "Who did it?"

"His own friend, Simon of Montolif."

"What of his wife and five children?"

"They are in Agios Sergios, outside of Famagusta, from what I hear, waiting for a galley to take them to her brother's court in Armenia." He paused. Then, "He's coming back."

"Who?"

"The king! Henry is coming back from exile. The Hospitallers have managed to bring him back without bloodshed! Everyone is going to Famagusta to welcome him. So are we. There will be great festivities for his return."

Lois looked at him, taken aback. "*We?* As in you *and I?*"

"Yes, my little White Venetian," he smiled fondly at her, caressing her cheek.

*

Lois felt as if she was stepping into a fairytale when the coach passed through the illuminated palace gate. A row of torches on both sides of the path lit up the magnificent gardens that were hemmed in by a thick line of cypress trees. Marble statues, cascading fountains, ponds with fish and water lilies spread left and right. It was a blend of bright colors, of blooming flowers, citrus, olive, carob, and pine trees. The infinite blossoms banished memories of the terrible drought two years ago.

Dressed in the latest fashion, the entire nobility, knights, and burgesses had gathered to welcome King Henry, eager to demonstrate their loyalty and move on to a new era, refusing to allow themselves to live the rest of their days filled with hatred or ill will. The four years of Amaury's abominable rule were over.

The air was filled with the smoky smell of roast game, and the chalices were never empty. The minstrels' voices filled the air, and everyone was in high spirits.

Nicholas heard someone call out his name and looked over his shoulder. "Seneschal!"

The last few years had not been kind to Philip of Ibelin. At first, he had been placed under house arrest, and later he was sent to Tarsus as a hostage. He gave Nicholas a warm embrace. "How are you, my boy?"

"I'm fine, my lord. I am happy to see you again. May I introduce you to my wife?" he said, turning to Lois.

"Lois? Is that you?" Philip hardly recognized her dressed as a lady, and Nicholas smothered a smile.

Lois curtsied. "Indeed, my lord."

"You look beautiful, my dear," Philip said admiringly.

She thanked him and rewarded him with a broad smile that he returned bashfully.

"And how is your father?" Philip turned his attention to Nicholas again. "Is he not here? I have not seen him."

"Father has passed on," Nicholas said solemnly.

"I'm sorry to hear that," Philip said. "I would like to visit his grave."

"He's buried in Famagusta."

"Famagusta? Not in the *casale?*"

"I'm afraid not," Nicholas said and explained in a few words what had happened.

"That snake!" Philip spit out the words. "The pain is yours, my boy, but the outrage is mine! I will have a word with Henry. That *casale* belongs to you! You will hear from me soon," Philip said with his customary authority and walked on to speak to more friends.

Lois' eyes sparkled. "Getting the *casale* back would be wonderful! We could have the house for the orphans built there."

"Indeed, but let us wait and see ... You have made quite an impression on Philip," Nicholas said, and Lois glowed with pleasure. Not just on Philip, he thought, proud of her and her impeccable manners.

Henry asked the queen mother to dance with him, and the floor was open to all the nobility thereafter. One by one, the couples took to the dance floor.

"My lady, may I have the pleasure of this dance?" Nicholas asked Lois, offering his outstretched arm.

Lois looked at him stunned. Though he had taught her how to dance, and they sometimes enjoyed dancing in the evenings, she had never imagined that one day they would dance at the palace. He smiled at her encouragingly.

"It would be my pleasure, my lord," she replied, curtsying and accepting his arm.

ABOUT THE AUTHOR

Lina Ellina has worked as a lecturer at the University of Trier
in Germany and at Intercollege in Cyprus as well as a business
consultant. Together with her husband, she has created The
Olive Park Oleastro, specializing in organic olive oil.

At various stages, Lina's interests included sports, music,
painting, reading, and theater. Today she's more into
history, culture, food and wine.

ALSO BY LINA ELLINA

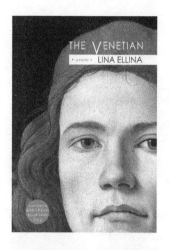

The Venetian

(Listed for the EUROPEAN BOOK PRIZE 2012)

A Renaissance-era mystery unravels in this story-within-a story, linking present day characters to history's most romantic intrigues.

A king's wedding and a present day chef's holiday are interwoven beautifully as details emerge about an inter-generational connection as delicate and rare as the Italian and Cypriot landscapes that form the backdrop for this literary rumination on life, love, food, and fellowship.

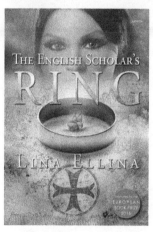

The English Scholar's Ring

(Listed for the EUROPEAN BOOK PRIZE 2016)

A crusader. A riddle. A ring.

Justin needs to spend three consecutive months in his deceased father's estate on the Mediterranean island of Cyprus — where he must solve a riddle to claim an extravagant inheritance, rich with history — and gold.

Unexpected help comes from a woman named Zoe who may hold a clue to Justin's own mysterious past — though neither of them fully know the stakes of her involvement. Unbeknownst to the two lovers, someone else is trying to solve the riddle for his own benefit.

In an epic story spanning the ages from the time of Richard the Lionheart and the Third Crusade, to modern day Cyprus, reincarnation, history, love, and mystery collide.

CPSIA information can be obtained
at www.ICGtesting.com
Printed in the USA
BVHW031430300419
546961BV00001B/30/P